TRIBUTE OF DEATH

By the same author

Demon of the Air
Shadow of the Lords
City of Spies

TRIBUTE OF DEATH

SIMON LEVACK

First published by Lulu.com, 2007

Copyright © Simon Levack 2007. All rights reserved.

Author's website: www.simonlevack.com

This book is fiction. All characters and situations depicted herein are imaginary or are used fictitiously. Any resemblance to real persons, living or dead, is coincidental.

ISBN 978-1-84799-744-9

For Sarah and Isaac, with love

Acknowledgement

This fourth of Yaotl's adventures was the hardest to write. As ever, thanks are due to my agent, Jane Gregory and her team at Gregory & Co, for making sure I did not let the standard slip.

Rather belatedly I also want to thank my friends, the Forest Writers of Walthamstow, without whose support, encouragement and suggestions this book and its predecessors would have been quite different and not nearly so good.

And where would I be without my wife? Sarah can always be relied upon to tell me candidly *exactly* what is wrong with anything I write!

Certainly it is our mortality, we who are women, for it is our battle, for at this time our mother, Cihuacoatl, Quilaztli, exacteth the tribute of death.

The Florentine Codex, Book VI

I should rather carry a shield in battle three times, than give birth once.

Euripides, *Medea*

Author's Note

Tribute of Death is the fourth novel featuring Cemiquiztli Yaotl and set in the Mexico of the early Sixteenth Century, in the final years before the coming of the Conquistadors. At this time the region was dominated by the people we call Aztecs, but whose name for themselves was *Mexica*. They had made their home in the central Mexican highlands, on the site of modern Mexico City, building an impregnable fortress-city on an island in the middle of a lake. They called the city Mexico-Tenochtitlan, and used it as a base to conquer and subdue most of their neighbours.

We tend to think of the Aztecs – when we think of them at all – in rather grand, dramatic terms. All too often, they are presented as builders of pyramids and temples, practitioners of grisly sacrificial rites and players in the final tragedy that saw their civilisation overturned and their magnificent island city devastated.

Of course, the Aztecs *were* all these things; but they were also men and women with food to prepare, children to bring up, errands to run, debts to pay and relatives to squabble with. Domestic concerns probably loomed larger in their minds than the great and terrible events that were unfolding around them: in that, of course, they were no different from us.

The story I have tried to tell in this book has less to do with the great and terrible events and more with the daily lives of ordinary Aztecs, and with one aspect, in particular, which was sharply at odds with anything we are familiar with: their view of childbirth. For in giving birth – in risking her life to bring forth a child – a mother was likened to a warrior, hazarding everything to seize and drag home an enemy captive on the battlefield. And just as a flowery death in war or on the sacrificial stone of an enemy's temple transformed the soul of the warrior, so strange and terrifying things were thought to befall the woman who died in childbirth.

Much of the action in this story takes place in a *calpolli*, or parish, named Atlixco. Although there was a place called Atlixco, the precise geography of the one in my book is imaginary; I believe an Aztec would have recognised it as typical of his city, however.

VALLEY OF MEXICO

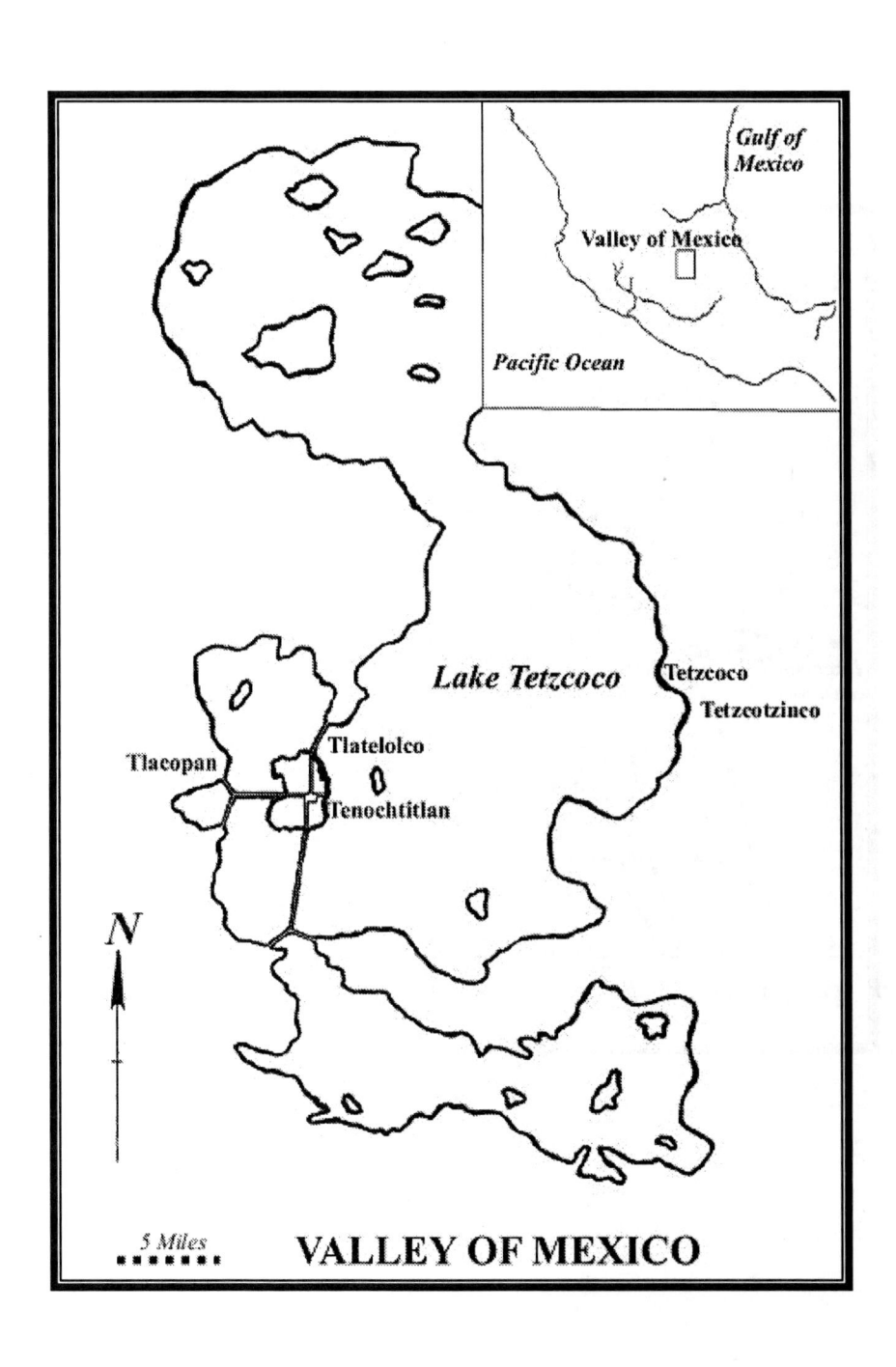

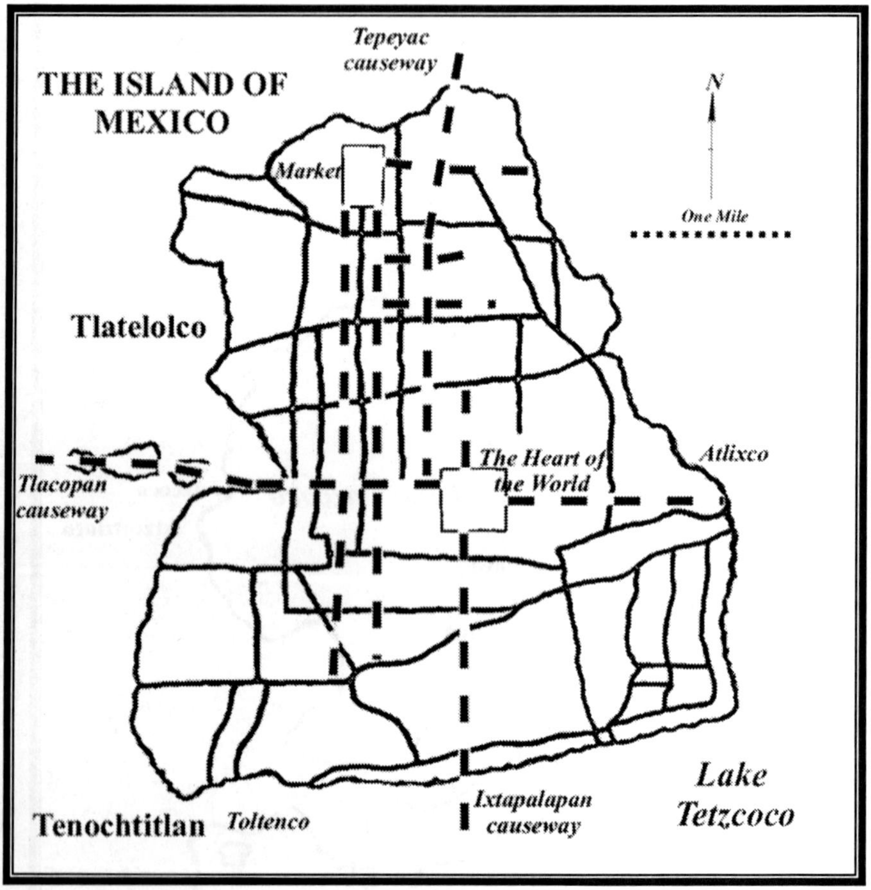
THE ISLAND OF MEXICO
Tepeyac causeway
N
Market
One Mile
Tlatelolco
The Heart of the World
Atlixco
Tlacopan causeway
Lake Tetzcoco
Ixtapalapan causeway
Tenochtitlan
Toltenco

*Path towards
the Heart of the World*

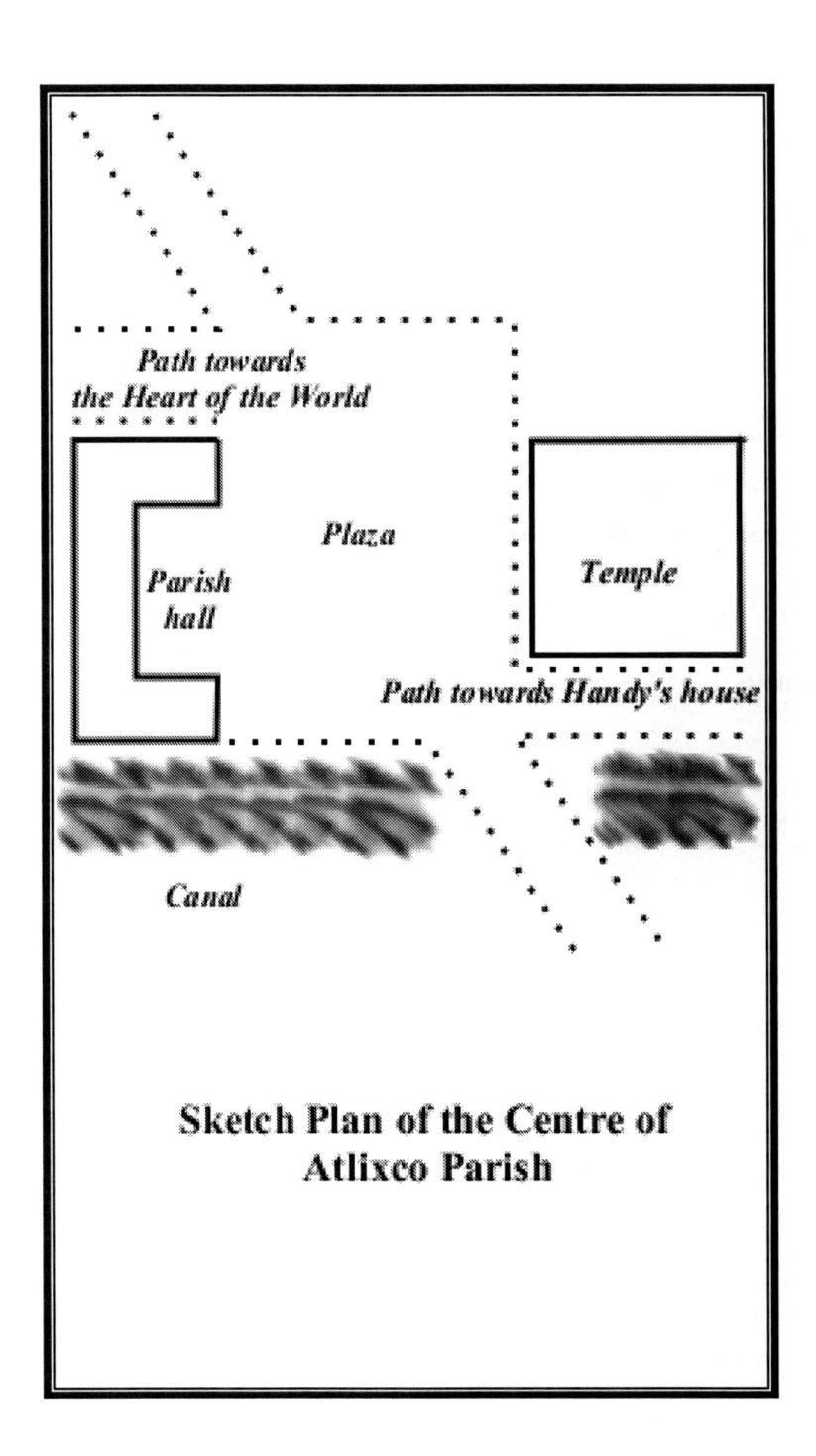

Parish hall

Plaza

Temple

Path towards Handy's house

Canal

**Sketch Plan of the Centre of
Atlixco Parish**

A Note on Nahuatl

The Aztec language, Nahuatl, is easy to pronounce, but is burdened with spellings based on Sixteenth Century Castilian. This note should help:

Spelling	Pronunciation
c	c as in 'cecil' before e or i; k before a or o
ch	sh
x	sh
hu, uh	w
qu	k as in 'kettle' before e or i; 'qu' as in 'quack' before a
tl	as in English, but where '-tl' occurs at the end of a word, the 'l' is hardly sounded.

The stress always falls on the penultimate syllable.

I have used as few Nahuatl words as possible and favoured clarity at the expense of strict accuracy in choosing English equivalents. Hence, for example, I have rendered *huey tlatoani* as 'emperor', c*ihuacoatl* as 'chief minister', *calpolli* as 'parish', *octli* as 'sacred wine' and *maquahuitl* as 'sword', and been similarly cavalier in choosing English replacements for most of the frequently recurring personal names. In referring to the Aztec emperor at the time when this story is set I have used the most familiar form of his name, Montezuma, although Motecuhzoma would be more accurate.

Finally I have called the people of Mexico-Tenochtitlan 'Aztecs', although their own name for themselves was *Mexica*, 'Mexicans'.

The name of the principal character in the novel, Yaotl, is pronounced 'YAH-ot'.

The Aztec Calendar

The Aztecs lived in a world governed by religion and magic, and their rituals and auguries were in turn ordered by the calendar.

The solar year, which began in our February, was divided into eighteen twenty-day periods (often called 'months'). Each month had its own religious observances associated with it; often these involved sacrifices, some of them human, to one or more of the many Aztec gods. At the end of the year were five 'useless days' that were considered profoundly unlucky.

Parallel to this ran a divinatory calendar of 260 days divided into twenty groups of thirteen days (sometimes called 'weeks'). The first day of each 'week' would bear the number 1 and one of twenty names – Reed, Jaguar, Eagle, Vulture and so on. The second day would bear the number 2 and the next name in the sequence. On the fourteenth day the number would revert to 1 but the sequence of names continued seamlessly, with each combination of names and numbers repeating itself every 260 days.

A year was named after the day in the divinatory calendar on which it began. For mathematical reasons these days could bear only one of four names – Reed, Flint Knife, House and Rabbit – combined with a number from 1 to 13. This produced a cycle of fifty-two years at the beginning and end of which the solar and divinatory calendars coincided. The Aztecs called this period a 'bundle of years'.

Every day in a bundle of years was the product of a unique combination of year, month and date in the divinatory calendar, and so had, for the Aztecs, its own individual character and religious and magical significance.

The Aztec name for the year in which this book is set is Thirteen Rabbit. In our calendar, it is the spring of 1518.

TWELVE VULTURE

1

It was a fine evening at the beginning of the year Thirteen Rabbit, after the winter rains had ceased but before the time for planting maize and amaranth. A few stars were out, sparkling frostily in the clear sky. In front of a little palace a girl kneeled to prepare chocolate, while I watched her and thought about fate.

On the day I was born, a soothsayer had told my parents that I would prosper and grow rich. This was on account of that day being One Death, which was sacred to Tezcatlipoca, the Smoking Mirror, the god who fixed our destinies and ruled our daily lives.

When I grew up, I learned exactly why the seer had thought that particular god would favour me. He would have consulted the Book of Days, the long screenfold volume which had every possible combination of day, month and year inscribed on its stiff bark paper pages. On the strength of his advice I had become a priest, which was a rare thing for a commoner's child but which my father had obviously thought a promising way to the fortune and renown that were my due.

As a priest I often had to look at the Book of Days myself, committing the pictures in it to memory: the glyphs for the days, months and years, and the harsh, angular, stylised images of the gods who presided over each of them. I knew exactly what the soothsayer had seen, and in his place would have made the same prediction. Nonetheless, on this evening in Thirteen Rabbit, as my eyes lingered over the sight of slim brown fingers gently turning a gourd bowl, then tipping it delicately until the warm, foaming contents spilled into another vessel, I asked myself what that learned man had actually done, all those years ago. Perhaps he had not looked my future up in a book after all. Why go to the trouble, when all he had needed to do was to take a few sacred mushrooms and give himself a vision of me as I was now, idling away my time on a marble patio, with half my attention on the game I was supposed to be playing and half on the girl and the rich aroma rising from those bowls. That, I thought contentedly, ought to have told him all he needed to know.

My opponent's peevish voice roused me from my reverie.

'Are you going to make your throw or do you intend spending the entire evening eyeing up that young woman?'

A torch, flickering behind me, caught the tiny hairs on the girl's arm, so that they glittered as she skimmed foam off the top of one of the bowls with a spoon and shook it into a third vessel. With my last, wistful glance, I caught what may have been the tiniest hint of a smile flickering across her beautiful face before I turned reluctantly back to the cross-shaped mat spread out in front of me.

'All right. Here we go... Oh, not again!' Four beans spilled out of my fist to fall, every one of them, white side up beside the mat. Nothing. I could not move.

The game was *patolli*: a race around a cross-shaped board where the first player to get all his counters back to where he started from was the winner. It resembled life, the centre and arms of the board representing the world's five directions, the fifty-two points on it standing for a full bundle of years, which however long a man actually lived was thought of as his natural time on Earth. It was seen as a means of revealing what the gods had in store for us, although as often as not we played it for fun or money.

'Bad luck, Yaotl,' the other player chuckled, as he gathered the beans for his own throw. He managed a four, his beans all landing with their black faces showing, which, since he had just one counter left on the board exactly four points from home, meant he had won. 'Your divine patron isn't with you tonight, is he?'

I grinned in spite of myself. 'I thought you told me it was a game of skill! But it's funny you should mention Tezcatlipoca. I was just thinking about all the tricks the god has chosen to play on me and what a funny one this one has turned to be!' I glanced about me, deliberately taking in all our surroundings, from the elegant house behind us to the girl who was now taking the foam she had skimmed off the surface of the chocolate and spreading it carefully over little clay cups full of the stuff. 'Do you think this is what he had in mind for us all along?'

I had served the god as a priest; but in my time I had also been a thief, then one of the water-folk, raking scum off the surface of the lake for a living, as well as a drunk, a prisoner and a slave. To the best of my knowledge no soothsayer had ever predicted any of that.

'You mean this place?' To my surprise, my opponent seemed to take me seriously. The weather-beaten face that the elderly merchant turned towards me wore a frown. 'I shouldn't count on it if I were you.

There's a reason why they use this game to foretell the future. Anything can happen! And remember, none of this is really ours. What the god or even the king gives us can be taken away, just like… that!' To illustrate his point he threw all the beans in the air.

We tracked them with our eyes as they dropped to the floor. They bounced and spun across the marble and for a few moments it was not clear what they were going to do. Even after they had come to rest, it was hard to take in what had happened. Then we both stared at them in shocked silence.

We saw the dark sides of two beans and the white side of a third, but it was the fourth that we both noticed, for it lay poised on its edge.

I had never seen such a thing before. It was so rare that if it happened during the course of a game, the player whose throw it was would win all the stakes.

Eventually I said weakly: 'I see what you mean!'

The old man's response was a whispered curse. 'Well, bugger me! How come that never happens when I'm playing for serious money?'

Then the girl announced that the chocolate was ready. At the same time, a soft footstep just behind me told me that my opponent's daughter had come out to join us.

2

The chocolate was perfect: neither too warm nor too cold, the froth whipped up until it would tremble but not break under my breath, the flavouring delicate, hinting at vanilla and honey and little marigold flowers. Yet when I sipped it that evening it seemed to have lost a little of its savour.

Icnoyo, the old merchant whose name meant 'Kindly', was telling his daughter about his last throw. The beans still lay where they had fallen, although the one that had landed on its edge had eventually toppled over. 'Can you believe it? I was just trying to remind Yaotl here how unpredictable life is and what happens? In all the years I've been playing this game I've never seen anything like it!'

The woman sipped her chocolate while she thought about her reply. Watching her was part of what had darkened my mood. Her name was Oceloxochitl – 'Tiger Lily' – and her handsome face and the hands that held her cocoa bowl might have made her father's point for him, if she had arrived a few moments before she did. Not all the lines that creased her forehead had been put there by age, although she was, like me, well into her middle years. Pain had etched some of them, stretched the skin a little more tightly over her high cheekbones and added a few extra streaks of grey to her dark hair. And she held the vessel clamped between her wrists because her bandaged fingers were still too tender to be of any use, and she was too proud or stubborn to let anyone else hold it for her.

The men who had hurt her, just a few days before, had been acting in the name of Cacamatzin, 'Lord Maize Ear', the king of Tetzcoco. But they had not been obeying his orders, and it had been the king who had rescued Lily, and me, from them. The lordly residence we were now living in belonged to him; it was near his retreat, on the beautiful wooded hill called Tetzcotzinco, overlooking the great lake that dominated the valley of Mexico. So we were drinking the king's chocolate, prepared by his servants, and as Kindly had pointed out to me, none of it was ours.

This was doubly true for me. My relationship with Lily and her father was a complex one. The woman and I were connected by loss – mine, of someone I barely recalled, years before; Lily's sharper, more immediate and irreparable: the loss of her son. What we knew of one another's suffering had thrown us together, and the repercussions of it, unexpected, hideously violent and culminating in the wounds she was still recovering from, had made us inseparable.

We had briefly been lovers and we both knew we might be again. However, I was still a slave. Lily had bought me out of a marketplace in Mexico, the great capital city of the Aztecs, where we both came from, to save me from a particularly hideous form of human sacrifice. The man who had put me up for sale, my former master, was Tlilpotonqui, lord Feathered In Black, who just happened to be the Aztec chief minister, the most powerful man in the world after the emperor Montezuma himself, and for reasons of his own he had been very much looking forward to watching my death throes. So Lily and her father, the old merchant, had brought me to lord Maize Ear's kingdom to escape lord Feathered In Black's fury.

As I thought about the dangers and torments that had befallen us, it occurred to me that here was a fine example indeed of the whimsical god of chance up to his usual tricks. All our lives had been imperilled and preserved so many times lately that I had lost count, and now even my status was in doubt. You could usually tell an Aztec's rank and occupation merely by looking at him: cotton and feathers for a lord; black-painted skin and unkempt hair for a priest; the soldier's mantle, breechcloth and jewellery, the emblems whose design told you exactly how many war captives he had taken. But if that soothsayer really had looked into my future and seen a vision of me now, there was no telling what he might have made of it. Did I look like a modestly dressed lord, or merely like a middle-aged, undernourished slave who had got above himself?

Lily set her cup down awkwardly before replying to her father. 'I don't understand why you were playing *patolli* with Yaotl in the first place, since he doesn't have a cocoa bean to his name.' Then she added, with a resigned sigh: 'All right, Yaotl, just how much do you owe him?'

I glanced down at the tally I had drawn, with a piece of charcoal, on the stone floor next to me. 'Um… five large cloaks, two small ones and seven bags of cocoa beans.'

She rolled her eyes in despair. 'Don't you ever learn?'

Kindly grinned. 'I'm trying to teach him! Double or quits next time, Yaotl?'

'Maybe.' I looked uncertainly at Lily, who had not been sleeping well. 'It's getting late.'

'It is,' she confirmed. 'I think we should finish the chocolate and go indoors before the raccoons and foxes come out.'

'Suit yourselves,' her father said. 'I don't think you'll see a fox or a raccoon up here, though. Even a centipede would have trouble getting past the guards at the bottom of this hill.' Lord Maize Ear lived in fear of assassination by one of his brothers, who had his own designs on the throne, and his retreat at Tetzcoctzinco was ringed day and night by fierce warriors. Lily and I both enjoyed the peace and quiet this gave us, though her father, who liked company, found it unnerving.

As I looked out over the edge of the patio in front of the palace and down the hill, however, I realised that our peace was about to be disturbed. 'It looks as if somebody managed to get past the sentries, though. Who's this coming up the hill? At this time of evening?'

'Some flunky, I suppose,' the old man suggested in a bored voice. 'The royal chefs probably ran out of newts or something like that, so they had to send out for some in a hurry. It won't be anything to do with us.'

Kindly's eyes were too poor to see much in the gathering gloom, but his daughter craned her neck to follow my gaze. 'Torches,' she said. 'And you're wrong, father. Whoever that is down there, he's more than a servant. Those men are carrying a litter! Yaotl, you don't think...?'

Lily's last words were spoken in a whisper, through a throat constricted by sudden terror, and when I stood up to stand by her, the hand I laid upon her arm for comfort was trembling.

Why we should both have been seized at that moment by the same sense of foreboding, I could not say. Perhaps it was something about the litter's painfully slow progress up the hillside, or the delicacy with which its bearers set it down in the forecourt of a small house set in the hillside below us, lowering their charge to the ground as gently as a mother laying her baby on his cradleboard.

My former master was a frail old man, who would demand that sort of care; but why should he be here?

'Lord Feathered in Black doesn't know where we are,' I said. The tremor I felt through the thin material of her blouse reminded me how much effort she was putting into living from one day to the next, and how close she still was to falling into the abyss that surrounded her, the memory of what she had just been through. 'And we're the king's guests, remember?'

'He could have changed his mind.'

'He made a promise, Lily. He ate earth.' I tightened my grip on her shoulder, wondering whether kings considered themselves bound by a form of oath that I myself had violated on occasion.

I stared down the hill, but in the gloom it was impossible to identify the person in the litter, which was draped in cotton and bedecked with feathers. A few human shapes moved about: the thick shadows of the litter bearers, the slighter forms of attendants with flickering torches, and another, whose brisk, determined stride gave him, even in the dark and at a distance, the look of an officer.

My breath caught in my throat when I saw which way he was

going, and I heard a startled gasp from Lily at the same time, for he was coming up the steps leading to our house.

I looked accusingly at Kindly. ' "It won't be anything to do with us," you said.'

'Can't be right all the time,' he murmured in a troubled voice.

' "Some flunky," you said. "Royal chefs run out of newts."' Fear made me fling the words at him. 'I suppose this man's here to borrow a cup of chocolate!'

Lily hissed: 'Yaotl, that's enough! We'll know in a moment.'

The lone man reached the top step and skirted the small pond at the front of our residence. His long cloak, glittering labret and earplugs and piled-up hair seemed to confirm my first impression of him: here was a veteran warrior, whose valour in combat had earned him much wealth and prestige in his own right. Only a king or a great lord could have sent such a man on an errand. I knew where the king of Tetzcoco was now: in his palace at the summit of the hill, and not being carried around in a litter like a cripple. If any other great lord had business with us, it was unlikely to be good news.

Still, as Lily had remarked, we would know in a moment. The officer stood on the edge of the pond, glancing at each of us in turn as though unsure which of us to address. Finally, with his eyes on the floor in front of him, he gave an embarrassed cough and began: 'My lords…'

I gaped at him. I wondered briefly who he thought we were, before blurting out: 'Oh, it's all right, he's got the wrong house. No lords here!'

Lily silenced me with a bony elbow in the ribs. Stepping

forward, she greeted the stranger graciously, with the customary words: 'You have expended breath to get here, you are tired, you are hungry. First you must rest and have some food.'

I giggled hysterically. 'We've got pots full of newts!'

'Yaotl, shut up!' my mistress cried, exasperated.

The soldier's astounded gaze swung from one to the other of us like a spectator's at a ball game, but at the mention of my name it came to rest on me. 'Yaotl,' he repeated.

I looked wildly around as though another Yaotl might have appeared out of the shadows beside me. 'It's a common enough name,' I said defensively.

'My lord...' he began again.

'No, look, there must be some mistake,' I protested, but I fell silent as I took in the expression on the man's face. For all his warrior's strength and vigour, his cheeks were hollow and his eyes darted about in their sockets as though looking for a means of escape. Something had terrified him, I realised suddenly: something he had seen very recently, perhaps this very evening.

I became aware that he was still speaking. I had not been paying attention: it had been some long, formal pronouncement, delivered in a monotone.

Kindly answered: 'An invitation? To what, though?'

'Lord Maize Ear, the Great Chichimec, lord of the Acolhuans...'

'The king, yes. Spare us all his titles, he's a friend of mine,' the old man lied outrageously. 'What about him?'

The officer looked wretched, his tension evident from the sweat glistening on his forehead. What frightened him was the possibility that we would not respond to his message as we were meant to, and he, the messenger, would get the blame. Kindly knew this and was making the most of it. I wondered if Lily's father had sensed that there was more to the man's fear than that, however.

He stammered: 'Although my master's house is mean, and he can offer but poor food...'

'You mean the king? Rubbish, he lives in a palace, of course. Mind you, if he's run out of newts again...'

'Father!' Lily snapped. 'Will you let the poor man finish?' She turned to the officer and smiled weakly at him. 'Forgive us,' she said gently. 'We haven't been the king's guests for long, and this is all new to us. He wants to see us, is that right? Just tell us when and where.'

The man seemed to gain a couple of fingers' breadths in height, like a porter straightening his back after untying his tump-line and dropping his burden on the ground. His formal manner vanished. 'Up the hill.' He jerked his head in the direction of the king's palace at the summit. 'Be there at dawn tomorrow.'

'Then please tell his lordship we will come...' Lily began, but in my agitation I could not restrain myself from speaking across her.

'You didn't come straight here from Maize Ear's palace, though, did you? You came from down there.' I gestured towards the house where we had seen the litter taken. 'So if this invitation is from the king, it includes someone else. Whoever it is, you asked him first, then you came to us. And I'm guessing as well that whatever it is that's put the wind up you, it's something more than whatever lord Maize Ear will say if he doesn't see our faces beaming at him over breakfast. So just who is this scary person? Who are we calling on tomorrow –

besides your king?'

He took a step backward, until one of his heels was over the water: any farther and he would have been in. No doubt he was not used to hearing slaves speaking like that. But he had an answer for me: a name. It was the one name guaranteed to silence me.

'Lord Feathered in Black.' His voice shook with awe. 'The chief minister of the Aztecs is here to see you.'

3

'But what does he want?'

I paced up and down in my agitation, my bare feet slapping the stuccoed floor of the small room Lily and I had retired to. The king's expensive feather and cotton wall-hangings deadened the sound they made, and for some reason I found that irritating, so I brought my soles down on the floor still harder until they hurt. This did not make me feel any better.

My owner and I shared a sleeping mat. We had not slept apart since we had come to Tetzcotzinco, not since the night, a few days and a lifetime ago, when we had been thrown into a cell in the dark prison in the heart of king Maize Ear's palace. In all that time we had not made love once, although we both knew, without either of us mentioning the fact, that this was likely to come. What we shared now was need. Lily had to know that when she fled from sleep, shrieking and thrashing about in her efforts to escape the monsters that haunted her dreams, I would be there.

I had never been given to flattering myself. I was a scrawny slave, and not a very reliable one at that, besides being a failed priest. My long hair was going grey and fast receding away from my forehead. As a man I had nothing to recommend me except this: I was a man, I was here, I was real, and she never had to tell me who or what she was dreaming about, because I already knew.

It had been possible to believe we had a future together, or at least pretend to believe it, so long as we were safely hidden. But now lord Feathered in Black was here.

Tetzcoco was an independent kingdom, and its king had offered us his protection. However, everyone knew lord Maize Ear owed his position to his uncle, the Aztec emperor Montezuma. My former master, besides being Montezuma's cousin, was also the emperor's chief minister. If he told the king to hand Lily, Kindly and me over to him, it would be hard for Maize Ear to refuse.

Lily looked up at me from the sleeping mat. 'It's obvious what he wants.' Her voice shook. 'He wants to finish what the king's servants started.'

I looked at her bandaged fingers and groaned. It was part pity, part remorse. 'Lily, I'm sorry. I got you into this. You and your father. You should have left me in that slave-dealer's cage!'

She shivered violently. 'Well,' she whispered, 'I didn't.' She looked down. 'Will he take us back to Mexico, do you think? Or has he brought the captain with him?'

The captain was my former master's favourite henchman. He was an otomi, a member of that select band of elite warriors who were among the most feared in the Aztec army. The otomies were berserkers, sworn never to take a step backwards in battle. They were instantly recognisable in the field by their close-fitting green cotton uniforms, their hair, worn piled up on their heads and flowing over the napes of their necks, and the towering feather-bedecked devices that they carried on wicker frames strapped to their backs. The mere sight of an otomi was usually enough to cow his enemies into submission. The captain was even more terrifying than most of his comrades because he had lost half his face and one eye during some particularly brutal fight many years before. The fact that he had survived the encounter at all was not the least frightening thing about him.

And he hated me. With my friend Momaimati, a commoner whose name meant One Skilled with his Hands or 'Handy', I had once humiliated the captain by leading him into a hostile crowd from which he had had to be rescued by a squad of Aztec warriors. The captain and his men had pursued me to king Maize Ear's kingdom of Tetzcoco. I knew that he would blame me for what happened as a result: a fight with the locals in which his followers had perished and from which he had been forced to flee. He would not rest now until one or other of us was dead.

'Perhaps we could run away,' I suggested.

'How? This hill is ringed with guards. Remember what my father said. If a centipede couldn't get in, how do you think we're going to sneak out of here? And where would we go? Back to Mexico? Where lord Feathered in Black is chief minister?'

'Then I'll have to fight him,' I said stoutly. 'Challenge him, maybe. Old Black Feathers likes to bet, you know. I could wager our lives on the contest – if I beat the otomi, the old bastard has to let us go!'

Lily laughed. It was a brittle sound with no humour in it. 'Don't be absurd! You're no warrior, and half the army couldn't take on the captain and win. Besides, would you trust the chief minister to honour the bet if you did win?' The laughter suddenly dissolved into the strangled, choking sound of barely-suppressed tears. 'It's hopeless,' she gasped. 'And I thought… No-one lives forever, I know, but you and I, we might have been happy…'

If I had been able to find any words, I would never have managed to squeeze them out past the constriction in my throat. I squatted awkwardly in front of her. I reached out to her as if to take her hands in mine, but then dropped my arms when I remembered how tender to the touch her fingers still were.

For a long moment neither of us said anything. Lily looked between her knees at the mat, while each of us waited for the other to speak. When she at last looked up at me, there was no more concealing the tears that started from the corners of her eyes and rolled silently down her cheeks.

I stretched my arms towards her again, this time to touch her face, cradling it between my palms. 'Lily,' I groaned. 'I'm sorry.'

THIRTEEN MOTION

1

The same messenger called for us just before daybreak, repeating his summons with the same awkward diffidence he had displayed on the previous evening.

'I'll say this for the Kingdom of Tetzcoco, you have the politest way of delivering a death warrant,' I told him sourly as we came out of the house. 'Where I come from, it's a lot less formal. They just throw you in a cage and leave you there till they get around to strangling you.' The man stared at me, looking gratifyingly shocked, but then for all I knew he genuinely believed he was inviting us to breakfast.

The four of us made a glum little procession as we climbed towards the royal Palace at the summit of the hill. Grey mist, rising from the mighty lake that filled the bottom of the valley of Mexico, swirled around us, wrapping us in darkness and making each of us clutch our cloaks tighter for warmth. Moisture dripping from branches and rocks made the ground slippery and treacherous. Even if we had not all been sunk in our own thoughts, we would have been too busy trying to keep our footing to speak to one another.

Near the top, steep steps had been etched into the rock, and our progress up them reminded me too vividly of the shuffling gait of captives being led up the side of the great pyramid in Mexico. It was the right time of day too, I judged. Around now, the priests would be hailing the dawn with trumpet calls and killing the first prisoner of the day, cutting his heart out to nourish the gods, in the hope that they would let the sun rise once more.

Sure enough, the sun was there to greet us when we reached the summit.

The officer strode on towards the king's palace. But he was used to this place. Kindly, Lily and I were not, and for moment we could only stand and stare at the things around us like little children at their first ball game.

None of us said anything until Lily let out a sob. 'It's so beautiful,' she whispered.

We had climbed above the mist. The valley below us was like a pale grey sea, empty save for the mountaintops in the distance, their slopes picked out in pink and gold by the newborn sun. Most astonishing of all, though, was what lay at our feet: for in the middle of the sea of mist was a lake.

Lord Maize Ear's grandfather had carved a huge reservoir out of the rock at the summit of the hill and built his palace on an island at the centre of it, in the shade of a grove of cedars. We had seen it once before, in moonlight, and then it had been lovely. At daybreak it was like one of the thirteen levels of heaven. The ripples on the lake glittered, the trees were hung with dewdrops that sparkled like jewels where the sunlight hit them, and the birdsong rising from the valley somehow made the foot of the hill, the mist-shrouded land below us, seem more remote than ever.

A causeway led across the lake to the palace in its centre. Against the gleaming surface of the water it was black, like a deep crack across the face of a gold statue. I hesitated to set foot on it, knowing who must be waiting for me at the far end; but the officer beckoned, and there was nothing we could do but follow.

Among the cedars, bathed in the morning's first rays of sunlight, two men sat on high-backed wicker chairs. One was in his twenties, tall, fresh-faced, his slight but well-muscled frame sheathed in a plain white robe of fine cotton and his brow crowned with the turquoise diadem of a king. His neighbour could not have looked more different: shrunken with age, with grey wisps of hair framing a face like an old leather mask, and his hands swollen and liver-spotted and shaking. My former master was dressed gaudily, as was his habit, in a blue mantle decorated with orange butterflies and a matching breechcloth, with grackle feathers in his hair. The effect was of a grotesque, overdressed doll – or it would have been, but for the eyes that shone out of that ravaged face, their gaze steady and bright with cunning.

Two girls in plain skirts and blouses, with their hair modestly bound up, knelt just behind the wicker chairs. They were obviously there to fetch food or drink or anything else the great men required. I saw no-one else. My head darted from side to side as I looked anxiously for the hulking figure of the otomi captain, but if he was there, he was hiding.

We walked slowly forward, my hand on Lily's arm and hers on her father's. She was trembling, but I was oddly calm, even numb. If I felt anything at all it was anger rather than fear.

'How could that young bastard do this to us?' I muttered. 'We're supposed to be his guests!'

'He's emperor Montezuma's nephew', Kindly reminded me. 'He probably doesn't have a choice. As soon as the chief minister learned we were here...'

'And how did he find that out, then?' I demanded. 'Who told him?' I could feel my fists clenching with barely suppressed rage, all the fiercer for my helplessness.

Before Lily's father could answer, the young king had got to his feet, speaking the ritual words of greeting in a soft treble voice: 'You are welcome. You have come far, you have expended breath to get here, you are hungry. Please, rest and have some food.' At the same time my nose caught the warm scent of freshly-made tortillas from somewhere within the palace at his back.

'You've got that wrong, my lord,' I said, removing my hand from Lily's arm. 'Victims are usually fasted before the sacrifice, not fed!'

The king could not have looked more shocked if I had stepped forward and spat in his eye. Beside me, Kindly drew in his breath with an audible hiss. 'Careful! Remember where you are!'

I ignored them both. I turned instead to lord Feathered in Black, my former master, to find those piercing eyes fixing me with an unblinking stare. My courage – a frail thing at the best of times and now sustained only by despair – almost failed me then, but I managed to stammer some more defiant words: 'I suppose I should feel honoured. What made you come in person, rather than sending some hireling?'

Young lord Maize Ear started forward, but surprisingly, my former master restrained him with a gnarled hand on his wrist. The old man did not shift his gaze. When he spoke, it was in the low growl that I had come, over the years, to fear more than his most thunderous rages.

'Prostrate yourselves before the king!'

I heard two bodies hitting the ground. Out of the corner of one eye I saw Kindly lying in an awkward posture, twisted sideways, as his knees had obviously given way on his way down, while his daughter was propped up on the heels of her hands in an effort to save her damaged fingers.

'You too!' the chief minister barked, and then my muscles seemed to give way of their own accord as I flopped forward onto the cold flagstones.

'That's better.' A faint creaking told me lord Feathered in Black was settling himself more comfortably in his chair. 'You're too soft, Maize Ear,' he muttered in an aside to his young relation. 'Your uncle the emperor would have had them all dismembered just for looking at him! And as for you, Yaotl, you ought to watch that tongue of yours. It will get you into trouble some day!'

I raised my head enough to see both the king and my former master. The former had resumed his seat. He was not looking at me. He stared sideways at the malevolent old man next to him, and I noted with interest how pale he was, and how the veins stood out on the backs of his hands, as though he were tense or furious.

'My lord,' I said to him, 'I am sorry. I forgot myself, seeing my former master here. It was a shock. I didn't think he knew where I was.'

'I will overlook it,' lord Maize Ear said absently. 'Although I may say that I had no idea that he knew where you were either!'

Lord Feathered in Black grinned humourlessly. 'Did you really believe, cousin, that lord Montezuma would let you reign in Tetzcoco without keeping a careful watch on your court? His concern for your welfare would never allow it!'

So our safe, comfortable resting place in the royal retreat of Tetzcotzinco had been an illusion. I groaned at my own naivety, and the king's. Old Black Feathers had known where we were from his spies almost from the moment we had arrived.

'Of course,' the old man went on, 'we lost touch with Yaotl when he first came here. Hence the unfortunate, er, misunderstanding...'

'Misunderstanding!' the young king cried. 'Your men invaded my kingdom...'

'Half a dozen hotheads are hardly an invasion, Maize Ear,' my former master said sharply, 'and anyway they weren't my men. I've explained that. They came of their own accord.'

That provoked Kindly into breaking his silence. 'You mean the otomi and his men, don't you? They came because you told them to look for us in Tetzcoco. You didn't manage to have Yaotl sacrificed the way you wanted, so you sent...'

'Not "sent", remember,' I said drily. 'How about "encouraged"?'

'Yes, that's a good word. You "encouraged" those madmen to come after us. And look what they did! Look at my daughter's hands!'

'Oh, stop babbling!' said lord Feathered in Black wearily. 'Yes, all that's true, but so what? I was angry and disappointed, and I really don't care for disappointment. Yaotl had let me down, so he had to be punished, naturally.' He sighed, and his eyes took on an unfocused, faraway look, as though he were seeing, in his imagination, something pleasant, a long way off, impossibly remote, never to be attained. 'And I'm still angry. Really, Yaotl, I'd still like to see you flayed alive! But there it is.' He sounded brisk, all of a sudden. 'We can't always have what we want, can we?'

'You can, it seems.' I had heard my former master's words but in my anger and bitterness had missed their meaning entirely. 'So where's your tame otomi? Did you bring him with you or is he at home in Mexico, roasting children for supper?'

Apart from a loud cough from Maize Ear, that remark was greeted by silence, until eventually lord Feathered in Black murmured, in a voice little more than a whisper: 'Ah. Yes, the otomi. Now…'

'And how come you're here, instead of him? I thought he ran your errands, not the other way around!'

His lordship's patience finally snapped. 'Shut your mouth, slave!' he roared in a voice that must have carried to the far side of the valley. 'Interrupt me again,' he added, more quietly, 'and I'll have things done to you that will make you curse the gods for ever letting you be born, do you hear? And that goes for you two as well!'

I heard movement from beside me. Glancing sideways, I discovered that Lily was as still as if she had been frozen solid, but her father was fidgeting and shuffling as though trying to put as much distance between me and him as he could.

Lord Feathered in Black went on: 'Yaotl, if you talked less and thought more it might have occurred to you to wonder why all three of you aren't already shrieking your lungs out in agony. Don't imagine I'm not tempted by the prospect! But the fact is that right now I need you alive more than dead. You asked me where the otomi was. Here's your answer: I don't know! So what do you think of that?'

It was just beginning to occur to me that the old man had not had us brought up here to kill us, after all, but I was too bewildered now to feel relief. My mind grappled with his last words. 'You've lost him.'

For some reason the old man seemed to find that funny: it set off a throaty, wheezing noise that I had learned to recognise as laughter. 'You might say that! I... what was the word? I "encouraged" him and his men to come here, as you know...'

'To kill me and Lily.'

'Yes, that's right.' It was typical of him that he could acknowledge this without a trace of embarrassment. 'Now, I have no idea what happened to him here. No doubt you know more about it than I do! He came back alone, without any of the men who'd been with him. I must say, Yaotl, that if you managed to dispose of a squad of otomies, there must be more to you than I thought!'

'Um, well, I didn't exactly...'

'Of course, I told him to have another go. But then he disappeared. I thought I'd heard the last of him then. I had the impression, when he was telling me – babbling incoherently, to be more precise – about what you'd done to him, that his nerve had gone. But then I started getting... reports.'

'What sort of reports?'

'Incidents – violent ones. People attacked in the street – always at night, alone, never with any witnesses. Rumours of a monster, a demon, creeping about in the city after dark. The fishermen are terrified: something's been raiding their nets, stealing their catches.' He paused, either for breath or for effect. 'The rumours are especially strong down by the lake, in the south of the city. And in two parishes in particular – Atlixco and Toltenco.'

'My parents live in Toltenco!' I burst out.

'So they do. And doesn't your friend Handy have his house in Atlixco?' The chief minister knew perfectly well where both my family and Handy's lived.

I had an unpleasant suspicion about what the old man might have in mind.

I had not killed the otomi's comrades, as it happened; but died, they certainly had, in a violent clash that only their leader had survived. He had been on the point of adding me to the pile of corpses when something had happened to him that, coming on top of everything else, must have driven him insane.

He had thought he had seen a god. Cihuacoatl, that most feared of goddesses, She of the Serpent Skirt, whose voice spelled doom to all who heard it, had called out to him out of the darkness.

The apparition had, as it happened, a perfectly mundane explanation: but for him, a typically superstitious warrior, a man who feared no human enemy but could be transfixed by an owl's call or the sight of a badger, mundane explanations did not exist. He had fled, gibbering, into the night. I had imagined that might be the last I would see of him.

I abandoned my prone position to rise to my knees. My former master watched me doing it but said nothing.

'You think he's given up trying to get to me directly,' I said slowly. 'He's going to get his revenge on my family instead. And Handy…'

'He has a grudge against him too, I gather, and of course he knows the commoner is a friend of yours.'

'How are you going to stop him?' I demanded. 'You have to catch him before anyone else does. Because if they do, and they start asking questions, it could be a bit awkward, couldn't it?'

'Assuming they can take him alive, yes. Some of the tasks I gave him and his men to do were a little, well, unorthodox. And he lacks a certain delicacy of manner, which is very necessary in an otomi warrior, but it can be taken too far.' He glanced sideways at the king, who sat looking straight ahead, his lips compressed in a grim expression. No doubt he was thinking of the havoc the captain had wreaked in his own realm. 'If it became known in the wrong quarters that I had been...' He hesitated as if searching for the right expression.

' "Encouraging" him?' I suggested. 'I can see the consequences might be a bit awkward. Fatal, even, if "the wrong quarters" happened to be anywhere near Montezuma!'

'Quite so. But as to how I stop him... Well, now we're coming to the point. I need your help.' He leaned forward as he said this, gripping the arms of his chair and talking very slowly and careful in his eagerness to be understood. 'Your help,' he repeated, 'in exchange for your life.'

I could only stare at him while my mind tried to grapple with what I was hearing. Surely, I thought, this must be some cruel joke. It sounded as though the chief minister were offering me some sort of deal, but the notion of lord Feathered in Black being anything less than ruthlessly, violently single-minded in his quest for vengeance was too surreal to bear. Less surprising to find that the gods had reversed the order of night and day or replaced the mountains with rolling hills.

It was Lily who spoke, while I was still trying to remember how my tongue worked. 'You want Yaotl to find the captain for you?' She had levered herself up on her elbows to glare defiantly at the old man on the chair, and she did not take her eyes off him even as I unthinkingly helped her up into a kneeling position. 'Why? You have enough men of your own you can call on. Why don't you just send them after him?'

'Because if he's hiding where I think he is – at the edge of the lake, among the marshes and the *chinampa* fields – then it would take an army to flush him out. It's a labyrinth there, as you well know. And I can't send an army. I'd have to tell far too many people exactly what they were searching for, and why!'

'So how do you plan for me to do this, then?' I asked.

'Come back to Mexico,' he replied airily. 'Go about your normal business and wait for him to find you. A couple of my men could follow you. At a discreet distance, naturally.'

'Discreet enough so that it takes a conveniently long time for them to get stuck in, you mean? Time enough for him to finish me off and rid you of two problems at once?'

'Oh, you do make everything so difficult!' old Black Feathers replied petulantly. 'I'm sure we can come up with some way of reassuring you, and it would be well worth your while, you know. I can offer you – all of you – a lot more than just your lives. How long were you going to stay here, in Tetzcotzinco? What would it be worth to you, to be able to live here in Mexico openly? Do you really want to be exiles, or be forever skulking in the shadows, afraid someone will recognise you?'

The wheedling tone he had adopted did not impress me; but his words themselves did. I had been living on my wits ever since I had run away from him. I was tired. I wanted to stop running and hiding. And above all, I wanted to go home.

No Aztec would ever feel at home anywhere but in Mexico. In the scant few bundles of years since the war-god had brought the Aztecs to the island in the midst of the lake, shown them an eagle perched on a cactus and told them that it was to be their dwelling-place, my ancestors had turned Mexico's marsh and rock into the greatest city in the world. They had filled it with houses, temples, palaces and gardens and surrounded it with *chinampa* fields, ever-fertile plots made of mud dredged from the river bed. Every street, every canal, every wall bore the stamp of my people; every plaza rang with voices chattering, cursing and laughing with the accent I knew. In Mexico I had been hunted like an animal, abused, imprisoned, tortured and threatened with death; but suddenly, now that the chief minister had shown me what my choice was, I realised the thing I dreaded most of all was exile. I had left the city and had felt safe for a while, but I did not want to accept that I would never be back.

I knew, without needing to look at them, that Lily and her father would feel the same way as well. They were merchants, but beneath that, they were Aztecs.

'How do we know we can trust you?' I asked cautiously.

I heard that harsh, cackling laugh again. 'Yaotl, I'm not so naïve as to think for one moment that you'll ever trust me! But you don't need to. Remember those rumours I told you about. Just go to the marketplace in Tetzcoco and ask any visitor from Mexico. You'll soon learn that I'm not making it up. Are you going to abandon your family to a monster?' He did not wait for an answer. 'This is the deal. If you do as I say then I'll promise to leave you and Lily and her father alone. It's not much I ask: just come back to Mexico, let people see you – no skulking in shadows – just until the otomi takes the bait. And we'll be watching over you, of course.'

'And if I don't?'

My former master grinned nastily before turning to his young cousin. 'And if he doesn't, Maize Ear?' he purred.

The young king looked down, apparently taking a sudden interest in his knees that were drawn up together in front of him. 'I'm sorry,' he mumbled. 'But it seems that you will no longer be my guests.'

'And where will you go then?' My former master asked. 'Even if you're prepared to leave your family to their fate, Yaotl, do you really want to go wandering among barbarians? Tarascans, Zapotecs, Mayans, scum like that? ' He grinned once more. 'Don't make things any more difficult for yourself than they have to be. I want you alive, at least for the time being. I may have further uses for you!'

2

It was early for breakfast, but the king insisted we eat, ordering his attendants to fetch tortillas for us from the palace kitchen. The bread was delicious, still warm from the griddle, but apart from lord Feathered in Black, who devoured his ravenously, talking all the time, nobody appeared to have much appetite. Kindly, Lily and I nibbled politely and in silence until the chief minister's flow of palace gossip and his meal were both finished.

My former master excused himself abruptly after that, remarking that wealth and power were no protection against the afflictions of old age. Two of his bearers were summoned from the palace to help him out of his seat. As soon as he was gone, the king stood up.

'I think,' he said ruefully, 'that means we are all dismissed! Come, I'll walk with you to the end of the causeway.'

We walked in silence for a few moments, while the waters of the lake lapped gently around us. There was too much anger and resentment for the peace to remain undisturbed for long, however.

'That – that bastard!' I burst out. A tiny stone lay on the carefully swept path in front of me. I aimed a kick at it with my bare foot, sending it into the water to vanish without so much as a 'plop'. 'He has me brought up here, convinced I'm going to have my heart cut out, but oh no, even that's not good enough for old Black Feathers. It's too much trouble for him, I suppose, so I've got to arrange my own death by going one on one with the otomi. I'm even expected to find the bugger myself, because our ever-vigilant chief minister's managed to lose him!'

Kindly peered curiously at me through his filmy eyes. 'What are you complaining about? We're in this too, and we didn't do anything to offend the old man in the first place. Besides, you're still alive, aren't you?'

'I don't care!' I cried irrationally. 'And I won't do it. I'm not going back to Mexico to face that madman. I'd rather lie in wait for old Black Feathers and throw him and his litter down the hillside.'

'I'd like to see you try it!' Kindly laughed. 'I wonder what odds I could get on your chances?'

Turning to the king, Lily said sharply: 'You promised to protect us!'

'Not forever,' the king said. 'I'm sorry, but I'm not free to do what I want, any more than you are. Lord Feathered in Black's spies told him where you were almost the moment you arrived here. This hill must be crawling with them, and I didn't even know! How long would I last if I defied him now?'

'Your father wouldn't have let old Black Feathers push him around!'

'Things were different in his day,' Maize Ear replied bitterly. 'My father didn't have a brother with his eyes on the throne and half the kingdom loyal to him, and the Aztecs didn't rule most of the world then either.' Then he smiled grimly. 'No good will come of it, though. For all their chief minister and my uncle the emperor can do, the

Aztecs have angered too many people. One day their enemies will combine against them, and Mexico won't be a good place to be then. You might want to think about going to live among barbarians after all!'

Kindly laughed again. 'I'm too old! No, I'm for going home. I'm going to sit in my own courtyard with my *patolli* mat and a gourd full of sacred wine, and if our enemies or avenging gods do come then I expect I shall be past caring.'

The king looked at me. 'Apart from mugging your chief minister on his way home,' he asked, 'What do you intend to do?'

We had reached the edge of the lake by now. I turned and stared moodily back at the palace, but there was no sign of my former master. Having made his wishes plain, he had presumably lost interest in us.

'I don't have a choice, do I?' I said bitterly. 'He's not wrong. We need to go back to Mexico sooner or later. And I need to find out if he's telling the truth: if that madman really is threatening my family, not to mention Handy and his brood.'

'Can't your brother look after them?' Lily asked. My eldest brother, whose name was Mamiztli – 'the Mountain Lion' – was a distinguished warrior, who had fought his way up from the obscure origins we shared to the high office of *Atempanecatl*, Guardian of the Waterfront. 'If anybody's capable of taking on the captain, it's him and his bodyguards.'

'Only if he knows what's going on. He'll have heard the rumours, of course, but old Black Feathers won't have told him what's behind them. He and my brother aren't friends. It would be like telling the whole city. I need to warn him. I ought to warn Handy as well.'

Something disturbed the air above us: a small flock of ducks, their wings beating heavily as they headed west towards the great lake in the bottom of the valley, with the mighty city at its centre. Ducks are reluctant fliers, and their laboured progress looked like an omen. We had to go that way too, whether we wanted to or not.

The noise caught Lily's attention as well. When she turned to watch the birds out of sight, the rising sun at her back caught the white strands in her hair, making them seem to glow briefly. The last few days appeared to have added to their number, I thought sadly.

'If we have to go,' she said abruptly, 'then let's get on with it. Yaotl, you need to see your parents in Toltenco, and your brother, and Handy in Atlixco – where to first, then?'

'I think Handy's place,' I said thoughtfully. 'He still runs errands for lord Feathered in Black from time to time. He may be able to tell me something useful. But I'll go alone.'

'Oh, no, you won't!' she cried. Her dark eyes glittered when she turned them on me. 'We're all caught up in this thing now, aren't we? What if you don't manage to find the otomi? What will old Black Feathers do to us then?'

'No more than the otomi would if he caught us all together,' her father muttered. 'Besides, I'm not in any condition to go paddling through the marshes after some madman, and nor, young lady, are you.'

'Don't talk to me as if were a child!' she shouted at him, stamping her foot in as childish a gesture as I ever saw. 'I'll do what I want. If you want to go home and squat in your own courtyard guzzling sacred wine with your senile friends that's up to you. I'm going with Yaotl!'

The king looked from one to the other of them with eyes

narrowed in consternation. I decided I had better settle the row before it became a brawl that got all three of us thrown bodily off the top of the hill. 'Your father's right, Lily. There won't be much you can do: it's me the otomi wants, and I'll be safer on my own.'

'But what about the men lord Feathered in Black was going to have following you?'

'What about them? Chances are they don't even exist. If they do, I'm afraid I don't believe what I said to him was wrong. They won't lay a finger on the captain until it's far too late for me. My only chance is to do exactly what old Black Feathers told me not to do – skulk in the shadows, and I can't do that in company. You and Kindly should go straight back to Tlatelolco. Make sure your house is still in one piece!'

From the way she reacted to my words I thought I might have said too much. She rocked backward on her heels as though I had threatened to hit her and her lips trembled.

'You might get hurt!' I burst out, desperately.

She pressed her lips together, forcing them into stillness. 'I'm already hurt,' she said calmly. There was no need for her to show me her wounded hands to demonstrate the point, but she dragged the back of one of them across her eyes before adding in a small voice: 'I don't want to be alone as well.'

Then she tried to turn away, but I had caught her in my arms before she could move.

'You won't ever be that, lady,' I said hoarsely.

ONE FLINT KNIFE

1

In the event we did not leave lord Maize Ear's kingdom until early the following morning. The king had his own boatmen paddle us across the lake, Lily and her father to the merchant's quarter of Tlatelolco in the north of the city of Mexico, and me to Atlixco, the poorer parish in the south where my friend Handy lived. We left before daybreak. We were all keen to make an early start, and the king was just as eager to slip us quietly back into the city we had come from, as though we had never set foot in his domain.

Lily had eventually come to her senses and agreed that I should go alone to see Handy and my family. I could be back at her house by nightfall.

The king undertook to tell lord Feathered in Black where I was going, so that his men could be on hand to keep a discreet eye on me, and intervene in case the captain appeared. As I had made clear to Lily, I placed no reliance on this. I still suspected that if the chief minister had his way, any action his servants took would come just a moment too late to prevent the otomi from finishing me off.

Trumpet calls filled the air around me as I approached Handy's house. They might have been an ironic fanfare to herald my arrival: a little man in a commoner's short cape and plain breechcloth. In fact the calls were made by priests blowing into huge conch shells as they stood at the tops of the pyramids, to herald the dawn.

There were a hundred thousand houses like this one in the city of Mexico All there was to see from outside was an adobe wall, its whitewashed surface pale in the weak light of early morning and featureless except for a single dark opening. There was no screen or cloth over the doorway. It was hard to see inside, but I knew what was there: a sparsely-furnished room opening out, at its far end, onto a square courtyard of hard earth, bounded on two sides by high walls and on the others by the few rooms in which Handy's family lived. There would be a few idols on low stone plinths and, against one wall, a small dome-shaped structure in dried mud: the sweat bath.

When I first saw the house I quickened my pace, afraid that I might miss my friend before he set out for his day's work. As I neared it, however, I slowed down and paused. Something was wrong.

I could hear nothing. Handy had nine children, I recalled, and the last time I had seen him there had been a tenth on the way; and he had nieces and nephews besides. Whenever I had been to this house, the place had been in a state approaching uproar. Piercingly high voices had sung, shouted or grizzled, while deeper ones had bellowed or sworn in frustration. And then I realised it was not even the lack of these sounds of a typically large Aztec family that had shocked me into stillness, but the absence of something even more basic.

There was no smoke billowing from the hole in the roof, no slap of dough on a griddle, no smell of baking bread. Nobody was making tortillas, and in a household in Mexico at daybreak, that was unthinkable.

I crept towards the doorway, fearful of what I might find. It suddenly occurred to me that the otomi captain might have been smarter than I had given him credit for, and there might be a sinister explanation for the silence and atmosphere of tension about the place.

'Er... Hullo? Handy?' I put a hand on the doorpost, peering past it while I nerved myself to leap backwards, whirl around and sprint away from the house if I had to.

For a moment there was no response. Then a pair of eyes gleamed, deep within the room's darkness. Someone shuffled towards me. A female voice snapped: 'What do you want?'

'My name's, er, Yaotl.' I hoped that was not the signal for my enemy to spring out of the shadows. I shot a nervous glance towards the flat roof, realising too late that anything could be lying in ambush just above my head.

'I know,' the woman told me. She came into the light. 'I asked you what you wanted.'

I stared at her.

I had seen her before. She was Atototl, or 'Goose': a pretty, lively, gossipy woman, the sister of Handy's wife. She was very close to her sister and much like her in temperament. At least that was how I remembered her, but to look at her now, with her eyes heavy-lidded and deep in shadow, her dark hair lank and tangled and her blouse and skirt looking as though she had not changed them in a month, I had to think again before I was sure she was the same person. It was plain that whatever was afflicting her, it had nothing to do with me. It was more like some great grief or fear.

'What's the matter, Goose? I just wanted to speak to Handy, to ask him a question, but...' And then I realised what must have happened, and I closed my eyes and groaned, a sound of pain, despair and remorse. 'So I'm too late. He's been here already. It wasn't yesterday, was it?' Had the captain struck while Lily and her father and I dawdled for a whole day in Tetzcoco?

She stared at me, her heavy eyelids blinking slowly as though she were getting used to the light. 'What are you talking about?'

'The otomi. Did he come here yesterday?'

'What's an otomi got to do with my sister?'

It was my turn to stare now. 'Your sister? Citlalli?' Star, her name meant: the mother of Handy's children. 'You mean it's Star, not Handy, who's...' Finally I understood. When I groaned for a second time, it was out of grief, for someone I had only met twice, but had liked, and whose sharp tongue, easy humour and stout courage I suddenly feared might be gone forever.

Handy, I recalled again, had a tenth child on the way.

'It's the baby, isn't it? Something's happened to her and the baby.'

A kind of pall always hung over Mexico at this time of year, during the Month of the Ceasing of Water. Long poles had been set up everywhere, with sharp points at their tips and strips of paper dashed and spotted with liquid rubber dangling from them. They stood in most houses, in the forecourts of temples, in the Houses of Youth and the Houses of Tears, as stark as trees in a burned forest. They were a reminder to the rain god of what was required, their points seemingly pricking the sky to draw moisture from it. The forlorn creaking sounds they made and the rustling of those paper streamers were a reminder to us, too, of those who had to die to ensure the god took notice: the young children whose bodies were left on the mountains where the clouds gathered.

However, as I looked around Handy's courtyard, I saw no sign that any attention was being paid to the ritual. The pain that showed on the faces of those around me was not for the rain god's anonymous victims, but for somebody close. All eyes were on the small, dome-shaped sweat bath.

Handy squatted just opposite the entrance hole. He was a stolid, broad shouldered man, still strong but with the grey, thinning hair of middle age. Normally at this time he would be on his way to the waterlogged plot of land he tended at the edge of the city, getting it ready for the coming Spring. Now though he seemed fascinated by the wisps of steam still drifting out of the sweat bath to form thin clouds in the crisp early morning air. The fire that had been built against the side of the dome to heat the water inside it had become a few bright embers in a dark bed of ash.

Near to Handy, standing with ashen faces and downcast eyes, were an elderly, heavily jowelled man and a thin, bony woman whose fingers constantly twisted around each other. From their air of tension and the way they held themselves apart from the rest of the family I guessed they were Star's parents. A few youngsters squatted or kneeled nearby. I recognised one of them as Itzcoatl or Obsidian Snake, one of Handy's younger sons, a boy of eleven or twelve years. I frowned as I noticed his slight figure: I was accustomed to see him looking lively and alert, but now he was hunched silently among his brothers and sisters and they all looked dejected and weary.

When I reappraised the scene I realised that apart from Handy and Goose, everyone was arranged in a rough semicircle against the walls of the courtyard. As Goose kneeled heavily on the earth floor with her nieces and nephews, I sidled across to speak to her, leaving her brother-in-law alone. I wondered what we were all distancing ourselves from: was it whatever was happening in the sweat bath, or was it Star's husband and his grief?

'There hasn't been a sound from them since the last of the stars went out,' the woman whispered, without prompting. She was not looking at me. 'Not even a groan.'

I looked at the dome in the corner. It seemed too small to contain one person, let alone two. 'What went wrong?'

'The opossum tail didn't work.'

'I don't understand.'

Childbirth was a mystery to me. It was not something I had ever been concerned with in my former life as a priest. It was the preserve of midwives, who had their own mysteries and rituals.

'The opossum tail,' she repeated dully, 'and before that the *cihuapatli*, the women's herb. Everything seemed to be going so well. She felt her first pains yesterday, just when she was due. All her children have been like that, never any problem. But something seems to have gone wrong since they went into the sweat bath. The midwife was shouting...' Goose paused for a long, shuddering breath before continuing: 'When we sent for my sister's midwife, we were told she couldn't be found. My niece had to go to the Pleasure House, to ask the women there if one of them would come instead. She was lucky to find Yolyamanqui.' The name was an appropriate one for someone in her profession, I thought, as it meant 'Gentle of Heart'.

Out of the corner of my eye I saw Handy move, leaning forward as though he had seen or heard something.

'She knows her work, and she's done her best. She brought the women's herb and the ground-up opossum tail. But it doesn't seem to have done any good. She thought the baby might be adhering to the womb. She took my sister into the sweat bath at midnight. I know she's doing everything she can – we could hear them from out here, my sister crying out and the midwife shouting at her – but everyone knows that if the opossum tail doesn't work there's nothing to be done. It was horrible, Yaotl, but this is worse. This silence…'

If she said anything else I did not hear it. A sound had erupted from the sweat bath: a loud, convulsive sobbing. I, like everyone else in the courtyard, was on my feet, starting instinctively towards the source of the crying. Then we all froze, everyone, it seemed, realising at once what that noise meant.

Only Handy approached the dome in the corner, but even he stopped when a woman emerged, crawling, through the hole in the wall. When she stood up I saw that she was not Star. She was a woman in late middle age, whose greying hair framed features that might normally be soft, the eyes wide and the nose a gentle curve, but whose face was now crumpled into a mask of anguish. The hem of her skirt and her legs were darkly spotted with what I took to be blood.

She had a small, cloth-wrapped bundle in her hands.

A gasp broke from Goose's throat. One of the children called out: 'Father!' but Handy seemed not to have heard him. He just stood and stared at the midwife as she cradled his child.

Goose stepped towards the woman. 'Gentle Heart, what has happened? Is my sister…'

The midwife looked at her and frowned. 'Your sister?'

'My sister, Star!' Goose was almost screaming. 'How is she?'

The other woman suddenly seemed to come to her senses. 'I'm

sorry. Please forgive me, I'm very tired.' Then she turned to Handy, who stood just a couple of hands' breadths away from her, his body swaying slightly, like a sapling rocked by wind, but his face as rigid as if it had been carved out of basalt.

'I'm sorry,' she said again, but this time deliberately, so as to leave her listeners no room to doubt what was to follow. 'I did what I could. But it doesn't seem to have been enough.'

A loud groan escaped the man. The old couple behind him both looked as if their faces had been slapped.

'The mother is with the Turquoise Prince, the sun, now; she has joined the Divine Princesses. She has paid her tribute of death. And the child...'

Gentle Heart's words fell on me like a blow, leaving me – a visitor here, not much better than a stranger – speechless and shocked out of any real awareness of what was going on around me. Sights and sounds seemed for a moment to come from a great distance away, or to be something imagined, made up from a story I had been told by someone else, as if I had not been there. I saw Handy dropping to his knees, his head bent as if he were being sick, his sister's eyes widened into pale, blank discs and his parents-in-law grasping each other with the force of drowning bathers seizing hold of a low branch. They all seemed fixed in place, like figures in a frieze or a mural: the background against which Gentle Heart alone acted out a forlorn ritual.

'The child,' she said, in a low, faltering voice, 'has obeyed the will of Tezcatlipoca, whose slaves we are. He has returned whence he came, to suckle from the divine milk-tree until it is his time to be born on Earth.'

2

Handy was still on his knees. His wife's parents spoke to the midwife, his mother-in-law cradling the inert bundle in her arms as though it were not entirely beyond comforting. From behind me I heard Goose's voice chattering as she tried to usher her nieces and nephews out of the courtyard. I stood rooted to the spot, ignored by everyone, which was probably just as well, as a fierce argument was developing.

Handy was looking up now, squinting into the face of his father-in-law as the old man stood over him, berating him over something. The midwife seemed to be trying to get in between them while the baby's grandmother stood by, still clutching the child's body protectively to her breast.

'I knew it!' the old man raged. 'I knew it, as soon as the midwife said he was stuck in the womb! You couldn't leave her alone, could you? Now look what you've done! My daughter, gone, and all because of you, because you couldn't keep your filthy hands off her, you animal, you stinking, shit-eating dog!' He spluttered incoherently into silence for as long as it took to draw breath. 'And the baby as well! I could kill you with my bare hands for this!' he shrieked, but as his trembling, swollen fingers clawed the air in fury, Gentle Heart interrupted him.

'You can't blame him, Ocelotl.' she protested, while Handy merely groaned.

'Yes I can!' shouted the old man, whose name meant 'Jaguar'. '"Stuck in the womb," you said! Do you think I don't know what that means? He was forcing himself on her, wasn't he, like a beast, even after the fourth month, and we all know what that leads to. That's why the baby wouldn't come out, isn't it?'

'Well, perhaps, but it is not an easy thing we ask, and for a couple who have conceived ten children…'

'I always found it easy enough!' the old man thundered.

'It's not true,' my friend said suddenly, in a dull voice, as though he did not much care whether it were true or not. 'We knew what was proper. We brought nine children into the world, didn't we? Do you think we didn't know how to control ourselves?'

Somebody pushed past me and rushed towards the little group in the middle of the courtyard: Goose, carrying a large pot and with a clean blouse and skirt draped over one arm. She strode boldly up to the old man.

'Father,' she said, 'You can't help Star now, and you're just going to make yourself ill if you carry on.'

The man's face was almost black with rage. 'Don't tell me what to do,' he snapped, but before he had got the words out his surviving daughter had already turned away from him. 'Where do you think you're going?' he demanded.

'To wash and dress my sister,' she said, without turning her head, and ducked into the sweat bath. The midwife watched her for a moment and then turned to Handy.

'The baby?' she said simply.

For a moment the commoner seemed to have no idea what she was talking about. Then he looked at the little bundle in his mother-in-law's arms. 'I don't know…' He looked away again quickly.

Star's mother spoke, for the first time in my hearing. 'Put him with his mother for now, in the sweat bath,' she suggested. Hearing her speak, sounding so much as her daughter might have done at such a time – not unkind, but practical – only added to my own sense of what had been lost.

Handy hesitated in response to his mother-in-law's suggestion, before making a noise that may have been assent. The old woman and the midwife turned towards the sweat bath. Star's father made as if to follow them, but he seemed to change his mind suddenly – perhaps realising that what they were about was women's work – and stalked into the interior of the house instead. He did not spare Handy or me a glance.

The bereaved husband got up off his knees slowly, moving like a man about twenty years older than he was. He and I were now alone in the courtyard.

I was acutely aware of this fact because I looked quickly about in the hope of seeing someone else. Measured against his grief and shock, my errand seemed almost too trivial to be worth troubling him with. However, as there was no-one else and no excuse not to, I made myself go on.

'Er, Handy…'

He looked at me quizzically. 'What's that? Oh, it's you, Yaotl. I thought you'd left the city.' He did not sound surprised to see me, nor much interested.

'I had to come back. Look, I'm sorry about Star.'

He shut his eyes for a moment. 'Do you think she's gone, like the midwife said? Gone to Heaven, to join the sun?'

'Of course,' I said hastily. I wondered whether to go on, to explain that his wife, dying to bring forth a child, had had a flowery death, the same as a warrior on the battlefield or on the sacrificial stone of an enemy's temple. She would rise again as one of the Divine Princesses, to greet the sun at midday and escort him toward the western horizon, surrounding him with war cries and dancing feet.

I was still trying to form the words when I sensed he was not listening.

'We were laughing about the baby only yesterday. She thought he was going to do well, arriving on One Flint Knife – that's not a bad day to be born, is it? But in the end, he missed it.'

I glanced at the sweat bath, but although I thought I heard muffled voices from that direction it was impossible to tell what was happening in there. I wondered what had gone wrong. Then I dismissed the thought, telling myself that it was beyond mending and was none of my business. I had come here to find out what, if anything, Handy knew about the captain's movements, and to warn him of the possible danger to himself. Then I wanted to be off straight away. I felt exposed here, in the parishes in the south of the city where I presumed the otomi would be looking for me. The sooner I was at Lily's house, even if it was only temporarily while we figured out what to do next, the happier I would be.

But then Handy said: 'Do you know the custom? What we have to do, if… when a woman dies giving birth?'

'Handy, I'll come to the point. Lord Feathered in Black… The custom? What do you mean?'

'I mean what we have to do with the body.'

I frowned. 'Well, yes, I mean I know what you're supposed to do, in theory at least, but…'

'Only, we're going to need your help.'

'What do you mean, help? Help with what… Oh, no!' It suddenly dawned on me what he was going to ask me and the thought of what that ritual would involve filled me with horror. 'No, look. I'm just passing through, you know. I only wanted to deliver a message…'

'Only I don't know whether I can get enough men together right now, at short notice, and as you know we need four for the burial.'

'I'd like to be there,' I said insincerely. 'But I'm very busy just now, and my time isn't my own, you know – did you hear Lily bought me? As I was saying, when we were in Tetzcoco…' I made as if to stand up, but only managed an awkward half crouch.

Suddenly Handy became, just for a moment, his old self. 'What are you talking about?' he growled irritably. 'My wife's dead in the sweat bath and you come barging in, like you were a neighbour come to borrow a pot of honey, spouting some bloody nonsense about Tetzcoco – who do you think you are, anyway?'

'That's not fair,' I said, taken aback by the outburst. 'I didn't know what was happening – how could I? I only wanted to give you a warning – and if this is all the thanks I'm going to get, I won't bother!'

The man suddenly let out a groan, and passed a hand in front of his eyes as if he were brushing away a cobweb. 'Yaotl, please,' he continued, in a voice suddenly small and hoarse, 'I'm sorry, it's just that… It's the shock, you know? I can't believe she's gone, and now there are these things I have to do, and I can't do them by myself.'

'I know,' I said, sympathetically.

For some reason I could not quite bring myself to get up and walk out. I glanced longingly over my shoulder at the doorway that led through the front room of the house to the street, to freedom and peace of mind, but I could not get there because my feet seemed to have glued themselves to the ground.

I made one more effort to talk my way out of this. 'Look, I'll come back later – in a few days, maybe. And if there's ever anything I can do…'

'There is. I told you, we need help with the burial. Her sister's washing her now. She'll be ready before nightfall.'

'I meant anything apart from that,' I muttered.

'Yaotl, I'm just asking you to do one thing. Just one. If you won't do it for me, can't you do it for Star?'

And then out of the sweat bath came Handy's sister-in-law, accompanied by her mother and the midwife. Gentle Heart was carrying the bowl Goose had taken in with her, but it was covered with a crumpled skirt and blouse.

The women were not weeping, but dark tracks stained both their cheeks. 'We've cleaned her and put a new skirt and shift on her,' Goose said quietly. 'Gentle Heart says she has to stay in there, alone, until nightfall. Then you have to bury her.'

'Yaotl will help,' Handy said quickly.

Goose gave me a weak smile. 'Yaotl, thank you. Star would have appreciated that.'

'Don't mention it.' I sat down heavily. I looked at the ground, not out of modesty, but so that I could swear silently without any of them noticing.

'I'll be back at sunset,' the midwife said. She put her bowl down by the doorway. She seemed to hesitate then, as though there were something she wanted to say. Star's mother went inside the house to look for her husband.

After a long, uncomfortable silence, Goose and the midwife both spoke at once.

'Look, Gentle Heart, you mustn't blame…'

'I tried to save them both! Believe me, I did all I could! If only…' Whatever else the woman had been about to say dissolved into a long, desolate howl. She turned and stumbled away from us, finishing up leaning against the courtyard wall with her face buried in her arms.

Goose darted towards her while Handy's eyes, wide with horror, followed them both.

'Listen to me…' Goose was pleading with the distraught midwife, shaking her by the elbow to get her attention. Eventually Gentle Heart turned, slumped against the wall with her back to it and lifted her glistening face to the sky.

'Why?' The words were whispered and barely intelligible. 'I did everything right, I know I did, so why?' Suddenly she looked down again, and her eyes seemed to bore straight into mine, although I am sure she hardly knew I was there.

'She was fine, and then she was… sick. And *I just don't understand what went wrong.*'

3

Goose had left Handy's children and her own at a relative's house. With the youngsters gone, the atmosphere in Handy's courtyard became more subdued than ever.

It was still early morning, the last of the stars only just gone out, and there was nothing to be done for Star now until nightfall. Handy and I rested against the wall, opposite the sweat bath, while from inside the house a slapping sound told us that Goose was belatedly preparing tortillas. Death might interrupt the daily routine but the living still had to be fed. The moment she had returned, the woman had set about her work in grim silence, giving the dough her undivided attention as she flung it onto the griddle.

Handy stared moodily into the entrance hole of the sweat bath. Much of the time he was silent, and when he spoke it was not always clear whether he was talking to me, to himself, or someone else whom he alone could see.

'Nothing we could have done,' he mumbled. 'What were we supposed to do, wait until a better midwife came along? We couldn't get hold of Piazticuechtli.'

' "Slender Neck"?'

'Star's midwife – the one she's always gone to before. I sent one of my girls to her house but they said she was ill. She had to go to the Pleasure House to see if any of the women there could come instead.' He gave a short, dry, mirthless laugh. 'Imagine, my daughter had to go to a Pleasure House!'

'At least she came back again,' I said unfeelingly. I was not looking forward to the burial, and resented being pressured into helping with it. Otherwise I might have reassured my friend that the marketplaces his female relations all no doubt frequented were probably riskier than the Pleasure Houses. These were the official establishments that our successful warriors were allowed to visit as a reward for valour. The girls were clean and eminently respectable. Some indeed were destined to become concubines or even wives of exalted commoners or even nobles. Others went on to become midwives. The midwives' profession was centred on the Pleasure Houses, where their skills were naturally much in demand.

Handy ignored me. The big man was so wrapped up in his own thoughts that he seemed to be speaking to himself most of the time. 'Gentle Heart knew what she was about, didn't she? She came as fast as she could. In fact she must have run all the way, I think, because she was here before my daughter had got back from the Pleasure House. And she did her best.'

I wondered whom he was trying to convince, but I was spared the need to think of an answer by Goose, who had finished her work for the moment and joined us in the courtyard.

'The bread will be ready soon,' she announced tonelessly.

I watched her out of the corner of my eye, but I did not know what to make of what I saw. She was kneeling, with her hands together in her lap. She was not looking at us, or at the sweat bath where her sister's body lay. Her eyes were pointed towards a blank wall, but narrowed slightly, as though inspecting something. They were dry but the effort she was putting into keeping the tears back showed in the thin line formed by her lips.

When she spoke, it was in answer to Handy's last words. 'I think Gentle Heart did all she could. Maybe Slender Neck might have done more, but who knows? Gentle Heart tried her best. She thought the baby was stuck.'

'It wasn't true!' Handy suddenly blurted out. 'What the old man said, it wasn't true! I didn't touch Star, not after the fourth month, when Slender Neck told us we mustn't … Goose, you believe me, don't you?'

I looked from one to the other, as baffled now as I had been by the scene in the courtyard earlier, when Handy's father-in-law had stood over him, shouting obscenities. 'What was that all about?'

Star's sister looked at the knees she had folded under her. 'If the baby was stuck, that can mean… I'm sorry, Handy, but…'

He sighed. 'I know what the midwives and curers say: we already had nine children, remember. Your father thought Star must have been accepting my seed after we had finished forming the baby – after the fourth month. But I'm telling you I didn't touch her!'

I said: 'Don't take too much notice of your father-in-law. He's probably forgotten what it's like!'

'I'm telling you we didn't!' Handy snarled. He turned back to his wife's sister. 'Tell me what happened.'

Goose hesitated. 'When it all started to go wrong, and she thought the baby was stuck…' She let out a long, shuddering breath. 'Oh, Handy, are you sure you want to hear this?'

'Go on,' he said, in a strained voice.

'She was trying to turn him in the womb, but he wouldn't move, and Star was getting weaker. She was struggling hard, and then not so hard... Gentle Heart said she tried everything, grasping her by the neck and shaking her, kicking her, shouting at her – we heard her, until long after midnight...'

' "Shouting at her"? Is that normal?'

'Childbirth is the woman's battle, Yaotl. Ask any mother. She has to have the courage and strength of a warrior. And my sister fought.' This with a note of pride, her face upturned, as though defying either of us men to argue. 'She fought! I saw the bruises. But the Giver of Life would not grant her her victory. Have you ever heard a midwife speaking to a woman, when she salutes her after the birth? *"Now our lord hath placed thee upon the eagle warrior reed mat, upon the jaguar warrior reed mat. Thou hast returned exhausted from battle, my beloved maiden, brave woman..."'* Goose got up abruptly, turned sharply away from us, and ended in a voice we could barely hear: 'Only she didn't, did she? She didn't return, never got to hear the words... not this time.' She began walking away. 'I've got to see if those tortillas are ready.'

Handy watched his sister-in-law dumbly.

I hesitated over what I was going to say next. However, I still had my message to deliver. For all the danger it implied for himself and his household, I wondered whether it might not do the grieving husband good to have something else to think about.

Diffidently, I began to describe lord Feathered in Black's visit. At first Handy seemed not to be listening, but eventually he turned his eyes towards me, and by the time I asked him whether he knew anything about the captain and his movements, he was frowning.

'I've not seen anything. I've heard the rumours, of course, but then so has everyone else. But as for the otomi – to be honest with you, Yaotl, I'm not sure I'm the right man to ask. I carry messages and run errands for old Black Feathers, but he doesn't take me into his confidence, and I haven't seen the captain since that business in Tlacopan.' His frown deepened. 'Do you really think he'd be after me, on account of that?'

'According to the chief minister, yes. He ended up looking a fool on account of what I did, and you were with me, and to his mind that's enough.'

He curled his lip. 'Doesn't seem fair,' he said indifferently, as though his present troubles made the prospect of meeting an inhumanly strong sword-wielding psychopath look insignificant. 'I mean, I can imagine him wanting to skin you like a rabbit.'

'Thanks,' I mumbled. 'I never knew you had that much imagination!'

His frown cleared a little as he thought of something else. 'I'll tell you who you do need to watch out for, though: lord Feathered in Black's steward.'

I snorted derisively. 'I'm not going to worry about him!'

'He's a three-captive warrior, Yaotl.'

'So what? He took his last prisoner ten years ago, at least. Now he's a sad, fat old man full of wind. What's more he's so stupid he can't pick his nose unless he's looking in a mirror. I can deal with him, don't worry about that.'

'Well, you may have to. That's all I can say.'

'Thanks,' I said neutrally. I felt that I had come here in vain.

Handy did not seem to care about the captain, and had nothing to tell me about him. And for this I had burdened myself with the horrible task of helping to bury a dead mother. I wondered what my chances were of getting back to Lily's house before the next morning.

'That's all right,' Handy was saying. 'I really appreciate what you're doing for us. I mean, I know it isn't a nice thing to have to do.'

'I had to do worse things as a priest,' I said lightly. 'Compared to sticking maguey spines through my tongue or wading through ice-cold lake water, I'm sure this is nothing! But are you certain you need me? Can't any of your sons help, or your brothers?'

'My sons are too young, apart from Cuicuilticuauhtli.' The young man's name meant 'Spotted Eagle'. 'My brother-in-law – Goose's husband, Xochipepe – will help. I've no brothers living, though, and by the time my father-in-law's finished with them I don't suppose any of my wife's relatives will talk to me. And it's a difficult thing to ask of a friend or a neighbour.' I wondered what that made me, in Handy's estimation, but before I could voice the question aloud, we were interrupted.

'What about me?'

Both Handy and I started at the sound of a man's voice. A moment later I heard Goose crying shrilly: 'You can't come in here! Don't you know what's happened?'

'Oh, yes, I know,' said the stranger grimly.

I turned around to see a tall, heavily built man whose weathered skin and grey-streaked hair were those of someone of about the same age as Handy and I. He was formally dressed: barefoot, because he was a commoner and so forbidden sandals in the city, but his carmine coloured cape with its tasselled orange border marked him as a Master of Youths, a soldier who had taken three war captives. His entry into the courtyard was curious: he moved with determination but also with a limp, and he had Goose scampering anxiously behind him, her hands waving and all but clutching at the trailing hem of his cloak. He seemed unsure of himself. His head kept jerking from side to side as if looking for signs of an ambush.

Handy was on his feet. 'What do you want, Tlapallalo?'

The newcomer took a step backwards, almost colliding with Goose. 'I came to help… and to say goodbye.'

'Goodbye it is,' Handy said coldly.

The man whose name meant 'Red Macaw' looked at the ground for a moment. When he looked up again I saw that his eyes were raw, and he was biting his lower lip. He took a deep breath. 'Look – I know we've had our differences. But I want to help now. You're short-handed for the burial.'

'No I'm not,' Handy snapped. 'And why should I give a shit for what you want? Goodbye, I said. Now get out of my house!'

He took a step towards Red Macaw. For a moment I thought the other man was going to retreat, but he stood his ground. They ended up with their noses almost touching, baring their teeth at each other. I got to my feet, wary of the fight that seemed to be about to break out, while Goose scurried around the two men, pleading with them both to calm down for her sister's sake.

'Why do you think I came here?' asked Red Macaw, without taking his eyes off his antagonist.

Handy responded: 'I don't know why you came here. There's nothing you can do. There never was, Red Macaw. Now get out, before Yaotl and I throw you out!'

'Wait a moment!' I spluttered indignantly. 'I may help you bury your wife but nobody said anything about joining in a fight! I'm in enough trouble already!'

Red Macaw seemed to notice me for the first time then. He looked me up and down and was clearly not impressed by what he saw. 'So who's this then?'

'None of your business!' snapped Handy.

'Listen, both of you.' I could hear my voice going up in pitch, in bafflement and confusion. 'Handy, if you expect me to help you shove this man out into the street you might at least tell me why. And as for you, Red Macaw, I don't know why you came here or what Handy has against you...'

'You mind your own business too, Yaotl,' Handy said menacingly.

I could only stare at him, suddenly lost for words. Fortunately Goose chose that moment to intervene again. Stepping up to the two men until she was all but standing between them – indeed I was sure she would have stood between them, if there had been space enough – she looked imploringly up at them both: 'Please, remember Star. Would she have wanted this?'

For a long moment no-one moved or spoke.

When the tension was finally broken it was by Red Macaw, who lowered his eyes from Handy's face and squeezed them shut as if to hold back a rush of tears. He turned away.

'You're wrong. There's something I can do – more than I can tell you. But if you won't let me... Look, just guard her very carefully, won't you? There could be trouble tonight.'

'Sod off,' Handy growled quietly.

With that the other man limped out of the courtyard, the pain of whatever injury he had sustained obvious now, and without a backward glance. The last words I heard him mutter were: 'You say there never was anything I could do… That isn't true, and you all know it.'

I stared after him, aware that my mouth was gaping like an idiot's but lacking the will to do anything about it. Slowly, I turned towards Handy, to see him glaring fiercely at me.

'Don't ask me, Yaotl,' he said simply. 'Just don't even ask, that's all.'

'What did he mean about trouble, though?'

'I've no idea. Like I said, don't ask!'

Bewildered, I looked at Goose, but she was already hurrying indoors, muttering something about tortillas.

4

There was nothing else to be done at Handy's house that day except eat and wait for nightfall. That seemed to be enough for the commoner, who soon lapsed into a torpor, slumped against the wall of his courtyard with eyes wide open but focused on nothing.

I had other concerns, however. I was no nearer to finding out the truth behind the chief minister's warning, or to alerting my family to the danger. And I was concerned about Lily. I had promised to return to her that night. Every moment I was delayed would be torment for her, and if I did nothing else, I had to let her know what I was up to, and reassure her that I was safe. I could not do any of these things in Handy's courtyard.

I stood up and looked down at the other man. 'I have to go,' I said hesitantly. 'I'll come back, but there are a couple of matters I have to attend to first. I don't know how long it'll take, though – I mean, I'll be back tonight, of course. But I've got to see my family, and get a message to Lily, the sooner the better.'

Handy became animated. He sat upright and looked at me with narrowed eyes. 'Don't worry about Lily. I'll send one my sons. It's not as if I'm going to get any other work out them today.' He paused. 'But are you sure it's wise, going to see your parents? What if old Black

Feathers is right? What if the captain's watching their house? It's too dangerous.'

'Old Black Feathers has men watching my back, remember.'

'Does he? They must be well hidden, then!'

I chose not to respond to that; it echoed my own fears too faithfully. Instead I said obstinately: 'I've got to warn my parents. The otomi might get bored, just watching their house.'

'But you don't even like your family.'

'That's not true!' I cried, in a wounded tone. 'Well, I'm quite fond of my little sister, anyway.'

'The last time you saw them you tried to push your father into a fire! I know, I was there.'

'I was only making a point, and anyway, he started it.' I laughed nervously. 'You're just afraid I'm going to get myself killed before tonight and the funeral.'

For a moment he looked as shocked as if he had been stung by some insect he had previously failed to notice. Then his features settled into a grime smile. 'Well, you'd be no use to Star dead.'

I was spared from having to think of a reply by the dead woman's sister.

I had not noticed her come back out into the courtyard, and nor probably had Handy. She asked us what we were talking about. This startled us both and had the effect of prompting us to appeal to her like two litigants before a judge.

'He's trying to run away!' said the commoner.

'No, I'm not,' I protested. 'I have to see my family. I'll be back.'

Goose looked at me shrewdly. 'Will you, though?' she asked.

'Of course! I'll eat earth...'

Tribute of Death

My voice trailed off before the woman's unblinking gaze.

'Go ahead then,' she commanded me quietly. 'Eat earth.'

Goose's was not obviously a large or imposing presence, but there was something about her stern, unflinching stare that compelled me to obey. I found myself performing the ritual, stooping to touch the ground with my fingertip, and bringing the fingertip to my mouth, and feeling all the time that the anger of the gods might be the least of my worries if I broke my oath. And getting killed would not be taken as an excuse.

5

Toltenco meant 'At the Edge of the Rushes'. The parish had been built on low-lying, marshy ground that Lake Tetzcoco continually threatened to reclaim for its own, and in fact some of the houses at its edge stood on stilts.

The place where I had grown up lay at the southern edge of the city, and it was past noon by the time I reached it, after threading my way along narrow canal paths and across still narrower bridges. It would have been quicker if I had not been casting continual nervous glances over my shoulder, ever on the look-out for a one-eyed giant with murder in his sole eye. I saw no sign of him. What was less reassuring was that I saw no sign of the men lord Feathered in Black was supposed to have following me, either. I was becoming more and more convinced that these men had never existed.

After a while I stopped worrying about what my former master might or might not be up to and turned my thoughts instead to the things I had seen and heard that morning. I recalled Star's death, and what had surrounded it: the absence of her own midwife; her father's furious reproaches to her husband and Handy's own row with Red Macaw; my getting caught up, against my better judgement, in the funeral arrangements.

Tribute of Death

I knew what Kindly would have made of it all, had he been there. Fate, he would have called it: an instance of the gods making the cocoa bean stand up on its end. How else had a strong woman, who had already brought nine healthy children into the World, suddenly been taken ill? And just when the midwife who attended her could not be found? Coming on top of my own troubles, at the very moment when I had been forced back into Mexico to confront my enemy, it surely showed Tezcatlipoca, the Smoking Mirror, the god of chance, at his most malicious.

I had always been less ready then Lily's father to accept chance and fate as the rulers of our lives. As a priest, I had been dedicated to Tezcatlipoca, and I knew the god well. I thought I knew when his influence was making itself felt and when it was not and when some human agency seemed to be at work. What had happened in the last few days surely had to be coincidence: there was no way Star's death could be connected with my return to the city. However, something about it made me uneasy. In some way I could not have explained, it did not feel like the work of a god.

I toyed with these ideas as I walked, until at last I found myself within a few streets of my family's home, experiencing the familiar sensation of not having the vaguest idea of what to do next.

The obvious course of action was to walk directly to my parents' house, which was only a few streets away, and deliver my warning, but I felt wary of doing that. I had had enough surprises for one morning. 'Too obvious,' I muttered. 'What if there's someone watching the entrance? Or both of them?' The house had a street entrance direct into the principal room, which in turn gave onto a small courtyard surrounded by other rooms, and at the rear of the courtyard was a second opening that led, via a small wooden landing stage, to a canal. If one was being watched then it was safe to assume that both were.

'Think about this, Yaotl,' I told myself. 'You can't walk in through the doorway. So what's left? Over the wall?' I tried to picture the area around the house. There were no trees overhanging the courtyard, and it stood apart from its neighbours, so that I could not hope to drop in from next door's rooftop. I would not have wanted to try it anyway. It would have meant trying to creep into a stranger's property unobserved, and I had no desire to be taken for a thief.

Thoughts of somehow trying to get into the house from above prompted me to glance in the direction of Toltenco's temple, a small shrine with a threadbare thatched roof that stood on top of a stumpy pyramid in the centre of the parish. It was just high enough to provide a vantage point from which I could see into the surrounding streets and canal-paths. If there were any dangerous characters loitering in the vicinity, I thought, it would be good to be able to spot them before they caught sight of me. And I had known the priest, Imacaxtli, 'the Worthy Man', ever since I was a child. Even if I could not see much from the shrine, it would be worth talking to him anyway. Very little happened in his parish without his knowing about it.

The pyramid stood in the middle of a little plaza that had weeds growing up between its flagstones. It was not an impressive sight. Most of my memories of it were from childhood and it had seemed much taller then. Even the thread of dried sacrificial blood running down its side seemed thinner than it had used to.

I began striding purposefully in the direction of the little pyramid. However, I was too nervous about being seen to keep this up. By the time I got there, I was shuffling, bent over as though that would somehow make me less visible. It was probably a good disguise as it must have made me look like a cripple. I stayed in the shadows for as long as I could, slipping furtively between them whenever I had to cross open ground. There were a few people about, standing or squatting in what passed for the marketplace in this parish, but from what I could see of them none looked like a warrior, and none of them took any notice of me.

Worthy, the old priest, was standing in front of the shrine at the summit of the pyramid. He was not an imposing figure: he was a little shorter than I and running slightly to fat, which made me suspect that he did not always fast as rigorously as he ought to. However, his hair was as long and unkempt as any priest's, and a black scab on his cheek showed where he had recently pierced his earlobe to offer his blood to the gods. His face was stained with pitch, which made it hard to read the expression on it as his eyes tracked my approach.

I halted just short of the top step.

'Do you remember me, Worthy One?'

'Cemiquiztli Yaotl?' He called me by my full name: the date of my birth, One Death, followed by my given name: Yaotl, 'The Enemy': one of the things we called the god to whom I was dedicated. 'Of course I remember you. But we all thought you were due to be sacrificed!'

'I believe that's what lord Feathered in Black had in mind at the time. It didn't appeal to me, though.'

The old man chuckled. 'Really? You surprise me. Still that's the young all over, isn't it? No sense of obligation.'

'Shocking, isn't it? I blame the parents.'

'Ah, talking of which, have you been to see your family, yet?

They seemed quite worried about you last time I spoke to them.'

This surprised me, since my father in particular seemed unable ever to set eyes on me without flying into a rage. I cast an involuntary glance in the direction of my family's home.

'No, I haven't. In fact, that's what I wanted to talk to you about.'

'I have things to do first.' He regarded me shrewdly for a moment before going on: 'Do you remember what today is?'

I frowned, puzzled. I glanced about me, noting the poles standing in the courtyards around us. 'It's the month of the Ceasing of Water,' I offered hesitantly.

'Yes, yes, of course. But that wasn't what I asked. What day is it? One Flint Knife!'

I remembered then. 'The sacrifice to the war god!' I cried, like a child repeating a lesson.

It was the day sacred to Huitzilopochtli, the god who had guided my ancestors through all the long years when they had wandered as outcasts, before showing them where they were to found their city, granting them the vision of an eagle perched upon a cactus as a sign that this was the place. All over Mexico, on this day, the images of the War God were taken out, cleaned and exposed to the sun; for the War God *was* the sun, and so it was as if he were being asked to inspect them, to satisfy himself that they were being taken care of by his people.

The old priest sighed wistfully. 'In another life, I might have been officiating in Huitzilopochtli's temple at the top of the great pyramid, offering the god flowers and food and feathered cloaks. But I was never ambitious enough. Still, even in this parish we can manage a quail. You can help me – if you want.'

Tribute of Death

The old priest knew what had happened to me. He had been instrumental in getting me into the harsh school for priests we called the House of Tears. I would not have thanked him for that at the time, but I had been a priest for a score of years, and for all its rigours, squalor and privations – the long ritual fasts, the daily offerings of my own blood to the gods and the poverty – I had grown to love the life. It did not matter that my cloak was threadbare and stained with blood and sweat, or that my hair was tangled and greasy, when the mere sight of these things would make commoners jump out of my way and lords speak my name with respect.

Worthy also knew how it had ended, when I had been judged inadequate and purged from the priesthood for a violation of ritual. Now he could not fail to know what he was offering me, when he handed me his long-handled incense ladle and a bag of copal resin. 'You know what to do,' he said quietly.

I looked wonderingly at him before taking the ladle. As he turned away to attend to the evening's sacrifice, I thrust the ladle into the brazier, scooping up a bowlful of hot coals and throwing the resin over them. As I held it aloft, the air around me filled with a cloying aroma. I raised it four times towards the eastern horizon, then four times towards the west, and repeated the gesture in the other two directions: the Left Hand of the Earth, which was South, and the Right, or North. Finally, with a cracking noise and a shower of sparks, I cast the contents of the censer back into the fire.

From behind me there came a thin piping call, followed by a sound of desperate fluttering.

I turned to find that Worthy had made the sacrifice. The quail he had beheaded still flapped feebly on the stone table behind the brazier.

As we watched, its thrashing motions became more feeble and the spurt of blood from its gaping neck slowed to a trickle.

As I silently handed back the censer, Worthy said: 'Which way would you say it was going?'

I looked at the smear of blood the headless bird had made in its last struggle. 'West, I think.'

'Really? Looks like it may have been north.' I shivered, recalling that north was the most ill-omened direction, a sure portent of death. Worthy seemed to reflect for a moment before adding: 'But we'll give ourselves the benefit of the doubt and call it west, shall we?'

I agreed eagerly, but as he picked up the pathetic little body I could not help wondering whether he was right. And if he was not, then whose death had the bird been hinting at?

Worthy said: 'Now, what was it you wanted to ask me?'

I told him about my recent adventures and the mission that had brought me back to Tenochtitlan. 'I need to find out what's really happening down there, and warn my family as quickly as possible.'

Worthy stroked his chin thoughtfully. 'There have been some funny goings-on around here, now that you mention it. You don't exactly have the whole city spread out before you here, like they do in the great temples in the Heart of the World and Tlatelolco, but I can keep an eye on the neighbouring streets. I do seem to have seen more armed men than usual skulking about.'

'Did they include a huge man with one eye?' I demanded anxiously.

'It's hard to count people's eyes from up here. Huge man, eh?'

He stroked his chin thoughtfully. 'Well, come to think of it I may have seen one or two huge men about lately…'

'So he has been here.' I gulped nervously. 'I'm going to have to go down there. I just wish I could be sure of being able to reach the house without being seen.'

'Difficult one. You won't be doing it by way of the front gateway, that's for sure.' He paused, before a sly smile began to spread across his face, opening little cracks in the pitch that coated it. 'Now, I wonder…'

6

I looked at the object the priest had given me with mounting concern.

'I really don't think this is going to work.'

'Why ever not?' he said impatiently.

'For one thing, I'm not a great swimmer.'

'That's the beauty of it. You don't need to be.'

Worthy's scheme was a simple one, in principle. I was to wade along the canal at the rear of my parents' house, going on my knees so as to keep my head beneath the surface – the water would only come up to my chest otherwise – and breathing through the long hollow drinking tube the old man had put into my hands.

'It's foolproof. You'll be invisible. You can sneak right up to the rear entrance and be inside the courtyard before anyone even knows you're there.' Worthy sounded pleased with himself as he enthused about his scheme. 'You know how, at the sacred wine sellers' festival, the old people sit around big bowls sucking the stuff through these straws…'

'They're for drinking through,' I objected. 'Drinking's not the same as breathing, is it?'

'I don't see why not. If the sacred wine doesn't leak out through the tube then water won't leak in, will it? It stands to reason.'

'Well, maybe, but if I'm underwater how can I see where I'm going?'

'It's a narrow canal, Yaotl. You get in the water a reasonable distance from where your parents live and just keep going forward. You can't get lost.'

'It'll be cold!'

The old priest looked at me scornfully. 'So what? Didn't you get used to being cold when you were a priest?'

It was true that some of the rituals I had had to undergo had included baths in the icy waters of the lake at midnight, and this ought not to be as bad as that, since it was early afternoon, with the sun still high in the sky. On the other hand I had been much younger then, and I had not had a chance to get used to the rich food, chocolate and lazy routine of lord Maize Ear's palace.

'Have you ever tried anything like this yourself?' I asked suspiciously.

Worthy laughed. 'Me? You must be joking!'

I had been right about its being cold. The plunge into the still, dark water of the canal was shocking. I shot out into the air again, gasping and plucking long streamers of something wet and slimy from my face.

'What's the matter?' asked Worthy innocently.

'It's bloody freezing and it smells!'

'What do you expect? I don't know, young people...'

'Oh, don't start that again. If I *were* young it might be different. I'm getting too old for this sort of insanity. Where's that tube?'

'Tube? Don't tell me you dropped it in the canal?' Then, hearing my groan of despair, the priest added with a chuckle: 'Only joking. Here it is... Good luck! And don't forget to keep the top of it above the surface!'

I accepted the long, hollow reed from him. After looking at it doubtfully for a moment, I took several deep breaths, stuck it in my mouth and kneeled down.

It did not take long to realize that wading along the canal breathing through a pipe was not going to be the simple proposition that Worthy had supposed. First, there was the sheer terror I felt when my eyes dropped below the surface. I was convinced that my first breath would fill my lungs with the evil, brackish stuff. I held my breath for as long as I could, and then, when I felt as if I would burst, I found myself taking rapid, shallow gasps like a dying fish. And the moment the water closed over my head, I was plunged into darkness. I wanted to stretch out my hands in the hope of at least touching one side of the canal, just to remind myself where it was, but I had them clamped around the tube, holding it rigidly upright for fear that its top might dip below the surface of the water. I was completely disorientated. It did not help that in order to hold the tube in place I had to keep my neck craned at a ridiculous angle so that I was looking up all the time.

Finally, water kept leaking into my mouth, and it tasted foul. I began to worry about whether I would reach my parents' house without poisoning myself.

I do not know how long I remained where I was, fighting the temptation to scramble out of the water and give up the whole reckless scheme. Eventually I decided I had better just get it over with.

No sooner had I begun to creep forward, scraping my knees

painfully across the stones and rubbish on the canal's bottom, than I discovered the last, fatal flaw in Worthy's plan.

He had been right, up to a point, in saying that I could not get lost. Although it was terrifying and confusing it was impossible to wander off my route once I had picked my direction; I only had to follow the canal. I knew exactly which way I was headed. However in a matter of moments I realised that I had no way to tell how far I had gone.

I had estimated the distance I had to travel to be a couple of hundred paces, but a pace on foot was a different matter from my shuffling crawl, and anyway I soon lost count of how many times I had forced my knees to bend and stretch. I may have been invisible to anyone watching the house but this was of little use since I could see nothing at all.

I began to feel as though I had been crawling through mud and filth and icy, brackish water for ever. When I dared to break the surface to look around me, though, I found that I had gone maybe a dozen paces. If my mouth had not been filled by one end of a reed pipe I would have groaned aloud. I forced myself to take slow, deep breaths. In order to restrain myself from trying to look around me again before I had made any real progress, I shut my eyes and tried to remember some of the old hymns I had been forced to learn in the House of Tears. After a while the metre of the words and the rhythm of my breathing became indistinguishable. I started to lose track of time, along with all sensation in my arms and legs as the numbing cold seeped through them. I went on reciting the hymn but it became more and more mechanical. Part of my mind turned the words over again and again, and part of it made my legs move and my chest rise and fall, and the rest of me seemed to have gone to sleep.

Something tugged sharply on my breathing tube.

My eyes snapped open, peering uselessly into the darkness. My hands clutched at the hollow reed. But it had been a long time since I had felt anything through my fingertips and the first I knew that the reed had been snatched from my grasp was when water flooded into my mouth, down my throat and into my lungs.

I choked, gasped and retched. I could not think of what to do and no instinct helped me. I could not jump out of the water because I did not know which way was up. I flapped about as wildly as the quail Worthy had killed earlier on, with my hands snapping at empty air as they searched vainly for the breathing tube.

I might have drowned there, kneeling in a stretch of shallow water within shouting distance of the house I had grown up in, if a pair of strong arms had not locked themselves firmly around me and hauled me upright.

At first all I could do was flop forward against them, coughing and spluttering while my feet slithered under me, scrabbling for a purchase. Then, as I brought my painful gasps for breath under control, it occurred to me to wonder who had grabbed me. I tried to turn, but was held fast.

A voice I did not recognise rasped in my ear: 'Hold still, you!' From a little further away a second voice called out: 'What have you caught, then, Ollin? It's not an *ahuitzotl*, is it?'

'No such luck. If this is a water-monster then I'm a Huaxtec. It's just some clown crawling along the canal. I told you that tube sticking up there looked all wrong.'

I made another effort to twist round. In response the man holding me released one of his arms so that he could hit me, striking the side of my head so hard that my teeth were knocked together. 'I told you not to move!' he snapped.

'Who are you?' I blurted out hoarsely.

I was swung around to face the man who stood on the bank, and there was no mistaking the hair piled up on his head in a veteran soldier's haircut, or the glittering blades of the sword he was brandishing.

I had failed, I thought bleakly. The man who had caught me was a warrior. He was not the captain but it was not difficult to guess whose orders he was acting on.

The man's voice rasped in my ear. 'See that man there? I'm going to put you on the bank in front of him now, and if you try anything clever he'll cut your legs off at the knees and we'll make you crawl back the way you came, without your breathing-tube. Understand?' Without waiting for an answer Ollin lifted me up and tossed me bodily out of the water.

I threw up my hands in an effort to control my fall but I was an instant too late. I flopped helplessly against the wooden pilings at the edge of the canal, catching one of them against my midriff and sending a foamy mixture of air and water spraying from my nose and mouth.

I gasped and flopped over sideways, doubled up in agony, while the warrior on the bank seized one of my arms just below the shoulder and pulled me fully onto dry land.

'So, what's your game, then?' he hissed.

Something tickled my ear. I lay quite still, realising that what I felt was the sharpest edge in the world: the blade of an obsidian-studded sword. I began trembling uncontrollably, either from the cold or from fear, and the ticking became a sharp pain.

'Careful,' breathed the man holding the sword. 'Nearly took your ear off.'

'Let me get up,' I croaked.

'Not till you tell us what you thought you were doing.' The chill was worse out of the water than it had been in the canal. The pain was like darts in my numb flesh and my right leg was twitching in the first stage of cramp. I could hear myself whimpering, while tears started uncontrollably from my eyes.

'I was just going home,' I sobbed.

'You were *what*?' the man in front of me said incredulously.

Ollin said: 'Down the middle of a canal? I don't think so. Who sent you?'

'Better search him for weapons,' his comrade advised.

Ollin scrambled out of the water and began tugging at my sodden breechcloth, looking presumably for a concealed knife. 'What are you, a spy or a hired killer?'

'He doesn't look like an otomi to me,' the other warrior said. 'No muscles on him at all.'

It began to dawn on me what was happening. These men had been expecting some associate of the captain's or maybe even the dreaded otomi himself – which, of course, meant that whoever had stationed them here, it could not be my enemy. I opened my mouth to cry out my name and tell them that they had got it all wrong, but just at that moment the cramp struck my right leg with full force and I fell to my knees, squealing in agony.

Ollin casually stuffed a rag in my mouth to shut me up and continued rummaging inside my breechcloth for weapons. As I struggled at his feet he shoved me the rest of the way to the ground with a heel between my shoulder blades.

'No knife or anything.'

'Tie him up,' Ollin ordered his comrade, 'and leave that gag in his mouth. We'll take him to the house and see what they make of him there.'

7

Before I could move or utter a protest the two warriors had trussed me up like a deer, lashing my legs to my arms with a coarse rope that they must have brought with them for the purpose. They carried me between them, bouncing me carelessly up and down as they strode briskly alongside the canal. At first I tried shouting through the gag, but I soon gave up. I knew I would be able to speak soon enough. I was face-down and could not see where I was going, but I had guessed by now that they were not going to take me very far.

They turned away from the canal path and into what looked like a courtyard, judging by the clean swept earth floor just beneath my nose. When they dropped me on the ground, I managed to turn my head to one side just quickly enough to avoid anything worse than a bruised cheek.

'We've got one!' crowed Ollin, his words echoing off the walls around us.

A male voice replied: 'Well done, Ollin. Who is he?'

'Don't know that yet,' the warrior admitted. 'We thought we'd bring him back here to question him.'

'Good idea! We'll get a fire going and throw some chillies on it. We can smoke the truth out of him.'

As I grunted in impotent protest I heard another voice, this one a woman's, saying: 'Don't you think we'd better take his gag off first? No point asking him anything if he can't speak.'

I knew the speaker. She was my elder sister, Quetzalchalchihuitl or 'Precious Jade'. The man she had spoken to was none other than my eldest brother: Lion, the Guardian of the Waterfront, my family's pride and joy.

Ollin and his comrade had carried me to my parents' house. The moment I recognised Lion's voice I knew who the two warriors were: members of his bodyguard. He must have left them on sentry duty outside the house.

My elder brother's plan would have involved building a fire in the courtyard, throwing some dried chillies on it, and then holding me over it until the choking and the pain in my nose, mouth and eyes had loosened my tongue. Fortunately, my gag was off and I was able to speak before the fire was hot enough.

'Yaotl?' my sister said, as soon as I had finished shouting. 'What are you doing here?'

'My brother,' Lion said dully, as though his disappointment were too much to bear, before turning to his men. 'I don't believe it. You bagged my brother!'

I looked at Ollin and his colleague balefully while I tried to massage some feeling back into my legs and other members of my family emerged, one by one, through the doorways that surrounded the courtyard. All my relations seemed to have gathered there, as though for a festival. My mother and father stood together in one corner of the courtyard. The old woman's faded blouse and skirt hung loosely from her frail-looking frame, while her husband stood upright, wrapped in the ancient orange two-captive warrior's cloak that was still his proudest possession. Neither of them was quite what he or she seemed. My mother was vigorous enough to take her own wares to the market every day. My father was no weakling, but his left knee had been destroyed by a javelin, and being too stubborn to use a stick, he had taught himself over the years to stand without one. His infirmity was obvious the moment he took a step.

Also watching me were my brothers and sisters. I saw Tlacazolli, the second of my three brothers, a large, slow man a year or two younger than I, whose name meant 'Glutton'. Near him were Copactecolotl, 'Sparrowhawk', a youngster proudly sporting the single lopsided lock of hair that meant he had taken one captive in war, and my younger sister Neuctli, or 'Honey.' Jade's husband, Camaxtli, was there too, next to my elder sister; they were flanked by their grown up sons. Camaxtli and a couple of my nephews carried obsidian-tipped spears.

'I don't understand why you keep these two idiots around,' I muttered, turning to my elder brother and gesturing towards Ollin and his comrade. 'They'd be more useful as sacrifices!'

'That's not fair!' the warrior appealed to his chief. 'We saw him creeping along that canal. How were we to know he wasn't up to no good?'

'You weren't,' Lion replied shortly. 'Yaotl, what in all the thirteen heavens possessed you to try sneaking up on us like that? And where did you get that stupid idea of trying to breathe through a straw?'

'Worthy suggested it. He said he'd seen the otomi and thought it would help me sneak past him... What's so bloody funny?'

Tribute of Death

My brother's laugh sounded like a stone shattering in a fire. 'You believed him! You fool, I was talking to him only this morning. He hasn't seen a thing – hardly surprising, considering how old he is. I doubt he can see his hands in front of his face! It's good to know he hasn't lost his sense of humour!'

'I like that,' I retorted, 'coming from someone who wouldn't recognise a joke if you'd just been introduced!'

'I wouldn't need an introduction, brother,' he responded coolly. 'I've known you since you were born!'

'That's enough!' my mother snapped. 'Yaotl didn't come here just so that you could insult him.'

'I'm sorry,' Lion replied meekly. Our mother was probably the only human being he had ever been afraid of. 'Though to be fair, he does make it very easy.'

I sighed. My brother relished his rare jokes. He was capable of terrifying rages, but I was starting to think I liked him better angry than when he was in a good mood.

I looked around me.

Apart from Lion, who was still enjoying his private joke at my expense, everyone appeared to be scowling.

I sighed. 'Why isn't anyone here ever pleased to see me?'

The last time I had come here my arrival had precipitated a family quarrel, with my father trying physically to throw me out of the house, and this occasion looked like going the same way. The old man lurched forward. 'Pleased to see you?' he snapped. 'After the trouble you've caused? Last time you were here I told you I didn't want to see you ever again, and that was before all this started! Ollin, you can put him back in the canal where you found him!'

My brother's bodyguards looked taken aback at that. 'But our chief said Yaotl was his brother,' Ollin managed at last. 'You can't really mean that!'

'Do you want to bet?' I muttered.

Lion had composed himself by now. 'He doesn't mean it,' he said, with a glance at my father. The old man grunted and looked away: head of the family though he was, he would let his distinguished favourite son have his own way.

My brother turned back towards me. 'Now, Yaotl…'

I interrupted him. 'Just a moment.' I looked nervously at my father, afraid the mere sound of my voice would send him flying into a further rage. 'You said "before all this started." All what?'

The old man did not deign to answer me. It was my mother who spoke. 'Look around you, Yaotl,' she said quietly. 'What do you see?'

I did as she told me, frowning in puzzlement. 'I don't know… It doesn't look any different… About time that wall was whitewashed… I give up!'

My father growled. Jade said hastily: 'It's us she means, you fool! Look at us!'

'When's the last time you saw all your brothers and sisters here, together?' snapped my mother impatiently. 'Lion included? And his bodyguards as well?'

'It's like being under siege in my own house,' my father rumbled. 'And all on account of you!'

Lion said: 'I told them to gather under one roof: it makes them easier to look after. I wanted them to come to my palace as it's more defensible, but father wouldn't leave.'

'My father built this house in the first Montezuma's time!' the old man cried. 'I'm not quitting it now, not for anyone!'

'You mean you *knew* about the otomi?' I shouted. 'Then I needn't have come here at all!'

There was a moment's silence before Lion and Jade both spoke at once.

My brother leaned towards me. 'You mentioned the otomi before. What do you know about him?'

Jade said: 'Why did you come here, Yaotl?'

'I wanted to warn you about him,' I told her. 'My former master – lord Feathered in Black – told me he thought he was haunting the marshes near here, and at Atlixco, and he thought he might come here.' I gave them a brief account of my meeting with the chief minister outside Maize Ear's palace. 'I was trying to find out for sure, and I wanted to make sure you were all safe. I suppose I've wasted my time. You obviously know more than I do!'

'Well, I should hope I know what's going on in the marshes,' Lion replied dryly. 'I'd not be much use as Guardian of the Waterfront if I didn't!'

'So it's true, then? The captain is out there?' I felt strangely let down. I could not have said what sort of reception I would have anticipated from my family. I would have been surprised if it had been especially cordial, but the last thing I would have expected was to be told that everything I had come to warn them about was already provided for and that my mission was unnecessary.

'It sounds that way,' my brother said. 'I don't know for sure what's out there, mind you, but whoever or whatever it is, it's certainly got old Black Feathers worried. He even took the trouble to warn me about it, and normally he and I aren't on speaking terms.' He frowned.

'The only thing that puzzles me is why he took the trouble to warn you as well. What did he expect you to do?'

'I'm bait,' I said bleakly. I explained that part of the chief minister's plan.

'He's got men shadowing you?' Lion asked incredulously.

Ollin spoke up. 'We didn't see anyone else, Chief. I think we'd have noticed.'

'He was probably lying,' I said. 'He claimed I was more use to him alive, but he didn't say how much more.'

'That would be a first, either way.' my father mumbled. 'You've never been much use to anyone before!'

My mother scowled at him and he fell silent.

Lion said: 'I should think your former master was lying, Yaotl. He lured you here in the hope that the otomi would kill you. Then he probably expects me to avenge you and get rid of that maniac for him in the process. Which I suppose I'd have to do,' he added, in the weary tone of a man acknowledging the need to do some unpleasant job he has been putting off too long, such as mending his roof in the wet season.

'You'd better stay here,' my mother suggested. 'You'd be safe.'

'Not from me, he wouldn't,' my father snapped rebelliously.

She glared at him again. 'He may be a failure and a slave and have brought disgrace upon our house, but he's still our son!'

'Thanks,' I said sullenly. 'I can't stay, though. I'm needed elsewhere.' I told them about Star and the promise I had made to her husband, to return to help him bury her. There was a moment of shocked silence.

'The poor woman,' Jade said softly.

My mother hung her head and murmured: 'It's true what the midwives say: *"Certainly it is our mortality, we who are women, for it is our battle, for at this time our mother, Cihuacoatl, Quilaztli, exacteth the tribute of death."* ' She looked up. 'You'd better go and see what you can do for her family, then.'

Sparrowhawk, my youngest brother, had had nothing to say up to now, and when he did finally open his mouth I wished he had kept it shut.

'The chief minister laid a trap for Yaotl,' he said as solemnly as a poet revealing the deepest mysteries of life and death. 'That's what all this amounts to, isn't it? But if it's just him they're after, why does it matter to the rest of us?'

'If you knew the kind of people we're talking about, you wouldn't ask such bloody silly questions,' I snarled at him.

'What do you mean?'

'Because the threat to you lot is the one thing old Black Feathers certainly wasn't lying about. The otomi would have as much hesitation before slaughtering you all and burning this place to the ground as you would before cracking a flea between your grubby nails. And if I do happen to fall into his hands, how much are you willing to bet that he'd stop then?'

Sparrowhawk blinked.

'These two lads,' I continued, indicating Ollin and his partner, 'and the rest of you are all very well, but if the captain ever does come here… Lion will tell you what he's capable of!'

'If he's an otomi,' my elder brother said darkly, 'then he's capable of anything.'

Anxious looks and a nervous shuffling of feet greeted his remark.

It was my mother who replied. 'So what do you intend to do about him, Yaotl?'

'Do? What do you mean? I've done it, haven't I, warning you...'

'You've told us you think he may come here to avenge himself for what you did to him,' she said crisply. 'We knew that already, thank you. Now you've also told us that there's nothing your brother's bodyguards and your brothers can do. So it's up to you, now, isn't it? Whatever this threat is, you'd better deal with it.'

I gasped, astonished at her reasoning, but my mother did not wait for me to reply. 'You made this mess, Yaotl,' she told me, as though I had just upset a bowl of maize gruel over her newly swept courtyard, 'and now you'll have to clear it up.'

'But I can't!' I cried. 'What do you suggest I do? Take on that madman with my bare hands?'

'I could lend you a spear,' Sparrowhawk volunteered. My sister told him to shut up.

My mother made an exasperated noise, somewhere between a sigh and a groan. 'Yaotl, don't pretend to be stupid,' she said to me. 'You can't do that, obviously. But you try to find him before he finds you, can't you?'

'I can help,' Lion offered. 'Lend you a couple of men. Can't spare any more – we're at full stretch trying to catch this lunatic as it is.'

'Men like these two?' I scoffed, looking at Ollin and his comrade. 'Forget it, brother. They'd just get in the way.'

'Suit yourself.' He sounded hurt at my rebuff, and the tone of his next words was scornful. 'After all, it's not as if you'll need help. You'll be on familiar territory, after all – didn't you used to gather stone dung for a living?'

I did not reply to that. It was true, though. Stone dung was what we called scum scraped from the surface of the lakes. It was formed into cakes and sold in the marketplace as food. For a while after I had been slung out of the priesthood I had made ends meet by collecting it. It was revolting work which had given me a lifelong aversion to eating the stuff.

'You can at least find out what the otomi wants,' my mother said. 'Maybe you can reason with him.'

'I know what he wants! Me! Preferably in bite-sized pieces, in a stew topped with beans and maize! And as for reasoning with him…'

'Just keep talking,' my father murmured. 'You can bore him to death!'

8

The afternoon was moving towards evening when I left my parents' house. The air was becoming chilly. My skin was still damp from my adventure in the canal, although my mother had grudgingly lent me a dry cloak.

Ollin and his comrade escorted me at first; but their presence was not enough to save me from an ambush.

I ought to have expected to find someone lying in wait for me, but I was too preoccupied. It was hard to come away from a meeting with my family without feeling that I was in some way a terrible disappointment to them all: Yaotl the failed priest, the wastrel, the slave. And what my brother and my mother had said disturbed me. I had never allowed myself to believe lord Feathered in Black when he said that he wanted me alive, but that had not stopped me from wishing it were true, and that the men he supposedly had following me were real and would protect me. I had been naïve, I realised, wanting to accept what he had told me because it made it easier to do what Lily, her father and I really wanted to do, which was to go home. But my former master had had me put in a cage once, with every intention of having me gruesomely killed. Why should he have changed his mind now?

Tribute of Death

My mother had made it clear that I must confront the otomi, for my own sake as well as my family's, unless I wanted to spend the rest of my life looking over my shoulder. But I would have to face him alone, it seemed, and where would I begin to look?

My thoughts turned naturally to the woman who might be the only person in the world who cared whether I lived or died. I surprised myself, then, by how much I missed Lily, although I had been away from her side less than a day and still intended to return before the next morning. I just wanted to hear her voice again. To be reminded of what we two had endured together and how we had come through it might have made the otomi seem less fearsome, my parents' lack of regard for me less hurtful and Handy's despair at the loss of his wife less overwhelming.

I was so caught up with thoughts such as these that I did not see who was waiting for me in the street until it was too late to get away. The two warriors with me missed him as well, because they were looking straight ahead rather than down.

'Hello, Yaotl.'

The sound of my own name, spoken by someone immediately behind me, was as shocking as a blow between the shoulders. I stopped, tensing, not turning around because for a moment I was too startled to move.

The two warriors recovered before I did. They both whirled, swords at the ready, but relaxed visibly at the sight of the speaker.

'Hello, youngster,' Ollin said. He took a step forward, with his sword now dangling loosely in his hand. 'What are you doing there? What's your name?'

'I came to meet Yaotl.'

The speaker was one of Handy's sons: the youngster, Obsidian Snake, whom I had seen at his father's house that morning. The pang of fear I had felt on hearing my name called was replaced by anger, but that soon subsided into a kind of sullen resignation.

'Your father send you to check up on me, did he?'

He gave me a bland look. 'He just wanted to be sure you were all right.' His expression changed to a puzzled frown. '*Are* you all right? There's a funny smell – did you fall in a canal?'

'It was an accident,' I said shortly.

Ollin looked at each of us in turn. 'Do you need us, then?' My brother had told him and his comrade to make sure nobody sprang at me out of the shadows on my way out of the house, but they were plainly uncertain what to make of the boy.

'No,' I sighed. 'I'll be fine. After all, it looks like I'll have an escort from here onwards!'

I walked briskly in the direction of Handy's house in Atlixco. The boy scampered after me on his young legs. As he caught up with me I muttered at him out of the corner of my mouth: 'Handy didn't need to send you after me. Did he think I wouldn't come back for the funeral? I said I would.'

'He wanted to make sure you did,' Snake replied, with more candour than an adult would have shown. 'Besides, I wanted to come.'

I watched him curiously. 'Why?'

'I thought you could use me. Father said you had enemies in the city. And I'm a good lookout.' Perhaps it was a skill he had practised while his brothers were stealing fruit or tortillas from market stalls. 'Anyway, I had to get out of the house. It's no fun at home at the moment – when we came back from my cousins', my aunt and my grandparents weren't even talking to each other and my little brothers and sisters were all making an exhibition of themselves, weeping and tearing their hair out. It was driving me crazy!'

'What about your father?'

'Just staring at the walls, the same as when you left him. He's got my oldest brother with him – not that he'll be of much use. They can be miserable together.'

I looked sharply at him, wondering now at his easy, relaxed gait, and the casual note, the sneer almost, in his speech.

Snake's hair had been shaved close – it was the custom, and it helped control head-lice – but the single tuft that would shortly mark him as old enough for the House of Youth was beginning to sprout at the back of his head. It was not much more than a fuzz around the nape of his neck but it would be enough to distinguish him from his younger brothers and cousins and it probably made him feel grown up. Perhaps that explained it, I thought, the lad already practising the arrogance of Aztec manhood, the confident air of warriors whose mere reputation was usually enough to put their enemies to flight.

Perhaps.

'And what about you?' I asked softly.

I had met Snake while his mother was alive, and liked him: he was a shrewd, quick-witted lad, small for his age, more of a talker than a fighter, who had reminded me a little of myself as a youngster. Perhaps that resemblance was why his words troubled me.

'What about me?'

I stopped walking. He carried on for a couple of paces before looking around.

'Snake,' I said deliberately, 'I'm sorry about your mother.'

'My mother was a warrior,' he informed me coldly, 'and I'll be one too, soon.'

'Even warriors are allowed to mourn their dead comrades.'

'A warrior has to grow a heart of stone,' he said stubbornly.

'It's not the truth, though. It's what they say, I know. It's what you're supposed to show to the other warriors – especially your enemies. But no man really feels that way, or he'd be mad. Your father doesn't.' I hesitated before adding: 'I was sent to the House of Tears when I was not much younger than you…'

He looked startled. 'You were a priest?'

'I know – astonishing, isn't it? But when I went I was told I must not weep: I must not keep looking back at my home and my parents. It wasn't my home any more.' I smiled ruefully at the memory. 'My eyes were like waterfalls! And so were all the other youngsters'. You could have held the lot of us over a pile of burning chillies and no-one would have noticed the difference.'

'What are you trying to tell me?' The boy searched my face as if looking for some meaning there.

'I'm just saying that when you're told you have to have a heart of stone, that's not really how anyone is, not if they know what's good for them. Or if they are like that, it's because stone is strong, not brittle like obsidian. If you go on pretending things that matter don't – if you keep telling yourself you don't miss your mother – then sooner or later you'll snap like a used razor.'

The boy blinked. He did not look convinced. I hoped he was smart enough to remember what he was told and sooner or later learn from it.

But as we walked on it occurred to me that there must be some who never had grasped the difference between obsidian and stone, the ones who had never understood that to be hard and sharp was not the same as to be strong. Whatever I might say, there was a place for men like that in the ranks of our armies. They could be found among the berserkers, the warriors who fought with no pity and who valued their own lives only a little more than they minded anybody else's, which was scarcely at all. Such men might be mad, but so long as their madness was turned on the enemy, that was all right.

What made a man like that in the first place, though, I wondered – what produced a creature like my enemy, the captain of the otomies? Might it have been the sort of loss that Handy and his sons had suffered?

9

Snake and I returned to the house in Atlixco just before nightfall.

I found Handy standing in the middle of his courtyard, with his best cloak – the one he had been presented with years before, after taking his second enemy captive – draped around his shoulders. He was fidgeting nervously, shifting his weight from one foot to the other and fiddling absently with the hem of his cloak, like a man about to undertake some task that he feared might be beyond him.

With him were two men I did not know.

Handy introduced the younger of them as his son, Spotted Eagle. We studied one another coolly. I could make little of what I saw. Spotted Eagle was a typical Aztec youth, slim and muscular, his lips seemingly frozen into an angry pout and his eyes into a resentful glare, but still bearing the unblooded warrior's telltale tuft of hair on the back of his closely shaved head.

Handy's other visitor turned out to be his brother-in-law Xochipepe, or 'Flower Gatherer'.

'Yaotl,' I said, answering the other man's unspoken question. 'Friend of the family. Handy asked me to help.'

Flower Gatherer's appearance surprised me. For some reason I had imagined Star's sister to be married to a man like Handy, a commoner, but a successful warrior in his day, a respected veteran with a captive or two to his credit, and now a stolid, reliable member of his community. Instead I saw a small, rough looking individual, with his bowed head shaved in a tonsure: a sign that he had never dragged a prisoner home from the battlefield and, given his age, surely never would. He was marked as a failure, in other words, condemned to menial work and poverty. His cloak was short, ragged and so threadbare it was almost translucent, and his grubby breechcloth was not much better.

'You're Goose's husband?'

I must have betrayed more surprise than I had intended to, because he looked up, scowled and barked back at me: 'Sure I am. You another one who doesn't think I'm good enough?'

I took a step backward, almost bumping into Goose, who had emerged from the interior of the house with an armful of fresh bread. 'No, I didn't say that!'

He scowled at me like a sulky child. 'Why not? Everyone else does. Her parents' – he glanced at his wife – 'her sister, all of them. Just because I never got lucky on the battlefield.'

'That's enough, Flower Gatherer,' Handy growled. 'And you'll leave Star out of this, if you know what's good for you!'

His brother-in-law glowered at him, but he lowered his head and said nothing else.

Goose stood in the middle of the courtyard, still holding the tortillas. She looked wretched, her face drawn and her hair dishevelled. In a painfully obvious effort to change the subject she told her husband and Spotted Eagle: 'That Red Macaw was here earlier, trying to poke his nose in.'

'Him?' A slight lift in Spotted Eagle's voice suggested mild surprise. 'I suppose you told him where to go?'

'I did.' Handy's voice had an edge to it, reflecting the tension the man must be feeling. He clearly did not want to pursue the topic. 'Has the sun gone down yet? Good. Gentle Heart and the other women should be here soon. I'm going to get the hammer, and Spotted Eagle, you had best come in and pay your respects to your grandfather and your grandmother.' He turned, leaving his eldest boy to follow him, and they both went indoors.

Flower Gatherer watched them go with a defiant curl of his lower lip. The three of us left outside stood in the courtyard, avoiding one another's glances. None of us dared to speak until, for want of anything better to say, I posed a question that had been on the tip of my tongue since the morning: 'Does either of you know what it is between Handy and Red Macaw?'

'Not my quarrel,' the man muttered. 'You'll have to ask him in there.'

Goose said: 'Why do you ask, Yaotl?'

'I just want to know why I'm a better candidate to help with the burial than he is, that's all. And he seemed to think he could help – in fact he almost insisted.'

Goose said: 'Don't take it personally, but as far as Handy is concerned a half-wit with only one leg would be a better candidate than Red Macaw!'

I could not resist trying to probe further. 'He's injured, isn't he? What was it, an old war wound? Was that anything to do with it? Were they in the army together and…'

'Yaotl,' Goose interrupted me, 'Look, I'm sure you mean well, but this isn't going to do any good. And now really isn't the time.'

'But...'

'Besides, it's too late,' she added firmly. 'I think they're ready to start now.' As Handy came out of the house, with a stone-headed hammer dangling from his fingers, I realised I could hear female voices from the far side of the courtyard wall at the back, and that the ritual was about to begin.

Handy wielded the hammer himself. He grunted as he swung its head against the wall of his courtyard, his face twisting with effort and something that may have been rage. I wondered where his fury was directed: at the gods whose callous whim had snatched his wife and child away from him, turning what should have been a joyous day into an occasion for mourning; at Red Macaw for an offence no-one was prepared to name; or just at anything that might distract him for a moment from his grief?

The hammer smashed into the frail adobe wall, each stroke landing with an echoing thud and raising a cloud of white dust. It took just four or five blows to make a hole big enough for a man to step through; or to carry a corpse through. The dead woman must not leave the house through the doorway, lest her spirit – the Divine Princess she was to become – return that way to torment her living relatives.

As the last fragments of plaster clattered to the floor, the voices from beyond the wall grew louder. Shrill screams, yells, howling: they were war cries, but the voices uttering them were not men's. Gentle Heart, the midwife, would have gathered her own army, mostly older women from the Pleasure House, fellow midwives and curers. These were the comrades in arms of the dead woman, come to escort her to her last resting-place on Earth.

A face appeared in the hole: a young woman's, one I did not recognise. As those behind her maintained their terrifying cries, she clambered over the rubble into the courtyard and surveyed the scene around her as if inspecting it.

'The sun has descended to the Land of the Dead,' she told Handy. Her voice was soft in contrast with the noise from the other side of the broken wall and hard to hear above it. 'The little woman's comrades, the Divine Princesses, are ready to receive her.'

'Who are you?' Handy replied shortly. 'Where's Gentle Heart?'

The woman's face darkened a little in embarrassment. 'She's unwell. She was taken ill this morning.'

Goose said: 'I'm not surprised. She didn't sleep all night.'

'But we need her!' Handy cried desperately. He looked wildly at Goose and the stranger in turn. 'She has to be here. Who's going to lead us, if she can't? Will you?' His eyes settled on the face of the young woman in front of him.

She looked away. 'I don't know how to. I was only taught the words I've just said.'

'I'll do it,' Goose said.

'You?' Her brother in law stared at her.

'I've taken part in one of these things before.'

'But... Shouldn't the midwife...'

'She isn't here! I am!' Goose's voice was hoarse with strain. 'Handy, what does it matter? We have to do this. It's the only thing left that I can still do for my sister. Now let's in the name of all the gods get it over with!'

Tribute of Death

Spotted Eagle had dragged a thick reed mat from the house, and now he tugged it along after him as he followed his father, leaving it by the entrance to the sweat bath while they scrambled into the dark, cramped space beyond.

I had been dreading the moment when the woman's body was pulled out into the open. I was used to death and the bodies of the dead, but I remembered Star as she had been when I had seen her last: spirited, unafraid of anybody – even my elder brother, who intimidated almost everyone else he met – and laughing at the antics of her busy household. I had wanted to hold onto that image of her and not replace it with the sight of her as a corpse, but I had no choice now, because I had felt sorry for her husband and her sister, and I had agreed to help bear her to her grave. At least we were spared seeing her dead child: his body had been left in the sweat bath for now, to be disposed of separately, as was the custom.

'They've not even covered her up,' Flower Gatherer complained.

Goose heard him. 'It's not the custom to wrap women who die in childbirth.' She busied herself over the body, straightening the skirt and blouse it had been dressed in like a mother fussing over her daughter on the morning of her wedding. I wondered how much of this activity and the brisk tone of her voice was a mask for her grief. 'We washed and clothed her, that's all.'

The dead woman's parents were nowhere to be seen. I hoped they had managed to say their farewells before now, because they would not have another opportunity.

Star's sister and her mother had got her into a sitting position and since then the stiffness had set in. When her husband and son had manoeuvred her into the courtyard and set her upon the mat, she remained seated, with her eyes closed and her hair loose. Apart from her wide-open mouth she looked as if she were resting.

I felt a thrill of horror as I noticed that she seemed to be trembling, but it was the shaking of the two men's hands as they placed her on the mat that caused it. They laid her gently on her side so that she would not topple when we picked her up. Then, as if obeying a command, they both turned, stumbling away. Handy stood up and gasped. His son bent forward as if a heavy weight had dropped onto his shoulders.

Handy turned towards his sister in law. 'We're ready,' he said gruffly.

'Then we have to go as quickly as we can,' the woman said. 'You know where?'

'Yes. There's a crossroads in Atlixco we can use. It's by our pyramid, and it has a shrine to the Divine Princesses. We'll bury her there.'

'Then let's hurry. Every youth and sorcerer in the city will know what happened here by now. They'll be gathering, waiting for their chance ... Handy, do you understand?'

She looked sharply at the commoner. His large frame seemed to have shrunk during the day, and now he appeared to have scarcely the strength left to stand, as he swayed silently back and forth, his gaze fixed on the floor. It seemed an age before he replied softly: 'I heard you.'

Star had to be buried in the place that was now her own: before one of the shrines to the Divine Princesses that stood at every crossroads. We had to get her there quickly because the body of a woman dead in childbirth drew the most desperate of thieves. Parts of it – the right middle finger and the hair in particular – would make a warrior invulnerable if he inserted them in his shield. To the youths in particular, still dreading their first venture onto the battlefield, such a charm was irresistible. Worse than the young warrior was the sorcerer, the thief: he would take the whole forearm, and carry it with him when he burgled a house, because it had the power to render the occupants unconscious.

It was hard to have secrets in our crowded city; to keep them in the intimate world of a parish with its tangle of family ties and mixed loyalties was impossible. Goose knew, as we all did, that the moment word got around that a woman had died giving birth, the sorcerers and the young warriors would start to gather.

This was why we had to hurry, and why Star would have an escort of midwives, mature women, many of them mothers themselves, who would fight to protect their charge.

'We must go,' she said quietly.

Flower Gatherer and I stepped towards the mat. After a brief hesitation, Handy and his son did the same. Each of us grasped a corner, and at a word from Handy we took up our burden.

Even with four men carrying her Star was heavy, and getting her through the hole in the wall was horrifyingly difficult. To have dropped her would have been unthinkable, but as we stumbled over the rubble created by her husband's hammer blows, it was impossible to stop her from wobbling alarmingly.

Somehow we pulled her from her home, intact, and then our ordeal began.

Women shrieked around us, waving torches whose flames traced painfully bright shapes on the indigo sky. As we walked away from the house they closed in, surrounding us on all sides, leaving just enough room in their midst for the four men, the body, and Goose. Star's sister did not fall into step with us, though. As we got under way she began to become more and more animated, darting back and forth, watching and calling to her comrades like a vigilant war captain encouraging his troops.

Watching her, I recalled Handy with his hammer and Snake with his air of harsh indifference. I wondered how long these people could keep on holding their sense of loss at bay. Sooner or later the bitterness and the frenzy would wear off. How would they cope then, when the pain came rushing on them and they had nothing left to oppose it with?

I had both hands hooked into my corner of the mat. The other men did the same. All our arms strained under the weight we bore, with our muscles and sinews standing out and our shoulders bowed. Every step was announced with a grunt.

That walk to the crossroads still haunts my nightmares, but it is the women, not the pain in my shoulders or the strain in my back, whose memory brings me to wakefulness crying and soaked with sweat.

It should have been reassuring to have an escort that few men in Mexico would dare to interfere with, but it was terrifying. High, ferocious cries tore the air around us: 'Not so bloody brave now, are they?' 'Where are you, you men? Hiding in the shadows?' 'Come out here, come dancing out here, showing off your manhood now. Ha! You can show it to this pine torch!' 'If she doesn't burn it off, I'll bite it off!'

' "Bloody, painful are the words of the women," ' grunted Flower Gatherer, quoting an old saying.

'It's not their words that scare me,' I muttered with feeling. 'What if they really mean it?'

There was nothing artificial about their rage: it was born of bitterness, anger and hate, and there could be no mistake about where it was directed. When women detached themselves from the crowd to hurl themselves into the surrounding darkness, brandishing torches or clawing the air with their fingernails, I knew the foe they sought need not be a sorcerer or a warrior. It was a man: any man at all. We four were exempt so long as we held onto the body of the dead woman, but I had no idea how safe we would be once we put her down. Men had a part to play in this ceremony, but it was the women's night.

Goose stayed in the midst of the crowd, prowling back and forth within the open space at its heart like a captive jaguar patrolling its cage. Every so often she would call out, although her voice was lower and her words more measured than the other women's. She seemed almost subdued in comparison, as though her anger, having burned more intensely than the others', was already starting to exhaust itself. Only once did she appear to give way to the hysteria that surrounded her: when a shrill voice near the back of the crowd suddenly cried out: 'There's one! Look, over there!'

We all stopped. I could not turn without dropping my corner of Star's mat but I could twist my head around, as did the other three men. It was hard to see exactly what was happening through the press of bodies behind us but at least two of the women had broken away, bearing torches, and were running back towards whatever it was one of them had seen. A moment later somebody pushed past me: it was Goose, racing to join in the pursuit, skirts flying, torch waving and spitting sparks, voice raised as she strove to make herself heard over the other women's screams.

The cries diminished with distance. A strange stillness descended over those of us who remained, as heads were turned and necks craned in an effort to follow the drama unfolding behind us. I could not see what the women were chasing. Then they vanished around a corner.

There was a brief pause. I turned to look at Handy, Spotted Eagle and Flower Gatherer. All four of us were frowning in puzzlement, as we tried to work out what had happened, and whom the women had seen: a sorcerer, a warrior, or some poor innocent engaged on business of his own, who had just happened to find himself in the wrong place at the wrong time. Around us, female voices began muttering and growling.

'We'd better put her down for a moment,' Handy said. 'We don't know what's going on.'

'I'm not sure I want to,' I replied as I lowered my corner of the mat. 'Whatever it is, it won't be pretty!'

There came a shout from somewhere out of sight, followed by a high-pitched, quivering cry: a triumphant sound, which was rapidly picked up and amplified by the crowd until the air seemed saturated by unearthly shrieks. I cringed, and with both hands now free I clapped them over my ears. The cries told me that the hunters, Gentle Heart and her followers, had caught something, and I shuddered at the thought of what they might be capable of in their fury.

There was a disturbance in the crowd and then Star's sister was beside me. Her face was flushed and the torchlight made the beads of sweat on her forehead gleam.

'Here!' she cried, and threw something at my feet.

Handy, the other two men and I looked at it with a mixture of wonder and slowly gathering shock.

'We chased him over a wall. He just about made it, but one of the girls caught hold of this.'

'I nearly pulled him back, but the cloth tore first.' The other woman was panting, forcing the words out between deep gasps. 'Lucky for him!'

The thing on the ground in front of me was a scrap of cloth: carmine-coloured, with a strip of orange along its hemmed edge and part of an emblem that had been destroyed when it was torn. It was a design I knew: the wind jewel.

The cloth had been torn from a cloak. The cloak had been of the kind awarded to a three-captive warrior.

'Red Macaw,' Handy spat. 'He won't give up, will he?'

10

'I think there were two of them,' Goose said.

'I thought so too.' The woman who claimed to have caught the man and torn his cloak looked over her shoulder with her teeth bared in a feral expression. She was young with large, dark eyes and might have been pretty on any other night. 'There was definitely *something* else out there.'

' "Something"?' Spotted Eagle echoed weakly. He looked around at the other men, his eyes wide with terror. 'What did she mean, "something"?'

There was no hint of fear in the young woman's voice when she replied, but only rage as she spat the words out. 'I don't know what I saw. Something moving. Not a man, it was too tall. Too big and slow to be an animal, though. And no face – I didn't see a face. Whatever it was it was up to no good, I'm sure of that.'

'Not a man, and not an animal either.' I repeated, suppressing a shudder. 'You think it was a demon?'

'Or a sorcerer: a man with two souls, in the form he cloaks himself in at night.' The young woman's words brought a gasp from her hearers. Everyone feared the creatures of the night: owls, raccoons, badgers, all were dreaded as portents of death for anyone who came across them. Worse, some of these animals were thought to be not what they seemed, but sorcerers: men and women endowed with a second soul that enabled them to change themselves into animals and go abroad in the darkness to work mischief. Such mischief, I realised, might well include stealing a dead woman's forearm to use as a charm.

'It was a sorcerer,' Goose put in firmly. 'They were lying in wait for us. Look, we're practically at the crossroads.'

I looked around me, peering between the women in an effort to make out whatever lay beyond the flickering glow of their torches. We were at the edge of an open space, with a small pyramid looming over its far side.

We men picked up our burden and walked on. The women's cries had subsided now to whispers and muttering, as though some of their anger had been spent in the chase. The crowd started to disperse, and as the torch-bearers spread out, scattering light over the space around us, I saw more of Atlixco's plaza. Streets led off it, more or less at right angles to each other. They were little more than paths, interrupted by the canals that boxed the little square, but their junction would still serve for a crossroads.

'Well, we're here,' I said as we brought Star into the middle of the space and settled her carefully on the ground. 'The burial ground. We made it.'

I did not hear the first part of Handy's reply. He was staring at the body. To begin with, I did not think he was speaking. I imagined he was taking the opportunity to look at his wife for the last time before she went underground forever, and that all her thoughts were with her. I took a step backward, away from him, supposing he would rather be alone.

Then, however, I realised his lips were moving, and I heard the whispered words: 'Four nights.'

Four nights: that was the period for which custom demanded the woman's grave be guarded against robbers. My sudden feeling of unease intensified when the commoner tore his eyes from the corpse to look directly into mine. 'Yaotl...'

I looked at him in alarm. 'Oh, no. I said I'd come this far, Handy, but four nights...' Four nights away from Lily and the relative safety of her house in the northern part of the city; four nights in Atlixco, with the captain prowling in the streets nearby.

He did not shift his gaze. 'Yaotl, please. We need you. Star needs you. You were trained as a priest, you must know better than any of us what we've got to guard her against, and why.'

Spotted Eagle, who had been standing nearby, brooding silently over his mother's body, responded before I could speak: 'They won't have gone far, all those sorcerers and young warriors. They'll be waiting until the women have gone. Then they'll come back. Do you want that to happen to my mother?' He fixed hard, bright young eyes on mine, challenging me to argue. 'You want her body to be torn apart by thieves and her soul left to wander around in the Nine Hells, trying to find her way across the river?'

Handy contradicted him harshly. 'No, not the Land of the Dead. She won't go there. Her soul will left behind, won't it, Yaotl? She'll be reduced to prowling the streets, haunting her old home. She'll be lost, angry. She'll want us but won't be able to get near us, except by sending us sickness and death.' His voice changed, became louder and more shrill. 'And she'll do it, because it's all she can do. That's what she'll be reduced to. My wife,' he concluded with a sob, 'turned into a demon!'

'Handy...' I protested as his son recoiled and then glared at me.

'You heard that!' Spotted Eagle cried. 'You can't leave us now!'

'I don't have a choice. I made a promise. I've got to get back to Tlatelolco tonight.'

'No, you haven't'

'Lily will...'

Handy produced something like a ghastly parody of a smile. 'No, she won't. When Snake took your message to her I had him say you wouldn't be back tonight.'

I stared at him, shocked. It was not so much the way I had been manipulated that I was reeling from as his apparent callousness. I could imagine Lily's face crumpling at the news that I was not coming home, that she would be alone tonight, with no-one to turn to when the nightmares threatened to overwhelm her.

'You bastards,' I muttered feebly. 'Do you think no-one else hurts, apart from you?'

'Maybe,' Handy said indifferently. 'My own hurt's all I know about, though.'

Goose interrupted us. 'Are you ready now? There are digging sticks and shovels here.'

The women had found a burial site, near the base of the stumpy pyramid. Atlixco's temple was very similar to the one I had visited that afternoon in my home parish: half dozen steps leading up to a platform with a little thatched shrine and a brazier in front of it, emitting frail glowing tendrils of smoke. In front of the temple a paving slab had been prized up, leaving a square of bare earth for us to dig.

We four men set to with a will, determined to get our task over with as quickly as we could. We worked to the sound of crackling torches and under the gaze of Goose and her comrades, and well intentioned though they may have been it felt like being watched by vultures.

At last we had a hole deep and wide enough to lower Star's seated body into.

I observed Handy's face as we dragged the mat with his wife's corpse on it to the hole, and as we lowered her into her grave, moving her body with hands as gentle as her own might have been if she had lived to hold her newborn child. The man's eyes were now dry and hard and his expression revealed nothing except concentration and physical effort. It was as if at this moment, when he had to say farewell once and for all to the woman he had loved, he found himself drained of all feeling. Or maybe this was one occasion that anger was simply not equal to.

Whatever priest presided over the shrine, he had relinquished it for tonight, leaving the midwives to their mysteries. Only we, who had buried her, were to hear the last words anyone would address to Star.

Goose must have seen more than one of these ceremonies, I realised. She knew what to say. She spoke clearly at first, her words measured and deliberate: 'My little one, my dove: thou hast done thy work, the will of thy mother Cihuacoatl. Thou hast taken up the shield which thy mother gave thee. Now...'

And that was when the anger failed, and her self control finally broke, along with her voice. For a moment her words were almost unintelligible through the sobs that suddenly racked her, almost drowned by the rising moans of her comrades: 'Awaken! Arise! Array thyself, go to the happy place, home of thy mother, thy father, the sun!

Go, accompany the sun! May the Divine Princesses bring thee to him!'

On the last word she burst loudly into unrestrained tears. She shuffled away from the graveside, whimpering, into the arms of an older woman; and it was that woman who took up the speech where she had left off, speaking in a tearful whisper, the wisps of her grey hair shivering in time with her words: 'My little one, my dove: thou art tired, thou hast suffered like a man, thou hast gained the place of destruction, thou has merited the precious death. Diest thou without purpose? Thou wilt live forever, among the Divine Princesses. Now farewell, beloved child! Enter among the Divine Princesses! May they receive thee! Bring joy to our mother, our father, the sun!

'Thou hast left us bereft, we old women, we old men. Remember us in our misery, we who are imprisoned here on Earth, to endure the cold, the wind, the heat of the sun, the wind, our unendurable hunger. Thou hast gone to rest in peace, in a good place, a pleasant place; noble lady, come back to us!'

As she fell silent, Goose stepped forward again, and with a signal commanded me and the other men to begin shovelling soil back into the grave. Only Handy stood back from the work now, watching silently as we hid his wife from view for the last time.

'She is happy now,' Gentle Heart whispered, but Handy seemed not to hear her. His wife was gone, her spirit headed now for the Land of the Women, far away beyond the western horizon.

And never again would be able to watch a sunset without thinking of her, for it would be her task now, along with all the other mothers dead in childbirth, to rise up every afternoon, to escort the sun on his downward journey from the zenith to the Land of the Dead beneath the Earth.

And that, I reminded myself, would happen only if he succeeded in preserving her body from attentions of thieves. If he failed, then the horrors that would await the dead woman and the men and children in her family would be too ghastly to contemplate.

We replaced the slab over the grave. It was a solid block of limestone that it took all the strength of four grown men to shift. The midwives departed, their work done, although the sky was still full of stars.

We had a single torch, which would go out before morning. This was not a good place for a man to spend the night, beside a shrine to the Divine Princesses and the body of a woman newly dead; and the pale, flickering light and the wavering shadows it cast on the other men's faces seemed to emphasise the weariness and strain we all felt.

After the shouting and the fury that had surrounded us for most of the night, the silence and stillness that enveloped us now were startling. At first, it felt as though we were the only living, breathing things in the city. I knew how much of an illusion that was. Many priests would be awake, keeping watch from the tops of pyramids, nervously scanning the horizon for signs of hostile spirits. After a few moments I heard the sound of distant chanting: warriors and youths practising in a House of Song, I assumed.

And nearer at hand, there was at least one creature prowling the streets around us; possibly more than one.

'What do you think it was?' Flower Gatherer asked fearfully.

'What?' I asked.

'The monster that woman saw. The one following the warrior.'

I shivered. 'It was probably nothing.' The lie was meant as much for me as for the others. 'Trick of the light. They imagined it.'

Tribute of Death

When Handy frowned, the long shadows thrown by the torch exaggerated the expression, drawing a thick black line across his brow, like someone using a charcoal stick. 'I don't know so much. Goose isn't the sort to imagine things, even if the others are.'

'So what do you want it to be?' I snapped. Fear made me peevish and I had been angry with him already. 'What would be scary enough for you: the goddess Cihuacoatl, come to eat us all alive? I told you there was nothing there – just leave it at that, can't you?'

'What about this otomi warrior you're afraid of?' Flower Gather suggested.

'He's a man. The girl said what she saw was taller than a man. And It didn't have a face,' Handy replied darkly.

There was no answer to that save a moody silence. For a while only our breathing and the crackling of the torch disturbed the empty air.

Eventually Spotted Eagle asked: 'What should we do? Stand shifts?'

'No,' his father said. 'Not tonight. It's too late and we're too tired. If one of us tried to stay awake by himself, it's a bag of mouldy cocoa beans to a boatload of emeralds he'd be asleep before he could count to twenty. We all need to be awake tonight, it's the only way we can stop each other dropping off.'

I wondered whether he was right. I suspected the terror we all felt, the fear of whatever might be lurking nearby, would be enough to keep us all alert.

Yet there was no denying that my eyelids were getting heavy, and my mind kept wandering, drawn by the flickering torchlight into some warmer, more comfortable, peaceful place, where the smell of

Simon Levack

pitch-pine drifted about me like cloud embracing a mountain.

11

I awoke with a start. My eyes opened on nothing, and when I blinked, it did nothing to dispel the darkness around me. I felt a spasm of fear, which jerked me fully awake.

'I can't see!' I gasped.

From very close by came a throaty whisper: Handy's voice. 'That's because the torch has gone out, you silly bugger!'

I looked wildly about me, still disorientated. 'How long was I asleep?'

'I don't know,' the commoner muttered. 'I nodded off too. We all did. Now keep your bloody voice down!'

I gazed in the direction from which he was speaking. After a moment I realised I could just make out his bulky shape. There was a fine mist in the air, glowing feebly with reflected firelight from the braziers burning outside the city's many temples. I could see the man next to me but little else.

I lowered my voice obediently. 'Why are you whispering?'

The answer came from Spotted Eagle, who was somewhere in the gloom beyond his father. 'I heard it again. I think it's closer now, by the foot of the pyramid.'

'Shit!' Flower Gatherer yelped. 'That's only a few paces away.'

'What is?' I demanded. 'What did you hear?'

'It can't see us properly,' Handy's son suggested. 'It's trying to figure out where we all are before it makes its move.'

'What is?' I demanded again. 'Will someone answer my questions? Have I lost my voice or something? Hey...'

'We ought to split up,' Handy said abruptly.

The suggestion came a moment too late.

Suddenly the air around us was split by a horrible, bubbling scream: a sound of pain or rage that could scarcely have come from a human throat. Then came footsteps, the smack of leather on stone, the sound of sandaled feet running. Something appeared, shockingly close: a looming shape bearing down on us out of the gloom. I caught the briefest glimpse of its towering figure before panic overcame me and I was on my feet and running too.

I took two steps and blundered into something. Flower Gatherer shouted curses in my ear and shoved me aside. Then he was gone, and I was racing into empty darkness, not knowing where I was going, not caring, only wanting to put the monster far behind me and leave it there.

Fear kept me going until my legs felt as heavy as gold and every breath was like having a spike driven through my chest. Eventually I staggered to a halt, doubled over with pain and nausea, my calves twitching painfully.

After gasping for air for a few moments I stumbled on, my pace reduced now to a shambling walk. Even now I dared not stop altogether.

I forced myself to think about my surroundings. Somehow, I had managed not to crash into a wall or stumble into a canal, but I had no idea how far I had run or where I had ended up. I suspected I had not being going in a straight line and my sense of direction, which was normally reliable, had failed me entirely tonight.

'Got to rest,' I wheezed. My legs had reached the point where they seemed to be moving by themselves, even though every step was agony, because it would have been even more painful to halt; but I made them stop now, leaning panting against a wall and looking fearfully about me. I could see a little: the first hint of twilight was appearing over the mountains in the East, although the mist and shadows around me were all but impenetrable still. My ears and sense of smell were working, however, and as I drew breath and listened I caught a whiff of rot and marsh gas and heard a splash, as of some animal or bird slipping into the water. I had reached the edge of the city: the shore of the lake must be a few paces away.

I felt a vague sense of disquiet. The marshes and the waterlogged maze of *chinampa* fields that bordered the city were dangerous country for me now. They were where my enemy might be hiding.

A moment later I found a more pressing reason to be afraid. I was being followed.

I could not have said what had I noticed first; the sound of breathing perhaps, the scrape of a sandal sole on hard earth, or whatever sense it is that makes a rabbit bolt an instant before the hunter can seize it. All I knew was that fine hairs on the back of my neck were standing up and a sick, hollow feeling had taken over my guts. I froze, not daring even to turn my head.

I could not hear anything. But that could just mean that whoever or whatever was behind me had stopped at the same time as I had.

I looked about me quickly. I had no wish to glance over my

shoulder; I told myself there would be nothing to see in the darkness and if there were, I was not sure I wanted to see it. I did not think I had the strength left to run. What I wanted was somewhere to hide.

There was just enough light to see that the path I was on was bounded by a canal. I thought of jumping into it but the splash and the ripples would give me away, and in the water I would be helpless. Opposite the canal was the blank wall of a house. It was too high to climb, so I darted around the corner instead

My bare feet padded over the short distance in silence, but betrayed myself by a hollow thump and a clatter as I crashed into something large and wooden with an impact that scraped skin from my knee.

Only terror held me back from cursing out loud until I recognised a rare stroke of good luck. I had run straight into an empty maize bin.

There was no time to think. I scrambled over the side, ignoring the pain as the top caught my wounded knee, and tumbled in. A cloud of dust filled the space around me, making me blink and pinch my nose to avoid sneezing.

Half-crouching, I cautiously lifted my eyes above the top of the bin. From here I could see to the corner I had just rounded.

A moment later I realised I had not been mistaken. I could hear hoarse breathing, the scratching sound of a sandaled foot on the path, and another noise I could not identify, a faint mixture of creaking and rustling. Then with a thrill of terror I realised I could see my follower as well as hear him, even with eyes watering from the dust in the maize bin.

Something stood at the corner: a large, irregular shape, taller than a man and bulkier. It seemed to be swivelling this way and that, like a hunting animal seeking its quarry. There was nothing animal-like in its ponderous, jerky movements, however; nor in the one thing I recognised about it, a thin pale sliver of something catching the faint twilight as it turned. It was the unmistakable gleam of an obsidian blade. Whatever manner of creature was seeking me, he – or it – was carrying a sword.

We stayed like that until I was gritting my teeth against the pain in my awkwardly bent legs. I reached up and clung to the top edge of my hiding place, to take some of my weight on my hands, and was rewarded with splinters in my fingers. My bladder began to ache and still the thing stood there, only paces away.

All I could see distinctly was the sword. I could not take my eyes off its obsidian blades, lethally sharp razors set into the weapon's hardwood shaft, giving it a cutting edge that could sever a man's neck with one blow or peel off his skin in layers. They fascinated me so much, each blade catching the light in turn, that I did not at first grasp that they were moving slowly towards me.

And then the monster was almost upon me. I ducked quickly, lowering my head and crouching deep inside the maize bin in silent terror while I listened to the creature's slow, heavy breathing.

When the breathing formed itself into a throaty whisper and the whisper became a word, something between a question and a gloat, I knew I was a dead man.

'Yaotl?'

At the sound of my own name I started so violently that my hiding place shuddered. The thing outside could not have failed to notice that. Even as I threw myself frantically against the side of the wooden container, trying to knock it over in a desperate bid to make it roll into the nearest canal, I heard the whisper transformed into a roar of rage and triumph.

The first blow knocked my teeth together and set my ears ringing. With a crack of shattered wood the maize bin split. I heard a swish of air as the sword was raised for a second strike. I slithered from the wreckage, hands and feet scrabbling to propel me out of the way with all the strength they still had. Then came another crash as blades sank once again into soft wood. More blows followed, each more frantic than the last, but now they had a different note, duller, with a hollow ring. The monster had got his sword embedded in the remains of the maize bin and was swinging the whole lot against a wall in an effort to free the weapon.

I seized my chance. I scrambled to my feet and ran. Luckily whatever sound I made was inaudible beneath the noise my assailant was making, the thumping and splintering and his own shouted curses.

I stumbled blindly through the streets until there were no streets, and I was wading knee deep in icy water and pushing aside stiff rushes that were taller than I was, and even then I kept going, never daring to look back but imagining the huge figure trudging relentlessly behind me, slashing at the stems with great sweeping strokes of its sword.

Eventually my legs gave up, slipping from under me in the mud and pitching me face-down in muddy water. I hauled myself out by my arms, using them to drag my sodden, exhausted body onto a foul-smelling pile of muck that had been dredged from the lake bottom to make a channel for a farmer's or a fisherman's canoe. It only just broke the surface of the water but it was the only more or less dry place I could find.

I knew I had to go on. I could not allow myself to rest here, in what might be my enemy's country, among the wetlands where the captain was rumoured to lurk. Gritting my teeth against the pain in my legs, I urged them to lift me up once more.

It was no good. I was at the end of my strength.

I collapsed on top of the heap of silt and was unconscious in an instant.

TWO RAIN

1

One of the rituals we priests had had to undergo to appease the rain god had involved throwing ourselves into the icy water of the lake at night and then running, naked, back to the House of Tears, where we would sit, shivering, until noon, covered only by a thin blanket. I had done this every year for twenty years, and it may have saved my life, for if my body had not been hardened by my priest's training the chill and damp might have killed me long before the sun had climbed high enough to share any of his warmth with me.

I groaned, squinted and turned my head away from the brilliant disc. I had no idea where I was or how I had got here, and for a moment did not care. It troubled me that the surface I lay on was so rough and soggy, as if someone had taken both my sleeping mat and the roof of my house away in the night, just before an unseasonable downpour; and there was an unpleasant smell in the air. Still, I was not going to worry about it. I wanted only to turn around and go back to sleep.

'Who are you? How did you get here?' The voice sounded like a child's: a little girl's. I replied with a grunt.

'You're not drunk, are you?'

If I could have summoned up the energy then, I would have

shouted at her to go away and leave me in peace. All I managed was another grunt.

'My brother said he thought you might be sleeping it off. I said I thought you might be ill.'

I forced myself to turn over and open my eyes. The pale blue of a late morning sky and the bright light of the sun shining between tall stems made me squint.

'But my brother said he'd go and get the parish police, because they'll have you beaten to death. That's what happens if they find you drunk. I know, my dad told me.'

It took a moment for the girl's words to penetrate my fogged, aching head, but when they did they were enough to jerk me at last into wakefulness. I did not need the girl to tell me what would be done to a commoner found drunk in public without a lawful excuse. It had happened to me once. I had been hauled off to the emperor's notorious Cuauhcalco prison and had barely escaped with my life. I sat up with a cry of terror.

'No!' I yelped.

The girl leaped backward in surprise. She looked to be about seven or eight, old enough to wear a blouse and skirt, both of which had evidently been made up out of material cut out of larger garments and roughly sewn together and patched.

I glanced around anxiously. 'Your brother – Where is he now?'

'Over there. I dared him to come and wake you up but he wouldn't. He's scared.'

'Nothing to be scared of,' I declared hastily. There was a boy of about ten in a short cloak and breechcloth peering nervously at me from between two rushes. He appeared to be ready to bolt if I threatened him. 'I'm harmless, really. I wouldn't hurt a beetle.' I smiled ruefully. 'That's even if I had the strength to! And I'm not drunk.' I hesitated before adding the unavoidable question. 'Er... that doesn't mean I have any idea where I am, though. I sort of got lost. Can you tell me?'

The girl looked at me through eyes that had suddenly narrowed with suspicion. 'This is Atlixco, of course. Or at least the wetlands belonging to it. How come you don't know that?'

So I had gone around almost in a circle, ending up not far from where I had set out. Blundering aimlessly through darkened streets, it would have been easy to do. At least I had saved myself a long walk back.

With the memory of how I had come to be here came all the other things that had happened in the night: the funeral procession, the terror that had snatched me and the other men from sleep, the chase across the darkened city; all that, and the knowledge that whatever monster had been after me, it had known my name. I had not just been another unfortunate caught out of doors at night, at the mercy of ghosts and malicious spirits. I had been the thing's intended quarry. But what had it been? What little I had seen of my pursuer had not looked human; and as Handy had pointed out, the captain, whatever else he might be, was a man. Or had he somehow been transformed – by sorcery or by the will of a god – into something else?

'Who were you?' I whispered. 'How did you know where to find me?' I was struck by another grim thought. It was too much of a coincidence for my follower and me to have encountered each other by chance, at night in a part of the city I had not been to lately. But where had he – he or it – picked up my trail? At Handy's house? At the shrine? Earlier?

'What are you talking about?' asked the girl. 'Are you sure you're not drunk?'

'Quite sure. I don't suppose you have any food?'

'He has,' she said, tossing her head to indicate her brother. 'We were taking our father his lunch, because he forgot it again. But my brother won't share it with you, because father will tie him up and stick cactus spines in him if there's any missing.' I considered offering to buy some, thinking a bagful of cocoa beans would be enough to deflect her father's anger, but then I remembered I had no money.

'Never mind.' I stood up. 'Where is your father now?'

I did not want to scare the children off by telling them what had happened to me but I asked them whether they had seen or heard anything out of the ordinary. They had not, but as the girl, whose name was Xochiyotl – 'Heart of a Flower' – pointed out, they had only just come out from the city. Their father was more likely to be able to help me, having been fishing at the edge of the lake since before dawn.

We found him where the rushes thinned out and gave way to open water, forlornly inspecting his mostly empty nets. At the sound of our approach, the splashing and slurping noises our feet made and rustle of tall stems being pushed aside, he whirled around as though in fear of being attacked from behind.

I saw a solid looking man in a frayed and soiled breechcloth. When he first caught sight of us his eyes widened in shock, but they quickly narrowed with anger. His first words were to me: 'Who are you? Where did you find these two?'

'Well, it was more the other way round...' He was not listening to me. He had already turned on his children, scolding them: 'What are you doing here? Didn't I tell you it's not safe at the moment? I said you weren't to come out here until it was over. What was your mother thinking of, letting you anywhere near the lake? I've a good mind to...'

His son retreated several steps, his face pale with fright. His sister ignored her father's outburst. 'You forgot your lunch,' she said, proffering a small cloth bag.

'Never mind my lunch! There are worse things than hunger, don't you know that?' The man was sweating, although it was not warm, especially for someone in water up to his knees. 'It's dangerous out here!'

I peered between the rushes and out across the lake. Its surface was a flat as a polished copper mirror, with scarcely a ripple except what was made by the occasional duck or heron. Nothing nearby broke it except fishing nets strung between poles. Beyond its far side loomed the mountains that edged the eastern side of the valley, with their foothills dotted with white houses. Among the many towns and villages on those hillsides was lord Maize Ear's capital, and not far from it, the retreat where Lily and I had found refuge. From where I stood that shoreline was a tantalising sight. It looked so peaceful, and there was not so much as a canoe between it and me.

' "Dangerous"?' I echoed, suppressing the wave of nostalgic self-pity that threatened to overwhelm me. 'Dangerous how?'

He scowled at me. 'Who are you?' he asked for a second time.

At that point his son finally nerved himself to speak. 'I think he's a drunk,' he said importantly.

'No he's not!' piped Heart of a Flower. 'He told us he got lost.'

The fisherman looked at me incredulously. 'No-one gets lost out here. You only come here if you're a fisherman or a farmer working on one of the *chinampa* plots, and we all know this place better than our own courtyards. So what are you really doing here?'

I had to tell him. Apart from anything else I wanted to ask him whether he had seen anything like the monster that had attacked me. As I described the encounter I glanced out of the corner of my eye at the two children. The little girl was gazing at me with wide, awe-struck eyes, while her brother crept closer to his father and shivered.

The man listened to me in grim silence. Then he said: 'You'd better come with me.'

We did not have far to go, briefly wading through brackish water until we reached a spot where a few broken and flattened stems showed where a small craft had been pushed into the rushes to hide it.

'Here you are,' the fisherman said.

'I don't get it.' I looked at him sharply. 'There was a boat here, I take it. Where is it now? Has it been stolen, is that what you're showing me?'

'Father, there's nothing here.' Now that his father seemed to have forgotten his anger the boy had become bolder.

'I'm not in the mood to play games,' I said, trying to sound menacing and succeeding only in provoking a chuckle, until the man decided he had had enough fun at my expense and pushed his way cautiously into the gap in the rushes.

'Here,' he said, stooping, 'you'll have to grab the other end.' I stared at him for a moment. Then I realised that his hands were beneath the surface and tugging at something heavy.

With the children looking on in silence, their father and I hoisted the wreck of a canoe into the air. I held onto my end for just long enough to see what had happened to it – to note the large, jagged hole in its bottom, a hole that must have been made by some tool such as an axe – before dropping it and letting it fall with a loud splash.

It might not have been an axe, of course. The boat had sunk again before I had time to examine its timber for any flakes of obsidian that might have become lodged in it, but I knew it could just as easily have been sunk by a strong man wielding a sword.

'That,' the fisherman said, as he led us back to his nets, 'is why I don't want you children coming out here. This has been going on for days. It's not safe. The boat's only the latest thing to have happened.'

'But who'd do something like that?' I muttered, half to myself.

'You tell me! Not to mention all the other fishermen and bird-catchers – they'd like to know too. Let me tell you, there are men who've been making their livings off the water all their lives who won't so much as dip a toe in it now, they're that frightened. See this?' He yanked a net out of the water. It held no fish, and the reason was obviously something more than bad luck.

'Something's torn it,' Heart of a Flower observed.

I looked at the net and the gaping holes in it, that made what was left of its mesh hang from its poles like limp rags. 'Torn?' I mused aloud, as I waded towards it for a closer look. 'Torn or...' I picked a section of it up, peering at ropes where they parted. I looked at two ends, frowned, and held them together, noting the way they matched.

'You see?' the fisherman said over my shoulder.

'This was cut,' I said, dropping the net. 'It's been slashed by something – a knife, something like that.' I regarded him thoughtfully.

'It's not the first time, is it? And it's not just you.'

'That's right.' He looked about him, fearfully surveying the tranquil scene surrounding us. Nothing stirred, but it was difficult to see between the tall, dense rushes: who could tell what might be hiding among them? 'Everyone who fishes this stretch of the shore – here, where it borders on Atlixco, and all the way south at least as far as Toltenco – it's the same story for all of them. Someone or something has been raiding these nets, cutting them, stealing the fish, if there are any, and just ripping them apart if there aren't. Anything like that boat that's left unattended is smashed up. It's not just theft – it's as if whoever, whatever is doing this is trying to do more than just forage for food. It's like he's trying to scare us all away.'

I recalled the strange, hulking form that had chased me, how its movements had not seemed quite human. 'You said "or something". What makes you think…' My voice faltered at the look on the man's face, the widening of his eyes, the slight slackness of his mouth and cheeks that betrayed the horror he felt.

He hesitated before speaking again, and when he did open his mouth it was to whisper in a confidential tone, as though he did not want his children to overhear him. 'I don't know what it is. I haven't seen it, but the ones who have, or who've heard it moving about… they don't think it's a man.'

'What do they think it is, then?'

'How should I know?' His voice became hoarse with strain. 'I don't know if it's a water monster, an *ahuitzotl*, or something worse, but from what I've heard… It moves wrong, it's too big, it's the wrong shape, and the one man who thinks he saw it up close – before he ran for his life, that is – he told me *it doesn't have a face.*'

2

I left the fisherman squatting disconsolately on a bank at the water's edge, picking at the severed strands of net and trying to splice them while his children ate his lunch. The only other thing I learned from them was that so far as anyone knew, whatever man or monster was prowling among the rushes had so far only ever struck at night.

I assumed a fish-thief, whether human or not, would be driven by hunger: a motive I could easily understand. But what reason could he or it have for sinking a canoe? That looked like an act of pure spitefulness – unless, of course, the fisherman had been right, and the intention was to scare people away from the neighbourhood.

'Why would anyone do such a thing?' I asked myself, but the answer was, unfortunately, all too obvious. Whoever or whatever lay behind the reports the chief minister and my elder brother had told me about was hiding out in the marshes, and the fewer people there were about, the less chance he had of being found. So this was no petty thief or vandal. There was a purpose behind what had happened: a purpose which evidently involved me. I, like the fisherman, was afraid of something that had appeared at night and had not seemed human, and it was hard to believe this was a coincidence. 'Why me?' The last thought came with a rush of self-pity. 'As if I haven't got enough to worry about!'

I needed to decide where to go next. I thought of returning straight away to Lily in Tlatelolco, but there was somewhere else I had to go first. I had to find out what had happened at the shrine and to Handy and the others guarding the grave. Once I was out of the marshes and able to think of something other than my own immediate peril, I began to be afraid that whatever had attacked us all might have finished them off before coming after me. 'Maybe there wasn't time for that, though,' I told myself hopefully. 'If it was really me he was after, maybe he left them alone.'

I returned to the centre of Handy's parish in the middle of the morning, to find it busier than I would have expected, its paths and canals choked by a chattering throng, nearly all commoners to judge by their haircuts and plain dress. I fell in with them readily enough, as they seemed to be heading in the same direction as I was – towards the plaza in front of the temple where we had buried Star, and where the parish's marketplace would be – but it surprised me to find them here now, with sun so high. Most traders and their customers would have arrived before dawn, and there was something in the way some of them walked, the men taking long, rapid steps and women tugging impatiently at the children's hands, that told me whatever they were after, it was not just cheap cloth or dried chillies.

'What's happening?' I asked an old man hobbling arthritically in the crowd's wake. 'Where's everyone going?'

He glowered at me. He probably thought he needed all his breath for walking and resented having to waste any of it on some tramp who looked and smelled as though he had been sleeping rough for a month. 'Haven't you heard?' he wheezed.

'No, I only just got here.'

'Then it's probably none of your business.' He kept his eyes on the people in front. 'But a man had to bury his wife here last night, and there was a lot of running about and shouting at daybreak, so work it out for yourself.'

I stopped, staring at him in astonishment. 'What happened?' I demanded. 'Was anyone hurt?'

'If I knew that I wouldn't have to go and look now, would I?' he responded irritably. 'But what I heard was, the body was stolen and two of the men guarding it have disappeared.'

'Two of them?' I yelped, but I was too late: he was still going and I was speaking to the back of his neck.

But it was obvious enough what had happened. I shut my eyes then, as if that could keep at bay the horror I felt creeping towards me. For all our and the women's care, someone had interfered with the body. And assuming I was one of the two who had supposedly vanished, then it seemed as though my attacker might have claimed another as his victim.

I hesitated at the corner of the plaza, peering furtively around the edge of a wall while I tried to make sense of what I saw.

If the old man's words had not given me reason to suspect as much before I got there, it would not have taken me long to realise that something was wrong.

The small square in front of me was full of reed mats spread with merchandise, but largely empty of people. They were all packed into the space in front of the temple, where we had buried the woman. Those on the edge of the throng were milling about and jostling each other as if trying to press forward into the middle, perhaps in order to get a better view of something.

Although I looked for Handy, Flower Gatherer and Spotted Eagle, it would have been hard to recognise any one person among the crowd. The only man who did stand out was of a kind I had learned over the years to avoid. He was a tall, thickset, rugged-looking man, whose square jaw was fringed by a thin dark wisp of beard. His long orange-and black-striped cloak emphasised the message of the hair piled up on top of his head: a veteran, a four-captive warrior. He carried no cudgel or other weapon and had no need of them: his reputation and status, advertised by the clothes and other marks of distinction he had earned on the battlefield, were enough to command respect anywhere in Mexico. He was trying to get men and women to move aside and make some space for someone in their midst, and he clearly expected them to do what they were told.

'Wonderful,' I thought. 'I'm already hiding from the captain, not to mention some monster from the marshes, and now I have to run into the parish police.' The man's dress, which was that of a veteran warrior, combined with his manner, convinced me that he was the authority in Atlixco, the official charged with maintaining law and order in the parish.

I did not like policemen. I had fallen foul of them too often ever to feel comfortable around them even when I had not knowingly done anything criminal. It was Handy I wanted to talk to, not some official who would just bark questions at me and hit me if he did not like the answers I gave him. However, even as I hesitated over what to do, I realised it was too late to avoid the man, as he was already looking keenly in my direction.

Tribute of Death

I took a step away from him, looking nervously left and right, and undoubtedly giving a very clear impression of a man with something to hide. Probably I was the only person present whom he did not know by sight, which must have sharpened his interest in me. The filthy, ragged state I had been left in by the night's adventures would have caught his eye too.

I had more sense than to try running away as he stepped between the traders' deserted pitches to stand in front of me. We examined each other in silence for a moment.

From the way he looked me over I gathered that his mind was engaged in trying to match some offence to the scruffy, shifty-looking individual in front of him, who smelled of foetid mud from the lake and was apparently given to lurking suspiciously at the edges of plazas.

I blurted: 'Er, look, let me explain…'

'Explain what?' the policeman said, pleasantly enough. 'I've not asked you anything.'

I tried grinning disarmingly. 'Oh, that's all right then. Only, I thought…'

'You thought what?' he wondered out loud. 'Let me see if I can guess. You thought I might wonder why you were lurking here like a thief. Not thinking of making off with any of the market traders' stuff while they're looking the other way, were you?.'

I glanced at the pitch beside my feet, a mat spread with lengths of cheap, poorly finished maguey fibre cloth. 'Do I look that hard up?' It was an effort to lighten the mood that I regretted at once.

The man growled at me. 'In a word, yes. To look at you I'd say you have just one thing left in the world.' He expected me to ask what that was. It seemed safest to oblige him.

'The one thing you've got,' he replied, smacking his lips as he relished his joke, 'is a chance to tell me what you're doing here. If I were you I wouldn't waste it by lying!'

'I'm not at thief!' I wondered why I sounded so unconvincing when for once I was telling the truth. Perhaps it was because I was more used to lying. 'I'm a friend of Handy's. You must know him. I only came back to see whether he and the others were all right. We were guarding his wife. Someone or something attacked us. I spent the night running away from him, it, whatever.' When he said nothing I added hastily: 'I came back as soon as I could. And they all ran off too... I think.'

There was a new keenness in the man's expression when he looked at me now. 'You must be the one they called Yaotl. The scrawny one with the mouth.'

It was almost a relief to hear him say it. It was not a flattering description but it was one I was familiar with. 'That sounds like me, yes.' I hesitated. 'And the others. What happened to them?'

'You'd better come with me.'

It was not an invitation. The policeman marched me across the plaza and right up to the crowd, and then through the press of people as they parted respectfully before my escort.

About sixty men, women and children were gathered in the small open space in front of the shrine. All were commoners. Some had tools, spades and digging sticks and hammers, suggesting that they had been on their way to the fields or some building site before something had caught their attention and drawn them here. It was easy to imagine them passing through the plaza and stopping, one by one, to stand and stare at the same spectacle.

Tribute of Death

They had left a small space clear in their midst. I felt the blood drain from my face as the policeman pushed me into it.

Ever since following the crowd into the plaza I had been nerving myself for the gruesome sight of a freshly exhumed corpse. It was no preparation for what greeted me as I stood by Star's grave, though.

It had been robbed. The flagstone that we had hauled back into place after backfilling the hole had gone. Loose dark soil was strewn around as if someone had dropped a large sack full of it from a great height. Here and there I noticed smudges that may have been footprints although the soil had been churned up so badly, possibly by the crowd standing around me, that there could be no way of telling who had made them.

There was no sign of the dead woman.

3

Handy had not been part of the crowd. He and Spotted Eagle had kept themselves apart, squatting by the base of the small pyramid at the corner of the plaza. They had both got up and started pushing their way into the centre of the mass of people as soon as I had reached the site of Star's grave. The first I knew of their appearance was when I heard Handy's voice snarling my name from somewhere close by.

I glanced at him absently. I was still struggling to understand what I had seen.

'Yaotl!' the commoner snapped. 'Where have you been?' Neither his expression nor his tone of voice sounded particularly welcoming.

'You're relieved to find me safe and well, then,' I said irritably. Tiredness and the strain of the night's events had exhausted my patience.

It was Spotted Eagle who answered. 'You ran away,' he said scornfully.

It was a mistake to laugh, but I could not help it. The youth's face and posture were as savage as any warrior's in the presence of the enemy, the upper lip curled contemptuously, one bare shoulder thrust forward to show off the muscles bunched under the skin, the fists clenched, his hands brought together as though he wielded an imaginary weapon. Yet it was so incongruous, when the back of his head still bore that tuft of hair, the mark of one who had yet to take a captive in battle.

'Too right, I did!' I said cheerfully. 'Don't tell me you didn't!'

The lad screamed: 'I didn't run! I'm a warrior, you bloody coward!' Then he threw himself at me.

He was young, strong and fast. Nonetheless, if I had been expecting his assault, then I could probably have defended myself, because he had no skill at all. His body crashed into mine, winding him as badly as me, and his hands clawed ineffectually at my throat as he tried to grip it. We both fell over. I was thrown into the man standing behind me, who uttered an explosive grunt as my head drove the air from his lungs, and then I was on the ground, staring at my assailant while his ferocious, snarling, spittle-flecked face filled my vision.

The fight can only have lasted for a few moments before the feeble grip on my throat was released and the body on top of mine hauled clear. My head flopped backwards onto the hard stone floor of the plaza as the face of the policeman swam into view before my misted-up eyes. From beside me came a sound of convulsive sobbing.

'That's enough,' the four-captive warrior said, as I got to my feet, rubbing my bruised neck. He turned to Handy. 'You obviously know this man.'

The big commoner was looking at his son. Then he passed the backs of his hands over his eyes and shook his head sharply. 'I do, Cuixtli,' he admitted. He turned to me. 'I thought you'd gone back to Lily's house. Where did you go? What happened? And did you see

Flower Gatherer?'

A muttering in the crowd told me that I had an attentive audience for whatever I was going to say next. There was silence then, broken only by a faint snuffling from Spotted Eagle.

At least the policeman now had a name. 'Cuixtli' meant Kite; a good choice, if his eyes were as sharp and all-seeing as they ought to be.

'Flower Gatherer's missing, then,' I said in a low voice.

'No,' said Kite heavily. 'We just like to play this guessing game with strangers. We ask you where someone is for no reason at all. Then if we don't care for your answer we put you in a cage and prod you with spears until you come up with one we like. Of course he's missing! Would Handy have asked you if he wasn't?'

I felt wearier than ever; too much so to match wits with this large, powerful man in the middle of his own parish, when he was surrounded by friends and loyal followers. I mumbled an account of my night's adventures, aware all the time of all the eyes upon me, glittering with barely suppressed hostility. Each of them felt as though he himself had been attacked and was eager to retaliate. They might easily turn their anger on the only stranger in their midst.

I wondered what would happen if they believed that I had brought the trouble upon them. The thought made me hesitate, faltering at the point in my story where I was cowering in the maize bin.

Someone took the opportunity to interrupt me with a question. I recognised the voice as that of the old man I had spoken to on the way to the marketplace. 'You said this monster was following you. Where from?'

'It must have been from here, unless it picked up the trail earlier.

The midwives though they saw something strange following Star's funeral procession. It could have followed me all the way from Handy's house.'

'Why? And why you?'

The speaker was bent with age, so that he had to crane his neck to watch me, as if his eyes on my face would help him catch me out in any lie. I looked away, preferring to confront the policeman instead. 'I don't know, but I've an idea. And I do know it was me he was after.' I explained how I had heard the hoarse, whispering voice utter my own name.

Then I told them about the otomi.

The reaction was as I had feared. There was an angry sound in the air; the rustling and shuffling noise of a crowd of people fidgeting impatiently and nudging their neighbours. I was becoming more nervous. Star had been a popular figure in this parish and if the feeling that I had somehow been responsible for what had happened to her started to spread, there was no telling what might happen next.

I appealed to Handy. 'Look, I helped you bury your wife last night because you asked me to. I could have gone away. If that thing – man – whatever, was following me, maybe he'd have come after me somewhere else. But he was here before I was.' I looked at Kite. 'You know what's been happening in the marshes. I talked to a fisherman and his children – Heart of a Flower and her brother.'

'Zolin's kids,' he said automatically. The name meant 'Quail'. There was a hissing sound from the crowd: my implicating still more of their neighbours in my adventures had not endeared me to them any more.

'You can't pretend you don't know what I'm talking about,' I insisted.

'I've heard things,' he said non-committally. 'But this... whatever people think they've seen, it's never spoken to anyone before.'

'You should lock him up.' The speaker was that old man again. 'Or take him away. Hand him over to the chief minister. He's supposed to run the city for the emperor. And you'd get this man out of the parish then.'

I shivered at the mention of my former master. If the men lord Feathered in Black supposedly had watching over me had been nearby during the night, then they had done nothing to protect me. I was more than ever convinced they had never existed. It was not a surprise, to have to conclude that my former master had lied to me, but the thought did not make me any happier. Nor did it make the prospect of being handed over to him as a prisoner any more appealing.

There was a movement in the crowd, and suddenly I knew that things had come to a crisis, for there were two large men standing in front of me, arms already reaching in my direction. They looked like the identical twin offspring of a union between a mountain and a bear: blank faces set on torsos so heavily muscled as to be almost shapeless.

'Leave this to us,' one of them rumbled, the voice seeming to come from somewhere in his bowels while his lips barely moved.

I tried to back away but the press of people around me made movement impossible. I tensed, sensing that the massive, callused hands that were about to drag me away would not be gentle. I only hoped they were both going to pull me in the same direction, as they looked as though they could rip my arms and legs off without effort if they chose.

However, the policeman was having none of it.

'That's enough!' he barked.

The two large men froze. They slowly turned their heads – something of a feat, considering neither had anything resembling a neck – and stared at each other.

'Behave yourselves, you two. Isn't it time you were back at the quarry? And as for you' – he glowered at the old man, who looked defiantly up at him but said nothing – 'this man isn't going to the chief minister or anybody else until I say so! This is my parish, do you hear?'

Somebody coughed discreetly. There was an awkward shuffling of feet. Some outlying members of the crowd, sensing that their policeman had ruled that the fun was over, disappeared unobtrusively. The giants who had been so keen to arrest me shuffled uncertainly away. Out of the corner of my eye I saw Spotted Eagle opening his mouth as if to say something, but he thought better of it.

'Now,' Kite said, 'I want to know what happened here last night, and what happened down by the lake as well, and I'm not minded to let anybody go anywhere until I get some answers. So who's going to start? We know what happened to Yaotl. Handy, what have you got to say?'

The commoner was looking morosely at the hole in the ground where Star's body had lain so briefly. 'My wife,' he muttered thickly.

Kite's expression softened at that. 'Yes, I know,' he said in a gentler tone. 'I'm trying to find out, old friend.' He glanced at Spotted Eagle. 'What can you tell me?'

The young man started, as though he had been woken from a dream. After a moment he said sullenly: 'We were guarding the body.

Then this – the slave calls it a monster, but I don't know what it was – it came out of nowhere…'

'We don't know where it came from.' I corrected him. 'We were all asleep.'

Spotted Eagle bristled. 'I may have closed my eyes for a second!'

'While a freak gust of wind blew the torch out?'

'Now listen…'

'Shut up, both of you!' the policeman bawled. 'Just tell me what happened after you woke up.'

'We were attacked.' The youth would not meet his eyes. 'Yaotl ran off…'

'What did you do? Your father? Flower Gatherer?'

Handy answered. He was still staring into the empty grave. 'We all ran,' he said quietly. 'We scattered. It was the surprise, and the noise. The scream…' He shuddered. 'By the time Spotted Eagle and I came back here, they were gone: Yaotl and Flower Gatherer.' There was a brief pause. 'And her.' I glanced at the grave; I believe we all did, prompted by Handy's last words. It occurred to me that there was something wrong with the way it looked; quite apart from the obvious absence of a body, I felt there was something else odd or out of place, that I could not quite identify.

I dismissed the thought as another occurred in its stead. I turned to Kite. 'Where's your parish hall?'

The central meeting place of Atlixco would, I knew, be close by. This was where the parish's elders gathered, where its records were kept – every birth, marriage and death entered on screenfold books made of stiff bark paper – and where its officials, including the police, would have their headquarters. He indicated a long, low stone building at the far corner of the plaza, right next to the canal.

'How come none of you heard anything?'

'You may well ask! The answer is, we were all at the House of Song, singing to celebrate the war god's day.' I remembered the snatches of song that had come to us in the night, after the midwives had left. 'By the time I was back here it was nearly daybreak. The traders were setting up in the market, and Handy and his son were wandering around in a daze. It seems no-one else had seen or heard a thing, apart from you three, Flower Gatherer – wherever he is – and whoever attacked you.'

'And one other,' I said. In answer to his questioning look I added: 'Remember the women thought there were two men following the procession. They got part of a cloak from one of them – a three captive warrior's cloak.'

Kite looked thoughtful. 'Red Macaw's a three-captive man,' he recalled.

Handy looked up then. 'Red Macaw didn't have anything to do with this.'

We all stared at him.

'What makes you say so?' I said. 'He was very anxious to be here yesterday. Practically begged you. Why, though?'

For the first time since I had seen him that morning, Handy became animated. He rounded one me, trembling, and raised his voice: 'He just wouldn't, that's all. I told you not to ask about him, Yaotl.' He turned to the policeman. 'Whatever else he might have done, I'm sure he wouldn't have done this.'

Kite met his gaze. Then he said slowly: 'Well, I don't know. I assume whoever took your wife's body was after a charm for a sorcerer or a warrior. And Red Macaw…'

'I'm telling you, this has nothing to do with him! We don't even know that it was his cloak!' The commoner was sweating and his hands were shaking with tension. The policeman watched him the way a man might watch a trapped snake thrashing about as he waited for the best moment to stoop and grasp it behind the head; but he said nothing.

I wondered aloud: 'What about Flower Gatherer?'

'What about him?' Kite asked.

'Did he run away? Could he have anything to do with what happened to the body?'

Spotted Eagle snorted loudly. 'Why would he do anything like that? He's her brother-in-law!'

Kite was watching me, saying nothing until I had begun to find his unblinking scrutiny unnerving. Finally he said: 'You'd better answer the young man's question.'

'I don't know,' I admitted. 'I'd never met him before last night. He didn't seem all that keen on what we were doing, though. Maybe he resented being dragged into the funeral and seized the chance to get his own back.'

'He was attacked as well,' Kite pointed out.

'It could have been faked. Set up to make him look like a victim as well.'

'So where is he now?' the youth demanded. 'What did he do with… with what he took? What's he going to say to my aunt when he comes home?'

'I don't know!'

The policeman intervened. 'The trouble is, Yaotl, or whatever your name is, I'd thought of your theory already, but there's no reason why her brother-in-law would have done anything like that.' He looked at the body. 'What the thief took were charms for a sorcerer or a warrior, that seems pretty clear. Flower Gatherer was neither of those. He was just a peasant, and married to the woman's sister. The boy's question is a good one. How's Goose going to react if she thinks her husband was behind this?'

'Is he likely to care?' I responded. 'Maybe he's not planning to come home at all. What other possibility is there?'

'You could have done it,' Spotted Eagle said shortly.

'What?' I gasped, so shocked that I could barely get the word out.

'It seems to me,' Kite said calmly, 'that there are two possible explanations for Flower Gatherer's disappearance. I think he ran away, like the rest of you. Either he ran fast enough, in which case he'll be back eventually, or he didn't, in which case he's dead.'

I frowned. 'But if that's so, where's his body?'

'You tell us,' spat Spotted Eagle.

I had to suppress a sudden, hysterical impulse to laugh in the young man's face. Fortunately I remembered what had happened when I had done that before. 'You think I did something to Flower Gatherer, and then dug Star up? That's ludicrous! Why would I have done a thing like that?'

'How should we know?' replied the youth. 'I don't know anything about you. Why *wouldn't* you have done it?'

I sighed. 'So where would I have put the man's body? What did I do with your mother?' I appealed to the lad's father. 'Handy, you know me. You don't really think I had any part in this?'

He could not look at me. For a moment his glance fell, perhaps involuntarily, on his wife's body. He turned away with a shudder. 'I don't know what to think any more.'

'The slave used to be a priest,' muttered Spotted Eagle sullenly. 'He could have done it. He knew what we had to do last night and why it mattered. He knows all about charms and how to make them...'

'No I don't!' I was genuinely shocked. 'I was a priest, not a sorcerer.'

'What if he went away,' the young man went on doggedly, 'and then came back and moved the body while his 'monster' made sure we didn't interfere?'

'But... but...' Outrage reduced me to stammering incoherently for a few moments, until I got a grip of myself and began again. 'If I'd wanted to steal Star's body, then why would I have gone to the trouble of walking all the way to the lake and back? Why would I have come back this morning?' I took a deep breath and looked imploringly at Handy one last time. He appeared as though he was about to be sick. 'I'm not a thief or a sorcerer, and I'm certainly not a warrior. I liked Star, Handy, you know I did. I've no use for her hair or her arm. And what did I do with Flower Gatherer?'

The commoner seemed beyond speech. He seemed to sway as I spoke to him, the way he might if my words had been blows. He let out a groan and stretched out a hand towards Spotted Eagle, who seemed about to launch into another tirade. Quietly he said: 'That's enough, boy.'

The policeman was staring into the open grave. 'I don't know what to do,' he confessed without turning around. 'What happened to the woman is one thing. She's already dead – I'm sorry, Handy – but there's this monster or whatever it is in the marshes, and even if I don't believe a word this stranger tells me, the fishermen are obviously afraid of something. And what about Flower Gatherer?' He seemed to be thinking aloud. 'Someone's going to have to find out what happened.' He looked at me. 'I still don't know about you, Yaotl or whoever you are. Handy tells me you're a slave, and you've been in trouble before. So I wonder if I shouldn't think about putting you in a cage until Star's brother-in-law turns up. A cage…'

A cage: he let his tongue linger over the word, while my imagination conjured up the image of a tiny wooden box, barely big enough to crouch in, inside a damp, stinking, dark prison. Did he know how well I knew such places? The dread of being put in one, of never getting out or even being able to get a message to Lily, made me catch my breath.

'I want them found,' he said quietly. 'I'm not arresting anyone just yet. But until the missing man turns up and someone tells me who the thief is, I may change my mind at any time.' His eyes swept the faces surrounding him. 'I don't think there's anyone here who doesn't understand what I'm saying.'

The crowd had largely broken up, but those who remained understood him, and would pass the word to others, and if I knew my city's parishes and their inhabitants, every man in Atlixco would comply – at least until their local official told them he had changed his mind.

I was to be left alone for the time being, but what the policeman had said was that I was still a suspect, and I had better take care, and not think about leaving Atlixco at any time soon.

Unless, of course, I could help him find the answers he wanted.

4

'We have to take her home.'

'I have to get another message to Lily.' It was about midday. The crowd had dispersed, and now Handy and I were holding two separate conversations. He just wanted to attend to his wife's body. I wanted to reassure my mistress. I wondered whether she had got any sleep during the previous night. And I wanted just as much to escape whatever was haunting the lake shore, but I knew that was not going to be easy, if the locals were watching my every move and reporting it to the police. I thought of what my mother had said, how I had to find the otomi. However, if he had somehow turned himself into the monster that had attacked me, there was less chance than ever of convincing him to see reason.

I knew I had been set up. I did not think the policeman really believed I had had anything to with killing Flower Gatherer or stealing anything from the grave. However, the idea had got into the crowd's mind, and he had been happy enough to let it stay there, giving me a powerful incentive to help find the real thief. I wondered what had made the policeman think I would be of any use to him. Perhaps Handy had told him of previous occasions when I had found – or stumbled over – the solutions to mysteries.

Tribute of Death

The commoner spared me only the briefest of glances before turning to his son. 'We need to go home. There are things to do. There's still the baby...' He swallowed once, before continuing: 'There's still the baby to be buried.'

'You can't have heard me,' I replied. 'I need to tell Lily where I am. She'll be worried.'

Handy suddenly seemed to lose his temper. 'Don't you ever think about anyone or anything except yourself?' he cried, taking a step towards me and stooping so that his face was close to mine and I could feel his breath on my cheek. 'You want to run away, don't you? You brought this thing with you, and now you want to go crawling back to your mistress and beg her to save your lousy skin. Never mind what might happen to the rest of us!'

'That's absurd! I didn't know what was going to happen. How could I have done?'

'Oh, I'm sure you didn't *know*.' His voice cracked and I could see that he was on the verge of tears. 'You never do, do you? As long as I've known you, you've been surrounded by complete and utter mayhem, but of course it's never been your fault. But see what's happened here...'

'This is where we started this morning,' I started to protest. 'It's not as if I did it!'

'Didn't you?' muttered Spotted Eagle sceptically.

His father continued: 'What happens to a woman like Star if a thief or a sorcerer gets her body, do you know that? What happens if she loses her hair and forearm? I don't think she's going to be greeting the sun at noon until she's buried again – whole. Now you know about these things – tell me I'm wrong.'

'I don't know. I told you before, I was a priest, not a midwife.'

'Tell us!' It was Spotted Eagle's turn to insist. 'What's going to happen to my mother?'

There was no policeman about now to restrain the young man and in his present mood I did not trust his father to step in. 'I'm not really sure,' I said reluctantly. 'But I suppose you could be right. If a thief took parts of her body for charms, then some of her power must go into those things. But what do you expect me to do, Handy? If I wanted to help you find her, and I'm not saying I don't, where would I start looking?'

'That's your problem. You heard what Kite said. Help find my wife – and that useless turd of a brother-in-law of mine too, if you must. You can do it. You're good at looking for things – you found those sorcerers after they escaped from the emperor's prison, didn't you, and that featherworker's daughter from Amantlan. Then you'll be free to go.'

'You forget,' I said drily, 'I'm a slave. You can't go around setting slaves free when they don't belong to you.'

Spotted Eagle let out a growl, which was no doubt intended to sound threatening. He clenched his fists, raised one of them to emphasise his words. 'If you won't listen to my father, you'd better listen to me! You do what we want or...'

I barely looked at him. 'Or what? You'll beat me up, is that it? Well, go ahead. How will you stop me running away afterwards? And what are you going to do while I'm searching, follow me around the city kicking me every time the trail seems to be getting cold? It won't work.'

I enjoyed the look of confusion that crossed the young man's face for a moment, but when I shifted my glance from him to his father I saw an entirely different expression. His cheeks were grey and sunken with fatigue and sorrow, which only made his raw, swollen eyes stand out more. I had not seen or heard him weep since his wife had died, but perhaps he had shed his tears silently in the night when it was too dark for them to be seen. There was no shame in weeping, but I could imagine him wanting to avoid adding to his family's grief by letting him see his own. Or perhaps he simply wanted to spare himself the sort of well-meaning expressions of sympathy people are prone to utter when confronted with another's distress. I knew what such misplaced offers of comfort were like, having heard enough of them from my family after I was thrown out of the Priest House. It never does any good to have others tell you how bad you must be feeling, when only you can know the measure of your own suffering. It just makes it worse.

I suddenly realised that all Handy's bitter words and threatening tone were bluster. He was not truly angry with me or anyone else, although that might come. He had no settled plan to recover his wife's body, let alone the determination to carry it out or the ruthlessness to force me into helping. What I saw in his face was bewilderment, shock, and a huge, gaping, hollow feeling of loss. And his words to me had been driven by desperation. There was only one thing he could do for his wife now, but he could not see how to do it. I was the only person he could turn to for help, and he thought that all I wanted to do was to get away.

'We used to be friends,' I said quietly, for want of anything better to say.

Before he could answer, a woman's voice from behind me said:

'Where are they? I came as soon as I could.'

The speaker was Goose, Handy's sister-in-law. He and his son both started, as I did, at the sound: they had been too engrossed in their argument with me to notice her.

She looked as weary, drawn and haggard as her brother-in-law, and she was breathing heavily and sweating, as though she had run most of the way from Atlixco. 'I had to make sure the children were all right,' she explained, 'but I'm here now. Tell me what happened. Where's my husband? What did they do with my sister?'

Handy groaned. 'Goose, didn't they tell you about Flower Gatherer?'

She hesitated. She looked quickly at each of us in turn, scanning our faces as if searching them for some clue to what we knew, so that she did not have to hear it spoken. Eventually she replied, in a low voice: 'They told me he was missing. Has anyone found... Is he dead?' The last word was forcibly ejected from the back of her throat.

'No,' her brother-in-law said hastily. 'No, there's no more news. I'm sorry.'

She bit her lip. 'He's not come home,' she informed us unnecessarily.

'Is that unusual for him?' I asked.

'It's never happened before. My husband wouldn't go wandering off anywhere. It would mean having to fend for himself. He's never been any good at that!' She turned to Handy. 'I want to see the grave.'

She walked towards where the body of her sister had lain. Handy was standing between her and her goal but he moved aside without another word.

We all gathered around her as she stood over the empty grave, with her head inclined. She said nothing, although I could hear her breathing. It was slow and deep as though each breath required an act of will. Glancing sideways, I realised that her eyes were closed.

When she finally turned away it was to face me. She looked straight into my eyes, in a gesture that in other circumstances might have been thought impolite.

'Thank you for helping us find her,' she said quietly.

My jaw dropped. Neither Handy nor his son said anything. They gave no sign of having heard her. I felt my face growing warm with embarrassment. 'I haven't done anything... I mean, Goose, I wouldn't know where to start...'

'But you will,' she sad simply. She smiled weakly. 'That's what matters.' She turned to her brother-in-law. 'You have to come home. The baby needs attending to. Then we have to look for Flower Gatherer. And what the thief took.'

Handy, his son, Goose and I walked slowly back towards the commoner's house.

Handy and Spotted Eagle had lapsed into a moody silence. Goose was quiet as well, making no obvious effort to persuade me to help in the search for her sister's corpse, and indeed scarcely looking at me: she preferred staring silently at the walls and gardens that we passed, content, until we were nearly at our destination, to leave me to my thoughts.

Death was no stranger to me. As a priest I had seen many men and some women die on the killing stone in front of a temple, and had accepted what I had seen as necessary, the price the gods exacted for letting us, their creatures, live on Earth. More recently, it had sometimes happened that I found myself looking at a body and wondering how the death had come about; and on occasion I had been the one to uncover the answer. What had befallen Star had been no mystery, so far as I was aware, but was beyond my experience, taking her into a realm that no man would ever know.

Star had not merely died. She had begun to transform herself into a Divine Princess, just as a warrior who had a flowery death in battle or on the sacrificial stone earned his place in the morning sun's entourage. I did not truly understand this process. I could not have said what stages the woman's soul had to pass through on its passage from the body to the Land of the Women beyond the western edge of the world, or how far it would have got. If its journey had been interrupted, where would that leave Star? Was some part of her still residing in a ruined, decomposing thing, even now being dragged carelessly across the city, or hacked to pieces for its magical properties? Or was it somehow caught between two worlds, the one it had inhabited in life and the one it yearned for, lost, confused and angry at whatever was dragging it back?

It may have been a movement in the air, or merely my own hunger and exhaustion pricking my imagination, but I glanced nervously upwards, seized suddenly by the conviction that her spirit, the part of her that ought now to be with the afternoon sun, was somehow hovering above my head.

It was an Aztec belief that the Divine Princesses sometimes came back to Earth to bring sickness to men and children, and there were four dates in our calendar in particular when no man would go out after dark for fear of them. What might she do to me, I wondered, if she knew I had done nothing to help her?

Tribute of Death

'I'll try,' I said. I meant the words for Star, wherever and whatever she now was. The answer I came from close beside me, however.

'I know,' said the dead woman's sister. 'I never doubted you would.'

5

In a short space of time the house in Atlixco had seen so many losses: Handy's of his wife and stillborn child; his children's of their mother; Goose's of her sister, perhaps also of her missing husband; and her parents' of a daughter. Each loss would have to be taken in or made good somehow, but it was hard to guess where this might begin.

At first, Goose appeared to take charge. Issuing her orders firmly, but in a voice hoarse with strain, she rounded up the children, whom we had found scattered like their own abandoned toys about the courtyard, and drove them indoors, commanding the girls to attend to their work and the boys to get out of the way. Her manner, even when directing Handy and me to squat in a corner while she fetched a broom, put me in mind of my mother's, when she had made me and my brothers and sisters line up before setting out for some ritual celebration. I suspected that telling others what to do was how Goose sought to master her own bewildered grief, and treating the adults around her as children was the only way she knew of doing it.

Handy appeared to have withdrawn into himself. He slumped obediently in a corner, beside the sweat bath where his wife had died. I squatted by him, seeing the exhaustion in his haggard face and resisting the temptation to yawn and rub my eyes.

Spotted Eagle was almost as tired as his father, but he was alert enough to look around him with a critical eye. 'My brothers haven't made a very good job of that wall,' he muttered.

I noticed that some attempt had been made to stop up the hole Handy had knocked in his courtyard wall. It was a crude effort, little more than a heaping-up of the rubble left over from the earlier demolition. I guessed from Spotted Eagle's words that two or more of his brothers had been left with the job of closing up the exit their mother had taken. The hole made for her had to be sealed as quickly as possible, in case her ghost used it to return and bring disease and death to those still living in her house.

'It'll do,' I said. I had no idea whether the attempt to fill the opening in would be adequate to stop a vengeful female spirit or not, but I was too tired to start shifting broken masonry in order to improve it now.

Goose came outside with a couple of stale tortillas. 'We all need to eat,' she said as if we needed the reminder. 'Handy, you still have work to do.'

For a moment the man did not react. He remained in his squatting position with his eyes lowered, neither looking at nor touching the bread his sister-in-law had put before him. It seemed at first that he had not heard her, but then he slowly turned his ashen face towards us and peered at us with his shadowed, bloodshot eyes.

'What?' he asked quietly.

'The baby.'

'The baby.' He repeated the words dully. 'Is it still in the sweat bath?'

'You should bury him.'

The man blinked once, but for all the other emotion he betrayed he may just have got a piece of grit in his eye. 'I'll do what's fitting,' he confirmed stiffly.

Goose turned to me. 'What will you do?' The urgency in her voice contrasted sharply with her brother-in-law's lassitude.

'I'm not sure.' I muttered. 'I'm sorry about your husband.'

'I'm worried about him,' she admitted, with downcast eyes. 'I don't know what we'll do if anything's happened to him.' She looked at me again, as though she thought I might have an answer to that. 'But he'll turn up, I'm sure. I expect he just got frightened, out there by himself with only the Divine Princesses for company. He's no warrior, I know. He probably just ran away. After all, if he'd... if anything had happened to him, he'd still be there, wouldn't he? But there wasn't anyone except Star. So he must be hiding.'

'Yes,' I admitted, although even as I said it, I had my doubts. What would have scared even an undistinguished commoner such as Flower Gatherer into running so far away that even now nobody knew where he was? Yet I dared not voice again the suggestion I had made by the empty grave: that Flower Gatherer may have had a hand in the theft.

'But what will you do?' she asked again.

In spite of the misery that surrounded me the repeated question made me smile wryly. How could I answer it when there were so many things that needed my attention? I had to get word to Lily. I had to confront whatever had hunted me in the night – with or without the chief minister's men watching over me. And I had to help find Handy's wife, and not just out of compassion for her family. To fail would be to risk incurring the displeasure of beings far more powerful than Atlixco's parish policeman: none other than the Divine Princesses themselves. The feeling I had had as we walked back from the plaza returned, bringing with it a chill that took the smile from my lips.

Handy lifted his head. 'We need you here.'

'I know,' I said. 'But first I have to get a message…'

'To your mistress. I know. One of the boys can take it for you.'

Goose had sent Snake indoors when we arrived, but he had obviously been listening by the doorway, as he sprang out at the mention of his name. 'I'm ready,' he said briskly. A moment later a second youthful head appeared, peering cautiously out of the shadows behind him. I recognised the slightly rounder, heavier features of Snake's elder brother Mazatl, or Buck.

'No, I'll go.' Buck's voice had a gruff note: it was in the process of breaking. 'You went last time.'

Snaked would not spare him so much as a glance over his shoulder. 'Exactly! So I know the way!'

'You can both forget it!' I told them. 'What story are you going to make up this time?'

'Don't be silly,' the boy said scornfully. 'I don't need to lie.'

'I always tell the truth,' Buck declared.

'Only because you haven't got the brains to make anything up!'

'That's enough,' their father said wearily. 'If you're so keen, you can both go.'

'Handy, there's no need…'

'Yes there is, Yaotl. I can't let you go yet.'

I rounded on him, exasperated. 'I've already told you I'll help you find the thief! What more do you all want? But at the moment I've no more notion of who or where he is than you have, not until he sprouts green feathers from his ears and runs through the streets shouting "I did it! It was me all along!"'

I paused for breath and a brief glance at the shocked faces around me: my outburst had stunned the family into wide-eyed silence. In a quieter tone I added: 'Does it matter so much if I run a simple errand first?'

'Yes. There's something that needs doing before anything else.'

'Anyway, you can't send your sons. It's dangerous.'

'Not for me, it isn't!' Snake cried indignantly. 'It was you the monster was after, remember?'

'Ask the fishermen how safe they feel!' I retorted, but it was of no use. I could guess what task Handy had in mind for me, whose urgency was such that it could not wait. The prospect made me want more than ever to be away from here, at least for the moment; but Spotted Eagle was already standing nonchalantly between me and the doorway, as though daring me to try going through it.

'You have to help us bury my child,' Handy whispered.

Before I could say another word Snake and Buck had vanished.

Probably the boys' eagerness to carry my message for me, whether I wanted them to or not, was not entirely selfless. They may well have been reluctant to stay for the dour little ritual that went ahead in their absence.

Handy fetched a digging stick and two spades from inside his house. Then he and Spotted Eagle broke up and shovelled the hard earth by the entrance to the courtyard, next to the maize bins, until there was a shallow hole there.

Children appeared from within the house, although no-one had called them. They may simply have sensed that something important and solemn was taking place. They stood in a loose group, watching their elders from a respectful distance. The smallest boys were too young to be wearing breechcloths, and cannot have had much idea of what was happening, but they had sense enough to keep quiet and wait.

Goose went into the sweat bath and emerged with a tiny bundle, its contents mercifully hidden inside cloth wrappings. She stood beside her brother-in-law and his son. The three of them looked silently into the hole, Handy and Spotted Eagle still holding their spades. Handy's face appeared set in stone, although I could see the strain he was feeling in the bulging of the muscles on either side of his lower jaw. His son darted quick glances about, as if afraid some assailant was about to spring out on him. Goose chewed her lip nervously. They all seemed to be waiting for something. I had an unpleasant feeling they were expecting me to tell them what to do next.

Then, sure enough, Handy turned to me. 'Yaotl, what do we say?'

I stared uncomprehendingly at him. 'Why are you asking me?' I turned to his sister-in-law. 'You knew the words for your sister, last night. Don't you know what to do now?'

'I've seen it done,' she acknowledged, in a low whisper. 'I've seen it done… for others. But my sister's child…' Abruptly she turned away and hid her face in her hands. For the first time since I had come to the house and learned of her sister's death, I heard her let out a sob.

'It's not right!' she cried in a muffled voice. 'It's not right! Yaotl, help us. You were a priest.'

I spread my hands in a gesture of helplessness. 'I can't! Midwives do these things, not priests.'

'You must know what to say!' She turned her glistening eyes towards me. 'When my friend Tiacapan lost her little girl, what the woman did then, when they buried her – it was so empty. Please...'

I could only stare dumbly at her, watching the tears falling silently on her cheeks, not knowing what I could say to help or even comfort her.

Spotted Eagle dropped his spade with a clatter and started towards his aunt, as though to offer her some comfort; but when he saw her eyes were fixed imploringly on mine, he rounded on me instead. 'You don't even care, do you! That was my brother!'

He was mistaken, but I should simply have agreed with him. I was usually ready enough with a lie when it suited me. This time, though, something compelled me to tell the truth. Once again I thought of Star's spirit lurking somewhere nearby, of whatever care she might have for her dead child, and of her fury if it were thwarted. 'I do care,' I insisted. 'But you don't understand. That's not your brother. It never was. His destiny is...'

'What?' The young man was almost spitting with rage. 'You brought all this upon us and now when my aunt asks you to do a simple thing all you can do is talk nonsense!'

'Brought all what upon you?'

'All this!' He made a sweeping gesture that took in the courtyard around us, but what he meant was the grief and pain felt by the people in it. 'You turn up, my mother dies...'

'Don't be absurd!' After the farcical scene at his mother's graveside I was not afraid of this young man. His temper was alarming, but it had begun to provoke my own. 'How could I have had anything to do with that?'

'Then, someone robs her grave...'

'Oh, that was me, of course. While I was down at the lake running for my life. After I'd rushed out of the darkness and attacked myself!'

Ignoring me, he continued to rant. 'And who's left without even a body to bury? He is, my father, that's who, and do you care? Do you know how much he's hurting?' The young man's father was watching us through the heavy-lidded, bloodshot eyes of a man too tired to feel hurt, or anything else.

Spotted Eagle stood in front of me. I could see the tongue working behind his teeth as he shouted, and when he turned, the tuft of hair on the back of his head almost brushed my nose; and that, I thought, explained a great deal.

This was a young man with much to prove: an unblooded warrior, no doubt used to being praised by his instructors at the House of Youth, and to winning his practice bouts, but with no experience of a real fight. And now, to the nagging self-doubt that, for any Aztec man, could only be dissolved on the battlefield, had been added the sight of his father's helplessness and pain.

It was no use reasoning with him. It was equally futile mocking him. All I could do was look around me in the hope of finding something to divert his attention from me. For once I was in luck: a distraction appeared.

'Handy,' Gentle Heart called from the house entrance. 'I'm sorry, I would have come earlier, but I met Nopalli, and he wanted to come too – I thought he might be able to help.'

We all turned to look at her and the stranger she had brought with her.

Nopalli's name meant 'Cactus.' He walked behind the woman and a little to one side of her as she came forward, as though unwilling to move out of her shadow, and so it was a moment before I was able to see him properly. Then I saw that he was dressed as a commoner, in a short, undyed cloak, although his hair was as long and almost as lank and greasy as a priest's. He was not thin but his overall appearance was one of neglect. His clothes were patched and frayed and he was none too clean. A dark smudge under one ear showed where he had offered his blood to the gods and some of it had dried on his cheek.

Handy took a step towards them and stopped, agitation showing in the working of his jaw. At first he did not seem to know what to say. At last it came out as a brusque question: 'Where were you last night?'

The woman was prepared for the question; as well she might be, I thought. She looked into his face and spoke quietly but clearly. 'I couldn't go through with it – not after what I'd seen. I know I should have been there, but...' She faltered for a moment, before adding in a lower voice: 'I know others suffered as well, yesterday. And I heard what happened. But I couldn't... Please understand... I sent the others on in my place.'

'I had to lead the ritual,' Goose said coldly.

The midwife flinched. 'I'm here now,' she said hastily. 'Perhaps I can help.'

Spotted Eagle had forgotten about me for the moment. 'Who are you?' he asked Cactus.

The stranger smiled. 'I'm a curer. I'm a friend of Gentle Heart's – we work together sometimes. She told me about your loss.' He looked about him, his eyes lingering on each person he saw in turn before he spoke to Handy. 'I'm sorry,' he concluded simply.

The commoner thanked him, but looked confused. Gentle Heart explained: 'Cactus finds herbs for me sometimes, and casts auguries. He thought he might have something to alleviate your distress, so I agreed to bring him.'

Goose said: 'But why did you come?'

'To see if there was anything I could do,' the midwife said.

I seized the chance to say: 'There is! Handy was asking me about what words to use for his... for Star's unborn baby. I was trying to explain why I didn't have any.'

Her expression when she looked at me was queer. It was a look of alarm, her eyes wide open and shifting left and right like a trapped animals. She licked her lips and swallowed once. 'Words?' she asked. 'For what?'

'For the child,' Goose said. She was still holding the bundle she had taken from the sweat bath. Now she walked over to the midwife and deposited it in the woman's hands before Gentle Heart had a chance to ask her what she was doing.

Gentle Heart looked at the body, but did not start to unwrap it. I was afraid she was going to drop it; but eventually she said gruffly: 'Poor little one.'

'We don't know what to do,' Handy said. 'He doesn't even have a name. And when we asked Yaotl here we got some nonsense about him not even being Spotted Eagle's brother, as though we'd somehow' – he took a deep breath – 'somehow picked up the wrong baby!'

Out of the corner of my eye I saw the curer, Cactus, glance at me curiously. I squirmed. 'Look, I was just trying to say...'

The woman shut her eyes and frowned as though trying to remember something she had heard once, a long time ago. 'I think he meant…. it was not the will of Tezcatlipoca that this child be born to your family. Isn't that right?' When she opened her eyes it was to look at me.

'Yes,' I said.

'Go on,' Spotted Eagle ordered.

The woman took a deep breath. 'The lord of the Here and Now is… capricious. Yes, that's the word. He gives and takes life at a whim.' She looked at the hole by the maize bin. 'You have found the right place for his body, but I don't think his soul ever entered it.'

'So where did it go, then?' the young man demanded. 'Where is it now?'

She seemed to have no answer for him. Seeing his tension in the way his hand trembled, I spoke up instead. 'It's back where it came from, ready for another life.'

The midwife took over again, with what sounded like a burst of renewed confidence, and eager to please, to tell these people what they wanted to hear: 'That's why I can't name him, you see, because he didn't live to see his name day. But you mustn't be distressed for him. He's getting ready to be born again. It's a terrible disappointment for you and a terrible loss, but the child is well.' And with that, she stooped, and in a quick, simple gesture, placed the body in the hole.

'Is that all?' Goose started forward. 'But there must be…'

'There aren't any words for him,' Gentle Heart went on, still looking into the tiny grave. 'He doesn't need any.'

'But we do!'

The midwife looked, for a moment, as baffled as I had felt, and more afraid; but at last I had understood what was required, and why my clumsy attempt to explain the dead child's fate had only angered his family. Belatedly I recognised that if I knew of no ritual for this occasion, then I had better make one up.

Half closing my eyes, I intoned solemnly: 'The Giver of Life has taken the little one, the precious feather, the jewel, has taken him back and guided him to the great Milk Tree, and shown him which of its countless teats to suck on until it is his time to appear on Earth.' It was the truth, as far as I was aware, and if the words were not right I could not see that it mattered now.

If Star's spirit was listening, I could only hope she approved.

6

After my little improvised speech, the household slowly resumed something resembling normal activity. Goose and the eldest of Handy's daughters hurried into the house, with a muttered apology from the woman about being so slow providing food and drink. Spotted Eagle and his father took up their tools again and began to fill in the hole they had dug. The other children, sensing they were no longer wanted as spectators, looked about them uncertainly for a moment until Gentle Heart went over to talk to them.

That left me alone with the newcomer, Cactus.

I looked at him curiously, taking in his unkempt appearance and trying not to wrinkle my nose too obviously at his odour. He must have been on a fast, I realised, when in addition to starving himself he would have been forbidden from washing. 'What kind of curer are you?' I asked.

'Why?' he replied guardedly. 'What kind would you like me to be?'

It was a strange answer. I frowned. 'There are so many different sorts of curer, aren't there? Bonesetters, midwives, doctors, soul doctors. Even some sorcerers work as healers, some of the time. I was just wondering…'

'I'm not a sorcerer,' he said hastily. 'A soothsayer, yes, in a small way, but... Sorcerers are different, you know that.' Sorcerers turned themselves into animals, haunted the streets at night, broke into houses while their inhabitants slept.

They also robbed graves.

'You've been fasting,' I observed.

'It's because of the herbs I have to gather.'

'Really? Which ones?' I looked at him with genuine interest, trying to remember, from my priest's training, what plant could only be gathered by a fasting man. For the moment nothing came to me. My scepticism must have been apparent.

He looked shamefaced. 'Oh, all right. I'm not really fasting at all.' He lowered his voice to an anxious whisper. 'I just try to look that way because it impresses my patients. You won't tell anyone, will you?'

I should have been more surprised. However, I knew of so many ways to pretend to treat a sick person, from casting an augury by throwing maize kernels into water and seeing if they floated to pretending to suck a stone out of the patient's body. The thing I had always found odd was that provided the invalid was not obviously dying to begin with, these fake cures often worked, as if one could lie to an illness as easily as to a human being. Or perhaps it was merely Tezcatlipoca rewarding a fellow trickster.

'I won't say anything if you give me a reason not to,' I said.

He looked hard at me. 'What do you mean?'

I glanced sideways at the midwife, who seemed to have got over whatever had made her so nervous beforehand and was now leading the younger children in some kind of game. There had been something curious about her performance this morning, I decided, and her explanation for her failure to appear the previous night did not ring true. If every midwife refused to attend the funeral of one of her patients, none would ever be buried.

'Tell me how you know her.'

'We work together sometimes. When she delivers a baby she recommends my services to the parents, to help them choose his name-day. As I said, I'm a soothsayer. I know the Book of Days, or most of it, anyway. And I supply her with herbs, sometimes.' He shot a furtive glance at the father and son shoving the last few spadefuls of earth into the hole, and produced a bulging cloth pouch from beneath his cloak. 'Talking of which... I heard about the bad business yesterday, and last night. I brought something I thought the husband might like to try. Do you think...'

He was interrupted by a loud 'crack' from the direction of the maize bins, accompanied by what sounded like a grunt of pain. Turning, I saw that Handy had brought his spade down on the loose earth that covered the stillborn child's grave so hard he had broken it.

'I think I'd forget it if I were you,' I suggested.

'But these herbs might help him forget.'

I frowned at the soothsayer. 'It may be he doesn't want to. Look, I've been in this household since yesterday, and I've seen how he's dealing with it. There's no telling what he'll say if he thinks you're trying to use his grief as an excuse to push jimson weed or morning glory seeds on him.'

'I'm not...'

'No, I'm sure you're not.' I had no wish to spare Handy a row with this fake magician only to get involved in one myself. 'Maybe some other day. I'll mention it to him later, if you like.'

'That's kind of you.' He seemed mollified. 'I've a pitch in Atlixco marketplace at the moment – been there for a while now. He can find me there any time.'

'Were you there this morning? Did you see anything?' It occurred to me that a trader setting up before dawn might have noticed some clue; maybe even seen the thief making off with Star's body.

I was to be disappointed. 'I heard about it. But I arrived late today. I had to see someone first. All I saw was a big crowd by the shrine and that policeman trying to calm everybody down.'

'You mean Kite? You want to keep on the right side of him,' I suggested. 'He's after whoever took the body. If you were to see or hear anything it wouldn't hurt you to have a word with him – especially if you want to go on trading in his marketplace.' I looked at him significantly.

Some sorcerers healed the sick, when it suited them. Some curers were sorcerers. I was sure there were others, especially those given to fake fasts and unreliable fortune-telling, who were not above pretending to be sorcerers. I wondered what circles this man moved in, and whether, if I mentioned Kite's name now, some rumour might find its way to the thief. I had no idea what would happen if it did but I thought it might alarm him, and perhaps prompt him into making a mistake.

'Oh, sure,' he said carelessly. 'I don't know what you'd expect me to see, though. It's not as if I know anyone who's likely to steal a dead mother's body.' He frowned. 'I told you, I'm not a sorcerer. I don't know any, either, and as for warriors…'

'I don't know what you might come across while you're out

looking for peyote buttons.' I grinned, trying to make a joke of it. 'Just ask anyone you meet if they happen to have robbed any graves lately!'

'Oh, sure,' he muttered peevishly. Then he suddenly brightened. He leaned towards me, like a man about to impart to secret, even while I was turning aside to get my nose a little further away from the smell of stale sweat wafting from his torn cloak.

'I'll tell you something, though. Pass this one to the policeman and tell him it's from me, won't you? If whoever robbed this woman's grave is a sorcerer, he must be a very strange one.'

'What makes you say that?' I asked curiously.

'Why did he take the body?'

'For the forearm,' I said automatically. 'It's well known what a sorcerer can do with a dead woman's forearm: he can dance with it and the magic can lull an entire household to sleep.'

'So why not just cut the arm off, then?'

I frowned. 'Well, because…'

He chuckled, delighted at his own cleverness. 'You see? A sorcerer wouldn't want to drag a whole corpse across the city when he could easily conceal an arm under his cloak. Doesn't make sense.'

I thought about this. 'There are other things he might have wanted,' I pointed out. 'The hair, a finger…'

'A sorcerer would have no use for them. They're warriors' charms.'

'Maybe the thief thought a warrior might buy them from him.'

'No, I don't think so. After all, how's the buyer to know for sure how the woman died, or whether she even had any children?' He asked the question as confidently as any man used to pitching his wares to sceptical customers. 'She could have been anybody. If you were a warrior about to go into battle would risk your life on a charm unless you were sure it was genuine?'

'So you think a warrior must have taken it. No, that doesn't make sense either,' I said impatiently. 'The hair and finger would be even easier to carry than an arm. Why'd a warrior have taken the body?'

He curled his lip. 'Can't help you there,' he admitted cheerfully. 'But I thought I'd save you and our policeman wasting your time looking for the wrong man.'

'Thanks a lot,' I said insincerely. 'I'm beginning to wish I'd not mentioned Kite now. Tell you what, forget what I said about helping him. If you want any favours from him just offer him a bribe!'

And I was about to add under my breath a fervent wish that Kite would be mortally offended by the offer and beat this cynical impostor until there was no longer an unbroken bone in his body, when a horrible thought made me catch my breath.

Suppose Cactus were right. It made no sense for either a warrior or a sorcerer to take a whole body when he only wanted a single, easily portable part of it, but what if he wanted more than that? What if he did, indeed, have a need for the hair as well as the arm because he was both a warrior *and* a sorcerer?

'Perhaps he had time to take just one charm,' I muttered. 'You could cut off an arm or a scalp, but how long would it take to get both? Maybe it was easier to take the body, after all.'

'What are you talking about?' Cactus asked. I ignored him, appalled and mesmerised by the idea that had occurred to me.

To be on the trail of someone who was both invincible by day and invisible by night. It was almost too frightening to contemplate, but I forced myself to admit that it made sense of one thing that had happened to me.

    The creature that had attacked me during the night, the being that had no human shape, had carried a sword.

7

Goose's niece had emerged from the house with her aunt, and was standing next to me holding a basket with some dough balls in it. There were not many of them and they did not look appetising – unevenly shaped, burned in places, almost raw in others. Nonetheless she proffered them as correctly as if she were serving at a feast, balancing the basket in her right palm, with her eyes downcast in a modest expression.

I accepted one out of politeness, taking it left-handed and looking around quickly for Goose, who had the bowl full of dipping sauce. 'Thank you.'

'Tlacotl made these herself,' Goose told us.

'Well done. They look delicious.' Cactus sounded more sincere in his appreciation than I would have done, although when I bit into one of the cakes I found it tasted better than it looked.

I looked at the little girl, whose name meant 'Osier Twig'. She appeared slightly older than I had thought at first: perhaps ten or eleven, almost ready for her first day at the House of Youth and old enough now to be of some use to her mother about the house in the meantime. Then I remembered, with a pang that almost made me choke on my dough ball, that she no longer had a mother.

'Thank the gentleman, Osier Twig,' her aunt prompted her.

The girl looked up at Cactus, to speak to him, and her lips parted, but the only sound she made was a faint 'Oh!' of surprise as she quickly hid her face again.

Goose frowned in annoyance. 'I'm sorry,' she started to say, 'but my niece has had a trying couple of days…'

Cactus had recovered himself, however. 'I didn't realise we'd met!' he said, addressing the girl.

'Where?' Goose asked sternly. No doubt she was concerned to learn that her niece had had an encounter with a strange man.

'No, no we haven't,' the girl said, stammering in confusion while the remaining dough balls shook so vigorously in their basket that two flew out onto the floor. 'I've never seen him before.'

'Yes, you have,' the curer said. He caught Goose's eye and said: 'Oh, I'm sorry, madam. It's perfectly innocent. I saw her the day before yesterday, running through Atlixco plaza. You were looking for a midwife,' he reminded the girl.

'I thought your father sent you to the House of Pleasure?' I said. I assumed Osier Twig was the girl Goose and Handy had both told me about.

'Yes,' said the girl wretchedly. She looked as though she would rather be anywhere than where she was now, with not one but two men talking to her. 'The plaza is on the way. I had to run through the marketplace. I heard a couple of people calling out. This man could have been one of them but I – I didn't stop.'

'Not for me,' Cactus conceded. 'But you did for one of my customers.'

'There was an old woman,' the girl said hastily. 'She only asked me what was the matter. And I talked to her for a moment, that's all – just long enough to tell her about mother – and then I went straight to the House of Pleasure. I ran all the way, honestly!' She wailed the last word before bursting into tears, as though voicing some awful confession.

'I'm sure you did,' Goose said soothingly. She laid an arm on her niece's shoulder, trying to still the violent shivering that had overcome her. She looked venomously at Cactus, who was staring at the girl as if he wanted to say something more. A glance at her aunt was enough to silence her, however.

'I ran all the way there,' Osier Twig snuffled, 'and all the way back.'

Goose squeezed her shoulder. 'You got there soon enough,' she said. 'Look how quickly Gentle Heart came!'

'She did that,' I mused. 'In fact she must have passed you on the way back to the house.'

The girl turned her tear-streaked face up to look at me. 'Yes,' she whispered. 'Yes, that's right. She did.'

'That's enough.' Goose was still trying to soothe her niece but there was an edge to her voice that I took to mean there had better be no more questions. 'And what happened wasn't your fault.' She heaved a deep sigh and looked in the midwife's direction. 'Not your fault...' she repeated under her breath.

Gentle Heart had stopped playing with the children. Now she stood by herself, a few paces away from where Handy and his eldest son were stamping on the child's grave, flattening the earth so as to obliterate all trace of it. The midwife met Goose's eye. She seemed to flinch momentarily, but then, gathering her courage, she walked slowly towards us.

Osier Twig proffered the basket unbidden, like a good hostess. Gentle Heart accepted a dough ball and began chewing on it mechanically.

'Thank you. I haven't eaten or slept since last night.' She looked exhausted, her eyes red and their lids puffy. 'I keep thinking about your poor sister,' she told Goose, 'and what I might have done differently, but I just' – I thought she was going to choke on the mouthful she had taken – 'I just can't understand it.'

Seeing her niece's wide eyes and trembling lip, Goose no doubt thought she was about to burst into tears again. 'Go indoors, child, and fetch some bread for your father and Spotted Eagle.'

As the girl fled she turned back to the midwife. 'Giving birth is the woman's battle,' she said stiffly. 'Tezcatlipoca and Cihuacoatl will not always grant us victory.'

'I tried. You have to believe me. I tried everything I know,' Gentle Heart said imploringly. 'Your sister did fight – I fought too – there wasn't anything I could do!'

'You could have helped us afterwards!' Goose hissed. 'You didn't come back, last night, when her husband needed you. What were you doing then?'

'I couldn't,' the midwife replied in a voice half-choked with sudden tears. 'I wanted to. I wanted to say goodbye, to tell her what I've told you – that she had fought, that she'd died like a warrior – but I couldn't. Don't you understand?' She looked around at us all, her eyes wide with distress, and something in them moved me to reply. Perhaps it was the eyes themselves, the redness of their rims and the jagged, broken veins that had coated their whites in a pink wash. They reminded me of Lily waking from a bad dream, wanting only to be held.

'You were afraid you'd get it wrong, that you'd forget the words,' I said quietly.

'But she's got to know what to do!' Goose said impatiently. 'You must have had this happen before.'

'No, I haven't.' Gentle Heart protested. 'I only know what others have told me. I've never – Star was the first who's ever…' She ended on a sob.

Cactus stepped towards her. 'It's all right,' he murmured. 'It's all right. You've been through much. Let me help. Look, I can make you feel better…'

He was fumbling for that cloth pouch once more. I told him to keep his bloody weeds out of sight. Turning back to Gentle Heart I said: 'How long have you been a midwife?'

'Since I was too old for the House of Pleasure – for the warriors who came there, I mean.'

'That must have been a few years ago,' Goose said tartly.

'And before that?' I persisted.

She looked at me gratefully. 'I'm from Chalco originally. But Goose is right – that was a long time ago. I was a tribute slave. I think I was intended to be sacrificed, but someone thought I'd be better employed entertaining warriors in the House of Pleasure than dancing and dying at a festival.' She seemed a little more composed: the remote past was easier to talk about than the events of yesterday. Goose, by contrast, looked as though she were about to give way to tears again.

'But you were in the Pleasure House long enough to learn your trade?'

'We all learned. We helped each other, and the older ones taught us. Some of us ended up as warriors' wives or concubines to great lords, of course, but we all knew we might have to make our living looking after other women. Many wanted that, anyway. It's a privilege no man can ever know.' She sighed. 'Goose, please try to understand what I'm saying. I know my work, I really do. I know what will happen if a pregnant woman chews gum or looks at anything red. I can tell her when she must accept her husband, to form the baby, and when she must stop. I can attend her in the sweat bath, turn a baby in the womb, offer the herbs when they're needed...' This recital of the midwife's skills came out in a single breath, and I wondered whom she was trying to convince. 'I've brought so many children into the World, Goose, and yet I have never seen anything like what happened to your sister. It was as if... It was as if, when we struggled to bring him out, there was someone else in there with us, fighting us. Can you believe that? I was scared!' By the time she had finished, Gentle Heart was no longer looking at any of us. She had buried her head in her hands and was weeping silently.

I looked helplessly over her shoulder towards where Handy and Spotted Eagle were finishing up, but there was no comfort for anyone to be found there. Father and son were staring, grim-faced, at their handiwork, and had no eyes for us.

The ground over the grave looked as though it had never been broken, if anything stamped harder than the earth around it. The sight reminded me of that other grave, in front of the shrine in Atlixco plaza. And that was when I realised what it was that had looked wrong; the thing that had looked out of place, or rather, that had not been in the place where it should have been.

8

By the time Gentle Heart and Cactus had left, the sun was well past its zenith. It was the time of day when labourers in the fields would be putting their lunch-bags aside and getting back to work.

I tried to explain to Handy what I thought might have happened to his brother-in-law. I was rewarded with a sceptical stare. 'You've changed your mind, then,' he remarked. 'You thought he'd just run away before.'

'I don't know for sure,' I said. I looked towards the doorway leading into the house, where Goose was listlessly going through the motions of some domestic task.. 'I don't think we should tell her until I've checked. So the sooner I can go and find out, the better.'

'One of us had better go with you.'

'It's not necessary,' I protested. 'I'm only going to see your policeman, and he's hardly likely to let me get into any trouble.'

Handy was not taking any notice, however. He was looking at his gateway, and his young sons running through it.

Snake and Buck were both panting slightly, having raced each other all the way back from my mistress's house. 'We found the place!' Buck called out, when he got his breath back.

'Only because I told you where it was,' Snake gasped.

'Liar! You got lost twice!'

'How was Lily?' I snapped impatiently. 'What did she say?'

Buck stared at me as if he had forgotten why they had gone to Tlatelolco in the first place. His brother grinned at me. 'Oh, I wouldn't be you. She's livid!' From that I took it that one of them at least had had the wit to pass on the message.

'What do you mean, livid?' I asked, an odd mixture of trepidation and hope stirring in me.

'I mean when I told her you were staying here to help us, she said who gave you permission?'

'And who do you think you are?' Buck put in.

'And you can sleep out in the courtyard when she's done dragging you home by the heels...'

'...if she hasn't pitched you into a canal on the way. And another thing...' I never found out what the other thing was, because I was laughing too loudly to hear it. I went on laughing until the tears were running down my cheeks, heedless of Handy's and Spotted Eagle's mute, astonished stares.

The image of Lily in one of her immense, foot-stamping rages was funny in itself; but what was so much more precious, what made me laugh and weep until my sides hurt, was relief. For her to be that angry, I thought, she must be feeling better.

I was spared an escort when I went to see Kite. Both Snake and Buck were too exhausted after their run to do any more than collapse in a heap against the courtyard wall. In the process they brought down some of the hastily built-up masonry that had blocked the hole made on the previous night. While Handy and Spotted Eagle rushed into the billowing dust-cloud this produced, I took the chance to slip away, darting nimbly through the gateway and running along the canal-path outside until I was out of sight.

I had every intention of helping to find out what had happened to Star's body. I had every reason to do so. It was not merely that I feared risking the anger of the dead woman's spirit and pitied her surviving family. Whoever or whatever had attacked me during the night must have had something to do with the theft. At the very least it had scattered the men watching the grave for long enough for the thief to do his work. However, if the fear that had assailed me when I talked to Cactus the curer had any foundation, then what the thief had taken might make the monster that had hunted me still deadlier than before. An invisible, invincible warrior out for my blood!

As I trotted back to the centre of the parish I thought longingly of the relative security of Lily's house in Tlatelolco, but I realised that safety was almost certainly an illusion. Neither I nor anyone close to me could afford to rest until the mystery of what had happened to Star's body was solved.

The obvious place to look for a policeman in any parish in Mexico was in the parish hall. However, before I had reached the long, low building, skirting market pitches that were as oddly empty of traders and customers as they had been the day before, I realised that I would not need to go inside in order to ask after Kite. He was standing at the edge of the canal that bordered the plaza opposite the little pyramid, close to the bridge that took the path across it.

There was a small crowd gathered around the policeman, although he was doing his best to shoo the bystanders away as I approached. When I heard what he was saying, I felt sick, although it was neither more nor less than I had expected.

'All right, so you've seen it. You all know what a body looks like. Now bugger off, the lot of you, and let me get on with my work! And what do *you* want?'

The last words were meant for me. I heard mutterings from one or two people who remembered me from the day before, but nobody tried to stop me as I pushed my way through the crowd of onlookers to Kite's side.

'Look, Kite, I've been thinking. About yesterday. I'm afraid I was wrong. I'm not sure Flower Gatherer ran away after all. I think I know what may have happened to him. You'll need to dredge the canal.'

He folded his arms and looked down his long, straight nose at me. 'Oh, really? And what do you suppose I'll find if I do that?'

'A body. Weighed down by...' I heard my voice tail off as I saw where he was looking. I lowered my own gaze to follow his. When I saw what lay at his feet, I staggered, my legs having suddenly lost most of their strength, and might have fallen over if I had not toppled against a man standing just behind me.

The remains were scarcely recognisable as those of a man. The legs and the lower part of the trunk were exposed, apart from the groin, coyly hidden by what was left of a breechcloth. The upper part of the body too was swaddled in some tattered material. The stench rising from the corpse was enough to make me gag. Knowing the smell of rot and piss was mostly that of the pool of canal water surrounding the body did not make it less nauseating.

I swallowed hard. The stink was not the worst of it, by a long way.

Tribute of Death

Aztecs were not strangers to the sight of human blood. Priests in particular were used to seeing hearts ripped, still beating, from the chests of sacrificial victims; but at certain times anyone might see blood carried through the streets in gourds and daubed on the faces of idols, or men dancing in the flayed skins of captive warriors, or an enemy's flesh stripped from a severed limb and turned into the makings of a stew. Most men had been to war, and seen friend and foe alike pierced and mutilated. However, I would have guessed that nobody present had ever seen anything like this.

The condition of the body was horrific. Both legs were broken, the knees twisted at bizarre angles, and there was what looked like an extra joint in one calf. Elsewhere the flesh was torn and gouged, criss-crossed by cuts ranging from grazes to deep gaping rents. What I could see made me thankful for the cloth covering the rest, which from the look of it was even more grotesquely misshapen. The cloth itself was so sodden with canal water and stained with dark blood that it was impossible to make out what colour it might have been before. It had been ripped, so that it looked little better than a rag, and part of it appeared to be missing altogether.

Something lay beside the body. Like the cloth it was heavily stained. It was rectangular, hard and smooth: a slab of dressed stone.

'Well,' I said quietly, 'I was right about the paving slab.'

A hand gripped my upper arm, not gently. 'Now, what was that about dredging the canal?' Kite's voice rasped in my ear. 'I think you'd better tell me what you know, don't you?'

Without taking my eyes off the body, I said: 'After we'd buried the woman, we put the paving slab back into place over the body. I realised that I hadn't seen it when I came back here this morning, after her body had been dug up again. Something that heavy doesn't just blow away in the wind. Flower Gatherer was missing. I wondered if the two had disappeared together.'

'The paving slab was tied to the body with this.' The policeman stirred the stained cloth with his sandaled foot. 'Anything to say about that?'

'If the slab was used to weigh the body down,' I said dully, 'then they had to have been tied together with something.' I looked up into the policeman's face. 'This looks like part of a cloak.'

'But what's it doing here, Yaotl?'

For all the orders Kite had been bellowing when I had arrived, the crowd around us had not dispersed. They were all looking steadily at me, and it felt as though I were surrounded by spears, their tips of flint and obsidian poised to be thrust into my flesh. I began to wish I had let someone from Handy's household come with me after all; at least I would have felt less alone.

I stammered through the best explanation I could come up with. 'When the monster attacked us it killed Flower Gatherer and threw his body in the canal. It must have used his cloak to tie the dead man to the paving slab.' I hesitated. 'I suppose this is Flower Gatherer's body? Did anyone recognise it?'

Kite laughed grimly. 'Look at him! His own mother wouldn't recognise him! But what are you saying? That someone else has vanished in this parish? I hope you're wrong. One missing person and one body, I can just about cope with. Two men vanished and one body wouldn't add up.'

'The women saw a three-captive warrior following us last night. They got a piece of his cloak. So why don't you go and talk to Red

Macaw?'

There was a stirring in the crowd around me. Somebody tittered, as though I had said something funny. It sounded incongruous, as Kite's own mirthless laugh had not, and the policeman's expression now was as bleak as ever.

'I can't talk to him,' he said slowly.

'Why not?' I stared at him. 'You can't mean he's disappeared too?'

'Not exactly.' The man looked troubled. His expression had not been tranquil before, but now, for the first time, I felt that he was not in command of the situation, and he knew it. He put a hand to his forehead and frowned deeply as if afflicted by a sudden pain between his temples. Then he whipped the hand away, and glared balefully at the people gathered around him.

'Didn't I send you lot about your business ages ago?' he snapped. He raised his arm in a fierce gesture. 'Go on, scram! Not the slave, though. You're coming with me!'

In one movement the arm descended and the hand seized my elbow in unbreakable grip.

As he dragged me towards the parish hall, visions of tiny cells swam before my eyes: open cages in airless, lightless rooms, filled with the stench of unwashed bodies and what came out of them. I squealed with fear, but nobody was listening.

9

The parish hall stood at the corner of the marketplace, facing the temple, with the waters of the canal lapping its rear wall. It was a long, low adobe building. Rooms opened onto three sides of its square central courtyard, the front being the outer wall dividing it from the marketplace, with the entrance in its middle. Opposite the entrance, a stairway led up to a broad flat roof. There was a doorway at ground level on either side of the steps.

Some of the doorways leading off the courtyard were closed by wicker screens. Others were dark holes giving no clue to what lay beyond them. I knew in general what such places contained: the parish records, weapons, quarters for local officials. I wondered which room held the stout wooden cages where prisoners would be kept. I was afraid that I might be about to find out, but that was not what Kite had in mind. Instead, he led me towards the steps leading up on to the roof. On the way he barked out orders to a couple of his deputies to go and clean up the mess by the canal outside. They moved reluctantly from where they had been squatting on the hard earth of the courtyard, two men who may have been the pair who had moved to arrest me that morning, or just two more who had been carved out of the side of the same mountain.

Tribute of Death

'Up here,' the policeman ordered.

The roof of the parish hall was decorated with plant pots. What grew from them were mostly hardy specimens. Many were desert varieties. 'A lot of cacti,' I observed nervously. 'What are they for, torturing prisoners with the thorns?' It was a genuine question. There were some forms of torment – beatings, pricking with maguey spines, drenching in ice-cold water – that I could endure, having known worse as a priest. If that was what the policeman had in mind then I could make myself ready for it.

'No, they just do well on the roof. I prefer dahlias, really, but it's too exposed for them up here.'

I stared at him incredulously. 'Next you'll be telling me you like sitting up here in the morning, watching the sun rising over the lake while you compose poetry!'

'And what if I do?'

Flower and Song, was what we called poetry. I supposed Cactus and Song would do as well. I was trying to think of some witty remark to that effect while the policeman squatted on the edge of his roof terrace and motioned for me to do the same.

'I didn't bring you up here to admire the blooms,' he said, 'nor to beat a confession out of you.'

'That's a relief,' I said weakly.

'I've not given up on that idea, though! However, there are things we need to talk about. Starting with Handy.'

There was an awkward pause while I pretended to admire a fat, globular Eagle's Claw, a variety normally to be found halfway up a mountain. Kite must take his hobby seriously, I thought. 'Handy's an old friend of yours.'

'I've known him a long time. But then, I've known most of them a long time.' He glanced across to the small pyramid, letting his gaze take in the busy marketplace spread out before it. 'They're like children,' he sighed. 'I have to shout at them and thump them sometimes and make them do things they don't want to do, but it's for their own good. And I can look after them. I don't need interference from your high officials – the palace, the chief minister, pompous upstarts like the Guardian of the Waterfront.'

I had to suppress a smile at the reference to Lion; I wondered whether Kite had any idea that he was my brother. Then I found the policeman was looking straight at me. 'I can't always keep the rest of the world out, though, can I? Let alone the rest of the city. Like when you turn up, for instance, and before you know it Handy loses his wife and maybe his brother-in-law, and there are monsters and thieves roaming around...'

'Not my fault!' I cried.

'Maybe not, though you can hardly deny some of this is connected with you. By your own account the monster, or whoever attacked you, called you by your name.'

A movement in the courtyard distracted him for a moment: his men bringing the body inside, mercifully hidden from sight by a blanket.

'Still,' he continued, 'about Handy. You were there this afternoon. How's he taking it?'

I thought about what I had seen and heard at the commoner's house. 'Not well. They're coping, I suppose. They don't understand what's going on around them.'

'They're not alone in that!'

'They had to bury the child this morning,' I added. 'They wanted me to help. Maybe I did, a bit.'

He looked at me curiously. 'I'd have thought that was the midwife's job.'

'It should be, just as Star's burial last night was. But she didn't turn up for one and she didn't exactly rise to the occasion for the other, either.' I was surprised at the anger I felt rising within me as I described the pathetic little ceremony beside Handy's maize bins, and Gentle Heart's arrival with Cactus in the midst of it. 'She didn't seem to have any idea! It's not just that she didn't know the words. For that matter, as far as I know there aren't any words. It's that she didn't seem to have much idea what it was all for. Neither did I, at first, but then I used to be a priest – my business was with gods, not men, and gods don't have any feelings at all.'

The policeman pursed his lips thoughtfully. 'And what about this character who came with her?'

'Cactus?' I thought about the curer, seeing his straggly hair and his grubby cloak again in my mind's eye. 'He's a fake at best. At worst…' I told him about the conversation I had had with Cactus, and about the terrifying possibility that had occurred to me, that thief of Star's body might be both a warrior and a sorcerer.

Kite took the hint. 'You think he may have been trying to put you off the scent? But that would make him the thief, then, wouldn't it?'

I shivered. I had been resisting the idea that I had stood within a few fingers' lengths of a sorcerer and had had a conversation with him. 'It's a possibility.'

'Well, I know what he looks like. Next time he puts in a appearance in the market, I'll bring him in.'

I still did not know quite why he had brought me up here. It was as though there were something in particular that he wanted to say to me but for some reason he was reluctant to bring it up. I decided to force the issue. 'Well,' I said, getting to my feet, 'It's getting late. Time I was heading back...'

A sinewy hand grasped the hem of my cloak hard enough to tear the material, had I made any real effort to get away. I looked down at the policeman, wondering why, when I was standing and he was still on his haunches, I still felt as though he towered over me.

'Not so fast,' he said quietly. 'I told you I wanted to talk about Handy...'

'You have talked about him. Then we moved on to Gentle Heart and Cactus. Then you said maybe the man I'd been talking to this afternoon was a sorcerer. I thought I'd go before it got really scary!'

'... Handy and Red Macaw.'

That silenced me.

'Now,' Kite continued, as I slowly lowered myself back into a squatting position, 'it's common knowledge that the two of them didn't get on.'

'I got that general impression.'

'Then you can see what's coming, and why I got you up here to talk about it rather than mouthing off in the middle of that bunch of gossipy old women down there in the plaza. I have one old friend – and he is, or was – who's just lost his wife in about the worst way you can imagine, and not taking it very well.'

'Yes.' I could not very well disagree.

'And I have an unidentified body which may belong to another old friend with whom Handy had a long-running feud.'

'What?'

'Red Macaw's gone too. That's what I meant when I said I couldn't talk to him.'

I gaped at him. 'Red Macaw's gone... where?' On occasion my gift for asking penetrating questions deserted me.

'If I knew that...' he began patiently. 'I can tell you where he *said* he was going. He came to see me yesterday afternoon. He'd heard there was to be a flowery war with Texcala. He wanted to join up.'

Texcala lay beyond the mountains to the east, a nation of proud warriors whom the Aztecs had never managed to subdue, although we kept their borders so tightly sealed that they lived in the kind of wretched poverty that produces the hardiest and fiercest soldiers. Every few years their army and ours would meet at a prearranged place for a formal battle. It gave both sides the opportunity to practise their skills and take the kind of prisoner the gods most wanted to have as sacrifices: men known to be mighty fighters, rather than effete barbarians.

Unfortunately our army had been badly beaten in the last clash, and many of our young men had long been clamouring for another one, to avenge their losses.

'He's too old to fight,' I objected. 'And surely with his bad leg...'

'The army would accept a three-captive warrior,' Kite assured me, 'if he can only catch them up; because they've already left, including the draft from this parish. All I could do was wish him luck. And hope he found what he was looking for.' He looked at me steadily as he said this, and I understood.

Red Macaw might be seeking fame or glory, but at his age his chances of finding either would be slim. It sounded to me as though what he had really been eager for was death: what our poets and priests sang of as the sweetest end a man could have, death in battle or on the sacrificial stone of an enemy's temple: the flowery death. I wondered what might have driven him to that.

Kite was saying: 'I need a reason why the body was hidden in the canal. If it is Flower Gatherer's body, then what would be the point of doing that, since everyone knows he was here last night?'

'Could be a double bluff,' I suggested, without much conviction. 'Slow you down, fool you into looking for the wrong man.'

'Maybe. It's possible, though, isn't it, that Red Macaw's fate overtook him before he even set out on the road?'

I was barely listening, however. I was too busy contemplating an unpleasant idea that had just formed in my mind.

Red Macaw – or someone wearing a cloak that looked just like his – had been seen following Star's funeral procession. If a flowery death was not what Red Macaw had wanted, then perhaps the ageing warrior had gone looking for something to protect him against the keen young braves he would have to face. He might have armed himself with charms to make him invincible – cut from a dead mother's body.

I lowered my voice deliberately, leaning towards Kite so that he could hear me whispering. 'You can't be suggesting Handy might have murdered him!'

'Why not? Do you know what they'd quarrelled over?'

'No, but I'm sure it wasn't anything to kill a man over!'

'Are you, though? You see, I've no idea what the matter was either. Not many things in this parish are secret from me, but this is. The two of them kept their mouths very firmly closed over it – except to each other, of course.'

Where was this going to end? I wondered. Bad enough to have been talking to a sorcerer. To have been talking to him while a murderer was quietly trampling the earth over his child's grave just paces away from me was still worse. I started looking for more arguments. 'Handy has an alibi. He wasn't alone. He had his son, and Flower Gatherer with him. His clothes would have been covered with blood...'

'He could have changed them. In the dark, who'd know? Spotted Eagle wouldn't speak up against his father. And Flower Gatherer's missing too, so he isn't going to tell.'

'Flower Gatherer could equally well be the killer.'

Kite laughed. 'If he was, then he's managed to fool a lot of people over the years. Nobody in this parish would have believed he had it in him!'

'Sorcerers are subtle.'

'They are.' His tone and his look were suddenly serious again. 'So much so that I'm prepared to believe anything now. Handy, Flower Gatherer, Red Macaw, you – as far as I'm concerned any of you could have been responsible for what we found in the canal. If you want me to believe otherwise, it's up to you to find me some proof.'

10

The afternoon was well advanced by the time Kite let me out of his parish hall. I stood in the gateway for a long moment, wondering at my freedom and doing my best to savour it while I watched the people of Atlixco parish going about their business.

The scene around me must have been repeated that day in many other small marketplaces across the city. Although it was getting late, most traders still occupied their pitches, their wares spread out before them on reed mats: cheap plates and sauce bowls here, obsidian blades there, lengths of rough maguey fibre cloth across the way. There were few of the luxury items you might look for in one of the big markets, such as that of Tlatelolco: no cocoa or feathers or cotton, because nobody here could afford to buy them. The men, women and children mumbling and shuffling between the pitches were a colourless lot: commoners, their feet bare, their clothes made of coarse cloth, the men's hair worn loose or tonsured to show they were not great warriors. They were ordinary Aztecs going about their daily lives.

One or two of them stopped to stare curiously at me, and then hurried on, leaving me feeling lonely and ashamed. Had I brought death among them, leading my enemies into their midst?

I looked up at the sun. The clear, brilliant yellow disk was descending now towards the West, and shortly it would vanish behind the buildings on that side of the plaza. I remembered the souls of the dead mothers who escorted the sun towards his rest each day. Star's might be among them; so far away, and yet for a moment I felt closer to her than to the living, breathing humans around me, because I thought she alone might understand what I was trying to do.

'I'm sorry,' I blurted out impulsively.

A woman, walking past with an infant strapped to her back and another clutching her hand, glared at me and quickened her pace, the twin tufts of hair over her forehead bobbing in mute warning.

I took a deep breath and stepped into the marketplace, meaning to cross it on the way to Handy's house. However, I paused when I saw someone I recognised.

'Quail!' I hailed him as much for the sake of having one of these people speak to me as because I expected him to tell me anything. 'Do you remember me? How are your children?'

The fisherman had been standing beside the canal, chatting to one of his fellows. From the morose looks they were exchanging I suspected that the monster in the marshes had ruined both men's catches, leaving them with little to do here but commiserate with one another.

Quail recognised me: that much was plain from the look he gave me, which was the sort that might have crossed a man's face on turning a corner to find an eviscerated dog in his path. 'Yaotl,' he said neutrally, as his companion slipped away.

'Did you hear about what happened?' I asked. 'About the body?'

'I don't suppose anyone in this parish will talk about much else,' he confirmed reluctantly. 'At least, until the next bad thing happens!'

He looked at me thoughtfully. 'You've been talking to Kite, haven't you? They're saying the body might be Red Macaw's.'

'It might be,' I admitted. 'But the state it's in, it could be anybody's. I'm sorry – did you know him?'

'No better than I know everyone else around here. Who does Kite think did it?'

'He doesn't know,' I said truthfully.

Quail glanced furtively about him, as though he wanted to make sure nobody saw him take a step closer to me. 'Listen,' he said confidentially, 'I don't care what anyone says: there's no way Handy would have done it. Kite ought to know that as well as anybody.'

I stared at him, mystified. 'Nobody said...'

Whatever I might have gone on to add was swept aside by the urgency in the man's voice. 'The policeman's a good man, but he doesn't know what it was between Handy and Red Macaw, and he's not going to know, you understand?'

'No, I don't.'

'All right, put it this way. Handy's a well-respected man in this parish. You want to know what I mean? Well, when I walked past his plot – he farms one of the *chinampa* fields on the edge of the lake, near where I set my nets – I saw someone turning over the soil. I didn't get a clear look at the man, because I was too far away and it was getting dark, but it wasn't one of Handy's sons, because they're all at home with him, so it must have been a neighbour. What's more, it looked as though he'd done something to fix up a little hut in the corner, though I know Handy hasn't troubled to repair the roof in years. Now what I'm saying is this: we're all busy with our own work, but one of his neighbours took the trouble to go and do that, turn over his field, because it's near the planting season and Handy would be in trouble if it wasn't done in time. If he wants to keep a thing to himself, there isn't anyone in Atlixco who won't go along with it. Do you see?'

'Enough to understand that I wouldn't want Kite's job,' I replied. 'And I get the general idea: no questions about Handy. Well, I'll pass that on, for what it's worth. Maybe he'll tell me what it's all about one day.'

'I wouldn't bet on it.' Quail stepped away from me, having apparently said what he had wanted to.

I was not prepared to leave it at that, though. 'What about Red Macaw, then?'

'What about him?'

'Is he as popular?'

Quail's brow furrowed. 'He's a fine warrior.'

'I'll take that as a "no".'

'They keep themselves to themselves,' the man said defensively. 'Nobody really knows them that well.'

'Who's "they"?'

'Red Macaw and his mother.'

'He lives with his mother?'

'She's his only family. He never married...' Quail shut his mouth with a snap, like a man who realises he has said too much already, and took another furtive look around him. 'Look, I've got to go now. Just remember you're a stranger here, all right? You can't expect people to tell you everything.'

As I walked back along the canal towards Handy's house, I felt extraordinarily weary. I found myself dragging my feet, scraping my heels on the hard earth of the path. It seemed that all the events that were happening around me – the mutilated body I had seen this afternoon, the monster that had pursued me in the night, the theft of Star's body, Flower Gatherer's disappearance, even in some way Star's death, all had some connection with this feud between her husband and Red Macaw. I was filled with despair at the prospect of trying to unravel a secret that the people of Atlixo would not share, even with their parish policeman.

It was while I was wrestling with these thoughts, with my eyes downcast so as to avoid the reproachful glances of the people around me, that I met an old acquaintance: one I would happily have avoided if I had recognised him in time.

'There he is!'

I looked up at the sound of a familiar voice. When I saw the face that went with it, my first thought was: 'Oh no, not you again.'

It was the old man I had spoken to in the morning, who had urged Kite to lock me up or hand me over to the chief minister. However, I dismissed him from my thoughts the moment I saw who was with him.

The old man was holding a conversation with someone in a canoe. It was that person who had caught my attention. He was looking directly at me. His jaw dropped as he took in my appearance, but he recovered from his surprise quickly, and a moment later he was out of the canoe and striding along the canal towards me. His cloak – a three-captive warrior's, like Red Macaw's – flapped around him and his long hair bounced at his temples in time with his steps.

I stared at him, horrified and amazed. He was none other than my former master's steward, Huitztic the Prick, the same man who had bullied and taunted me relentlessly during the years I had spent in lord Feathered in Black's household.

He stopped a few paces away from where I stood. The old man he had been speaking to and a few others trailed diffidently behind him, halting a respectable distance away and trying to peer over his shoulder.

The steward stared at me. It seemed to take him a little while to find his voice. 'Yaotl! What are you doing here?'

Having concluded that he had lied about the men who were meant to be protecting me, I had all but forgotten about my former master. The horror and terror I had experienced since the previous day had all but driven the chief minister and his servants from my mind. But it seemed he had remembered me. It had been inevitable that he would get to hear where I was, ever since I had returned to Atlixco that morning, and found myself the centre of attention. Now I was face-to-face with his steward and had to decide whether to cringe or to defy him.

I swallowed nervously and found my mouth had gone dry.

'Nothing to say? That's not like you.'

'He had plenty to say this morning,' growled one of the bystanders.

At last I managed to find my voice. 'I don't belong to your master any more, Huitztic. You know that. So does he.'

The grin faded but did not vanish. 'Of course we know that. Why should we care? That's what you should be asking yourself.'

The sneer in his voice made up my mind for me. 'So go away and leave me alone,' I said defiantly.

He sighed and narrowed his eyes as though something had made him sad, although the grin was still there. The resulting expression was as peculiar as anything I seen on any man's face. 'Yaotl! Is that any way to speak to the chief minister's servant?'

'No, of course you're right,' I said in a meek tone. 'How about this, then? "Try shoving your head up a dog's arse and barking!" Any better?'

This time the grin slipped. He took a step forward, with his fists balled, and the crowd stirred expectantly. I wondered whether anyone was placing bets and what odds were being offered on me to win. I was not much fitter than Huitzic and unlike him, I never had been much of a warrior.

The audience was to be disappointed. The man took a deep breath and stopped after that first step. He seemed to hesitate, deliberately looking away for a moment before continuing, speaking through gritted teeth: 'I'm not going to let you provoke me. What's the point? You and that oafish friend of yours have worse than me to reckon with, don't you?' Suddenly he laughed. 'Maybe I'll come along and have some fun with whatever's left of the two of you!'

I noticed a couple of the men standing behind the steward exchanging disapproving glances.

'What do you mean by that, Huitztic?' I asked innocently.

'I mean I'm not the only one who has a grudge against you and Handy, after what happened in Tlacopan!' He meant the incident where I had humiliated the captain. The Prick had been there as well, and if anything had come off worse than the otomi, adding a severe beating to the humiliation they had both suffered.

We were gathering a growing audience, whose members were becoming more restive. The steward never had had the sense to know when to shut up.

'Of course, that other poor fool's even more pathetic than you are, isn't he? I mean, for a slave like you, mooning over some merchant's old ugly daughter's ridiculous enough, but as for Handy...'

I might have tried my strength against his, just for talking about Lily like that, but even as I gritted my teeth and clenched my fists, I knew there would be no need. 'What about him?' I hissed.

'Why, don't you know? About him and that warrior, Red Macaw?' He giggled suddenly. 'You must be the only person here who doesn't! Why, if it had been me, I'd have...'

I almost regretted it when they threw him in the canal. He hit the water with a deeply satisfying splash, causing the surface to explode, waves and jets flying in all directions as though trying to get away from the wild, frenzied thing thrashing furiously at their centre. All the same, I reflected, as I leaped backwards to avoid being soaked, it might have been good to have heard a little more. It sounded as though he was in on a secret I should have liked to know about.

But then I could not help myself any longer. I started to laugh. Soon the roaring and hooting had spread through the crowd that had gathered rapidly around us.

'What's the matter with him?' someone called out. 'Why's he splashing about like that?'

With some difficulty I recovered enough breath between my own bursts of giggling to answer him. 'He can't swim!' I sobbed, remembering what had happened the last time I had seen the steward fall into the water.

'A man could stand up in that canal!' cried a small boy.

'I know! But he hasn't figured that out yet!' I gasped as a stitch caught my side. The pain was enough to make me catch my breath and remind me whose servant the man struggling in the water was. As soon as I could speak again I shouted: 'Huitztic! If they ever fish you out of there, tell your master from me – thanks for looking out for me last night, but if I ever want his protection, I'll ask!'

With that I turned and walked away, still chuckling at the thought of my old tormentor floundering in the stinking waters of a canal. It was not until I had turned a corner, putting him and the crowd of amused spectators out of sight, that I began to wonder just what my former master's steward had been doing in Atlixco.

And what did he know about Handy and Red Macaw? Had he somehow learned a secret that not even the parish policeman was privy to?

11

It was getting towards evening by the time I returned to Handy's house.

I found the courtyard full of members of the commoner's family. They were close together, as they had to be in the confined space, but they stood, squatted or kneeled in little groups that seemed to have no connection with one another. It looked as though something had pulled them apart: some quarrel, perhaps.

Handy was alone, huddled beside the wall, opposite the sweat bath. He did not look up at me. Spotted Eagle and Snake were talking together in a corner. They both fell silent at my arrival, their eyes tracking me as I searched the courtyard for an empty space to squat in.

Nobody remarked on my absence; nor did anyone express any surprise at my coming back.

Jaguar, Star's and Goose's father, stood beside the sweat bath, directly across the courtyard from his son-in-law, and glared silently at him. The old man's wife kneeled between two of the younger children, whispering to them. It looked as though she was telling them a story. She seemed distracted, though: she kept looking across at her daughter, and fidgeting, as though trying to resist the impulse to get up and go to her. And it was her daughter on whom my eyes rested finally.

Goose appeared to have been weaving, as a backstrap loom lay beside her. However, both the threads and the strap that had gone around her back to support the loom were in such a tangle that it looked as if she had thrown it aside in a hurry. The woman herself lay in a trembling heap on the floor. The hand I could see was formed into a fist that opened and closed spasmodically.

Suddenly her mother, after a brief glance at her husband, stood up and crossed the courtyard to where Goose lay. She put a hand on her shoulder.

'Don't grieve, love,' she said in a loud whisper. 'We don't know it was him. We don't know what happened.'

Goose said nothing, only shaking a little more violently. It was her father who responded, barking harshly at his wife: 'Leave her be, woman! Of course we know. It was Red Macaw's body in the canal, and Flower Gatherer ran off somewhere. Now stop making such a fuss, both of you, and get back to your work!' Clearly the story of what had been pulled out of the water had run ahead of me.

All her father's words did to Goose was to make her shudder. Her mother, however, looked up and scowled. 'How can you say that? She's just lost her sister and now her husband!'

'No, I told you: he's run away. He'll be back. Not that she wouldn't be better off without him! Besides, you've no higher opinion of him than I have. He's a good-for nothing, useless, improvident dolt.' As an indignant afterthought he added: 'And don't talk back to me like that, in front of others!'

'I'll talk however I like!' She put an arm protectively around her daughter's shoulders, squeezing them so hard that her own body convulsed in time with Goose's sobs. 'Whatever else he may have been he was – is – her husband. And we don't know whose the body in the canal was. You only want it to be Red Macaw's so that people will believe either Flower Gatherer or Handy killed him!'

The old man's red-rimmed eyes glistened as he stared at his wife. 'After what that beast did to our daughter, you can defend him?' he gasped.

'I'm not defending anybody.'

Handy himself said nothing. He barely stirred, even at the mention of his own name. He seemed too wrapped up in his own thoughts to care what anyone said.

His sons, Snake and Spotted Eagle, were another matter, both starting forward and speaking at once. Snake cried: 'Father didn't do it!' while Spotted Eagle shouted: 'He couldn't have – look at him!'

Handy looked up through dull eyes, and mumbled: 'It isn't true. What you said about me and Star – it isn't true.'

Jaguar responded with a contemptuous snort.

Spotted Eagle turned on me then. 'And what about him?' With the exception of Goose, everyone looked in my direction, fixing me with glances that ranged from hostile to curious.

There was a long silence. I broke it hesitantly. 'I don't know whose body it was, in the canal. But I gather you all know Red Macaw is missing too.'

'He went to join the army,' said Spotted Eagle coolly.

'That's what he told the policeman,' I replied. 'You obviously know as much as I do about that. But there's another thing. Handy, I ran into an old friend of ours.'

I told him some of what had transpired between me and Huitztic. Nobody laughed when I got to the part when he fell in the canal.

Handy merely grunted: 'What do you think he was there for?'

'I've no idea, and I don't care either. It certainly wasn't to ask after my health. In fact he seemed surprised to see me. Maybe he was here for you – you run errands for lord Feathered in Black, don't you?'

'His steward comes here to give me orders sometimes. I don't think he's ever had any other reason to be in Atlixco,' the commoner admitted. 'But I've not seem him lately.'

Spotted Eagle said: 'He was probably here to gloat over what's happened. He's always been jealous of you, father, ever since lord Feathered in Black started trusting you to carry his messages.'

'Huitztic's jealous of everyone,' I added. 'Before the chief minister put me up for sale his steward did all he could to make my life a misery. I don't know why. Maybe it was because I could count to twenty without having to sit down and stare at my toes!' Then I thought about what Spotted Eagle had said. 'You could be right, about him wanting to gloat. He said something about your father...' I hesitated. As I recalled the steward's words, I hesitated, realising that it would mean broaching a dangerous subject. However, I had said too much already.

Spotted Eagle took a step towards me and leaned forward, bringing his face near to mine. 'Go on, then. You'd better tell us what he said.'

I looked at Handy. 'I didn't understand it. It was something about you and Red Macaw.'

Since his wife had died, there seemed to be only one way guaranteed to provoke a response from the commoner, and that was any mention of the three-captive warrior's name. Handy was still slumped against the wall of his house, but a tremor ran through his body as though he had been stung. He looked up sharply. 'What does Huitztic know about that?'

I whirled around at the sound of a harsh, explosive laugh from a few paces away. It was Jaguar, Handy's father-in-law, who had made the sound; however, his look, the way his lips were spread into a narrow grin, was one of triumph rather than mirth. I stared at the grim smile on Star's father's face in shock, recognising then that if Huitztic had indeed come here to gloat he might not have done so alone.

'That's a good question, isn't it, Handy?' the old man crowed. 'What does he know about it? What is there to know? Why don't you tell us?'

The commoner glared at his late wife's father. 'You know why. And if you had any shame at all you'd keep your filthy mouth shut.'

'Shame!' Jaguar cried. 'I'll tell you who ought to be ashamed. You, that's who. And you are, too. So ashamed you can't bear to hear about it even though we all know what they did!'

Handy struggled to his feet. His elder son started towards him anxiously but he waved him away. 'I told you to shut up!' he hissed. 'This isn't the time or the place.'

'To share a secret the whole parish has known for a dozen years?' the older man spat contemptuously. 'Why not?'

I looked at Spotted Eagle, who was standing between his father and grandfather. The young man's head was darting from side to side as he looked at each in turn, and he shook with agitation. Suddenly he took a step towards the old man. He raised a hand and I was afraid he was about to strike him; but at that moment Star's mother intervened.

We had barely noticed her as she stepped swiftly and silently across the courtyard. She pushed her way into the space between

Jaguar and Spotted Eagle. She glared silently at her grandson before spinning on her heel to face her husband. 'That will do!' she hissed. 'Remember who's here!'

'I don't care! And don't tell me what to do, woman. It's time there was one less secret here! We all know what we're talking about...'

'There are some who don't!' the old woman snapped. 'Just remember who's going to be hurt.'

'Hurt?' Jaguar screamed into her face. 'I've just lost my daughter, have you forgotten about that? And you talk about hurt!'

He was silenced with a sound like a stick breaking in two as the woman struck him, swinging her open hand against his cheek so hard he staggered sideways. He gasped and stared at her.

For a moment everyone was still. Then Handy said slowly: 'Get out of my house.' The old man rubbed his cheek. He looked at his wife, his son-in-law, the sky and the floor; then, gradually, he turned towards the gateway, dragging his heels as he went.

His son-in-law slumped back against the wall, letting out a long, shuddering breath.

A low wail sounded from the far side of the courtyard. Goose had rolled over onto her back and was staring up into the air, crying aloud for the first time since I had come to the house.

'Come on, both of you,' the old man called from the pathway outside. 'We're going!'

His wife ignored him. She darted to her daughter's side, cooing anxiously as she crouched over her.

Jaguar's parting words puzzled me at first.

'Handy!' he yelled, in a voice that must have carried the length

Tribute of Death

of the parish, 'how do your turkey chicks go on these days?'

It was a strange question and all the more so since, for so long as I had known him, Handy had never kept turkeys.

12

Night was falling, a clear, starry night that promised to be bitterly cold.

Goose and her mother had gone to bed, at her mother's insistence. They had taken the younger children with them, and then the old woman had come back to summon Spotted Eagle and Snake indoors. She ushered them through the doorway, insisting against their protests that they warm themselves by the hearth.

Handy showed no inclination to move, barely acknowledging the others as they left.

I paced the courtyard for a while, unable to make up my mind what to do. I was tempted to leave, to abandon Handy's family to their grief and recriminations, and head straight for Lily's house, where I knew I would be welcome and relatively safe. What stopped me was partly fear of the thing I had encountered the night before. I knew that the streets were not safe at night. However, there was something else. I had the feeling that I had been left alone with the commoner for a reason. Judging by the way Spotted Eagle had glowered at me as he was all but pushed inside by his grandmother, he expected me to fulfil some role. It was not necessarily one he approved of, but his grandmother would not have it any other way.

Eventually I squatted beside Handy, noting as I did so that, hunched over miserably as he was and with his face made haggard by hunger and lack of sleep, he looked smaller than usual.

I shivered, but it was not from the cold. I was afraid. I felt exposed and vulnerable here. I wondered how much safety there was behind a courtyard wall; was my enemy waiting, just beyond that frail barrier, ready to break through at any time he chose?

If so, I thought, I could not face the danger alone. It was all the more reason why I had to try to stir the man next to me out of his apathy.

'Handy...' I began. I looked down at the hard earth floor between us while I gathered my thoughts. When I met his eyes again I began speaking in a tone that I hoped was both firm and gentle: 'What are you going to do now?'

'I don't know. Sit here for a little longer, I guess, till it gets cold. Go indoors then. What about you?'

There was a dangerous quality in his voice, a lightness that betrayed how far detached his words were from what was going on inside his head.

I ignored his question.

'And after that?'

'Go to sleep. I expect. What's it to you?' He turned away, not just his face but his whole body, shuffling around so that he was looking into the opposite corner of the courtyard. Well, I had achieved something, I reflected wryly. It was probably the most he had moved since we had come back to the house.

'You reckon on going to sleep, then? When was the last time you did that?' There was a long pause. I thought the only answer I was going to get was silence, but what the man did in the end was to heave a long, shuddering sigh.

'You know,' he said softly. He tried to look at me then, but he could not hold my gaze for more than a moment. Instead of turning away now, though, he raised his hand, passing it in front of his eyes as if to brush away tears.

'I keep seeing her, you see,' he whispered. 'When I lie down. I can't close my eyes... And if I dream...' The last word vanished into a high, thin whine, like the wind in a treetop. He swallowed. 'Do you understand?' he gasped. 'It's how she was... Not when she was here, but afterwards. When we put her in that hole.'

I watched him steadily, not daring to say anything, but thinking that perhaps this was what we had been left together for.

'I can't see anything else,' he went on. 'I daren't go in, where it's dark, because then she'll be there like that – cold, stiff. Not how I knew her.'

Then he lowered the arm and was staring at me, wide-eyed, seemingly oblivious to the tears now pouring down his cheeks. 'Yaotl, I want her back, you know?'

'I know,' I said again, helplessly.

He stretched his hand out towards me, but dropped it. 'No, you don't. I know she can't come back, not really, not alive, but that's how I want to see her, do you understand that? As she was, laughing, grinding maize, running around after the bloody kids...' He suddenly seemed to feel the urge to move; to rise or turn around, I was not sure which, but whatever it was it made him lurch forward like a blind man, off balance, and I had to put my arms out to catch him before he toppled over.

Tribute of Death

We ended up in a clumsy embrace, the big commoner weeping in my arms. At last, I thought, I knew what this had all been about, and I realised how difficult it would have been for me to leave, while there was anything that might still be done to find Star's body. It had nothing to do with the fate of her soul, with whether or not it was destined to dwell in the Land of the Women and dance with the setting sun.

It was Handy's soul that was in jeopardy now. He needed something to put out of his mind the horrible memory of his wife's burial and the terror that had followed it, because until he found it, he would remember nothing else of her; and the image of that pathetic corpse being dragged across the city, dismembered and abused, forever hanging in front of his vision like a lure, might be enough to drive his spirit from his body.

'It's all right,' I whispered. 'My friend, we'll find her. We'll see her buried as she should be.'

His body was still shaking uncontrollably when the sun went down.

I persuaded Handy to go indoors, to stretch out his sleeping mat by the hearth. Eventually, exhaustion overcame him and he slept. From the way he tossed and turned and muttered throughout the night his dreams were obviously troubled, but he settled at last, seemingly so deeply asleep that whatever was haunting him had lost him and given up.

Snake and most of Handy's other children were already slumbering. Only Spotted Eagle remained awake and alert. He glared at me suspiciously for a while and then got up and went out into the courtyard without speaking. The anger that had driven him to attack me by his mother's empty grave had not gone away. The young man himself probably could not have told me what it was he blamed me for. For the moment it was enough that I was here and an outsider, and that my coming had coincided with the moment at which everything had started to go horribly wrong.

Tired though I was, I found it impossible to lie still. I was too afraid and too agitated to sleep. Instead I paced back and forth in the room, until the fading light from the fire in the hearth became too faint for me to do so without the risk of treading on someone.

I had a lot to think about.

I longed to be back with Lily, but I was confined to Handy's house, at least until the morning, by fear of what might be lurking outside.

It occurred to me that Spotted Eagle had posted himself by the gateway in order to prevent me from sneaking away. A grown man might have realised that there was no need. Fear notwithstanding, I did not have such a heart of stone that I could not be affected by his father's grief, and as I paced I found myself thinking about its causes, and the mysteries that surrounded them.

Somebody, during the previous night, had stolen Star's body. Presumably – because I could think of no other motive – he had done so in order to obtain charms that might be useful both to a sorcerer and a warrior. Flower Gatherer had vanished. Someone had died and been hidden in the nearby canal, but it was impossible to tell whether this was Flower Gatherer, Red Macaw – who was also missing – or indeed someone else altogether. Until it was known who the dead man in the canal had been, there was no way to tell why he had been killed.

I needed to get to the bottom of the mystery because at its heart was a greater one. What was the being that had attacked us and followed me through the streets after Star's burial? It had to have some connection with the theft; yet it had been seeking something more than the body of a dead mother. It had followed me through the streets and called me by my name.

13

I woke up with a start.

I was not aware of having gone to sleep. The last thing I remembered doing was squatting beside the hearth, staring into the embers and pulling my cloak around me for warmth while I thought about the troubles that beset me: both my own and Handy's.

Beside me, the big commoner was still curled up peacefully on his sleeping mat. I could hear his snoring, and the regular breathing of Snake and the other children. I could see him as well, a vague, still form on the floor. In my confused state, having been roused from a deep sleep, I thought at first that it was daylight shining faintly into the room. As I became more fully awake I recognised the light's silvery quality. It was still night-time and the moon was up.

I was aware that a sound had woken me up. Since everyone around me was unconscious, it must have come from outside.

I crept cautiously through the open doorway.

There was enough light for me to see Spotted Eagle, who as I had guessed was wide awake and squatting by the entrance. The young man turned around sharply at my approach.

'Relax,' I said coolly. 'I'm not about to run off. I'm afraid you've got a long way to go before you're as frightening as that thing out there!'

'Shut up and listen!' he hissed. 'Did you hear it?' Coming closer, I saw the pale gleam of his eyes: they were wide with terror. He may have come out here with the intention of stopping me from going out but I judged that was the last thing on his mind now.

'I heard something,' I said. 'I was asleep. I don't know what woke me up.'

The young man licked his lips nervously. 'It sounded like a scream.' He seemed for the moment at least to have forgotten his hostility towards me.

I felt a pricking at the back of my neck. 'What sort of scream?' I asked stupidly.

Instead of answering, he turned his head, looking in the direction of the doorway. 'It came from out there – by the canal.'

The waterway that ran past Handy's house was the same as the one that bordered the marketplace. I peered at it around the courtyard wall, but could see nothing in the gloom. 'How close?' I asked.

'Close enough!'

Courtyard walls stood on both sides of the canal. They would trap and magnify any sound, making it hard to tell where it had come from. Baffled, I withdrew from the doorway. 'Could be anything,' I said. 'An animal, maybe.'

'What kind of animal?' His voice shook. There were creatures of the night as terrifying as any demon; owls, racoons, weasels. To see or hear any of these after dark was said to be portent of death.

'It may be something harmless, or not even an animal at all. Some fool blundering into a canal at night.' I gave a hollow laugh; Spotted Eagle's nervousness was starting to get to me. 'You know, some young lord with a gourd of sacred wine, or a merchant going home from a feast, so full of mushrooms or peyote buttons he thinks he can fly…'

The young man interrupted me, hissing fiercely: 'What's that, then? That's no drunk!'

I fell silent. After a moment I caught the sound he had heard, and it made the hairs on the back of my neck stand up. I could not identify it, but it sounded like a voice, crooning softly, maybe singing or chanting, and there was something else like a shuffling of feet.

'Now would be a good time to tell me which members of your family sing in their sleep,' I murmured.

'It's coming from outside, Yaotl.'

'What is?' Fear made my throat contract so that I had to force the words out.

Spotted Eagle lurched to his feet. 'There's only one way to find out.'

I stared at him. 'You must be crazy! You've no idea what's out there!'

Astonishingly, he grinned at me. 'You have, though, haven't you? Think it's the otomi, come to get you?' The hint of a taunt in his voice stung me, but not enough to make me volunteer to go and see for myself.

'Listen,' I said. 'If that's who it is then believe me, you don't want to get involved! And if it isn't then it's none of our business.' I was trying to persuade the young man to stay where he was. I had no reason to feel concerned for his safety, but if anything happened to him, I did not want to be the one to have to tell his father about it.

He walked towards the exit. 'You forget,' he said shortly, 'I live here. This is my parish.' Kite would have been proud of him. He stood by the canal, looking to left and right. Reluctantly, I followed him. I felt more vulnerable alone in the courtyard than I did joining him outside it.

I lowered my voice. 'Shouldn't we wake your father?'

'I don't want to disturb him.'

The water of the canal reflected the sky as a wide, pale streak in the darkness at our feet. Walls loomed around us, throwing deep shadows over the paths on either side of the narrow waterway and making it hard to see anything else.

'We'd better go along the path for a bit and see what's there,' Spotted Eagle muttered. 'I'll go one way. You go the other.'

'I don't think that's a good idea...' I began, but he was already moving. I stayed where I was for a moment, irresolute, watching him vanish into the shadows. I was not sure whether to do as he had said or to follow him because it felt safer being in company.

My mind was made up by a sudden noise from somewhere behind me.

I started and whirled about. At first I could see nothing, only hear the sound that had caught my attention: that shuffling again, but louder now and closer, magnified to a rhythmic slapping. It was the sound bare feet would make, dancing on hard earth.

Peering fearfully into the darkness, I noticed movement. About twenty paces away a dark shape jerked erratically, seeming to approach and recede, a little like a flickering torch flame but almost as dark as its background. I stared at it, baffled, until I noticed an object that moved in time with its movements and the slapping sound, a short, narrow thing that gleamed palely in the moonlight.

The breath caught in my throat as I realised what I was looking at. The pale thing was part of a severed limb. There was someone just in front of me, dancing with a dead woman's forearm.

It looked as though I had found part of Star's body, and the sorcerer who had stolen it.

I stood, paralysed with terror, as the jerking feet brought the dancer now forward, now back, but always a little closer. I could hear breathing now, but no words. The stranger seemed oblivious to my presence, absorbed in the ritual.

I might have stood like that until he was close enough to plunge a knife into me – not asleep, but as helpless as if I had been – if Spotted Eagle's cry had not jerked me back to life.

'Yaotl! Over here!'

I started and whirled around, forgetting the person in front of me for an instant. A grunt, like the noise of someone disturbed in mid-snore, told me the dancer was surprised as well.

Spotted Eagle was invisible in the shadows, but what I could see was enough to freeze the blood in my veins.

It stood on the roof of a house, a shadow cast against the pale sky. It was impossibly tall for a man. Its shape was conical, slightly curved, like some great twisted root, but it had limbs like a man's that were bent as if in a crouch. It was preparing to leap onto the path below.

I dashed towards it, screaming: 'Spotted Eagle! Look out!' The thing vanished from my sight as it fell, landing with a loud, ungraceful clatter and a bellowing cry that may have been part pain and part rage. Distracted by my voice, it had mistimed its jump.

Feet thumped the path behind me. I heard rapid, shallow

breathing. A hand seized the material of my cloak.

I remembered the dancer then. It was too late and my assailant was too close for thought. Still running, I turned, almost losing my footing, and struck instinctively with my fist. The blow connected with something soft, halting the shadowy figure in mid stride. With a snarl, the strange figure staggered back and thrust the pale shape towards me. It was only a finger's breadth in front of my face. I could smell it: raw meat and a hint of rot.

Furious now, I lashed out again, but my target was too far away. I heard a giggle, a peculiar, high-pitched noise. I wondered whether the sorcerer had taken sacred mushrooms as part of the magic that was supposed to lull a household to sleep.

Unable to hit the dancer again, I screamed instead.

It may have been my shout or it may simply have been bafflement and fear at the failure of the charm to render me unconscious; but for whatever reason, the giggling stopped. In its place came a shocked silence, and then a strange, babbling, gibbering sound as the stranger backed away, then turned and bounded off into the night.

I took two steps in pursuit. Then I remembered the creature I had seen leaping off the roof, which was now presumably somewhere on the path behind me. I spun around again.

'Spotted Eagle?' I called nervously.

After a long, dreadful interval the youth's voice, shaky but clear, answered: 'Here. I'm all right. It ran off.'

I hesitated, fearing a trap, before walking cautiously towards him. 'What happened?'

'I think it hurt itself when it fell. It landed with a bit of a crash, anyway. It took a swipe at me with a sword, but I think one of its legs must have given way. Then all that screaming broke out over there and it staggered off.' He added in a shamefaced tone: 'I was too slow getting after it. I wasn't expecting anything like that!'

Judging by the catch in his voice, the shock had just begun to affect him. 'Yaotl,' he gasped, as I got close enough to see him and notice how pale and drawn his face looked in the poor light, 'What *was* it?'

'I don't know,' I admitted. 'Some kind of demon? My friend back there must have brought it with him.' I told him what had happened to me.

'You saw my mother's arm?' he cried in a strangled voice.

'I think so. I was like you, though – too shocked to do anything about it.' There was a pause. I tensed, waiting for an explosion of wrath from the youth, a tirade about my failure to recover the arm, more bitter reproaches for drawing this horror down upon his family.

Instead he said: 'That thing would have got me if you hadn't yelled.' After a further hesitation he added gruffly: 'Thanks.'

'Don't mention it,' I replied, embarrassed. Looking for a change of topic I went on: 'You saw something first, though, didn't you? What was it?'

His answer should not have surprised me. I should have anticipated it, considering why we had come out here, but it still came as a shock.

'A body.'

THREE FLOWER

•••

1

Spotted Eagle said that one of us ought to go at once to the parish hall, to alert Kite and his men. He changed his mind when I asked him where he thought our assailants had got to.

'They may have run off,' I said. 'Then again, they may be lurking around the next corner. Do you want to risk running into them again?'

'Not particularly,' he admitted.

'Wait until daylight. We'll be able to get a good look at this body then, as well.'

'Who do you think this is?'

There would be no answer to that question until the morning. If the body had been left in the same condition as the one Kite had shown me earlier, there was every chance we would not know even then. 'I couldn't begin to guess,' I said unhappily.

'Flower Gatherer and Red Macaw are still missing,' the youth mused.

'True. If it was either of them then we may know later on. Or not. For all we know this was just some poor sod who got in the way. Maybe we can find out when there's light enough to see. Kite won't like this, will he? Another unidentified body on his patch!'

I knew parish policemen. They were old soldiers who had settled down to a quiet life of arresting drunks, making sure no-one was cheated too outrageously in the local marketplace and rounding up labourers when the call went out for men to work on some big public project. They were not used to murder. 'We'll just have to wait.' I looked sideways at the young man and gave him a cautious grin. 'Do you still think I'm about to run away?'

He looked startled, and then laughed nervously. 'No chance! You're no more keen on braving whatever's roaming around out there than I am!'

Until dawn we kept a largely silent vigil over the inert form on the path. I reflected that one mystery had been solved, as it looked as if a sorcerer had been involved in robbing Star's grave. That told me nothing about who he was; nor whose body had been found in the canal by the marketplace, nor who the unfortunate creature that now lay in front of us might be. Above all we had no clue to who or what kind of being this sorcerer's accomplice might be. All I knew about that was that I had seen it before, following me through the streets after Star's burial. So it seemed had the midwives, and the fishermen, and we all agreed on one thing: its form was not human.

Dawn brought Handy out of his house, blinking and yawning in the early morning sunlight of what promised to be a bright, clear day. He stopped and stared when he saw his son and me examining the body.

'Father.' The young man leapt to his feet and went to him. 'Are you all right?'

Handy grimaced and rubbed his eyes. 'Better for a night's sleep… what happened out here, though?'

Tribute of Death

Before Spotted Eagle could say a word, I said to him: 'You can run and fetch your policeman, now. You'd better warn him this isn't pretty to look at!'

The dead man lay on his back. He had been wearing a cloak, but it was bunched beneath him, exposing his skin except where it was covered by a breechcloth. In the daylight it did nothing to conceal the full horror of his injuries.

His flesh seemed to have burst open, leaving long, deep gashes whose edges were pink but whose middles were dark with welling blood. Jagged bone and slick organs peeped out of some of them. An arm hung loose, ripped from its socket, and part of it was misshapen, crushed, the flesh torn as if by the claws of some savage beast. The face was almost whole, but blood had poured from every orifice in it: mouth, nostrils, ears, even the corners of his eyes.

Handy and I looked at it together. I let my eyes linger on the face, noting the wide, bloodshot eyes, lips curled back in agony, but searching for more: for some trace of what it might have been in life.

The commoner swore under his breath. 'What happened to him?'

'I'd guess he didn't just trip over and hit his head. You don't know him, I suppose? He's not Red Macaw or' - I looked over towards the house, where I assumed Goose was just rising to attend to her daily chores – 'or Flower Gatherer?'

'I don't know. He could be either of them, or anyone else. The state he's in, it's hard to tell.' He took his eyes off the body and looked at me. 'What happened?' he asked again.

I told him. I hesitated when I got to the part about the sorcerer and how he had brandished what I was sure must be Star's forearm. To my relief he merely shut his eyes and sighed.

'I'm sorry I couldn't catch him,' I said.

'It could have been worse. If I'd lost the boy as well…' The man shivered.

I regarded the mutilated corpse again. 'Obviously, it must have been his scream Spotted Eagle and I heard. The creature, or whatever it was, must have carved him up. Your son said it was armed.'

'Why do that, though? He must have been slashing away long after the man was dead.'

'He, or it, must have been out of control. Something happened to make it angry.' I swallowed hard as an unpleasant thought struck me. 'Perhaps they – the sorcerer and the demon – weren't expecting this man to be here. They wanted to get into a house, but he surprised them before the sorcerer's spell could work.'

'Whose house?' His hushed tone told me Handy had guessed the answer to his own question.

'Yours,' I told him grimly. 'Somebody stole your wife's forearm in order to get into your own house!'

He stared at me, 'Why…?'

Before he could get the rest of the question out, another voice – the last one I would have expected to hear – interrupted him, calling out of the twilight: 'Where is he?'

I stood and stared and felt my mouth fall open stupidly as the speaker came into view, striding purposefully towards us out of the early morning shadows.

'Where is he?' the woman demanded again, and then she was in front of me, and although I should have felt joy and relief, I was too shocked for either.

Lily's black hair flew wildly about her head, her eyes glistened and her bandaged hands were raised as if to strike someone. 'What do you mean by this?' she screamed. The words were barely intelligible. 'What do you think you're doing?'

I cowered. I took a step backwards. 'Lily, I can explain…'

'You were supposed to be here one day! A day! That was two days ago. Do you have any idea…'

Handy tried to intervene: 'Didn't you get our messages…'

'Of course I got your messages. Why do you think I'm here? That's not the point!' Suddenly she kicked me, lashing out with a bare foot and catching my kneecap. I cried out in pain, and then she was in my arms, sobbing uncontrollably. 'Yaotl, I've been so worried. I couldn't sleep. Why didn't you come?'

'It's a long story,' I whispered into her hair. 'But why are you here? Don't you know how dangerous it is?'

I looked up to catch Handy's eye. After staring at us in mute astonishment for a moment he shook his head violently and said: 'Er… Have I got this right? This is Lily? You *are* her slave, yes?'

'That's a long story too.' I turned back to Lily. I was about to ask her again why she had left the safety of her own house to come here. However, I was distracted by the sound of running feet, the flat thump of sandals striking hard earth.

Spotted Eagle came into sight, his face nearly black with the exertion of running all the way to the parish hall and back. He was barefoot, naturally, as a commoner in the city. The sound had been made by the man following him: Kite the policeman, wrapped in his long cloak and brandishing an obsidian-bladed sword as though he were expecting a fight. He skidded to a halt when they saw us.

'Father!' The young man went straight up to Handy before

halting and staring at Lily.

'What's happened here, then?' the policeman demanded. In answer, Handy gestured towards the thing on the ground

Spotted Eagle had told the policeman what to expect. It ought not to have come as a surprise, but he faltered, turning slightly pale, when he set eyes on the corpse.

Beside me, Lily screamed. It was only long afterwards that it occurred to me that she had been so angry and delighted at the sight of me that she had failed to notice the dead man. I had to steady her now to prevent her from falling. She was as brave as any warrior, but what lay at her feet would have turned the stomach of the most accustomed butcher.

Kite looked the body over. He asked whether anyone recognised the dead man. Nobody did. He asked Lily who she was and what she was doing here. He made both me and Handy give our own accounts of what had happened in the night, although all Handy could say was that he had been asleep. From the way he barked his questions it was obvious that, as I had predicted, he was not pleased. 'So now I have another unidentified corpse, besides sorcerers, demons, thieves...' He glanced at me and gestured towards Handy's house. 'You think they were trying to get in here?'

'It looked that way.'

'Why?'

Handy said: 'I was just about to ask Yaotl that myself, before you turned up.'

The policeman had the answer to that. 'They were after you, weren't they?' he said, looking at me. 'You said the sorcerer – if that's what the dancer was – called you by your name. So did whoever followed you the night before last.'

Spotted Eagle's features suddenly twisted into a look of revulsion. 'You mean my mother's body was stolen just so that someone could break into the house and kill this slave?' He spat the words out disgustedly, but the energy that had been behind his attack on me of the previous morning had gone. All he could manage now was a half-hearted snarl. 'So you did bring this on us, after all.'

'I didn't mean to,' I protested wearily, 'and if I did, I don't understand how. Maybe the otomi captain had something to do with it, but how could he have known where to find me, and so quickly? I'd only been here a day the first time I was attacked.'

'I know.'

We all turned to look at Lily. She had recovered somewhat from her earlier shock and was standing unsupported, but there was an audible tremor in her voice all the same. 'It's easy, isn't it? The chief minister lied to you. He hasn't lost control of the captain at all. They're still working together. He knew you were likely to come here.'

For some reason – no doubt because it was such an unpleasant idea – this had not occurred to me. It made perfect sense, of course. Why should I assume that my former master had suddenly forgotten his grudge against me?

I tried in vain to protest: 'No, he didn't! Who'd have told him?' But it carried no conviction. How like the vindictive old bastard, I thought, to lull me into a false sense of security by pretending he and the otomi had fallen out. Now my situation was more hopeless than ever, trapped between the two of them.

Handy said: 'His steward saw you yesterday.'

Kite smiled humourlessly. 'Well, that would solve my problem.

All I have to do is hand you over to lord Feathered in Black!'

Listening to these two was like being left by a roadside with a copper knife stuck in you, and having passers-by come and twist it this way and that for fun. 'You can't do that!' I cried. 'I'm a slave, remember? Lily, tell him he can't do that!'

'You don't need to,' she assured Kite. 'I'll take charge of my slave. If I take him back to Tlatelolco, whoever's after him will follow us, surely? And I think we merchants can look after ourselves, otomi or no otomi!'

They were brave words, but I could see from the pulse in her neck that Lily understood just how dangerous that course of action might prove to be. Even the chief minister might hesitate to try his strength against that of the merchants, but the fact remained that lord Feathered in Black and the captain had once invaded the sanctuary of her house in Tlatelolco, and they might do so again. But I was denied the chance to say so.

My reply, together with whatever else anyone might have been about to say, was choked off by the sound of a scream.

Several moments passed before I recognised the woman who had just come through the gateway to Handy's courtyard as his sister-in-law. She looked as though she had been struck down by some wasting sickness. Her hair hung lankly about her temples, its strands as tangled and ragged as if she had tried to tear them from her own scalp. He eyes were red, her cheeks hollow, and her skin was as grey as a stone.

As I watched her stumble towards us, her sunken eyes fixed on the bloody mess on the ground in our midst, I realised that the sounds and smells of sweeping and cooking that normally echoed around an Aztec courtyard at daybreak had not been there this morning. Goose had not risen to do her customary tasks. She seemed to have forgotten about them.

We men watched her in stupefied horror, appalled at the change that had come over this woman. It was Lily who reacted, pushing me and Spotted Eagle aside and running to her side. 'What is it?' she cried, unthinkingly stretching her bandaged hands towards her. 'What's the matter?'

Goose stared blankly at her.

'Yaotl!' my mistress snapped, 'stop staring at us like a five year-old watching his parents on their sleeping mat! Come and help!'

Torn from my reverie, I stepped over to them, taking Goose's unresisting arm in mine. 'We must go into the house,' Lily told her firmly. 'There's food to prepare. Your children will be hungry.'

We led the stumbling, snuffling woman back into Handy's courtyard. Handy, Kite and Spotted Eagle were left to follow.

2

Goose kept apologising. 'I'm sorry. I'm so sorry. It was the shock, seeing him there... At first I thought...' The words tailed off into a series of dry sobs.

Lily had made her sit against a wall in Handy's courtyard, ordering me to lower her gently to the ground under the astonished gaze of her children, nieces and nephews. The youngsters had not been allowed to stand and stare for long, because my mistress had orders for them too. She set the boys to sweeping, ignoring their protests at being given women's work, while the girls were told to make the tortillas. Finally she sent Handy indoors to make sure nobody spilled any hot coals or kicked over a hearthstone, which would be the worst kind of bad luck.

As the household bustled into life around us, Lily said gently: 'You thought it was your husband?'

Goose wiped her eyes with the knuckles of one hand. 'Until I saw him.'

'You're sure it wasn't him?' I asked. 'How can you know?'

'I just know. Even after what's been done to him, there's no way that could be Flower Gatherer.' She let out a sound that was something between a moan and a wail. 'I was doing so well, until then, wasn't I? I knew someone had to keep it all together, and it had to be a woman, and with Star gone, that left me... Lily, you understand, don't you? I got so tired!' I remembered how she had been the day before, prostrated upon the floor while her parents and her brother-in-law argued around her.

'I know,' Lily confirmed, with the authority of a woman who, at various times, had lost her husband and her son and seen her father degenerate into an idle, drunken old reprobate. 'I know how hard it is.'

'I'm sorry,' Goose mumbled once more. 'I should be stronger.'

'Can we get anyone to help?' Kite asked. The policeman had been hovering awkwardly nearby, having apparently run out of useful things to do after sending Spotted Eagle back to the parish hall to summon assistance removing the body from outside the house.

Lily said: 'Could someone fetch your parents? Your mother...'

'No!' Goose cried vehemently. 'You can't ask my mother. She'd bring my father, and then there be sure to be a fight.'

'Over what?'

Goose frowned at Lily, as though unsure whether the question was a serious one. She forgot momentarily that my mistress had not seen or heard the clashes between Handy and Jaguar. Hastily, I tried to explain: 'Goose's father seems to blame Handy for what happened to Star. I got the idea they don't exactly see eye-to-eye on a lot of things.'

'My father didn't care much for either of our husbands – mine or my sister's. Hers especially.' She gave a watery smile. 'Odd, isn't it? Star made a better marriage that I did. Flower Gatherer was never anything but a labourer. Handy was a warrior – for a time, anyway. But I suppose they thought they'd made a mistake with him. They knew she could have done better.'

'How?' I asked.

For some reason the question seemed to confuse her. Her face, that had been pale, darkened, and she looked away. 'I don't know,' she muttered, almost inaudibly. 'Maybe she ought to have married a rich merchant.'

Lily, the daughter and widow of merchants, laughed shortly. 'Believe me, girl, she was better off as she was!'

'I don't understand, though,' I said. 'Last night they were arguing about Red Macaw. And this big secret that Jaguar was about to blurt out before your mother stopped him.'

Kite groaned and rolled his eyes. 'Oh, that!'

'Yes, *that*.' Goose's tone was earnest. She leaned forward, looking imploringly at the policeman. 'You know we can't talk about it. You know we can't even say why, Kite. And you know we trust you.'

He turned to me and Lily with an apologetic sigh. 'True enough. One of the first things you learn as a parish policeman is what questions not to ask!'

Avoiding Goose's reproachful eyes, I said: 'But it's different now, surely? Red Macaw's disappeared, Flower Gatherer's disappeared, you've got monsters and what not tearing up the place and two unidentified corpses. Not to mention the theft of a woman's body. Now when you know there's a long-standing quarrel between one of your vanished men and the dead woman's husband, how can you tell us you don't want to know what it's about?'

For the first time since I had met him, Kite looked ill at ease. 'I didn't say I don't want to know,' he said defensively, 'but you've got to understand – I have to look after these people, but I've got to live among them too.'

'Why don't you ask his mother?'

We all three turned to look at the speaker.

Snake, Handy's son, the one aged about twelve, had been put in charge of sweeping the courtyard. He had not been making a particularly good job of it, largely because he was more intent on what the grown ups around him were saying than on the sacred duty of brushing the loose earth into the street outside. Now he leaned on his broom and repeated his suggestion. 'Why don't you ask Red Macaw's mother? I bet she could tell you.'

'We could do that,' Kite said slowly. 'You talk as if you know her.'

The boy threw a fearful glance over his shoulder, looking towards the interior of the house, before approaching us and saying in a lowered voice: 'Don't tell my father.'

Goose appeared paralysed. She merely stared at her nephew while Lily assured him: 'We won't, if you tell us why.'

'You know what my father's like about Red Macaw,' Snake said warily. 'I'm not supposed to know anything about him.'

'But you know his mother?' Lily said.

'And I know where he lives.'

'How? Did you follow him home?'

The boy looked shamefaced then, lowering his eyes. 'Not exactly. More the other way around, really.'

'Snake, will you stop talking in riddles?' I said, exasperated.

'I'm not! I was coming back from the fields – my father farms a piece of parish land, a *chinampa* plot out on the lake, opposite Mixoacan island…'

'Do we need to know where your father grows his beans?'

'Just let him get on with it, Yaotl,' my mistress ordered.

The boy went on: 'This man called out to me, when I'd almost got home. I'd have taken no notice of him, but he was a three captive warrior, and I thought he might be the chief minister's steward. I know father works for lord Feathered in Black sometimes.'

I could not resist a brief chuckle at that. 'You thought Red Macaw was Huitztic? I doubt he'd be flattered!'

Kite said: 'So what did he want?'

'That first time? Not much. He just asked me how I was, how my mother was. He said he'd heard she was expecting another child.'

'And when was this?'

'Last year. Around the time of the Festival of the Sweeping of the Roads.' Late in the previous Summer, in other words.

'You've seen him since?' Kite asked.

'Sometimes. He's often about in Atlixco, in the marketplace or by the canal, especially if he knows father isn't around.'

'Where did he hear about your mother's pregnancy?'

'It's common knowledge in this parish. Anything like that is.' I could accept that. News travelled fast in the crowded parishes of Mexico, and Handy and Star would have had no reason to keep this quiet. I wondered whether Red Macaw had been asking after them, and if so for how long he had been more-or-less discreetly probing into their affairs; and why, more to the point.

'So he asked you how your parents were doing...'

'Mother,' the boy corrected the policeman. 'He didn't say anything about father.'

'So he asked after your mother. What else?'

Tribute of Death

'Lots of different things. What I was doing, when I was going to start at the House of Youth, that sort of thing. He said when I was old enough he'd show me some tricks with a sword.'

'What did he want to know about your mother, though?' Lily asked.

'He said he'd like to know when the baby was born. He offered to give me a present if I went and told him.'

Hearing Snake's words was like finding a juicy-looking custard apple only to discover, on breaking it open, that instead of soft ripe flesh the interior was a mass of mould and maggots. 'You were his spy,' I accused him.

'No, I wasn't!' the lad cried, stung. 'At least... I didn't mean to be. Honestly, all he wanted to know was that the baby had been born, and how my mother was, that was all. I thought it wouldn't matter. After all, we would all have run through the streets shouting it out when my brother was named, weren't we?'

It was the custom when the midwife baptised a new child for his siblings to announce it to the World. I contemplated Snake's face. It bore a strange expression, a mixture of fear, defiance and bewilderment. I realised the boy was desperate to be reassured that he had done nothing wrong, but he was also baffled by the turn events had taken. He wanted someone to tell him that his meetings with Red Macaw had nothing to do with what had happened to his mother and to her body afterwards.

After a few moments, he added, in a subdued, sulky tone: 'Anyway, it's not just me. Osier Twig knows them too.'

' "Them"?'

'Red Macaw and his mother. Who do you think the old lady was

– the one my sister met in the marketplace – when she was sent to look for the midwife?'

'Cactus told us she was one of his customers,' I said.

'She was at his stall, sure. But she told Osier Twig who she was. And to give me her regards, and her son's.'

Before I could speak Lily said: 'It doesn't matter. Neither of you has done anything wrong.' She frowned at Kite and me, silently telling us to keep quiet for a moment. 'Snake,' she said, 'Do you have any idea why Red Macaw might have wanted to ask these questions?'

'I've no idea. I knew father didn't like him, but I don't know what he thought about my family. He always seemed friendly enough. So did his mother, the one time I met her. They didn't want me to tell mother or father they'd talked to me.'

'And you didn't know anything about them, beyond what they told you?'

'No. I'd never heard of Red Macaw before he spoke to me, and before he came to the house after mother died, I didn't know for sure that father even knew him.'

'Did you ever go to his house?'

'Once,' the boy admitted. 'He asked me to. Are you going there now? Can I come?'

Kite said doubtfully: 'Don't you have chores? Things to do at home?'

The boy looked at the ground. 'There's nothing for me to do here except get in the way.'

'You could finish the job you were told to do,' his aunt snapped. 'And I've a good mind to tell your father what you've told us. What were you thinking of, talking to Red Macaw? Do you realise what that man's done?'

To my amazement, my mistress rounded on her. 'Of course he doesn't!' she snapped. 'That's the whole problem, here, isn't it? It's a secret. There are too many bloody secrets!'

Goose lurched to her feet and tottered towards Lily, her red-rimmed eyes all but popping out of her head in anger. 'This can't come out!' she hissed. 'Especially now, with the boy here.'

The broom hit the ground with a clatter. 'That's it!' the youngster piped, outraged. 'You can go on talking as long as you like! I'm going to ask her myself!' And before anyone could think of stopping him, Snake was out of the courtyard, running in the direction of Atlixco plaza.

Lily, Kite and I stared at each other. Without a word, we turned to follow him.

'Wait!' Goose cried. 'You don't understand!'

'If you have your way, we never will,' I muttered, but I did not say it aloud. I wanted all my breath for running.

Beside me, Lily panted: 'That poor woman. Don't they realise her son's gone missing too?'

3

Red Macaw and his mother lived in a house almost identical to Handy's. Lily, Kite, Snake and I reached it, just as the sun rose above the tops of the neighbouring buildings, by walking beside and crossing several other waterways that were all but indistinguishable from each other. By the time we arrived I was lost. This was no more than what I expected, but it was a reminder of how far my experiences as a priest and a great lord's slave had taken me away from the everyday life of the common people. A typical Aztec was born and died in the same parish, coming to know the same few streets, plazas and canals as well as he knew his own courtyard, and seldom venturing further afield unless ordered to, as part of a work detail or a war party. Even then, though the army took him half way across the world, he would be surrounded by men he had grown up with. I felt a moment's regret for a life spent away from home. It would be as much as I could manage now to remember how to get from my mother's hearth to the local market.

'It's this one,' Snake announced, before stepping up to the front doorway and calling out through the wicker screen that hid the inside of the house from our view.

For a long time there was no answer. Eventually, just as we were about to give up and go away, we heard a shuffling from beyond the doorway and a scraping sound as the screen was pulled back.

The doorway opened directly into a room, and in the gloom inside it was difficult at first to make out details of the person looking at us. All I could see clearly at was a pair of eyes, squinting painfully up at us from a position at about the height of my chest.

When she came forward into the light, we saw the silver-haired figure of an old woman, so stooped with age that she was bent almost double.

She looked steadily back at each of us in turn. 'What do you want?' she demanded querulously. I wondered whether she might have been more co-operative if Kite had brought his sword with him, but he had diplomatically left it at Handy's house.

I opened my mouth to respond, but shut it again without a word. Instead I found myself staring at the dark, wrinkled face in front of me, startled into silence. To my amazement I realised that I had seen this woman before, although at first I could not remember where.

Lily said: 'Xiuhtonal, We need to talk to you.' Snake had given us the name, which meant 'Precious Light.'

'If it's about my son, I've already told the police everything I know.' She glared at Kite. 'Unless you've come to tell me you found his body.'

'No,' The policeman replied quickly.

The old woman's expression did not change in response. I continued to gaze at her leathery features, squinting as though that would bring them into sharper focus. Where else had I seen them?

Kite added mildly: 'You didn't tell us everything.'

Snake cried: 'But it is about Red Macaw. Him and my father!'

Precious Light looked at him with interest. 'Your father,' she said slowly. 'You mean that man Handy.'

Lily joined in then: 'We're very sorry, but it's important.'

'It's not just about him and Red Macaw now.' Kite added. 'There have been deaths. There was one last night, and…' He might as well have been talking to himself, because the woman's ancient, red-rimmed eyes were fixed on my face. I found their gaze hard to meet. The moment I looked away was when she chose to speak. 'I've seen you before.'

I seemed to have been waiting for that to shake loose the memory. 'At Handy's house,' I said wonderingly. 'You were in the burial party. You led the women to the house, before Goose took over, and you spoke to him after they'd knocked the wall down And it was you who made the speech at the graveside.'

'I didn't do it for him,' she said softly. 'It was for her. I knew she would need us: the women. I bore her no ill-will. She might have been any of us.'

'Are you another midwife?' I asked.

The question seemed to surprise her. She paused before answering, and when she did it was in an even sharper voice than before, as though I had accused her of something: 'No!' she cried, so vehemently that I flinched. 'I'm an old woman, that's all. Just an old woman who's seen too many of her friends put underground.' She caught her breath, as though fearful that she might go on to say something she would regret, and turned deliberately away from me to talk to the boy. 'I was expecting you sooner, young man. You'd better come in. But I can't offer you any of you anything to eat. Now that I'm alone, I don't know where my next meal is coming from.'

Tribute of Death

Before any of us could ask her what she had meant, she had turned around and disappeared within her house, leaving us to follow.

Once through the doorway we found ourselves in a small, well-kept courtyard. Snake, Kite and I squatted, Lily kneeled, and the old woman remained standing, explaining that if she once got down on the floor it would take her a long time to get up again. She appeared to be alone in the house, but she had not been shirking her domestic duties, as the place was spotless, the whitewash on the walls gleaming in the morning sunshine.

Once we were all settled, an uncomfortable silence descended, persisting for a few moments until the old woman decided it was time to speak. I had the uncomfortable feeling that she was going to dictate whatever was said and done within her own walls, and that here not even the emperor's word carried more weight.

'You said this was about my son,' she said abruptly, 'but my son is dead.'

'We don't know that,' I put in. 'The police don't know whose the bodies are.'

'He is dead,' she asserted again. 'If not here, then in some other place: some mountain pass or freshly turned over field or at the top of some barbarian city's pyramid. You know this,' she said to Kite.

The policeman looked unhappy. 'He said he was going to try to join the army. I haven't seen him since, so I don't know whether he made it.'

'It doesn't matter. You know what he wanted.'

I remembered my conversation with the policeman on the rooftop of the parish hall, how he had suspected that the old three-captive warrior had gone looking for a flowery death. 'Why, though?' I wondered aloud.

She turned scornful eyes on mine. 'Only a slave would ask that. All warriors crave death by the obsidian knife. What other reason did he need?'

'But why now, after all these years?' Kite asked.

The old woman did not answer, but she did not need to. It was obvious, I realised, if we just accepted what she said, and took it for granted that her son had followed the warrior's calling. Then Kite's question was the only one left to be answered.

'What's changed?' I was thinking aloud. 'He hasn't fought for years, and suddenly decides to go to war one last time. Something prompted him to do that. Maybe it was a soothsayer casting an augury, but I bet it wasn't.' I regarded the woman once more, and this time it was her turn to look away. 'It was Star's death, wasn't it? How blind we've all been! That's what the big quarrel was about!'

I heard a small sound from Lily, a suppressed gasp. When I turned towards her I saw her staring at me, her eyes slowly widening as she grasped my meaning.

'What are you talking about?' Snake asked.

Red Macaw's mother looked carefully at him. 'Tell me something, boy.'

The youngster scowled at her rebelliously. 'What?'

'You knew my son, didn't you? He used to talk to you in the street.'

'Yes.'

'Did he ask you about your mother?'

'Sometimes. What's this all about?'

She turned away from him then and fixed her sharp, bright eyes upon Lily.

Lily met her gaze steadily and said: 'I understand.'

'Well, I don't!' the boy cried. He lurched awkwardly to his feet. 'What are you all talking about?'

Precious Light moved a brown, bony arm, the loose and wrinkled skin seeming to fall away from it like a fold of cloth as she stretched out a hand in Snake's direction. The gesture puzzled me, but my mistress caught her meaning.

'Er... Snake...'

The lad got to his feet. In a choked voice he muttered: 'I'm thirsty. I'm going to go and get some water.'

I never knew whether it was tact beyond his years, fear of what he might learn if he stayed or simple embarrassment that made him get up and leave at that point, but I watched him stumble from the room with a mixture of relief and pity.

'He'll be better off alone for a moment,' Red Macaw's mother advised us. 'And I want you to hear this, anyway. Then you judge for yourself what to tell the boy.'

She was looking at me again. Her gaze was uncomfortable. There was something in it that reminded me of my former master, the ancient lord Feathered in Black. Like his, her eyes seemed like those of someone much younger than she was, clear, sharp and bright with a feral kind of intelligence, and the old woman had the chief minister's way of staring straight at me that was rare among Aztecs.

'My son never married. Unheard of, isn't it? Especially for a successful warrior. It wasn't as if he couldn't have had his pick of the girls in this parish: I knew that much even when he was still at the House of Youth, before he'd taken his first captive. But Red Macaw didn't want to know. He never showed the least sign of wanting to give his stone axe to the Masters of Youth, though he could certainly have afforded to.' The stone axe was the symbolic price a man paid for his release from the House of Youth, traditionally presented at a costly feast, laid on at his family's expense, when he wanted to marry. 'I heard rumours – people were whispering about him, in the end, asking if he might be… might be a…' She found it hard to say the word, even now. Sodomy was a capital crime, punished by burning alive, and a great disgrace.

'But he wasn't, was he?' Lily said.

'No. No, it wasn't that. It was a woman.'

'Star.'

'I didn't understand it at first – not for years, in fact. But what stopped my son from marrying was that he'd fallen in love. And for some reason he thought that meant he couldn't have anyone else. And don't ask me where's the sense in that! I don't know where they met. Though I suppose it can't have been difficult, growing up within a few streets of each other. He must have seen her while he was on the way to the fields or the House of Youth and she was going to the market with her mother or taking flowers to the temple.'

'But she married Handy,' I said.

'Her family may not have given her much choice in the matter. If she was anything like me, she probably didn't even meet her husband until their wedding.'

And after that, I suppose, Star had made the best of it. I had a sudden painfully vivid recollection of how she had been in life: a busy, practical woman, fully occupied in supervising her large household even in late pregnancy.

Tribute of Death

'Well, it explains the turkey chicks, anyway,' I said.

Kite asked 'What turkey chicks?'

'Handy's father in law asked how his turkey chicks were doing. You know what they say: the presence of an adulterer kills them – they just fall over and die.'

Red Macaw's mother closed her eyes for a few moments, and I wondered what she was seeing behind their lids: her son as she had last seen him, perhaps, or as he had been as a young man, or possibly as he might be now.

'I'm not ashamed of what my son did. I'm too old for that. There were rumours. I heard them in the marketplace, and in other women's houses when I went visiting. Gossip, whispers that suddenly stopped when I entered the courtyard. I ignored them.'

'How did it happen?' Kite asked.

'It was years ago, twelve or thirteen, I think. Most of the men in this parish were called up to go to war. My son had been wounded on his last expedition and couldn't accompany them. So he stayed at home.'

I could guess the next part. 'But Handy went.'

'It seems so.'

'And while he was away…'

'Red Macaw was at home to start with, recovering from his wounds. Then he got better. There wasn't any work to be done in the fields, since it was winter. So in the end he was left without much to do except potter around the parish...'

'And go calling on old friends.' Kite completed the sentence for her. 'No wonder nobody would ever tell me what the big secret was.'

The old woman agreed. 'It wasn't a thing for a policeman's ears.

It would have meant death for both of them. Even her husband wouldn't have been able to save her.'

'How long did this go on?' I asked.

'All winter, I suppose, and into the spring. Throughout the campaigning season. Why she allowed it to happen in the first place, I don't know. She was bored and lonely, I suppose, and perhaps things between her and her husband weren't good. I gather her parents regretted their choice of a bridegroom for her quite quickly.' The last words came out with an unpleasant cackle. 'She ended the affair before the warriors returned – but I think it was a long war.'

'And what did your son do then?'

'Nothing. I couldn't understand it. It was as if he were waiting for something to happen. And even when it did, he seemed to go on waiting, and watching from a distance. I couldn't persuade him to move on, or let go.'

Lily asked quietly: 'What was the thing that happened?'

I glanced out of the doorway, towards where I supposed the boy to be lurking, assuming he had had his drink and not simply gone home. I tried not to think about how we were going to answer his inevitable questions. I tried to put myself in his position, asking myself how I might feel if I had just discovered for the first time that my mother had been an adulteress, but I could not imagine it. I was fairly sure that any man making improper suggestions to my mother could count himself lucky if she merely threw him into the nearest canal.

When I turned back to the old woman I found that she had been looking in the same direction as I had. And to my astonishment, I saw that she was weeping, tears making thin, glistening tracks over her cheeks.

'He was born nine months after they parted,' she whispered. 'He doesn't know.'

It was now obvious why Handy and his family had been so reluctant to talk about his relationship with Red Macaw. They had been trying to protect his dead wife's reputation and hide the truth from the child who believed he was his.

Precious Light was weeping for her grandson.

Snake rejoined us, to sit in brooding silence while Kite and I told Precious Light what had been happening in the parish since her son had left. She listened with apparent indifference while we described the bodies we had found and the attack on Spotted Eagle and me during the night.

'So now you're looking for sorcerers and monsters,' was all she could find to say when we had finished.

'And a three-captive warrior who lost part of his cloak,' Kite added. 'Which is what made us think of Red Macaw.'

'What would my son be doing following a woman's funeral procession?' Precious Light snapped. 'He'd have no use for a warrior's charm. He didn't want to be invincible!'

'Still, it needs explaining,' Kite persisted. 'Look at it this way. If it wasn't him the midwives saw, who was it? I'm afraid we have to think about the possibility that it might have been someone or something he'd run into earlier – someone who took his cloak from him, perhaps.' He paused to see how Precious Light would respond to that suggestion, but she did not so much as flinch. 'It could be you next,' he added quietly. 'Anyone capable of what these creatures have done is a threat to all of us.'

For the second time she uttered an unpleasant, cackling laugh. 'Not to me! I never go out at night!'

'You've lived here all your life, though,' I said, 'and you must know a lot of what goes on. Come to think of it, you do know Cactus, don't you? I'm not sure about him – he could be a sorcerer.'

Precious Light looked taken aback. 'Cactus?'

Snake broke his silence. 'You know. You're a customer of his. My sister met you both in the marketplace.'

The old woman's expression cleared. 'Oh, I remember now. Yes, I buy herbs from him from time to time. They're for making up poultices, for my back. It's all those years bending over a spindle! He's no sorcerer, thought, surely? Just a curer. But he's very good and very attentive.'

'Cactus, though. It's a coincidence that you know him.' I explained to Lily: 'I met him at Handy's house.'

'Its not really that odd,' said Snake. 'This isn't a big parish. I'd seen him before.'

'He's become quite a well-known figure,' Kite put in. 'He's taken to giving away free samples of herbs to drum up business. He's not done anything wrong that I know of.'

'Curers and sorcerers aren't so very different, though,' Lily said. 'You need to be careful. And if this one is going to start attacking people in their homes, then it doesn't matter if you never go out.'

'I've nothing to fear,' Precious Light replied scornfully. 'What have I got to live for anyway? It's not as if anyone would miss me.'

She looked down at Snake then, and it was hard for me to read her expression, but I noticed the skin stretching and slackening over her cheekbones as though a range of feelings were chasing each other across her face. 'We weren't like your mother and Handy, boy.' Her voice was calm but suddenly hoarse. 'My husband and I didn't have a houseful of healthy children to see us into our old age. We lost most of them while they still lay on their cradleboards. Then my husband died. Only Red Macaw survived. Now he's gone.'

Snake made a fist and let it drop heavily into his lap. 'We won't see our mother into her old age,' he said quietly.

The old woman gave him a thin smile. Perhaps it was intended to look sympathetic. 'I know,' she replied.

4

Lily was watching Snake. The boy walked quickly in front of us as we made our way back from Red Macaw's house towards Handy's. 'What do you suppose he's thinking?' she asked.

'Do you think he's guessed about Red Macaw and his mother then?'

She gave an exasperated sigh. 'Yaotl, the only person I know who would be too stupid to guess is you!' She quickened her pace suddenly and called after the boy. He stopped and half-turned his head.

'What was that about?' Kite asked me in a whisper.

'No idea,' I said wearily. 'I suppose I'm too stupid to guess what she meant!'

Lily had caught up with Snake. He acknowledged her without turning his head. 'What?'

'Snake, are you all right?'

'Sure. Why wouldn't I be?'

Lily faltered then, and even I could see that for now, the lad was probably better left alone with his thoughts. Hurrying after them, I asked: 'Where you going now?'

While my mistress glared at me in silence Snake mumbled: 'I'd better be getting back now. They'll be wondering where I've gone. I can find my own way, though. You don't have to come with me.'

'But we're going the same way,' Lily protested.

'What for?' the boy demanded. His tone was bitter. 'Haven't you caused enough trouble already?' His truculence reminded me of his eldest brother.

'Your father doesn't think so,' I said.

'What does he know?' The words burst from him, forced out between the sobs he was trying to suppress. Lily, crouching, extended a wounded hand towards him, but he brushed it aside. 'He didn't want me to hear about my mother. So I didn't, until you took me to that old woman's house!'

'Nobody took you. We followed you.'

He took no notice of my interruption. 'Now you're going to boast to him about knowing his little secret, I suppose!'

'Don't be stupid,' I said impatiently.

He was still flinging words at me. 'Of course you'll tell him how sorry you are, how much you understand how he's hurting, but it'll be you who's caused it! All you've done with your meddling is make everything worse!'

'That's enough, boy!' Kite snapped. He stepped towards him, glowering threateningly.

However, Lily was standing again now and the policeman found her barring his way, her expression stricken but determined. 'Be careful,' she warned.

The boy darted behind her. 'You're no better!' he cried. 'Have you done anything to find my mother's body? Do you have any idea where Flower Gatherer is? I don't think so!'

Kite clenched his fists, but there was nothing he could do unless he were prepared to shove the merchant's widow to one side in order to get at Snake; and Lily was not moving. 'It's not his fault either,' she said, in a trembling voice. 'Let him be.'

'You go where you like!' the lad called out, as he ran along the canal path towards his house. 'But don't come near me!'

Lily turned to watch him go. When she took her eyes off him, I thought Kite might spring after the boy, to fetch him a clip around the ear for his cheek, but all he did was let out a low whistle.

'I'm sorry,' my mistress said without looking around. 'But you have to let him go.'

'Oh, I know that,' the policeman assured her. 'But I do have to go back to Handy's house, anyway. I left my sword there.' He glanced at each of us in turn, smiling thinly. 'I hope after all that's happened we all know each other well enough for me to trust you not to go running off anywhere?' And with that he stepped delicately past the woman and walked with a measured gait the way the boy had gone.

As soon as he was out of sight I breathed a deep sigh. 'Well, that's that. Where do we go now?'

Lily stared at me. 'What are you talking about?'

'Snake's right about one thing. We haven't got any closer to finding out what happened to his mother's body or to his uncle. The trail must be getting colder with every breath we take. And we're no nearer to learning who's haunting the streets and terrorising the fishermen, or who the two dead men we've found were. And every moment I stay in Atlixco, I'm in danger. I wonder if we shouldn't just head back to your house in Tlatelolco.'

I gave what I thought was an encouraging grin. Lily's answering look wiped it away the way a large, sandalled foot would scrub out a child's drawing in the sand. 'You want to run away.'

'No!' I replied earnestly. 'Or at least, well, not exactly. But I can't see what more I can do here. And if that monster is still looking for me...'

'Then he'll find you, wherever you are.' She spoke harshly as she finished the sentence. 'Yaotl, what kind of a slave are you? You weren't bought for your strength and the gods know it wasn't for your looks, so it must have been your brains, yes? Well now bloody well use them! Why did we come back to Mexico to begin with?'

'I'm having trouble remembering,' I said, with mistimed flippancy. 'Maybe life in Maize Ear's retreat was getting boring.'

'It was for you and your precious family!' she cried. 'And now you're here, and your enemies know it. Whoever attacked you last night and the night before knows you're in Mexico, and for that matter so does lord Feathered in Black. The very most you've managed to do is stir whoever was after you up, so they're even more likely to want to kill you. If you leave now, what do you think will happen?'

I held up my hands. 'I give in! You're right. They'll keep trying to break into Handy's house, and maybe it'll work, and then I suppose they'll go to Toltenco and start on my parents. And no doubt if this is a real sorcerer then sooner or later he'll track me down to Tlatelolco too.' I groaned. 'I know all this. I don't want to drag you into it. And I suppose I thought it might be nice to have a rest, even just for a day. Lily, it was good in Tetzcotzinco, wasn't it? It felt like the first time in years I wasn't being hunted or threatened with death! I'm so tired of running away all the time... What's the matter?' I stared at her in consternation, for suddenly there were tears streaming down her cheeks.

'Nothing,' she gasped.

I held her arm gently. 'I'm sorry. We'll go back to Handy's house. We'll think of something else. Maybe I can have another word with Cactus. Maybe I can try my brother. Lion might know something. It's all right. I'm not going anywhere, I promise.'

Her shoulders were heaving. She bowed her head, and drew the back of a bandaged hand across her eyes to wipe away the tears. Then she gave a loud sniff and turned fully around to face me.

'Do you think that's it?' she asked softly.

'Well, isn't it?' Trying to grasp her meaning was starting to make my head hurt. 'Lily, I don't understand. You don't want me to run away and when I tell you I'm not going to, you burst into tears! Please tell me what you want me to do.'

She took two steps towards me so that her face was very close to mine. 'But I want to know what you want.'

'It doesn't matter. I'm a slave. I can only do what you tell me.'

'That's exactly the point! Don't you understand what I'm telling you, you silly man?' She shouted the words at me from about a finger's breadth away, and the force of it made me recoil. I nearly fell over. 'Why do you think I bought you out of the market in the first place?'

'Well, you did say it wasn't for my looks or my strength....'

'And apparently it wasn't for your brains either! But for some reason I thought your worthless life was worth saving, when your closest friend – if you ever had any! – wouldn't have given a mouldy cocoa bean for it!'

I gaped at her, probably looking as foolish as I felt. Suddenly I knew why she had been weeping, and what the look in her eyes now meant.

'What do you want?' she asked me again, in a much softer voice.

'You're telling me I have to start thinking for myself,' I said wonderingly.

'Yes,' she said hoarsely.

'About you?'

'About everything. Yaotl, you can't run all your life. Even if we live through this – afterwards – you mustn't be just a slave. I need more than that!'

Fortunately Kite was long gone and there was nobody about: no-one gardening on the surrounding rooftops or polling a canoe past us on the neighbouring canal. The sight of a middle-aged man and middle-aged woman embracing in the middle of the path, both of them seemingly laughing and crying at the same time, was an unusual one. It would have caused comment.

When we got back to Handy's house, we found Kite standing by the canal outside it. He had his sword and was turning it over in his hands, examining it and every now and then stroking one of the obsidian slivers set into its shaft or pinching it between thumb and forefinger. I did not much like the look of that: he seemed to be testing the blades, making sure none of them was loose, and the only reason for doing that was that he expected to have need of the weapon soon.

He glanced up at Lily and me as we approached. 'You two look happy.'

'We had a row,' I said.

'That explains it.'

Lily had been holding my arm loosely, as best she could with her damaged hand; she detached herself now, although she did not move away. 'How's the boy?' she asked.

The blades of the sword glittered. 'As well as you could expect. I understand he stumped into the house and hasn't said a word to anyone since. He'll get over it.' Kite looked at me. 'I'm glad you're here. I want you to look at something.'

He led us a few paces along the canal until we found ourselves opposite a corner of Handy's courtyard wall. A narrow alleyway separated the commoner's house from the one next door. Peering into it, I noticed how dirty it was. Little heaps of dust were banked against the whitewashed walls on either side, and I saw a couple of maize husks, the skin of a tuna cactus fruit and several smudges that may have been footprints.

'Oh,' said Lily mournfully. I shared her sadness. The litter was only a couple of days' worth, nothing that could not be shifted with a few moments' sweeping. Its being there at all was a sign of neglect. Star and the other women of her household would normally have kept the area around their home spotless; it was a duty owed to the gods, as sacred as washing the faces of the idols in their niches every morning.

I glanced along the canal. Between where we stood and the corner of the next house I saw three smudges like the one in the alley. As I looked at them, Kite said: 'I don't suppose either of you happened to notice whether these prints were here this morning?'

'No,' I said. I squatted beside the nearest of the marks, scratching at it experimentally with a fingernail. 'But that doesn't mean they weren't here. We were all looking at the body.' I looked at my finger, sniffed at it. 'This is mud. Dried mud.'

'Interesting, that,' the policeman said, 'considering we've had no rain lately.'

Lily was standing behind me as I stood up. 'Then whoever left these must have come from the lake.'

'Directly from there, and not very far,' I added. 'Or else all the mud would have been rubbed off before he got here.'

We both stared at the policeman. He used his sword to point to the footprints by the canal. 'If you look at them again you'll notice these are different shapes. See here? And here?'

'That one was made by someone wearing sandals,' I said. The flat oblong print was unmistakable. I glanced into the alley again. 'Did they both go around the corner, or only one?' I had an unpleasant suspicion that I now knew what Kite was getting at, and why he had been checking his sword so carefully.

'Some of the prints out here, by the canal, were made by bare feet. The ones in the alley are all of sandals. So just one of them went in there, I'd say. They split up.'

'Who?' Lily asked in a worried tone.

'Whoever attacked me and Spotted Eagle last night,' I replied grimly. 'The one who tried to jump on the young man must have gone around the backs of the houses here. That's why his prints go off into the alley.' I shivered as I contemplated the inhuman shape I had seen, perched on a rooftop. What sort of monster wore sandals? 'The sorcerer stopped here. In fact this is about where I met him last night.'

'If they did come from the lake, that's pretty suggestive,' Kite said, 'considering what's been happening to Quail and the others.'

'Have you been able to follow these back to where they started?' I asked.

'Not yet. The pathways around here have been cleaned since this morning, except in this spot. But I agree with you that the pair of them must have taken a pretty direct route from the lake. So what I thought we could do, is try to retrace it. We'll take the shortest path to shore and see if we can pick any more of these prints up along the way.'

' "We"?' Lily and I repeated simultaneously.

He hefted the sword. 'I mean Yaotl, me and Spotted Eagle. What do you think I was waiting here for?'

I was speechless for a moment. I felt Lily's hand rest on my arm again. 'You can't take my slave,' she said firmly.

The policeman sighed. 'Madam, I have to. He's seen the makers of these footprints. He seems to have been the reason they were here in the first place. He must know more about them than anyone else...'

'I don't,' I objected. 'And it's hardly my fault if they happen to know me, is it?'

'I wouldn't be so sure of that,' Kite said darkly, 'and what if you know more than you think? You might get a surprise if you come face to face with one of them in daylight.'

'I doubt if surprise is quite the word for it!'

'Yaotl can't go,' my mistress asserted. 'He's a slave. His tribute obligations were discharged when he sold himself and he only obeys me. And I'm a merchant, remember?' Her voice wavered slightly as she said this, but her words were clear, and moreover, she was right. It was one of the curious ways in which I, as a slave, was freer than most men. I could not be compelled to fight in the army, form part of a work detail or perform any of the other tasks that an ordinary commoner might be made to do at the behest of the emperor or anyone else. Only my owner could give me orders. And my owner was a merchant, from Tlatelolco. The merchants of the city's northern quarter were a law unto themselves. They had their own police, their own courts, and emperor Montezuma's special favour, in return for the wealth and intelligence they brought him. Even here, on his own ground, Kite had no power over Lily or anything belonging to her, and she knew it.

So did Kite. He looked away to conceal a scowl. 'Have it your way, then,' he signed. 'Spotted Eagle and I will have to go alone. It'll be more dangerous for just the two of us, but...'

Reluctantly, I drew away from Lily. 'All right,' I said, between clenched teeth. 'I'll come. But I'll need a sword. And can't you at least rustle up some more men?'

'Yaotl!' Lily cried. 'You can't! They'll kill you!'

I forced myself to look at her face, to see how her eyes suddenly misted over with shocked, angry tears. 'No, they won't.' I was not sure myself which of us I was trying to convince.

'What's got into you? Just now you were all for running away!'

'I'm sorry,' I said helplessly. 'I just remembered what my mother said, about having made this mess and having to help clear it up. And you said I couldn't keep running forever.'

'I can't fetch any more men,' Kite said. 'There's no time. If there are any more of these prints, we need to find them before they're cleaned up. But I'd already thought about arming you. Spotted Eagle's bringing his father's sword for you.... Speaking of which, here he is.'

'Yaotl,' Lily urged, 'you can't do this! I won't let you!'

I could not meet her eyes a second time. 'You will, though,' I muttered. 'You know I have to... Spotted Eagle, what is that?'

The young man hurried out of his father's house. He looked different from when I had seen him before, although the change was subtle. The unblooded youth's tuft of hair still marked the back of this head, and his cloak was still the plain one of a man who had yet to take a captive, but something about the lad himself was altered. The petulance that I had associated with him at first was gone, and even his grief seemed to have been submerged for the moment. A grin like a coyote's was fixed on his face, and he moved with the brisk assurance of the hunter who has seen his prey.

'Your sword, Yaotl.' Answering my question, he presented the weapon to me with flourish. 'Look after it! Father wants it back!'

He pressed it into my hands. I felt my fingers close around the handle, without my willing it, as I stared at the thing and wondered whether I had made the right decision after all.

I wondered what use Handy had put the sword to in the years since he had last wielded it in battle. Perhaps he had employed it as a digging stick, or to bang wooden pegs into the walls of his house, because it was grimy, with dark stains around the blades set into the shaft whose origin I preferred not to guess at. The shaft itself had a deep split running along half its length, and the two rows of blades were like an old man's teeth, because most were broken, loose and wobbly and many were missing altogether.

Spotted Eagle caught some of my consternation. 'It may not look much,' he said in a hurt tone. 'But it's won a few fights, and you won't find one better balanced.'

I twisted it experimentally, trying to remember what a sword ought to feel like. Like all priests I had trained for a while in a House of Youth, and I had gone to war, but it had all been a long time ago. Still, the boy was not wrong: the handle ended in a heavy wooden knob that balanced the long, flat shaft perfectly. If I did not drop it or cut my own arm off with what was left of its edge, it would be better than nothing.

I glanced at the young man's own weapon, its blades forming a single, unbroken line along either side of its immaculately polished shaft, and said sardonically: 'I'll treat it like it was my own.'

Lily took a step towards me. 'Yaotl, please,' she whispered. 'I won't order you not to go.' Of course not; she had too much pride. 'I'm asking you. You've done enough!'

I jerked my head roughly in the direction of Handy's house. 'Look after them in there,' I said hoarsely. 'They need help. And don't worry. The chances are we won't find anything and we'll be back before nightfall!'

Spotted Eagle said: 'Oh, I hope you're wrong.'

5

As Kite had said, we followed the most direct route to the water's edge. It was no great distance but the walk appeared to last an age. We kept halting while one or other of us squatted to peer at some mark on the canal path in front of us that would invariably turn out not to resemble a footprint, but it was not just that that slowed us down. We knew we were heading into peril; a greater peril perhaps than any of us had faced, since we did not know even whether our enemy was human. With every step I felt as though my feet had been glued to the ground. I supposed it might be like this for a sacrificial victim on the climb towards the summit of the great pyramid, where the fire priest and his flint knife awaited him. Even the bravest man could not know for certain what might lie beyond the moment when his heart was torn out: was it to be rebirth as one of the morning sun's companions, as the priests told us; or nothing; or something worse than oblivion?

These thoughts troubled me until the moment when I realised that there were no longer any houses on either side of us, but only greenery: tall reeds, and beyond them taller willow trees, planted in rows and carefully lopped so as to shore up the edges of the fields without denying the sun's warmth to the crops. Ahead of us, the path narrowed and petered out, becoming a rough bank against which green water lapped sluggishly.

From somewhere nearby, a crow cackled. Some larger bird, probably a heron, took flight, the splash of its exit from the water and the heavy beat of its wings coming to us muffled by the surrounding foliage. The air was laden with a smell like rotten turkey eggs floating in stale piss.

Kite walked along the path as far as he could go without wading. He turned this way and that, brandishing his sword. 'See anything?' he demanded.

'Nothing,' I called. I was still on dry land and intended to stay there. 'I guess we were too late. Or this is the wrong place altogether. Since we didn't find any footprints, we don't know they were ever here, do we?''

Spotted Eagle was standing next to me. I saw him pouting like a child who has been told he has had all his ration of bread for the day. 'We can't go back empty handed,' he objected. 'Let's at least look around.'

My enthusiasm for a confrontation with my enemies was starting to wane, now that I was standing on the edge of their territory. The end of my broken sword drooped as I gazed vainly at the green walls around me and wondered what might be peering back at me, unseen, through the cracks in them.

Kite took as step forward, planting his foot noisily into the thick, murky water. 'We'd better look around. Can either of you suggest where?' He spoke abruptly, making his frustration obvious.

I watched the muck swirling ponderously around his ankles.

The sight of it reminded me of something my brother had mentioned a few days before.

When I looked up again, I saw the same willows and tall rushes as before, hiding everything else except the malodorous water and the clear blue sky. However, this time they looked different. I had lived here, briefly, in the time when I had lived by scraping scum off the surface of the lake. So if this was my enemy's territory, then it had been mine too.

I knew how life was lived in the marshes; what the necessities were, and where they were to be found. Perhaps sorcerers and their tame monsters had different needs from those of men, but I doubted it. As I thought about it further, I saw one need that a dancer with dead woman's forearm might have that was unlike a normal man's. Then I remembered a conversation in Atlixco marketplace and saw how that need might have been met, out here at the waterlogged edge of the city,

I clutched the sword more tightly. If you are here for a fight, Yaotl, then get it over with, I told myself. Aloud I said: 'I can tell you where to go, but Spotted Eagle will have to show us how to get there.'

We splashed through mud that clung to our calves and ankles, clambered over slimy banks, and picked our way gingerly over fields that smelled as though they had been manured recently.

Eventually we found ourselves at the edge of one particular square plot, a pile of neglected, churned-up mud with a tumbledown shelter at one corner.

Kite, Spotted Eagle and I stood waist-deep in the waters of a narrow channel, each cowering behind a different willow, and peeped cautiously around the narrow tree trunks. 'You're sure this is the place?' I said in a loud whisper.

'Of course.' Spotted Eagle sounded unhappy. 'Do you think I

wouldn't know my father's plot? Though it doesn't look like it did last time I saw it.'

'I'd say it hasn't been touched in years,' muttered Kite.

'That's where you're wrong.' I repeated what Quail, the fisherman, had told me the previous day, when he had mentioned seeing somebody working here. 'And look at the shelter.'

It was the only building in sight, a crude round hut with a thatched roof. The thatch was ragged and threadbare at best and in places great dark rents were visible. However, some effort seemed to have been made to fill the holes in with crude patches made of the broad, flat leaves of maguey plants. It would not remain habitable for long, at least in the rainy season, but then, I knew it was not intended to.

The hut, where Handy stored his tools and anything else he needed from day to day, had been fixed up to meet the most basic need of any dweller in the marshes: somewhere more or less dry to lay his head.

I heard a catch in Spotted Eagle's voice. 'Are they there now?'

Kite observed: 'There's no smoke.'

'Around here, that proves nothing,' I pointed out. 'How easy do you think it is to start a fire in this muck?'

'I don't understand how it's got into this state,' Spotted Eagle complained. 'The field looks like a herd of wild pigs has been rooting around in it! How could my father have let it go like this? And what happened to that neighbour Quail mentioned? I can't imagine who that would have been – most men are too busy minding their own plots to worry about ours.'

The set of the young man's jaw and the firmness with which he gripped his sword belied the pain and disappointment in his voice. I took a deep breath before I spoke again, knowing that the disappointment at least would be short lived: he was about to find out that there was much worse to come. 'I'm sorry,' I said, 'but Quail was mistaken. The man he saw wasn't digging over the soil. He was burying something.'

'What do you mean?' Spotted Eagle asked.

Kite interrupted me before I could reply. 'We'd better go and look,' he said briskly, 'but I want this area scouted first. Spotted Eagle, you circle the plot from the left. Keep out of sight and keep quiet. If you see anything you don't like, then first, you run away, and second, you yell. Otherwise we meet up by the shack in the corner. Got that? Go!'

For a moment the young man merely stared at the policeman; but the tone of command, so much like what he must have heard many times from his instructors at the House of Youth, proved irresistible. Without a word he turned and began wading along the edge of his father's field, moving slowly so as to make as little noise as possible, while his head darted from side to side in search of an ambush.

'He's a good lad,' Kite murmured.

'Are you sure he'll be safe?' I asked anxiously.

'If I didn't think so, I'd have gone myself, but anyway, the boy needs to face up to his first real fight sooner or later. Now, come on. Let's get this over with.'

I had thought he meant to circle the field in the opposite direction from the one Snake had taken, intending to meet up with the boy as he had ordered. Instead he threw his sword onto the patch of mud in front of us and scrambled out of the water to collect it. 'I want to do this before the lad realises what we're doing. Now where do we need to dig?' he asked, as he beckoned me to follow him.

Between the willows, the edges of the plot were sheer, reinforced with wooden stakes that were slimy to the touch and difficult to get a purchase on. Eventually, however, Kite and I stood together, our feet slowly sinking into the mud.

The policeman repeated his question. 'Where, Yaotl?'

I noticed an area beside Handy's little thatched hut where the ground appeared particularly badly churned, the mud and silt heaped up in a low mound.

'You'll find Spotted Eagle's mother in there, I should think.'

Kite grimaced, hesitated, and then appeared to make up his mind. His feet made slurping noises in the mud as he strode towards the place I had indicated. When he got there he drove the flat end of his sword into the ground like a shovel.

'Come on,' he barked, as he threw as mass of black muck away from him. 'Hurry up! We don't have long.'

I bounded towards him and joined in. It was not long before we had a shallow hole, and not long after that before I felt my own improvised tool strike something other than liquid mud. I paused then to look at the policeman.

His face was ghastly. 'You've found her, haven't you?' he asked me under his breath.

'The boy will be here in a moment,' I said. 'What are you going to say to him?'

He leaned on his sword and looked down. 'I don't know,' he confessed. 'I just wanted to know before he did. For some reason I thought that might make it easier for him.'

By the time Spotted Eagle had appeared, forcing his way between the rushes close to the little shelter, we had scraped enough of the mud away to leave no room to doubt what we had found.

Partly exposed, curled up at the bottom of the hole we had made, half-submerged in black, stinking water, lay the pale form of a human body. The dark, sodden remains of a woman's skirt and blouse clung to it. Its features were unrecognisable, with all the bloated blandness of death.

The dead woman lay just where I had thought we might find her. Her right arm ended in a stump at the elbow. Her head was crowned with a dark mass of dried blood instead of hair. There was no doubt that the corpse we had found was Star's.

The young man stood at the side of the shallow grave in silence. Neither Kite nor I could think of anything to say to him. Spotted Eagle did not need us to tell him what we had found.

When at last Handy's son found his voice, all he could say was: 'So they brought her here.'

I watched the sword swinging loosely from his fingers and wondered whether I had done the right thing by leading him and Kite here.

'How did you know?' the young man asked in a whisper.

I looked at the policeman. He returned my gaze steadily.

'It was a guess,' I said truthfully. 'I remembered from my own time living in the marshes that you have to have some sort of shelter and somewhere to sleep – somewhere to lie low, for that matter, because you wouldn't be living here at all unless you were running away from something. But it's not that easy: there are too many people making their living off the lake to make hiding away anywhere around here an easy matter. And of course the sorcerer and the monster needed something more: they had to have somewhere to hide... this.'

Spotted Eagle did not react.

'They chose their ground well,' I went on. 'They knew this plot was likely to be neglected for a good while after Star's death. Handy can't have been here in days. Quail told me he'd seen someone else digging it over, but he didn't see who it was very clearly. It just occurred to me that there might be another explanation.'

'The thief,' Spotted Eagle hissed. 'Where is he now?'

'Obviously not here.' I looked towards the shelter. 'We'll take a look in there, see if we can find any clues inside.'

'Don't get any ideas, son,' the policeman warned. 'I understand how you must be feeling. But these are dangerous creatures we're dealing with.'

The young man looked at him resentfully from under lowered brows. 'As if I didn't know that,' he mumbled. 'But who are they?' He glanced at the body before turning hastily away from it. He swallowed hard. We had all done very well not to be violently sick, I thought.

'They took...' Watching Spotted Eagle's face, I picked my words carefully. 'We need to think about what they took. Cactus was right. The arm is a sorcerer's charm. The hair is a warrior's. Perhaps we are dealing with both.'

'You told us the thing that followed you had a sword,' Kite reminded me.

'True. But if that was a warrior, he didn't look like any I've ever seen.'

Spotted Eagle drove the end of his sword into the ground angrily. 'Stop it!' he shouted. 'It's my mother's hair and arm you're talking about, not a couple of freshly-laundered breechcloths that someone's pilfered while they were drying! Where are they now?'

Kite looked as nonplussed as I felt. 'I'm sorry,' I said, 'I don't know. But at least we found the rest.'

'We need to get her home,' Spotted Eagle asserted. 'Then we'll look for the other things.'

Merely thinking about descending into the hole to try to drag the body clear of the mud that still clung to it was enough to make me feel ill. 'I suppose we do,' I said. 'Though we could do with some help.'

'Or at least some tools,' Kite suggested. 'Are there any in your father's shed?'

'Spades, digging sticks,' Spotted Eagle replied absently. 'And I think there's an old rabbit's fur mantle in there too. He wears it when it's very cold out here in the winter. I'll show you.' For a moment I did not think he was going to move from the graveside, but then he turned and dragged his feet ponderously towards the open entrance to the shelter. 'He kept all sorts of junk in here...' He vanished inside the decrepit little building.

For a long moment we heard nothing more from him. Then he began yelling.

Kite and I stared at each other for a moment, while we strained to catch the words, although they were muffled by the walls of the shed. Finally we both rushed towards the doorway just as Spotted Eagle appeared in it. I staggered to a halt, slipping and stumbling in the sodden, churned up ground, and just managed to avoid running full tilt into the blades of the young man's sword.

His eyes were wide open. His mouth was opening and closing but now no words were coming out, only faint gasps.

'What is it?' Kite demanded, before pushing him aside and launching himself through the doorway.

The youth staggered sideways. He turned to stare at me. 'It's Red Macaw!' he cried in a strangled voice. 'He's in there!'

6

I do not know what I expected to find when I followed Kite through the doorway. All I knew was that Spotted Eagle had seen his father's old antagonist – his mother's former lover – in here, but I had no idea in what guise. For all I knew he might be got up as a sorcerer, his face painted black like a priest's, or transformed into some grotesque but still somehow identifiable version of himself, the warrior fused with the monster.

I did not see him at all to begin with, because it was too dark and my attention was caught by Kite. The policeman stood in the centre of the hut, hacking at the roof with his sword, while a litter reeds and damp moss fell around his feet.

'Need some light in here,' he said, 'and watch where you're putting your feet!' Automatically I looked down.

There was just enough room in here for a man to lie full length if his head were wedged into one corner and his feet jammed into the corner opposite. That was how I found Red Macaw.

At first I thought he was dead. An unpleasant smell rose from him; a smell of blood, rot and shit, worse than the inside of a temple after a busy day's sacrificing to the gods.

Kite wrenched a great lump of material from the roof, which I had to bat away to prevent it from landing on the man on the floor. In the daylight that flooded the space around us, I could make out two things. The first was that Red Macaw was still alive, for his eyes rolled weakly and a faint tremor shook his body. The second was that he did not have much time left.

He was naked except for the tattered, filthy remains of a breechcloth. Just above the garment, his flesh had been torn open. A fat grey loop of gut peeked obscenely through the hole. The floor would have been damp anyway, but now it was soaked with his blood.

I lifted my eyes from his ruined abdomen to his face. It was grey, the skin stretched so tightly over the bones that it looked as if it might burst. Dried blood caked the corners of his mouth and his upper lip. I would not have recognised him from our one meeting, but Kite and Spotted Eagle obviously knew him better.

His lips moved. The tongue that appeared between them was black.

'He wants a drink,' Kite suggested.

I thought about the medicine I had had to learn at the priest house and the wounds I had seen treated or neglected in the army. 'Even if you could get clean water it would probably finish him off.'

'Wouldn't that be kinder?' Spotted Eagle spoke from behind me. He was peering cautiously through the doorway.

Kite looked at him sharply. 'Don't stand there! Someone's got to keep watch outside! Whoever did this may still be around, remember?'

The young man vanished. I dropped to my knees, staring into the haggard face. The eyes tried to swivel to meet mine, but they kept rolling to one side.

'Who did this?' I demanded.

The lips moved silently.

I looked up a Kite. I felt sick, not so much from the sight and smell of the dying man as from what I knew I had to do. But I told myself it would make no difference now in any case. 'You were right. He's asking for water.'

'What do I do?'

'Find a bowl, or a cup, or anything.'

I turned back to Red Macaw's agonised features as the policeman rummaged through a pile of effects in one corner of the hut. Slowly and loudly I said: 'We'll get you water. But you have to tell me: who did this to you?'

I did not think he had heard me. The eyes rolled slowly in their sockets. Eventually they came to rest pointing in my direction, although they looked dull and unfocused.

The lips moved silently again.

'What's he saying?' the policeman demanded.

'I'm not sure. It's one word. And again... Shit, he's saying "Yaotl"!' For a moment the shock of seeing my own name form on the dying man's lips threatened to overwhelm me, but I managed to get a grip on myself. 'Yes, yes, it's me, Yaotl. Now tell me who did this!'

The lips moved again. ' "Looking.... Looking for you"?' I repeated.

'Here's a cup,' said Kite. 'But are you sure...'

'Here's your water, Red Macaw,' I called out. 'You can have it in a moment. Just a couple more questions, please.' I held the cup above his face, and watched the eyeballs tracking it thirstily. I hated myself then; but I knew that the first sip Red Macaw took from that cup would be the last thing he ever did, and there were things I had to know first.

'Who's looking for me?'

The eyes closed, as though he could not bear to look at the cup any more. I held it where it was, irresolutely, for a moment. I was on the point of weakening, of giving him his drink and his release, when I saw the lips move again.

I frowned as I tried to make out the words. They did not look like an answer to my question. 'Wanted... to.... see... her...'

I said nothing.

There was one more word to come: 'Stop.'

'Stop?' I said. 'Stop what? Who did you want to see?'

This time there was no reply.

After a few moments I looked at Kite. Some unspoken agreement passed between us. The policeman cradled Red Macaw's head in his hands while I tilted the cup towards his lips. Something like a smile passed over them, and he drank.

The result was less violent than I had feared. At first, nothing happened. Then his eyes snapped open. They rolled slowly up into his head. His body shook once, and from his mouth came a faint sigh and a thin dark trickle of blood.

I threw the cup against the wall of the hut. 'That's that, then! I've finished off the bastards' work for them!'

Yet I still think that at that moment, it was the only kind thing I could have done.

7

'Have a look over here.'

I took no notice of the policeman. I squatted by Red Macaw's inert body, with my head in my hands, trying to shut out the sight of the dead man but seeing only his face in his last instant of life. For the first time in all the years since the stuff had nearly done for me, I longed for a gourd of sacred wine. I wanted to get uproariously drunk, even though to do so would be to risk execution.

'Yaotl! Stop feeling sorry for yourself and look!' Kite barked. You need to see this.'

With a sigh I hauled myself to my feet and turned around. 'Kite, don't you realise...' I never finished what I was going to say because I had seen what he wanted to show me, and the sight of it stopped the breath in my throat. For a moment I forgot Red Macaw had ever existed.

The policeman stood under the hole he had made in the roof and held something up in the light. It was perhaps half as tall as he was, but he could lift it with one hand, because it was made of nothing more substantial than cloth stretched over a wicker frame. It was green, shaped like a huge teardrop with long green feathers – quetzal tail plumes, the most precious feathers of all – trailing like tassels from the tapered end at the top.

'You know what this is, don't you?' Kite said.

My mouth was too dry to form words.

'The rest is in that pile behind me: the green cotton suit, the sandals with the long straps, everything.' He lifted the wicker and cloth construction a little higher. 'How tall would a man look, carrying this on his back? Half again his own height? And you thought the monster that followed you was too tall to be human!'

'It's the captain,' I whispered, appalled.

'I'm right, aren't I?' Kite said in a tone of grim satisfaction. 'This is an otomi's back device. It's what he'd wear into battle.'

The marks of an otomi warrior were the hair piled up on his head and spilling down his back, the tall, conical back device, the green cotton suit that clung to his torso and limbs like a second skin, the heavy jewelled sandals. They ensured that he could be seen and recognised across the most crowded battlefield, so that his friends would rally to him and his enemies faint at his approach. Perhaps some of the younger and bolder warriors on the other side would see the captain's distinctive garb as a goad, and rush at him, keen to try their luck, but it would be all one to him: they would end up as corpses or captives.

I had heard this costume described and seen warriors sporting the clothes and the hairstyle, but never had I set eyes on a man wearing the full regalia, not even in my youth when I had served with the army as a priest.

'He's been wearing it in the city,' I said. 'Who's his enemy here?'

'You seem to have earned that honour!'

I squeezed past the policeman to look at the clothes on the floor. They had been neatly folded but were not clean. The front of the green suit was covered in dark stains. 'It looks as though others have got in his way. Including that poor bastard on the floor.' I squatted and stretched out a hand to feel the material, as though I wanted to satisfy myself that it was real and not something that belonged in the land of dreams. 'It's good cotton,' I said absently.

'The emperor would have presented it to him.' the policeman responded. 'He doesn't give out rubbish!'

'I hope he doesn't want it back, then. It's ruined now. Take a lot of cold water to get these stains out and then it'll probably shrink.' I stood up. 'Let's get out of here before he comes back for it, shall we?'

Kite had already started heading towards the doorway. 'I'll round up every man we've got and come back here for this stuff. We'll need to pick up Star and Red Macaw as well. Then you can explain to me what all this means!'

'It means we know who the warrior is,' I said. 'And he's not a monster after all, just a man.' Yet I felt no relief. Inside me a voice was shrieking hysterically: *What do you mean 'just a man'? This is the otomi you're talking about!*

My thoughts were interrupted by the sound of screaming from outside.

There was a rapid serious of wet slaps, as of feet running over mud. Someone called out and the shout was followed by the crash and rustle of reeds being shoved roughly aside.

'It's Spotted Eagle,' Kite said, 'doing what he was told – screaming and running away!' He paused, his head on one side, listening, and then I realised the sounds were not receding.

'He's not running away,' I said slowly. I still had my sword. Now I found I was gripping it so tightly my knuckles hurt.

'Idiot!' snapped the policeman. 'He's trying to divert him, to draw him off! Come on, we have to get out there!'

'No, wait...'

I was too late. Kite bounded through the doorway.

There was a sound like someone chopping wood, and then another scream, much closer.

I had no time to think. I just ran, hurling myself after Kite, swinging the sword in a wild, undisciplined arc and bellowing at the top of my voice – not a war cry, but a sound of pure panic.

The weapon connected with something. The impact jarred my arm all the way up to the shoulder. An indignant roar sounded in my right ear, and then a terrific force wrenched the sword away from me.

I held on to the handle for a moment too long. I was dragged forward after it, stumbling helplessly until a sandalled foot lashed out and caught me behind the right knee. Then I crashed face down into stinking mud.

8

Large, rough hands seized my shoulders and yanked me onto my knees. My right leg was weak and numb. It collapsed under me, sending me toppling sideways. My fall was checked by a savage cuff to the side of the head that knocked my teeth together hard enough to send a spasm of pain up through my cheeks. Then the hands were dragging me backwards, with my heels leaving broad tracks in the mud. When my back struck the side of the hut, the whole structure shook, showering me with dead leaves and pieces of reed thatch.

I stared anxiously at my right leg, which was beginning to throb. It lay stretched out before me, looking no more scrawny and twisted than usual, even if the knee was starting to look slightly swollen. I hoped it was not broken.

The policeman had been less lucky.

He had been put against the wall too, in the same position, although he had slipped downwards so that his head was jammed against the crumbling adobe and his neck bent awkwardly beneath it. His face had an ugly yellow hue, his eyes were hollow, and his breath came in shallow gasps.

'Kite!' I cried. His eyeballs swivelled at the sound of my voice, as Red Macaw's had done. They were bloodshot with pain and shock.

'Are you all right?' I asked. It was a stupid question: self-evidently he was not. The flesh at his hip had been torn open and a splinter of white bone jutting from the red, pulpy mass in the wound.

'Don't waste your breath on him,' a harsh, slurred voice rasped. 'He was lucky.'

I turned towards the speaker. 'You,' I said. It scarcely seemed worth the effort needed to come up with anything more original than that, since I was about to be killed anyway.

My enemy, the otomi captain, stood over me. He would have looked down upon me if I had been standing, but from where I sat now he seemed as tall as a full-grown cypress tree. He wore only a breechcloth, and that none too clean, and his hair had not long ago been cut short, but he was no less terrifying for that. His face was split by the lopsided grin I had learned to dread and hate so much. Mirth wrinkled half his features only; the rest was an immobile slab of dead flesh, left that way by some fight long ago. For some reason it occurred to me then that I had never found out who had inflicted that wound on him, or what had become of him. I hoped he had died quickly.

'What's so funny?' I asked.

'He is!' He jabbed Kite with the end of the weapon he was holding. 'If I'd used an ordinary sword instead of this, he'd have been cut in half! He's lucky he met me!'

I felt sick. I knew the captain's weapon of choice well, a long wooden club with four rows of obsidian blades set into it at right angles. He had obviously caught Kite with it as the policeman ran out of the shelter. If he had struck his victim with a sword, the force of the blow would probably have taken both his legs off.

'I'm sure he's grateful,' I said bleakly.

Then Kite spoke. With obvious effort he turned his head to face the captain. 'What happened to the boy?' he asked in a voice so thick and guttural I could barely make out the words.

'Don't worry about him. He's being taken care of!'

'Not by you, though,' I said. 'So the sorcerer came too.' In what guise? I wondered, with a chill. Was the captain's ally wading through the marshes on human feet or on an animal's; or even soaring overhead on wings? I remembered the large bird we had heard taking off from the lake's surface and wondered whether that had been as innocent as it sounded. 'Does he do your killing for you, these days? I'm not surprised. It can't be easy recruiting followers, after what happened to the last lot!'

The otomi stiffened. I tensed myself for a lacerating blow, wondering what had made me speak like that: why did I want to provoke him? Bloody awful timing, Yaotl, when you're lying at your enemy's feet with a leg that won't move.

The blow did not come. The grin broadened. 'You should watch your mouth. It'll get you in trouble soon. Very soon! But there's no hurry – I've plenty of time. Unlike you!'

A feeble groan came from Kite's throat. The captain looked at him.

I realised the policeman was asking what the otomi wanted. I repeated the question.

The great brute looked more amused than ever. 'You, of course,' he purred. 'I've been waiting for this for so long!'

I jerked my head towards the policeman. 'Well, you seem to have got me. He needs help, though.' Kite's breechcloth and the lower part of his cloak were saturated with dark red fluid. 'He'll bleed to death, if the shock doesn't kill him. And if that wound turns rotten...'

'Fuck him!' the captain shouted. A foot struck out, slamming into the wounded man's chest. His body jerked in response. 'He can live or die. I don't care. You, I intend to have some fun with. Just one thing I have to do first...'

He strode past me, casually swinging his foot against the side of my head as he entered the hut behind me. The blow was a token, only hard enough to make me flinch, and the moment he was out of sight, I tried to get up. I was going to run. I knew it meant leaving Kite to his fate, but unless I got help he was a dead man anyway, so I had no choice.

My right leg sprawled helplessly under me, depositing me back on the damp mud. Before I could move again the otomi had reappeared.

His huge form hurled itself outside. Mud flying off his feet spattered my face. He ran several paces before turning to face us, and when he did so, it was obvious that whatever he had seen in that hut had turned him nearly demented. His jaw was working, twisting the living part of his face, and his feet stamped and danced in the mud.

'He's dead!' he screamed. 'What happened? Tell me what happened to Red Macaw!'

I stared at him. 'You opened his stomach with that club of yours. What did you expect that to do, give him mild indigestion?'

He held the weapon high in the air. The blades glittered in the sunlight. Then he lunged at me.

It was my turn to scream, to cry out in terror, but the agonising, crushing blow was not to fall yet. Instead he stooped, seized my ankle and tugged at it. The next thing I knew I was on my back, staring into the sky, with my left leg raised and stretched. The ankle was held in an unbreakable grip and something sharp was tickling the skin. I gasped as I felt it do more than tickle.

'You tell me what happened, or I'll start flaying you alive from the feet up!' the otomi bellowed.

My courage left me then. The stinging pressure of the obsidian blades increased. 'All right!' I stammered out an account of the three-captive warrior's death. 'But he was dying! We couldn't have saved him, not with a wound like that! Why did you do it if you wanted him alive?'

The otomi's expression was always hard to read. At this angle it was nearly impossible, but I watched the muscles twitch and bulge and saw his agitation, even something that might have been remorse. At the same time the blades were biting deeper into my skin. I could feel blood running along the inside of my leg. Much more of this, I thought desperately, and he'll have my foot off.

What he said next was not meant for me. It was not even a question. 'I didn't intend killing him. I didn't know it was him! How could I? He crept up on me. I didn't have time to look!' He let out a wild groan. 'What do I do now?'

'Let me go!' I gasped. 'What can I give you, to let me go?' He ignored the pathetic squirming thing begging for its life at his feet. He went on talking to himself: 'Why did he have to come out here? I haven't got long now. If he'd just clung on a little longer. I've got to think!' He seemed to come to a decision. He dropped my foot. His war club swept towards my face, stopping still a hair's breadth from my eyes, so close I could not bring the blades into focus.

'Get up,' he barked.

Tribute of Death

'I can't, not with that club there. It'll take my nose off!'

The weapon was twitched aside. 'Get up! Any more wisecracks and you'll lose more than your nose!'

I tried to rise and fell backwards, gasping with pain from my leg. Suddenly it was not numb any more. The captain growled threateningly, and I forced myself to stand, bracing myself unsteadily against the wall of the shed.

'Now get in there and drag that body out. You're going to bury it, here, quickly. Any funny business and this fool starts to die – slowly!'

I looked at Kite. From the way his eyes were rolling under half-closed lids it was hard to tell whether he was conscious or not, but I knew the otomi would find a way of waking him up.

'Get on with it!'

I hastened to obey, only hesitating when I stepped through the door of the shelter and the smell of what was inside hit me once more. For some reason it seemed stronger and ranker than it had before. When I looked down I realised why. The captain must have taken some convincing before he would believe Red Macaw was dead. It looked as if he had picked the body up and shaken it in the hope of getting some response. What this had done to the dead man's innards is something I try not to recall at mealtimes.

There was no point in attempting to pack everything back inside the wound. I reminded myself that I had seen hearts torn, still beating, from the breasts of sacrificial victims. I swallowed the gorge rising in my throat, and applied myself to the job of dragging the body outside by the heels. I assumed the otomi would send me back inside for any parts that I left behind.

Where do you want him?' I asked, throwing the question over my shoulder like a servant carrying a wicker chest into his master's newly-build house.

The response was the swish of a sword swinging through the air and a soft thump that might have been made by blades sinking into unresisting flesh.

I dropped the body and whirled around, shocked and indignant. 'What are you doing? Leave him alone! I brought the body out, like you said...' I fell silent as I saw what the captain was doing.

He was not using his club to carve pieces from the policeman's body, as I had thought. Instead, he was standing over Star's grave, attacking the edges of the shallow hole so as to make it bigger. 'Get that thing over here,' he snapped, without looking up. 'Hurry up! And don't leave anything behind, do you understand?'

I did what I was told.

The otomi stood aside, swinging his vicious club suggestively as I rolled what was left of Red Macaw into the shallow hole. When I went back to scrape up the mess on the ground between the grave and the shelter, I noticed that he kept looking away, glancing at the dense growth of rushes at the edge of the field as though expecting to see someone emerge from them at any moment. I stared at him in wonder. It seemed that he was nervous about something, but that was almost inconceivable: what could this man be afraid of?

'You're scared,' I blurted out, unthinking.

He ignored that. 'Now get a shovel from in there and fill the hole in!' he barked.

'You don't want me to climb into it first?'

'Oh, no.' He prodded me with the blunt end of his sword. 'Once

Red Macaw's hidden, I'll start on you. I'm going to take my time over that, and I intend to make the most of it!'

When I emerged from the shelter for the last time, I was armed with a shovel. I looked at its fire-hardened wooden blade in despair. Against the captain and his obsidian-studded club, I still stood no chance.

I stood by the entrance to the hut and looked into the otomi's only eye. It glared, unblinking, back at me. 'Well?' he growled.

Something made me drop the shovel. As it fell with a soft 'plop' at my feet, I cried: 'Why are you doing this?'

The question did not seem to make him angry. If the twitch of his one eyebrow meant anything, it looked like bemusement. 'What do you mean?'

'I was right, wasn't I? You're afraid of something. You saw Red Macaw dead in there and it spooked you. Why?'

'It's nothing to you. Pick up that shovel!' He jerked his obsidian-bladed club threateningly, and I responded by stooping towards the tool I had dropped, which lay half-buried in the mud. It came up with a loud squelching sound and heavy with stinking ooze. I shook it once, to knock some of the muck off. I hesitated before shaking it again, much less vigorously, and at the same time I looked at the captain and spoke again, picking up my train of thought in an effort to distract him.

'You've got to hide this body quickly, before someone finds it. Why? You aren't afraid of any man. You'd tell the emperor to eat his own breechcloth if you felt like it. So it's something more than a man you're frightened of. It's not even lord Feathered in Black, is it?'

'You're the one who ought to be frightened,' he snarled. 'You're about to die. If you do what you're told it might not take as long, that's all! And this has nothing to do with the chief minister. I'm not afraid of him, not any more. With the edge I've got over him now, he'd better be afraid of me!'

'What edge?' My thoughts were racing, as I struggled to hold everything in my head at once: the shovel in my hands, the wounded and the dead who lay around me, the monstrous, disfigured warrior and the mysterious fear that had gripped him. 'That's it, isn't it?' I cried. 'That edge – that's what's got to you. It's the sorcerer! You're afraid of the sorcerer!'

He took a step towards me and jabbed me with the end of club again, hard enough this time to make me stagger backwards. 'I told you to fill that hole in! Now pick that shovel up and dig! I can take the rest of today and all day tomorrow killing you or I can do it in a moment, understand?'

I understood, but it no longer mattered.

When he prodded me with his club, the captain and I were as close as we were going to be. It would have to do, I judged. With all my strength I thrust the shovel towards him, jerking it sharply towards his ruined face. He did not so much as blink, but a gobbet of thick mud flew from the tool's flat blade into his one good eye.

He leaped back instinctively, howling in shock and fury. I threw the shovel at him, but did not wait to see whether it connected before turning and running blindly away.

I did not get far.

It is almost impossible to run barefoot through thick, churned-up mud. The stuff clung to my feet, relinquishing them only reluctantly with loud sucking noises. I did not know where I was going. I had had no time to think or pick a direction, instead merely turning towards the nearest canal in the vain hope of crossing it and losing myself in the fields beyond. Yet from behind me the furious roar and the splashing of massive feet striking the mud told me how futile this was, and the edge of Handy's plot, bounded as it was by the canal separating it from his neighbours, put an end to all thoughts of escape.

I hesitated, teetering on the edge of the canal, unable in that moment to decide whether to leap across or somehow try to hide. That moment of indecision was enough for the panting, roaring, splashing creature behind me to catch me up.

'Got you!' he shouted, his breath like a warm wind on the back of my neck. 'You're going to wish you hadn't done that!'

I could only turn to stare mutely at him.

Then a dart whistled past my head.

It buried itself in the wall of the hut with a soft thump. I stared at it for a moment. Then I came to my senses and threw myself flat on the ground as a second missile soared through the air to catch the otomi on the arm.

His scream split the air around us. I thought it made the willow trees shake, although that may have been a trick of the wind. Then he was on the move, his club raised high over his head, its blades flashing, his voice shrieking in an ululating war-cry as he raced towards his unseen opponents.

I glimpsed something moving in the reeds at the edge of the plot. The otomi bore down on them. He had covered half the distance towards them before he stumbled, and I saw that he had a dart buried in his knee. Almost without breaking stride, he bent down, tore the projectile from his flesh and hurled it back towards his unseen antagonist.

'Come out here, you cowards!' he screamed. 'Come and show yourselves!'

The only answer was a flurry of darts from whoever was concealed among those reeds. Two of them landed in the mud near where I stood, causing me to jump backwards in fright. One clipped the captain's skull, doing him little damage but causing him to stumble. He recovered without breaking his stride, but suddenly he was running, not toward the hidden marksman, but away from him.

One enormous leap took him clear across the channel separating Handy's plot of land from his neighbours', and then he was gone, reduced to a bellowing, splashing presence, somewhere out there at the edge of the lake.

9

First to emerge from the edge of the field was Spotted Eagle. He ran across the muddy plot in the captain's wake, yelling incoherently. He would have vanished into the greenery as fast as he had appeared if a strong male voice had not called him back.

The voice belonged to Quail, the fisherman. He crashed through the reads after Spotted Eagle, but unlike the young man, he was not chasing anybody. Instead he made directly for the shelter and the wounded man lying against it. He took no notice of me, dashing past the shallow pit I had been working on with barely a glance.

As Quail stooped over Kite, he shouted over his shoulder at Spotted Eagle: 'Get over here and don't be a fool, boy!'

The young man stood in the middle of the field, looking this way and that, clearly at a loss. 'But he's getting away!'

'Good! You'll never catch him and it'll be the worse for you if you do. Leave him to others. This man needs help! And you, don't just stand there, we need something to carry him with – can't you find a mantle or a blanket in that shed?'

The last words were thrown in my direction. I was about to splutter an indignant reply when I noticed that others were pushing the reeds aside to join us. Two were young men I did not recognise, but I was startled to see that the third was Quail's daughter, Heart of a Flower, and even more amazed to when I realised that she was the one carrying a throwing stick. She still held a dart between her right thumb and forefinger.

Spotted Eagle thumped the soil by his feet with his sword, but he did as he was told. 'There's a blanket in the shelter,' he said sulkily. I remembered that we had been intending to wrap his mother in it, but she was not likely to be needing it for warmth.

'I'll help,' I said, falling into step beside the newcomers. To the girl I added: 'That was good shooting.'

'It was crap shooting,' she said disgustedly. 'I should have put his other eye out! But it's harder than it looks when they're running straight at you.'

Her father was looking anxiously into the policeman's eyes. 'I'm no curer,' he muttered. 'But I think he's in a bad way. We need to get him out of here quickly.'

'I won't argue with that,' I said. Spotted Eagle beat me to the doorway and I let him go to look for the blanket while I added: 'How did you get here? What happened?'

'We heard someone shouting and blundering about among the rushes. Then the boy appeared, yelling something about murderers and thieves.'

'You didn't see who he was following?'

Spotted Eagle came out of the shelter with the blanket. Quail grabbed it. 'Help me get it underneath him,' he said to the men who had come with him. 'We'll use it to carry him home. Hope we can make it to the parish hall.'

'I was following the sorcerer, I think,' Spotted Eagle said in a low, chastened voice. 'But he disappeared.'

'Of course he did,' Heart of a Flower said contemptuously. 'If you understood the first thing about hunting you'd know better than to make all that noise! You probably ran straight past him!'

'That's enough,' Quail told his daughter reprovingly. He probably thought her outburst was not quite seemly in an Aztec maiden. 'We didn't see him either, remember.'

'I just did what Kite told me to do,' Spotted Eagle said defensively. 'Run about and make a lot of noise, he said. So when that monster appeared at the edge of the field, I did. Then I saw this movement in the reeds and went after it.'

'You didn't get a good look at him?' I asked anxiously.

The answer was interrupted by a loud yell from Kite as the three local men heaved him onto the blanket. Quail whispered some reassuring words to him; the two must have been old friends.

'No,' the young man said mournfully. 'It was all too quick. I don't know that he was moving that fast, but he obviously knows how to keep hidden. I didn't see anyone until I ran into these people.'

'We were gathering stone dung at the edge of the city,' Quail's daughter said. 'Father says it's as far out as we dare go at the moment, with the demon roaming about.' I realised they must be desperate. Gathering scum from the lake's surface was always a disagreeable, slimy job, and it required particular care the edge of the city because of all the jars of poisonous whitewash that got emptied into the water. 'I had my throwing stick just in case I had a chance to catch a bird. We've not had meat or fish lately.'

'You didn't see anyone else at all?' I asked.

'Only others like us. Mostly old people stooped over the water.'

Quail and his comrades lifted Kite off the ground and began carrying him slowly in the direction of the city.

'Wait a moment!' Spotted Eagle cried. 'What about my mother? We can't leave her here!'

'And Red Macaw,' I added. 'He died. He's in this hole too!'

Quail did not look back. 'They're already dead,' he said indifferently. 'Let's see if we can keep Kite alive. Then we'll worry about them.'

10

Dusk had fallen by the time Spotted Eagle and I had made it back to his father's house. Quail and the others had gone directly to the parish hall, while Heart of a Flower ran to find a curer. I hoped it would not be Cactus.

As we trudged wearily through the entrance to the courtyard, Lily came out and ran towards us. She stopped suddenly within a few paces of where we stood, and the whites of her eyes showed plainly as they widened with shock.

'Yaotl!' she gasped. 'What happened? You're hurt!'

'What?' I looked down and noticed that I was covered in blood. It soaked my breechcloth and cloak and was smeared over my belly and legs. The memory of dragging Red Macaw's partly eviscerated body out of that hut came to me, and for the first time it made me feel faint. I staggered forward, doubled over as if it had been my stomach the captain had opened up.

Lily cried out and darted forward, catching me and crying out again as she felt the pain in her fingers.

'It's all right,' I managed to gasp, although the world was starting to spin around me. 'It's all right, Lily. It isn't mine!'

Then I fainted.

I came to beside the hearth.

The sleeping mat underneath me was firm and dry. The mantle I was wrapped in smelled of freshly laundered cloth. Half of my body – the side nearer to the flames – was bathed in delicious warmth. A woman cooed gently in my ear, telling me to rest, and a hand – bandaged but still comforting – lay on my brow. I sighed contentedly, and turned over, to feel the fire's heat on my face.

A voice that was anything but soothing barked: 'Awake, is he? Come on, Yaotl. Up you get! We need to talk.'

Handy's voice shattered my mood. I groaned and rolled onto my back.

'Leave him be!' Lily cried. It had been her voice that had been on the point of lulling me back to sleep. 'He's tired.'

'We're all tired,' Handy said. 'But Yaotl's got some explaining to do!'

I sat up stiffly, shrugging off both the cloak and Lily's hand. 'All right,' I muttered irritably. I looked about me.

I must have been carried indoors and laid by the fire. A sweat bath would have done me good but it was too late in the day for that: a glance at the doorway showed me it was now dark outside.

The little room was crowded, mostly with members of Handy's family, although I recognised the face of Quail, the fisherman, among those around me. I caught a glimpse of movement through the doorway and sensed that the courtyard outside was crowded.

'It's busy in here,' I muttered.

Quail said: 'Kite told us all to come here, just before we handed him over to the curer and the bonesetter. He was afraid whoever was out there last night would try again. Well, the more fool them if they do! We've got just about every unoccupied man in Atlixco out there.'

Handy said quietly: 'What happened today, Yaotl?' I looked at him. In the weak light in that room his features looked sunken and more sallow than ever. His eyes seemed to stand out as having more life in them than the rest of his face, and in their unblinking gaze I saw an unasked question.

'We found her,' I said.

He seemed to hesitate. 'Yes. Spotted Eagle told me.'

I glanced at the youth. 'He'll have told you where...'

'Where,' the commoner agreed, 'and in what state. Yes, I know. We'll have to go and get her.'

'Not until tomorrow,' Quail advised. 'We had our hands full with Kite this afternoon. The demon – the otomi, apparently – is still at large, and you can't ask anyone to go out into the marshes at night while he's prowling around. How many has he killed now?'

'Three men, at least,' I said. 'Red Macaw and... Well, we still don't know for sure who the others are.' I glanced at a dark corner of the room where I knew Handy's sister-in-law was kneeling silently, no doubt wondering even now whether one of the mangled corpses we had found had been her husband's.

I explained what I had seen and done in the fields that day. 'Knowing that your demon is really the otomi accounts for a good deal,' I concluded. 'The monster Spotted Eagle and I saw, which some of the midwives glimpsed on the night of the funeral – the thing you fishermen are afraid of – it was just the captain in his full uniform. All we could make out in the dark was his shape, and with that back device he carries, it didn't look human. And all the people who said he didn't have a face had simply seen his bad side, where he was wounded all those years ago.'

'I don't understand why he'd have wanted to dress up like that, though,' Spotted Eagle said. 'Wouldn't all that clobber have slowed him down?'

I had wondered that myself, and when the answer had come to me I was not sure whether I found it encouraging or more frightening than ever; for no animal is more dangerous than one driven mad by fear.

'He's afraid. His nerve went, after what happened to him in Tetzcoco. Now he needs the uniform, because it's only when he's wearing it that he can feel like a warrior – brave, invincible, knowing everyone he sees will be more frightened of him than he is of them. Quail' – I looked gravely at the fisherman – 'if he'd been wearing it when your daughter started taking pot shots at him with her throwing stick, he'd have stood his ground, and we'd all be dead by now.'

'I know it,' Quail said. 'Though if you'd told us this at the time, we might have picked that costume of his up and brought it back with us!'

Goose spoke then, although her voice was so thin and shaky with fatigue that I had difficulty recognising it. 'Was it Red Macaw we saw, following Star's funeral procession?'

'I think it must have been,' I said. 'Though what he thought he was doing, I don't know. "I wanted to see her" - that's what he said just before he died. Maybe that was it. He just wanted to say goodbye.' I could not resist looking at Handy then.

The commoner returned my glance steadily. 'They're together now,' he said quietly.

'We'll go and get her in the morning,' Quail assured him.

Tribute of Death

'Why was Red Macaw out in the marshes anyway, when he was supposed to be trying to join the army?' Lily asked. 'Was he following the captain?'

'He may have been. But the otomi said he sneaked up on him.' I recalled how he had been when he had said this. 'It's odd. He went berserk when he found Red Macaw was dead – as though something dreadful was going to happen as a result. He clearly didn't intend to kill him. Then he wanted me to bury him as fast as possible, as though he wanted to hide what he'd done from someone – the sorcerer, I think, though I can't see why. Covering up what he'd done was even more important to him than killing me!'

'But why was Red Macaw there at all?'

'I don't know.'

Lily persisted with another question: 'You told us he said "Stop". What did he want to stop?'

'I've no idea, except I thought it had something to do with what he said before – about wanting to see "her". But he was almost dead. He probably didn't know what he was saying.'

'What about... What about the things that are missing?' Spotted Eagle demanded sharply. 'My mother's arm? Her hair?'

'The captain will have the hair,' I said. 'It's what he wanted all along – a charm to make him invincible. He needs that, and the uniform, and then on top of all that he has to have a sorcerer with him, a dancer with a dead woman's forearm – I'm sorry, with Star's forearm – to lull us all to sleep before he attacks. And all to conquer his fear, so that he can kill me.' I shivered. 'It's all fear, do you understand?' I could hear the tremor in my voice, reflecting my own terror. 'He's become afraid of everything. He's terrified of his ally, the sorcerer, whoever he is. I could tell that while we were out there in the marshes, burying Red Macaw. All that fear – and he's got it into his head that the one thing that will overcome it, that will prove to himself and everyone else and the gods that he's still the mighty warrior, is to kill me!'

'Well, he won't do it tonight,' Quail said stoutly. 'The courtyard's full of men and so's the street outside. There are even a couple on the roof. And we aren't about to be lulled to sleep, sorcerer or no sorcerer!'

They left Lily and me alone by the hearth. Handy and what was left of his family, along with their many guests, moved away, one by one, curling up to sleep in the corners, or creeping out into the courtyard to join the guards there or look for a space in one of the other rooms.

'Will they try again tonight?' the woman asked.

I lay on my back, watching the reflected light of the dying flames dancing on the roof overhead. 'The captain and the sorcerer? I don't know. At least the place is well guarded.'

'But if it isn't tonight...'

'I know.' I paused, listening to the sound of our breathing, the faint crackling of the fire, and a soft footstep from outside the room. 'If they don't come tonight, it'll be tomorrow, or the day after. Unless we can find some way to stop them first.'

'Would we get Star's hair and forearm back then?' she asked.

The question surprised me: it was hard to think of much beyond preserving our lives. Yet she reminded me of that other female being, Star's ghost, and the promise I had felt compelled to make to her, for fear of the vengeance that might follow if I did not. 'I hope so,' I said.

'I just wish I knew where to look. The captain must have abandoned Handy's plot by now – he'll be expecting the place to be swarming with men tomorrow, all out for his blood on account of what he did to Kite.'

'What about the sorcerer?'

I had to suppress a yawn. 'We don't have any idea who he is, even!' I heard a rustle of cloth. Lily had lain down beside me on the sleeping mat. Without thinking I rolled over and took her in my arms, and we lay still like that, side by side, letting the warmth of each other's bodies replace the fading heat of the fire.

Suddenly the woman mumbled into my shoulder: 'How did they know?'

I was drifting into sleep. 'Know what?' I mumbled.

'About Star. If they wanted a dead woman's hair and forearm all along – how did they know where to find them?'

I groaned and rolled over onto my back again. 'Sorcery, maybe?' I suggested blearily.

'Come to think of it, how do the captain and the sorcerer know each other?'

I frowned at the roof. 'There has to be some connection between them, I suppose. Lord Feathered in Black could have put them in touch – Handy works for him, so old Black Feathers may well have known his wife was about to give birth. Come to think of it, I expect he could have told them where Handy's plot of land was, too. Though the captain said something odd about my old master: something about not being afraid of him any more, about having an edge over him. So it didn't sound as if they were working together. Maybe old Black Feathers isn't the connection.' I yawned. 'Lily, I'm tired. Can we think about this in the morning?'

She had got hold of a train of thought, however, and was not about to let go. 'What about this man Cactus?'

'The curer?' I grunted in surprise. 'What about him? I can't see him being mixed up in this. He's just a small-time crook, a charlatan.'

'He knows the midwife.'

It was no use, I realized: Lily was not going to let me sleep until the talk had run out. Perhaps it helped to keep her own nightmares at bay. I forced myself to think about her question. 'You think Gentle Heart told him what had happened?'

'I think it may have been the other way around.'

'I don't understand.'

She made an impatient clucking noise. 'Think about it, Yaotl. How many children did Star have?'

'Nine… before the one she lost.'

'So she was well able to bear them, wasn't she? What suddenly went wrong this time?'

'I don't know… any number of things.' I frowned at her. 'What are you saying?' But I was beginning to understand, and the thought of it drove the last vestige of sleepiness away.

'Suppose you're a sorcerer. You need a charm in a hurry, because you need to break into someone's house. That means in turn that you need a dead mother in a hurry. You don't know of any, but you do know of a healthy woman who's just about to drop…'

'Now wait a moment – Lily, you can't mean…'

'Don't you think it's a bit odd, Yaotl?' She was speaking now in an urgent whisper. 'Star's regular midwife is ill. In her place, this woman she's never heard of just happens to turn up, and she dies, and then her body is stolen. The new midwife just happens to know Cactus, who calls himself a curer, but who *could* be a sorcerer as well. What if it isn't all just a coincidence?'

'But you're saying Star was murdered!'

'Not impossible, is it?'

'But that's... It can't be right, Lily. Nobody would do a thing like that.'

'The otomi would.'

I had no answer to that. She was right, of course. Only a madman would contemplate killing a woman in childbirth. That was like venturing into the realm of Cihuacoatl, the Snake Woman, and challenging the most feared of our goddesses to do her worst; and what kind of horrible vengeance would the dead woman's spirit wreak when she returned to Earth?

I asked myself whether the captain truly was mad enough to risk so much for the sake of killing me. I did not want to believe it. The thought that all the grief and bloodshed I had witnessed in the last few days, from Star's death onwards, might have been connected with me from the outset was terrifying.

I found that I was shaking. 'Lily, if you're right...'

I turned to towards her, to find that she had raised herself up on one elbow, and was looking down on me. There was not enough light to read her expression.

'What do I tell Handy?' I asked. 'If I'd known anything like this would happen...'

'You couldn't have done a thing.' Suddenly she lowered her face towards mine, and her voice became an almost silent movement in the air by my ear. 'You couldn't have helped. No-one could.'

'What do we do now?' I muttered miserably.

'Worry about it in the morning.'

'But…'

'In the morning,' she said firmly.

I felt the movement of her body next to mine on the sleeping mat. There was a sense of purpose to it, an urgency that I known before, which had nothing to do with keeping bad dreams at bay.

Then I rediscovered the wild hunger I had once found in her, that first time we had slept together. We were careful to begin with, I mindful of her hands and she of my tiredness; then we forgot about these things and just gave ourselves to each other.

Afterwards I had the best night's sleep I had had in years.

FOUR CROCODILE

••••

1

There was no attack on Handy's house that night.

I did not stir until after daybreak. A wonderful smell filled my nostrils: someone was cooking tortillas on a griddle. But what had woken me up was a peculiar sound, a kind of nasal warbling that put me in mind of some creature in inexpressable pain.

Cautiously I peered out of the doorway.

Handy was in his courtyard, calling out instructions to someone who I gathered was one of his daughters: It appeared she was the one making the bread. 'What's that strange noise?' I asked.

'It's your mistress,' he said, then lowered his voice to add in a shocked, even outraged tone: 'singing!'

The lady herself appeared then. 'Yaotl,' she called. 'Good, I'm glad you're up. I've been helping Goose to get this household moving again. Now we'll have fresh tortillas, and... What are you two staring at?'

For the first time since she had been rescued from king Maize Ear's prison, Lily looked healthy, and more than healthy. Her hair had been dressed, the ends caught up and taken forward over her brow to form two horns. One of Handy's womenfolk must have helped her with that, and with her change of clothes, into a matching skirt and blouse embroidered with blue flowers. Her skin appeared to have lost one or two of the folds and wrinkles that had grown on it lately.

Handy said: 'Yaotl wanted to know what the noise was.'

'Noise? I didn't hear a noise.'

'Never mind,' I said hastily. 'What are we going to do now?'

Handy said: 'Quail and the others have gone home to rest. As soon as they're back we're going to retrieve my wife's body.' He did not sound distressed, but determined. Whatever Star's remains meant to him, and however painful it might be for him to contemplate them, he had decided they did not belong in a muddy field. 'I'd better go and wake my sons up.'

As soon as he had gone, Lily said: 'Yaotl, we need to visit the marketplace.'

'You want to look for Cactus?'

'And Gentle Heart.' She smiled grimly. 'Of course we may have to ask at the House of Pleasure for her.'

'The House of Pleasure? That will be interesting. I've always wondered what the inside of one of those places was like!'

I was rewarded with a playful slap: a gesture only, because of the state of her hands, but it might have led to something more, as we had the courtyard to ourselves for the moment. However, the appearance of a familiar figure at the gateway put a stop to all that. We drew apart guiltily and watched, in my case in astonishment, as my brother's bodyguard, Ollin, stepped hesitantly into the courtyard.

He was dressed for battle, with his cloak flapping about him, his hair piled up on his head and his sword gripped firmly in his right hand. The lower parts of his legs and his sandaled feet were liberally spattered with mud. He looked uncertainly at both of us before clearing his throat with the air of someone who has something to say but no idea where to begin.

It must be bad news, I thought, and then: *Oh, no, not my family!*

Aloud I said: 'What is it? What are you doing here?'

'You're needed, Yaotl,' he replied abruptly. 'At your brother's palace. You're to come at once.'

Lily bristled at that. 'Who says so? Who are you to give my slave orders?'

'He's one of my brother's men,' I explained hastily. 'Ollin, what's happened? Not my parents, surely?' I felt sick. It suddenly occurred to me why the captain had not attacked during the night: he had been creating mayhem elsewhere.

Ollin was still staring at Lily, probably as confused as she had been and wondering why this woman was shouting at him. He took his eyes off her reluctantly. 'Your parents? No, nothing to do with them. It's Handy...'

'What are you talking about? He's been here all night. We saw him just a moment ago.'

'Will you let me finish?' he snapped impatiently. 'It's his wife. His wife's body, and that warrior's, what's his name?'

'Red Macaw. How do you know about them?'

'Your brother's Guardian of the Waterfront, remember? He heard about what happened yesterday and sent some men out there to secure the site. A good thing too, since I gather the locals are all still fast asleep!' His sneering tone was unfair, I thought, but I was not about to interrupt. 'We were too late, though. When we reached the place – one of those sodden little patches of mud out in the middle of the lake – all we found was the smashed up remains of a hut and a hole in the ground, full of water.'

Lily and I exchanged shocked glances. 'No bodies?' I said weakly.

'That's what I told you, isn't it? But that's not what I'm here for. It's not the bodies your brother wants to know about. I'm told there should have been an otomi warrior costume in that hut, but we pulled what was left of it to pieces and didn't find so much as a thread. Now why do you suppose that is?'

The answer to the question was obvious. The captain, or the sorcerer, or both had gone back to the field to collect it. What they might have wanted with the bodies, I had no idea, but by securing the uniform the captain had made one thing plain: he had not given up. And if I knew him at all, then driving him from his hiding place would have made him more reckless than ever.

2

Ollin had brought a two-man canoe. There was no room for Lily, who was going to be left with the unenviable job of telling Handy what had happened during the night.

As befitted a man of his rank, Lion lived in a palace, a sprawling single-storey compound close to the Heart of the World, the vast sacred precinct whose temples loomed over the centre of Tenochtitlan. It lay in the shadow of the Great Pyramid with its twin temples to Tlaloc the rain god and Huitzilopochtli the war god, and when the wind was in the right direction my brother could sit in one of his courtyards and smell the incense and the sacrificial blood.

Almost before the boat had coasted to a stop beneath the palace's stuccoed walls, Ollin and I leaped out and ran past the guards at the entrance. However, the sight that greeted us the moment we were inside made us both skid to a halt.

There were a lot of people about. This was no surprise in itself. It was a big house. I had expected to see women in the courtyards sweeping or weaving, men whitewashing the walls, messengers in their short formal capes, and enough guards to lend the household the dignity it merited.

All of these people were present. However nothing else about the house was as it ought to have been.

The women were not weaving. Their looms lay abandoned on the flagstones while they huddled in little groups in the corners. The men had dropped their pots of whitewash and were hovering by the warriors, trying to look important while avoiding catching the armed men's eyes. The only messenger stood by himself, apparently with nothing better to do than loiter here after delivering his despatch. The guards, instead of lounging idly by the doorways waiting to be relieved, were fidgeting and glancing nervously about them, the blades of their swords catching the sunlight and glittering as they twitched in their hands.

All of this I noticed out of the corner of my eye, but my attention was drawn to what I saw directly me in front of me. A small group of people stood or sat in the centre of the courtyard, surrounded by a large, clear space, as though no-one else dared to approach them.

My brother, the Guardian of the Waterfront, was formally dressed. He wore a long, yellow cotton cloak with a red border, tubular plugs in his ears, white ribbons in his hair, and yellow sandals with long, loose straps. His face and what could be seen of his body were stained black, although the pitch had not been laid on so thickly as to conceal his expression, which was ferocious.

Beside him stood a short, slightly plump woman of about my age: his wife, Papan, or 'Banner.' She was fidgeting, nervously shifting her weight from one foot to the other while two of her women wavered close by, impatient to be allowed to finish dressing her. Her cheeks were still brown because they had yet to apply their customary coat of yellow ochre, and her hair was a tangled mess.

Lion had made very few mistakes in the course of his career,

Tribute of Death

which had seen him rise smoothly from the humble origins we shared to his present eminence; but he was not perfect, and to my mind, marrying Banner had been his greatest blunder of all. It was understandable, of course: he had been the glamorous young warrior, sporting the finery he had just won by taking two captives single-handed on his first campaign, no doubt feeling very pleased with himself and entitled to the best his grateful city could bestow on him. She had caught his eye during the early summer festival of the Great Vigil, when the girls carried ears of maize to the temple of the goddess Chicome Coatl. Whether it was the glow of the pyrites stuck to her skin or the way she tossed her unbound hair, I never knew, but he had decided that she was the loveliest creature he had ever seen and therefore his by right. Her parents had agreed, partly I suspected to get her off their hands. Their wedding had been a conventional affair, the couple kneeling with their cloaks knotted together as they fed little maize cakes to each other, and the most remarkable thing about it was that she had somehow managed to stop talking for long enough to allow the ceremony to go ahead.

She was not talking now, although her mouth was open. She was staring with a mixture of astonishment and awe at the figure dominating her courtyard: a very old man, wrapped in a rabbit's-fur cloak against the morning chill, and huddled in a wicker chair that must have been placed here for him by the litter bearers who now stood behind it. His presence explained my brother's suppressed anger and my sister-in-law's nervousness, for he was none other than my former master, lord Feathered in Black.

If Ollin had not been standing next to me I might have turned around and left the moment I recognised the chief minister. The sight of his steward, Huitztic, skulking behind his master's chair as though hoping to use it to conceal himself, would only have encouraged me to walk faster. As the big, well armed warrior at my side was likely to object to my going, I stayed.

'It's a bit crowded in here, Lion,' I said loudly. 'Who else have you invited to this party?'

It was Banner who answered, trilling her way through the ritual greeting: 'Yaotl! You have expended breath to get here, you are tired, you are hungry. You must rest and have something to eat...'

'Nonsense, woman,' her husband growled. 'He's not exhausted because Ollin brought him in the canoe, and there aren't any tortillas yet because nobody in your household has done any work since our noble guest arrived.' The ironic emphasis on the word 'guest' reminded me that he and the chief minister had never been friends. Lord Feathered in Black's father had once been Guardian of the Waterfront and my former master hated the thought of a commoner like my brother holding the rank.

The old man in the chair had been looking at the ground. Now, when he raised his head, regarding me with hollow eyes sunk deep into his gaunt features, I noticed that he did not look well. Something must have happened in the last few days to age him dramatically.

'Yaotl,' he said. His voice was unusually hoarse. 'We've been waiting for you.'

'So sorry to have kept you waiting, my lord,' I said drily. 'Unfortunately when your steward came to fetch me I was busy. Of course if I were still your slave, it might have been different, but seeing that I'm not...'

My brother heaved an exasperated sigh. 'Yaotl, this isn't

Tribute of Death

helping...'

Lord Feathered in Black frowned. 'What do you mean, when my steward came to fetch you?'

'You sent him to Atlixco, the day before yesterday. I presume it was to drag me back here.' I raised my head to call out to the steward. 'You managed to get your cloak wrung out all right, did you?' The man behind the chair stiffened indignantly, but he said nothing. The litter bearers stared at him. My former master's frown deepened.

'I don't understand,' he said slowly. 'I didn't sent Huitztic to fetch you. He was supposed to give you a message, but he told me he couldn't find you. What's this about?' He half turned his head to glower over his shoulder.

I almost felt sorry for the Prick then. His adam's apple bobbed up and down spasmodically. 'I'm sorry, my lord... I, er, I must have forgotten to mention it...'

I laughed. 'Forgotten to mention you were thrown in a canal for insulting one of the locals? The water must have got in through your ears and softened your brains! And for that matter...'

'That will do!'

Infirm he may have been, but my former master had had many years' practice at imposing his will on others, and he managed it now by rapping out a few words. 'I will find out what happened between you and Huitztic later, Yaotl, but for now you might wonder what made me send my steward to Atlixco just to deliver a warning to a creature whose life I'd normally value about as much as a cockroach's.' He paused for breath. 'I take it he did manage to tell you what had happened?'

Momentarily subdued, I lapsed into silence. This was

unfortunate, because I had been about to add that it was odd if Huitztic had been ordered to find me, since he had seemed so surprised to see me when we met. If I had said that it might have cleared up a number of mysteries in one go. It might even have saved a life or two.

'Well?' the old man said impatiently.

'He didn't tell me anything.' I added defiantly: 'Though I don't suppose I'd have believed anything he said anyway. After all, you told me you were going to have your men follow me, and that was a lie, wasn't it?'

'No, it wasn't.'

'Yaotl....' My brother was about to warn me that I was going too far, but I was more interested in what the chief minister was saying now. There was an odd lack of indignation in his denial, as though he did not much care whether I believed it or not.

'It must have been a lie. If it wasn't, how come I didn't see them?'

'Because,' the old man said, as if he were talking to a child, 'you weren't *supposed* to see them. They were two of the most experienced spies in the city. And for all your famous ability to figure things out you obviously weren't smart enough to notice either of them when they were standing just a few paces away from you!'

I stared at him for a moment before, inevitably, whirling around to look behind me. 'So where are they, then?' I asked, bewildered.

'Dead,' he replied laconically. 'Unfortunately they seem to have met someone with better eyesight or more brains than you have.'

'But that must mean... no, wait a moment... when did all this happen?' An unpleasant suspicion had begun to dawn on me, which I was about to have confirmed.

Tribute of Death

'One of them vanished three nights ago: the night your friend Handy buried his wife. We lost the other one the night before last, while he was watching your friend's house. The first of them turned up the day after he disappeared, when the parish authorities in Atlixco fished him out of a canal. I understand you found the second.'

'They were *yours*?' I cried, as though we were talking about a missing pair of sandals.

'That's what I've been telling you.'

'But... they didn't look like warriors!'

'My understanding is that by the time they were found, neither of them even looked like men. What did you expect? They were spies, you idiot. They would have been dressed to pass for locals, commoners or even slaves.'

My mind reeled as it tried to grapple with what I had heard. It made sense enough: two bodies had turned up in Atlixco, but not been identified, and even in their mangled state that almost certainly meant they were outsiders. Also, so far as I knew there was only one native of the parish missing: Handy's brother-in-law, Flower Gatherer. 'So that's two mysteries solved, but what happened to Goose's husband?'

'Who?' lord Feathered in Black asked sharply. I tried to explain, but it soon became clear that he was not interested. 'I didn't come here to talk about some commoner,' he snapped, 'Or even my men. What I want to know about is what happened last night.'

'He means your adventures by the lake yesterday,' my brother added.

'I understand one of the fishermen told you about that,' I said to him. 'It's good to know your network of informers is functioning well.'

My brother shot a baleful glance at lord Feathered in Black. 'Mine isn't the only one, it seems! I sent Ollin there with a couple of men to investigate. They came back here to report, but they didn't have time to scrape the mud off their boots before his lordship heard about it.'

The chief minister smiled thinly. 'I am the emperor's eyes and ears. He looks to me to protect the city from its enemies.'

'Even if they happen to be your own servants?' I suggested.

'Even so,' he said indifferently. 'Though the otomi was never exactly my servant. More a tool.'

'Then it's a good job you're a noble rather than a carpenter!'

'Yaotl, please!' my brother almost howled. His wife took a step backward, bumping into one of her women. She looked about her in confusion, plainly torn between the desire to stay and listen and be noticed by the chief minister, and the urge to run away and hide.

Lord Feathered in Black said: 'Just tell us what happened to you yesterday. And before you're tempted to utter any more witty remarks, you may care to reflect on how much harder it'll be to crack jokes after I've had your tongue torn out!'

I mumbled hastily through an account of the expedition I had made with Kite and Spotted Eagle in the afternoon. The only interruption came when I described the policeman's wound.

'I know Kite,' Lion said anxiously. 'He's a good man. Is he going to be all right?'

'I don't know. Last I heard he was with a curer.'

'Get on with it,' the chief minister snapped.

There was a pause after I had finished.

Banner asked nervously if anybody would like anything to eat, but was ignored.

'Why don't you just tell me why I'm here?' I said at last.

'You know what Ollin found,' said Lion.

'He didn't find very much, by the sound of it.'

'Precisely,' my former master responded. 'And I know you will have worked out what that means.'

I had known the answer to that as soon as Ollin had first spoken to me. 'The otomi's still around, and probably more pissed off than ever. He managed to retrieve his uniform. Don't know why he took the bodies, though.'

'There may be more power in them than we know about,' lord Feathered in Black said darkly. 'But in any event, we have to work out how to protect ourselves from this madman. That's why I had your brother summon you here.'

' "Ourselves"?' I echoed. 'Why do you need protecting? It's me he's after.'

My brother said: 'Don't pretend to be stupid. Old Bl.... The chief minister is concerned that the otomi may blame him as well as you for his misfortunes.'

'I can't tell you how distressing I find that!'

My former master appeared to be examining his fingernails. 'What your brother means, of course, is that the captain may seek to avenge himself on me *after* he's finished stripping the hide off your miserable, writhing, shrieking *flesh*!' He ended on a shout that made all the men present flinch and Banner burst into tears. The chief minister ignored them all, leaning towards me while his hands gripped the arms of his chair. 'Now do you understand?'

I quailed. 'My lord, yes, of course, but what do you want me to do?'

'What you were supposed to do at the outset, before you allowed yourself to get distracted over some commoner's dead wife. Go after him. Get him before he gets you.'

'You must be joking!'

'I never joke,' growled lord Feathered in Black dangerously. 'What else will you do, wait for him to attack you again? How long will your luck hold? You will go in search of him. In spite of everything I still think you have a better chance of finding him than anyone else!'

'Thanks. You're probably right, if he's looking for me anyway. But if I get killed how is that going to help you?'

'You won't be killed,' he said airily, 'because you'll have an escort, one of the finest warriors in the city, and he won't be confined to skulking in the shadows either. I plan to have him stick to you as if you'd been glued together with bat guano. When your enemy comes, he'll have to take you both on at once.'

'Brilliant!' I cried. 'So now I'm going to have to go looking for a deranged otomi accompanied by the kind of rash idiot who thinks he can fight him! So who is this poor lunatic? Is he here?' I made a show of looking around me until my eyes lighted on my brother's grim visage and it dawned on me that I had my answer. 'Oh, no...'

'Oh, yes, brother,' Lion assured me. 'It seems I've been given the job of saving your skin once again!'

Banner's nerve finally broke. She hid her face in her hands and fled.

Lord Feathered in Black watched her go with a ghastly half-smile on his face. 'What's the matter? Does she imagine you won't come back?'

'Surely not,' I said drily. If I thought she might have been seized by panic at the thought of organising the catering for her husband's wake, I was not about to say so.

'It's not as if you're going to be entirely alone, anyway.' lord Feathered in Black's smile broadened into a quite cheerless grin. 'I'll send Huitztic along too – once I've made sure he's recovered his memory of that little incident you were telling me about!'

3

Lion and I went back to Atlixco in the canoe that had brought me to his house, although he insisted that I take the pole. It was unthinkable for the Guardian of the Waterfront to do the work while a mere slave lounged about in the bows as his passenger. He had his image to think about.

'Why can't we bring your bodyguards along?' I asked, as we set off.

He sat with this sword propped between his knees and looked morosely down into the bottom of the boat. 'They're needed elsewhere. Watching my house, watching our parents' house.'

'Couldn't old Black Feathers have spared us some more of his men? Huitztic will be as much use as a wax oven. And he worships the otomi – the captain's the only man he knows who's more mindlessly vicious than he is.'

He laughed bitterly. 'You don't get it, do you, Yaotl? The chief minister doesn't want us to succeed. How likely do you think it is that even the otomi could get near him, secure in his palace – even with a sorcerer on his side? His lordship probably has sorcerers of his own to protect him anyway. You and I, we've been set up. If we do kill the captain, I dare say the old bastard will be pleased enough. But

Tribute of Death

remember he's no love for either of us. He's probably tired of his steward too. If we all get hacked to pieces in the process I wouldn't count on him to go into mourning!'

Standing up in the stern of the canoe, I looked down on his greying head with concern.

Lion and I had fought continuously as little boys, until fate separated us by sending me to the priest house. We had been parted too young for the furious animosity of our childish squabbles to be tempered by any kind of mutual regard, and had seen little of one another as adults. For many years he had been the overbearing bully and I had been the uppity younger brother with the smart mouth.

Just a few months previously events had happened to alter our relationship. It had come as a shock to each of us to find anything in the other to respect, let alone like. But what I saw now was even more shocking. One thing I would never have expected, even in the days when he would hold my face under water with the sincere intention of drowning me, was to see him showing fear of any human enemy.

'You can beat him, though, can't you?' I said cautiously.

He looked up with wide open eyes, not troubling to conceal his nervousness, which if I had thought about it I might have taken as a compliment of sorts. 'I hope so,' he said quietly. 'But the truth is, Yaotl, I'm not sure. I'm not young, and I can't pretend I'm as fast as I used to be.'

'You're a match for men half your age,' I countered, because it happened to be true.

'Probably I am. But the otomi isn't half my age. He's got the speed still, and the experience, and the guts…'

'He's mad,' I pointed out.

That provoked another bark of mirthless laughter. 'Mad! Yaotl, you don't know the half of it! Did you ever hear what happened to him?'

Something in the way he posed the question made me shiver. I found my knuckles tightening around the pole, and had to force myself to loosen their grip, to let the long wooden shaft trail lazily in our wake, as it should if we were not to crash into the side of the canal.

Lion went on: 'I've been making some enquiries, asking about in the warrior houses. I thought there must be some veterans who knew of him. And it turned out there were plenty, but nobody who'd own up to being a friend of his, or having had much to do with him. Even his fellow berserkers – the other otomies and the shorn ones – even they looked away when I mentioned him, as if he were some kind of embarrassment to them.'

'But you found someone eventually,' I prompted.

'Oh yes. I found out who he was. And how he got his wound.'

'I always assumed he was in a fight. I often wondered what happened to the man who lost it.'

'No. It wasn't that. Let me tell you, Yaotl, if you think you're scared of him now, just wait till you hear the story!'

Lion had heard the tale in the House of Song, from a grizzled veteran who was too old to do anything now but lend his cracked voice to the verses our warriors chanted nightly, to keep our enemies in bad dreams. And this old man in turn had heard it from a prisoner of war: a warrior from Cholola, whose cage he had been guarding for a few days before he was taken to the summit of the great pyramid to be sacrificed.

Tribute of Death

Cholola was an independent city beyond the mountains to the East, one that the Aztecs had never subdued. They spoke the Nahuatl language, as we did, but like the Texcalans and the Huexotzicas, they were our implacable foes. We could not conquer them but fought them regularly, in what we called the flowery wars: formal clashes where both sides would test the mettle of their young men, honing their skills and giving them the chance to take a distinguished captive or earn the honour of a flowery death at the top of the enemy's pyramid.

Montezuma had sent an emissary there once, a young warrior named Pizotzin.

What his message had been, Lion's informant could not say, but it had not been well received. The Chololans planned to emphasise their rejection of it by sending Pizotzin home alive, but without either his hands, or the skin of his face and arms.

The Chololan prisoner had been one of those present when the mutilation had begun.

'He planned it. That's what's so terrifying, do you see?' My brother spoke in hushed tones. 'He lay there, on that stone bench, with five men holding him down, and he knew that once they'd started – once they'd begun to peel the flesh off his face – he knew they'd relax, loosen their grip, because they'd think he was so helpless from pain and fear that they wouldn't have to hold him any more.'

The otomi had not acted until half his face was hanging off by a thread of twisted skin. Only then, when any normal man would have fainted dead away and his guards had begun to laugh and joke among themselves at the expense of the tormented thing in their midst, had he made his move.

'Apparently it all happened too fast to follow. There was this loud crack which was someone's jaw breaking, and that seems to have been the man who held the obsidian knife. Then everyone was trying to grab Pizotzin, but they were getting in each other's way, and by then there was so much blood no-one could get a grip. The old man I spoke to said that, to hear this prisoner he was guarding talk, you couldn't rightly see what was happening, and in the end the Chololan just did what everyone else did: he ran for it. It was the shock. And funnily enough, no-one held it against him afterwards. What had happened was so bizarre that his fellow warriors all assumed it was sorcery, and there's no defying that.'

'How did the otomi – Pizotzin? – get away afterwards?' I asked.

'It seems nobody was prepared to try to stop him,' said Lion grimly. 'And is that surprising? There can't have been more than one man roaming around in Cholola at the time with an oozing mass of raw flesh where half his face should have been. Everyone who saw him would know who he was and what he'd done. They were terrified. In the end they let him go, and he made his own way back to Mexico.'

'Where he joined the otomies.'

'Of course. What else could they do with anyone who'd survived an ordeal like that, and come through it still able and willing to fight?' Suddenly my brother shuddered so violently I felt it through the dugout hull of the boat. 'But it's the man who went into that ordeal who scares me, Yaotl. What kind of man could lie there, while they were doing that to him, waiting for the precise moment when they'd be off their guard? That's not courage. It's not even madness. It's something beyond either, and that's what your old master expects me to go up against.'

'Old Black Feathers was right about one thing,' I said. 'It would be better for us to find the otomi than wait for him to spring out at us in his own time.'

My brother responded to my observation with a sardonic smile. 'I'm sure you're right. Do I take it you have some sort of plan, then, beyond blundering around in the marshes?'

When I explained what Lily and I had had in mind, he surprised me by turning pale. 'You really think that's a good idea – questioning Cactus and the midwife?'

'Don't worry. I don't think Cactus is a real sorcerer.'

'You don't?'

The eagerness in his tone reminded me that he had always been superstitious, and found anything associated with magic troubling.

'No. I've been thinking about this. The other night I got as close to a dancer with a dead woman's forearm as anyone ever did, and it didn't even make me feel drowsy. I think the otomi believes his ally is the genuine article – that's why he's so scared of him – but I don't. He's a fake. Which makes it all the more likely that Cactus is our man, because he's a fake too – not even a real curer. He's dangerous, of course, but only as a man.'

'Well, that's something. Mind you, it's not just him I'm worried about. You expect me to come to a House of Pleasure with you? Have you any idea what will happen to me at home if Banner finds out about it?'

I laughed in spite of myself. 'For a moment I thought you were worrying about something trivial! Now look – here's Handy. He looks as if he's been waiting for us.'

We had reached the commoner's house in Atlixco. Handy threw

me a mooring rope while I let the canoe drift against the bank. He raised his eyebrows when he saw Lion and I was afraid for a moment that he was about to prostrate himself before him: he had always been somewhat in awe of my brother.

Lion himself cut short any obeisance, scrambling ashore before the boat had stopped moving and demanding brusquely: 'How's Kite?'

Handy stammered: 'M-my lord...'

'Just "Sir" will do.'

'Sir... He should live, the curer thinks.' He looked at me wide-eyed. 'He didn't faint, did he? So with any luck his soul should be safe.' Whenever anyone suffered a severe shock there was always the fear that his soul would flee, leaving the body a shell, to wither and die from within.

I looked towards the house. 'Where's Lily?'

'Ah.'

I whirled to confront the man. He was studying the sky now as though finding something intensely interesting in its uniform blue. 'What?' I asked dangerously.

'I did try to persuade her not to. I said you wouldn't be happy, but she said... Well, I wouldn't like to repeat it word for word, but it was along the lines of who was whose slave and you didn't have to like it.'

'Where's she gone?'

He sighed. 'She didn't want to wait, that was all. And it didn't seem too dangerous, what she wanted to do – just to go and talk to that curer, Cactus, and Gentle Heart. Surely the marketplace and the House of Pleasure should be safe enough?'

Lion and I looked at one another. 'He's got a point,' my brother said cautiously. 'What harm can she come to?'

'Harm?' I cried, appalled. 'Do you have any what those two may have done?'

'No.' Handy looked at me curiously. 'I only gathered you'd be angry when you found out she'd gone without you... What's this all about?'

'We'd better go after her,' said Lion, gripping his sword.

The three of us ran all the way to the marketplace, where the sight of the Guardian of the Waterfront, armed and clad in all his finery, but panting and glistening with sweat, was enough to silence the small crowd of buyers and sellers we found gathered there, the hush spreading around us like ripples on a pond.

'Cactus!' I gasped. 'Where's Cactus?'

Nobody answered.

My brother raised his sword. Its blades caught the sunlight as he shook it in time with his words. 'What are you all standing there staring at us for? Where's the curer? Where's his friend the midwife?'

The people around us were a nondescript lot: commoners dressed in short, plain maguey fibre capes, and their womenfolk in equally rough but gaily-coloured skirts and shifts. The men were mostly scrawny, grey-haired individuals whose tonsured scalps meant they had never taken a captive in war. It may have been this that tempted my brother to try cowing them into answering our questions, forgetting that whatever else they might be, they were all Aztecs, and so born bloody-minded.

Two of the nearest stallholders, dealers in cheap crockery, to judge by their merchandise, looked at one another. 'Have you seen a curer and a midwife?' one of them said.

'Can't say as I have,' replied the other, scratching himself thoughtfully. 'Not that I'm sure I'd know what they looked like if I saw them. Do you know what they look like?' he asked Lion.

The innocent question had the effect of making Lion look foolish because, of course, had never set eyes on either Gentle Heart or Cactus. He was reduced to staring at me and Handy, in a silent appeal for help.

I looked about me and saw scowls and eyes narrowed with recognition. Some of these people must remember me from the morning after Star's funeral, I realised. 'Look,' I said, keeping my voice level. 'You all know Handy here, don't you?' I heard a mutter of assent. 'We buried his wife not long ago. Now we're just asking you to help us find the people who caused her death...'

Too late, I realised what I had said. I heard a choking noise from beside me. 'What?' Handy cried. 'Yaotl, what are you saying?'

'...And crippled your policeman,' I went on hastily, hoping to carry his questions away on a flood of words. 'You've all heard what happened out at the lake shore yesterday. Now Kite's injured, likely to die from what I hear. I don't expect you to do anything for my big brother here and I'm sure you won't do it for me, but Star and Kite, they're your own people, aren't they?'

I looked expectantly at the truculent faces around me while Handy lapsed into a pained silence.

Eventually a small voice – that of a young boy peering between the knees of two of his adult neighbours – replied: 'There was a lady here asking for Cactus and Gentle Heart too. Why don't you ask her?'

'A lady?' I caught my breath. 'You mean Tiger Lily?'

Tribute of Death

A woman, probably the boy's mother, judging by the way she had hissed at him when he spoke, replied: 'She didn't say her name, but she was looking for the same thing you were. We couldn't tell her anything, even though she knew how to ask nicely,' She looked significantly at my brother before adding: 'We've not seen either of them for a couple of days now.'

'Where did she go?' I demanded.

'She said she was going to the House of Pleasure.'

4

The House of Pleasure resembled a long, low stone palace, its façade topped with brightly coloured friezes, decorated with blooms in a pattern presumably meant to call to mind Xochipilli, the Prince of Flowers, the patron god of love.

For all the promise of its name and the reputation of the alluring creatures who inhabited it, there was nothing frivolous about the House of Pleasure. It represented part of the reward for valour on the battlefield. For that reason, it was forbidden to any man who had not earned the privilege of being allowed through its doorway, and guarded by hefty-looking warriors who were clearly jealous of their privileges. Even my brother, who might presumably have come here whenever he wished if he were prepared to brave whatever awaited him at home afterwards, had a hard time persuading them to let the three of us in.

Once through the doorway, Handy, Lion and I found ourselves in what might have been another world.

We were in a dimly-lit passageway. There was no-one about: 'Probably asleep, at this hour,' Lion suggested. It was early in the afternoon, when many people would be resting. 'Don't forget many of the girls will have been up all night! And the midwives and curers may well have been, too. What we have to do is creep about very quietly and hope someone can tell us if they've seen Lily or where to find Gentle Heart, before the guards decide our time's up and come to throw us out.'

The passageway led into a small courtyard, with a pond at its centre, surrounded by greenery: tall yucca plants and wild figs spreading their leaves and dropping them in the water. It was pleasant and shady, and here we were not alone. A number of women of varying ages draped themselves around the sides of the pool or sat on stone benches, chatting quietly in groups of two or three. The murmuring of soft female voices ceased the moment we appeared.

Three pairs of male eyes gazed intently at them.

Some men might have felt a sense of disappointment, perhaps. After all, this was the closest thing to a harem that I had ever seen. I might have expected to be treated to the sight of delicate, bare limbs, smooth skin the colour of honey and flowing like warm honey over soft curves, dark hair glistening like pitch and flashing, perfect, red-stained teeth; however, there was nothing of the kind to be seen here. Some of the women were young and were presumably pleasure girls, but they were dressed like fine ladies, in cotton blouses and skirts, with their hair, most of them, bound up in respectable style, with two loose tufts sweeping forward over their brows, or tied at the back with ribbons.

Yet disappointment hardly sums up the way I felt, looking at them. After all a beautiful woman is still a beautiful woman, even if she is dressed like a matron, and the eyes that looked boldly back into mine held as much promise as their half-naked bodies would have done. Which, admittedly, in my case was probably no promise at all. I had long since got used to the fact that whatever Lily saw in me was invisible to most women.

Handy had been trying to attract my attention ever since we had left Atlixco plaza, demanding that I tell him what I thought Gentle Heart and Cactus might have done. I had done my best to ignore him; now, however, he fell silent, overwhelmed by what he was seeing. I wondered whether his success in taking two captives had ever entitled him to come here.

I searched the faces of all the women as intently as I could without risking insulting them. However, neither my mistress nor Gentle Heart was among them. The fear for Lily's safety that had gripped me when Handy had told me where she had gone returned: if Gentle Heart was not here, then what was she up to, and was Lily with her or not?

The woman who stood up to speak to us was one of the older ones. Looking at her, it was hard to find any trace of the lovely creature she must once have been. Her hair was grey and the skin on her face was thin and mottled, and seemed to hang loosely off her bones as though she had lately lost a great deal of weight. One arm looked stiff and swollen. She got to her feet slowly, as though it required an effort.

'Gentlemen,' she croaked, 'You weren't expected, but please make yourselves comfortable. You have expended your breath to get here,' she added, more formally. 'You have come far, you are tired. Please rest and have some food. Right, now what's the meaning of this? How did you get past the guards?'

Lion and Handy both looked at me.

'We're looking for Gentle Heart,' I called out. 'And a merchant's

Tribute of Death

widow named Lily, who came here to talk to her.'

Nobody answered the question, but I sensed a stirring among the women and heard the faint rustle of material as one or two sat up and stared. Most were looking at the woman who had greeted us, as though they expected her to respond.

'Who are you?' she demanded.

'My name's Yaotl. I'm Lily's slave. This man is Lion, the Guardian of the Waterfront.'

'Lion! We know you by repute, but this is your first visit, isn't it? We are honoured!'

My brother coughed awkwardly. I continued: 'And this is Handy. His wife was Gentle Heart's patient.' After a brief glance at Handy I looked significantly at the woman and added quietly: 'She died.'

Her reply left me speechless. 'I know. She was my patient also.'

I stared dumbly at her while Handy answered for me: 'Slender Neck?' he said hesitantly. 'Is it you? What happened to you?'

She replied with a dry chuckle. 'Didn't recognise me, eh? Well, I'm not surprised.'

I looked from one to the other of them in confusion, eventually managing to stammer: 'You were Star's midwife? Her regular midwife?'

Slender Neck did not reply straight away. Instead she lowered herself into the position in which we had found her, as slowly and painfully as she had got up. Once she had settled herself she said: 'Yes, although Star hasn't been a patient of mine in a long time. It must be, oh, at least two years, I should think. But I told this to your mistress, Yaotl.'

'She wanted to speak to Gentle Heart,' I reminded her. 'Did she find her?'

'I've no idea. She wouldn't have found her here, and I told her that as well.'

'Gentle Heart's a midwife, though.' Lion put in. 'Where else would anyone look for her, but here?'

Handy added: 'When Star's time came, I had to send my daughter here to look for someone, because you were ill...' His voice trailed off into uncertain silence as the same thought occurred to him as it just had to me.

I put it into words. 'Osier Twig did find Gentle Heart here, didn't she?'

Slender Neck said: 'I can't tell you about that. As this man said, I was ill. Very ill!' She closed her eyes for a moment as though the effort of keeping them open were threatening to overwhelm her. 'But what I heard was that a young girl had called here, asking for a midwife to attend Star, and then later someone else came to tell us she was not needed after all.'

I frowned and looked again at Handy. 'Who would that have been, then?'

'I don't know. A friend of Gentle Heart's, maybe.'

'It must have been her, or someone she sent,' the commoner added, speaking to Slender Neck. 'If Gentle Heart works from here, wouldn't she send a message to say what she was doing, and whether she needed any help?'

The woman gave him a pitying look. 'Gentle Heart doesn't work from this house, because she isn't a midwife, and never has been.'

A sound broke from Handy then: a long, low, anguished moan; a great, deep sound that, perhaps, had been waiting for its chance to come out ever since I had let slip Lily's and my suspicions about the woman who had attended his wife.

Alarmed, I watched him swaying as though caught by a blow or a strong gust of wind, and I stepped towards him with my hand outstretched to stop him if he fell, and all the time the woman was still talking: 'I don't mean she doesn't work as a midwife. In fact I believe she does straightforward deliveries, and some of my colleagues use her as an assistant at times. I'm sure she's perfectly competent, but she was never examined by the midwives, and never admitted among us.'

'My wife,' Handy muttered, through clenched teeth. 'What did that woman do to her?'

'You couldn't know,' I said soothingly. I turned to the woman. 'What do you mean? You talk as though you know about her, but she's not one of you – why not?'

'Because she was expelled from the House of Pleasure while she was still a young woman. She was found to have been somewhat too particular with her favours.'

'You mean she was living with one of the warriors.'

'I think he was a Master of Youths. They beat him, singed the warrior lock off his head and expelled him from the House of Youth.' I thought I detected a note of satisfaction in Slender Neck's voice as she described the customary penalty for getting too close to a courtesan from the House of Pleasure, whose body should have been equally available to all whose warrior prowess merited it. I could understand the midwife's attitude: after all, the girl's punishment would have been to be slung out with nothing more than the clothes she stood up in.

'Not a real midwife,' Handy gasped.

'I don't say she was no good,' Slender Neck said

sympathetically. 'There are plenty of unofficial curers and midwives, and many of them are excellent. She made a mistake once, as a young girl, that's all. I'm sorry about your wife – I was so shocked when I heard about it, but it was far too late by then, of course. But it wouldn't be fair to lay the blame on Gentle Heart. I'm sure she did all she could.'

As Handy seemed incapable of any coherent speech I replied: 'You've no idea how it could have happened?'

'There are four hundred things that can befall a woman in childbirth. But as for Star herself – as I told you, I haven't seen her in a long time. She always seemed robustly healthy to me, though. You don't bear nine children if you're a weakling.'

'I suppose not, but what I'm asking is whether you think that maybe she didn't die solely because the birth went wrong.'

She hesitated, as if she had not considered this possibility and needed time to think about it. When she replied, it was with another question: 'What possible reason could a woman have for killing another woman and her baby?'

I hoped she was right. However, Lily's idea had planted itself firmly in my mind by now, and put down roots, and was growing strongly. It was all too much: the new midwife who just happened to be there when she was needed, Star's death, the plundering of her body. If Star had not died by accident, then Gentle Heart must be the culprit. The only alternative I could see was magic, which might act at a distance; but magic performed by whom?

Lion was trying to comfort Handy, in his own rough fashion, by grabbing his shoulders and shaking him vigorously. 'Come on, man. How will this help? There's nothing you could have done. Snap out of it.'

'My wife,' the big commoner groaned again. 'If only that stupid girl had just done what she was told. Why didn't she just come straight here?'

'Well, she didn't. You can't change it. It was fate, Handy, it was ordained by the gods...'

'It was bloody Cactus, wasn't it? That's what you didn't want to tell me about before! My daughter told him, and he sent for that woman!'

I was still looking at Slender Neck when he said this. I could not miss the way she suddenly stiffened and what little colour there was in her cheeks drained away.

'Did he say "Cactus"?' she whispered. Her hands had contracted spasmodically into fists.

'Yes,' I said. 'He heard about Star's being about to give birth from her daughter, and got word to Gentle Heart... Why? Do you know him?'

'I've met him,' she responded grimly.

'What happened?'

'He was peddling herbs, remedies for everything you could think of. He came to see me with a selection of things he said he thought I could use.'

Gentle Heart and Cactus: the woman who claimed to be a midwife and the man who had so vehemently denied being a sorcerer.

'He showed me the women's herb, so he said, and the opossum tail,' the woman added. 'Of course they were no such thing. I mean, they looked right but they didn't smell right or feel right, do you understand that? And when I tried to get him to tell me where he'd picked them, he wouldn't give me a straight answer. I didn't believe he'd gathered them himself at all: I thought someone else must have given them to him. Either that, or else he thought that if I knew where his herbs came from, I'd realise they weren't what he claimed they were.'

'He knew you were Star's midwife,' I said, talking mainly to myself in a voice that sounded hollow, even to me. 'He must have picked that much up in the marketplace. Or maybe he learned it from Red Macaw, who been told by Snake.' I heard a sharp intake of breath from Handy. Ignoring him, I explained: 'We know Red Macaw and Cactus knew one another: the curer was a regular visitor to Red Macaw's house. And yes, Handy, I'm sorry, but Red Macaw befriended your son – it wasn't Snake's doing, though, and I don't think the lad learned anything from Red Macaw that you wouldn't have wanted him to know.' As the big commoner looked stonily at me, I went on: 'Red Macaw made Snake keep him up to date on the news from home – including Star's pregnancy. There was no way the boy could have known that what he said would go straight to Cactus.'

'So it was that bastard Red Macaw, is that what you're saying? He told Cactus everything. He as good as killed Star himself!' Handy was twitching with anger now, and the colour was draining from his face.

'He may have,' I said carefully. 'But, Handy – listen to me! – he was duped as well, don't you see? As far as he was concerned Cactus was just a curer, a friend. He didn't know what the man was going to do with the information he was giving him.'

But what *had* the curer done with the information? I asked myself. Had he made use of it himself, or merely passed it on to another – such as Gentle Heart?

Slender Neck said: 'I told Cactus to go away, which he did, cheerfully enough. I thought nothing of it at the time – unfortunately.'

'Why "unfortunately"?'

'Because the next day, when I was coming back from the marketplace, someone bumped into me. I didn't see who it was. I felt a sharp pain in my arm, as though I'd got a thorn stuck in it, or been bitten by something. Then my arm felt as though it was on fire. When I looked I saw the marks, a couple of tiny wounds. I knew what had happened then, because the bleeding from them wouldn't stop. By the time I got home, I was shivering and wanted to throw up. The next thing I knew it was the next day, when I woke up here with every part of me feeling as if it was burning up and a mouth like a dried-up river bed.'

'I don't understand – are you saying you were poisoned?'

'Was I poisoned? Look at me now! It's no wonder Handy didn't recognise me. I nearly died!'

5

Gentle Heart may not have been based at the House of Pleasure, but she was well enough known there for one of the other women to be able to tell us where she lived. Lily, of course, had been given the same information.

We ran out of the building, under the astonished gaze of the guards at the entrance, and scrambled into the first canoe for hire that came past. The boatman's jaw dropped when he took in my brother's appearance. His amazement can only have increased when he heard the Guardian of the Waterfront's barked directions. Still, he seized his pole and set to with a will when Lion named the price he was willing to pay to be taken to Gentle Heart's house as quickly as ever he could go.

'Whoever attacked Slender Neck – it must have been either Cactus or Gentle Heart,' I gasped, as soon as I had got my breath back. 'One of them must be the sorcerer. They'll be in it together.'

Beside me, Handy sat stiffly in the bottom of the canoe. The vessel pitched and rocked as the boatman wove in and out between other craft, bumping into a few that responded too slowly to Lion's demands to get out of the way. The big commoner seemed not to notice the movement. 'He was in my house,' he muttered. 'Both of them were.'

Tribute of Death

'One of them poisoned Slender Neck, in order to leave the coast clear for Gentle Heart.' I was trying to piece together what must have happened while I talked. 'Once she was out of the way, you were bound to send to the House of Pleasure for a replacement. So Cactus stationed himself where he could intercept your daughter on her way there. Gentle Heart may have already been coming to your house, but he had to make it look as if she'd been summoned. I bet he was the one who called at the House of Pleasure afterwards, just to make sure they didn't send someone else who might have interfered with his plans.'

'But *why*?' The words broke from Handy as an anguished cry. 'Him, I can understand, if he was a sorcerer: he'd have had a use for her arm, at least. But why did she do it? And why us?'

'I don't know.' I admitted. 'He may have found her down on her luck and offered her a chance to make some money – a share of whatever he stole, perhaps.' There was another possibility, of course: the otomi captain could have recruited both of them. But then how, I wondered, had they all got to know of each other?

Lion had been listening to our talk, in intervals between shouting at passing boats and barking orders to his boatman. 'What did they do to Slender Neck?' he asked.

I had learned a good deal of medicine during my training as a priest. 'What she described sounded a bit like a rattlesnake bite. Cactus must have a supply of the venom.'

Lion said: 'I came across one of these once, in the broken country to the South. Horrible big thing, must have been as long as I am tall.' He shuddered. 'Never saw anyone killed with one before, though! How did he get hold of it? How did he use it?'

'Catching them is an art,' I said. 'I suppose it's one a sorcerer would learn, if he had a use for the venom. As for how you use it: I guess you'd have to be close, as close as whoever attacked Slender Neck was. I suppose you press the jaw closed on your victim's skin and venom flows through the fangs, even if the snake's dead.' I had learned a lot of curious things at the House of Tears, including enough about rattlesnakes to be grateful that I had never met one. 'It's not the most reliable way of killing anyone, or the quickest. Slender Neck survived, obviously. But it would have put her out of action for a while, which is probably all her attacker needed.'

'You make it sound as if Cactus might be a genuine sorcerer after all,' Lion said reproachfully.

'I know. I don't understand it, but that poison came from somewhere.'

'And Star? Was that poison, too?'

'It must have been the herbs. Cactus offered these herbs to Slender Neck and she didn't like the way they smelled. I suppose that was his initial plan: to get Star's own midwife to administer the poison for him.'

The canoe gave a sudden lurch, forcing me to break off and clutch the side to avoid being tipped out, as a shower of abuse gushed over us from the barge full of seed corn we had nearly rammed.

As I tried to recover my train of thought an idea occurred to me. 'Poison... It wasn't just Star and Slender Neck, you know. He tried to poison you too.' I was looking at Handy.

The commoner returned my look speechlessly.

'He was going to push some remedy onto you, when your child was buried. I told him not to, and he probably gave up because he didn't think you'd take it anyway. I should think it would have killed

Tribute of Death

you pretty quickly if you had.'

'You think he tried to kill Handy as well? Why would he have wanted to do that?' Lion asked. 'And what about those two men of lord Feathered in Black's? We thought all that was on account of you, if you remember. Why would Cactus or Gentle Heart want you dead? Neither of them knew you.'

'Maybe Red Macaw put him up to it.' The look on Handy's face had not changed but his knuckles were white with tension.

'Why?' Lion posed the obvious question.

'He was jealous. He wanted me and Star dead, because he couldn't have her. He wanted Yaotl and Spotted Eagle dead, because you helped bury her and he couldn't. So he got Cactus to do his dirty work for him – or maybe did some of it himself, while he was supposed to be trying to catch up with the army. And Red Macaw knew Cactus, didn't he?'

I frowned. 'According to his mother, he did, but how can he have had anything to do with the murders? I saw Red Macaw yesterday, remember, just moments before he died.' I winced at the memory. 'The captain killed him. What he could possibly have been doing out there in your *chinampa* field, I can't imagine, but one thing's plain: it's the otomi who wants us all to suffer, and has been all along.'

The big commoner suddenly squeezed his eyes shut. He looked as if he were trying to stem a sudden flood of tears. 'Why?' he whispered. 'I didn't ask for any of this. It's not my fault, what happened to him – I didn't lead him into that crowd of Tepanecs, who made such a fool of him. That was you, Yaotl. Oh, why did I ever meet you?' He let out a despairing groan. 'If it had been Red Macaw – him, I could have handled. I could have fought him and enjoyed doing it.

But the otomi... If it hadn't been for you, I'd never have set eyes on him. This would never have happened!'

'This isn't getting us anywhere,' Lion interrupted impatiently.

'Wait a moment.' I put a hand on my brother's arm, to get his attention. I looked at Handy. There have been times in my life when I could have given any man lessons in self-pity, and ordinarily I would probably not have spared him any sympathy. But his distress touched me because he was right: none of what had happened had been his fault. He had merely found himself in the wrong place at the wrong time once.

I had a vision of Lily's father making a point by throwing a handful of beans in the air, on a pleasant evening in Tetzcotzinco, just a few days before, although it seemed like a lifetime ago now. When I remembered how one of the beans had landed, freakishly, on its end, I understood what the old man had been trying to tell me.

'You aren't to blame,' I said, 'and I'm not to blame, because neither of us could have known what would happen. It wasn't even written in the Book of Days so some soothsayer or priest could warn us about it. It was chance, Handy. It was Tezcatlipoca.'

Aztecs believed a man's life was like a walk along a narrow ridge, with a giddying cliff falling away on either side. If you kept to the straight path you should have a good life, but nothing could guard you against the sudden side-wind that blew you clean over the edge, and that was the caprice of Tezcatlipoca, the Smoking Mirror, lord of the Here and Now. If you managed to survive, if you ended up, as it were, clinging to the cliff's edge by your fingertips, then all you could do was haul yourself back up and continue along the road.

'You just have to keep going,' I said. 'It's no use asking "why", or how you got here, or what you did to deserve it – even when times are good, you can only keep going. And the same will go for your children, and Goose, and maybe even her husband, wherever he is. We're all still alive.'

Handy looked at me then, his watery eyes narrowed into slits. 'So's the captain,' he managed to mutter at last.

'I know,' I sighed. 'And I still can't figure out how he fits into all this.' I voiced aloud the question that had come to me, not for the first time, a moment before: 'We know Cactus and Gentle Heart know each other, but what's their connection with the otomi?'

I did not have the time to reflect on this any further, however. The sun was dropping through the afternoon sky and our boat was bumping up against a landing stage. As we all scrambled ashore, I could only think about Gentle Heart and Lily, and hope that my mistress was safe.

The midwife's house was close to Handy's own parish of Atlixco. It was a neat, square box of whitewashed adobe, that from the outside at least had nothing to distinguish it from its neighbours or most other dwellings in Mexico. There was no screen over the only opening: either it had been pushed aside and left, or else the house's occupant did not value her privacy.

'Does she live alone?' I wondered.

I called the midwife's name softly from outside the house. When nothing came back out of the darkness inside, I tried again, a little louder.

I hesitated then, torn between concern and a curious feeling of relief. I was still fearful for Lily. On the other hand I had had no real notion of what I was going to do if I met Gentle Heart on her own territory, either alone or with Cactus. I dared not even contemplate an encounter with the otomi.

Lion said: 'So what do we do now, then?'

'If she's in, I want to know where Lily is.'

'And if she's not? Or she won't tell us?'

'Can we hit her over the head and search her house for clues?'

'Leave that to me,' Handy rumbled. I glanced uneasily at him before calling out again. Eventually, still unanswered, I put my head through the doorway and peered about me. I felt this only made me look foolish, though, so I stepped inside.

'Gentle Heart?' I said, for the fourth time.

I held my breath while I listened for a response. Perhaps she was in the courtyard, I thought, or the back room, and it was entirely possible that she had recognised my voice and was hiding. Nobody replied.

I looked around the room but my eyes had not adjusted to its gloom after the full daylight outside. What I could see looked normal enough, vague shapes that might be a wicker chest, a sleeping mat and a sack.

My eyes travelled around the dimly-lit space, taking in what they could. They returned to the sack. It lay in one of the far corners of the room, against the wall, as though it had been thrown there out of the way. While my gaze rested on it and I began to get used to the light it occurred to me that it might not be as normal as I had thought. There was something not right about its shape. What would you keep in a sack in a house, I wondered? Chillies, squashes or greens? But the thing I saw did not look like a bag of vegetables, all bunched together by the cloth that held them: it was somehow sprawled across the floor. Then I became aware of something else: there was a nasty smell in the room.

Behind me, Lion made a disgusted sound. 'What in all the nine regions of Hell happened in here? It's like someone kicked over a chamberpot!'

'Oh, no,' I whispered, as I stepped towards the thing. 'Lily? Not you as well. Please, not that...'

Part of me wanted to turn and run then, to forget about lord Feathered in Black and Handy and Mexico and even my family, just to go far away, far enough for me put all the horrors I had found in my home city out of my mind for good. Even while I was thinking this, with every instinct urging me against it, another step had brought me to the thing on the floor and I was plucking at the cloth with my fingertips.

I tugged at the material. I whimpered in grief and disgust as the smell flooded my nostrils and I felt the weight of a stiff, inert human body resisting my efforts. I dropped to my knees and reached out with both hands in an effort to shift the corpse, to get it onto its back and look it in the face.

The horror of what I had felt, imagining the body was Lily's, was swept away by what I saw when I finally had those sightless eyes staring upward into mine.

I was staring at a rigid mask, with its lips drawn back and its teeth clamped together in a mirthless grin. Spittle and dried vomit coated its chin. It was a woman's face. However, it was not my mistress's. And even as understanding dawned on me, I realized why it had been so hard to turn the body over. It was not one corpse at all, but two. Two human beings, a man and a woman, their stiff limbs forever locked in a last gruesome embrace.

I was too shocked to be relieved. I could only stare dumbly at the twisted, soiled features, the arms and legs grotesquely contorted, and try to find in them something I might have recognised in a living, breathing human being.

'Who is it?' Handy asked. 'Is she dead? What happened to her?'

Nausea threatened to overwhelm me. I felt as though I were about to fall over. I put a hand out to steady myself, inadvertently touching the body. 'It's Gentle Heart,' I said, in a hushed voice. 'And Cactus!'

'So it is,' said Lion coolly. 'But that rather upsets your theory, doesn't it, brother? Unless they killed themselves!'

'Maybe that's what happened,' I said. 'What's this?' A small, shallow earthenware vessel, decorated with bands of black and orange glaze, lay on the floor by my foot. It was the kind of thing that could be found in almost any house in the city; my mother probably had a shelf full of them. 'One of them dropped it, I think. See, it's cracked here? And there are some dregs in the bottom.' I lifted it until its edge was level with my nose for a cautious sniff. 'Smells like chocolate!'

'That's a rich man's drink,' Lion protested. 'What would a midwife and a small-time curer be doing with it?'

'I wonder...' I put a finger into the bowl to touch the residue at the bottom.

A piercing shriek split the air in the room. There was a sound of running feet, and then wild confusion as something warm – I realised it was an arm – was thrown around my neck and began tugging at me, pulling me away from the dead woman and shaking me until my teeth

Tribute of Death

rattled. The shrieking became words: 'Don't touch that! Did you touch it? Don't put that finger near your mouth. Yaotl! Are you all right?'

The faces of the dead became a blur as my head jerked backward, while a living woman's furious cries battered my ears, for a moment driving every thought out of my head.

'What are you doing?' Lion sounded as shocked as I was. 'You're mad, woman! Hey, stop... Handy! Help me get her off him!'

It was like being snatched out of a bad dream and having, all of a sudden, to take in what was happening around me and make sense of it.

The woman whose voice filled my ears and whose arm was locked around my throat, preventing me from answering her, was Lily.

She let me go with a violent jerk that pitched me forward beside the midwife's body. From behind me, there came a crash that shook the walls of the little house and brought plaster and sawdust down from the roof.

'Hold onto her, Handy, she's bloody dangerous. Just let me get up!'

Lily was sobbing now, hysterical tears choking her voice.

Groaning, I stood and turned around.

My mistress lay against the wall where the three of them had fallen, her face crumpled with distress. Handy stood over her, slack-jawed with bewilderment, while my brother got slowly to his feet, shaking his head and blinking.

I stepped across the floor to extend a hand. 'Lily,' I said loudly. 'It's all right. Look at me! I'm all right!'

She glanced up, fixing me with wide, glistening eyes. The sobs subsided. 'Are you... Are you sure?' she whispered fearfully, as I bent down and took her arm to help her up.

Lion was standing by now. 'Is one of you going to tell me what all that was about?' he inquired peevishly, as Lily and I hugged each other.

Over her shoulder I said: 'Someone gave Gentle Heart and Cactus the same treatment as Slender Neck!'

Lily mumbled thickly: 'I was afraid the poison would get you too!' She turned to look at Lion. 'I'm sorry,' she sniffed, 'I wasn't thinking.'

'Gentle Heart?' Handy repeated. 'But...' He stepped across to the body. He pulled a foot back as if to kick it, and then seemed to change his mind, recoiling and turning away in disgust. 'Why? If she was the one who killed my wife, then who...?'

'How long have they been dead?' I asked.

Lily said: 'I don't know. A couple of days? They're still quite stiff.'

Lion began inspecting the bodies. 'A couple of days is right, I'd say. Not easy to tell, of course.'

'She was alive when we buried the baby,' Handy reminded us.

'That's right,' I said. 'She must have died soon afterwards, though. Remember what they told us in the marketplace – neither of them has been seen for couple of days.' I thought for a moment. 'We know the sorcerer, whoever he is, was with the otomi yesterday. Maybe he finally took off with him after he did this.' I cursed suddenly. 'But why wasn't it Cactus? It would have made sense if it had been! We know he was trying to kill you, Handy, with those herbs he wanted to give you. And he's such an obvious fraud, he'd have been a perfect fake sorcerer!'

Tribute of Death

Lion frowned. 'You mentioned those herbs once before. It seems strange, that. Seems an oddly half-hearted way to try to kill someone. And didn't he give up rather easily?'

'I just put it down to him being a devious bastard,' I admitted.

My brother said mournfully: 'I suppose there's no way he could have taken his own poison by accident?'

'Or on purpose?' Handy suggested.

'I don't see how, or why,' I replied, 'Which means we've got to start all over again – and look for someone else altogether!'

6

Lily had found Gentle Heart and Cactus as we had seen them. She had examined them herself, as best she could in the relative gloom of the midwife's room, and had been considering what to do next when she had heard us outside.

'I hid out here and waited.' We had come into the house's tiny courtyard, and now squatted or kneeled on the well-swept earth floor, taking deep breaths of fresh air that smelled of nothing worse than the city's cooking-fires. 'I didn't want to show myself in case you were the killer, come back to make sure they were dead, though I should think he's done that already, long since. I was just checking, peeping around the edge of the doorway before showing myself, when I saw you touching the stuff in that bowl. I was afraid you were going to try tasting it.' She shivered. 'I nearly made that mistake! If I had…'

'What do you suppose it was?' Lion asked. 'Snake venom?'

'I doubt if it was that,' I said. 'Whatever it was, it killed them both fairly quickly.'

'What makes you say that?'

'They were clinging to each other. Do you suppose they were lovers? Maybe it was just for comfort. But the thing is, if the poison – whatever it was – hadn't hit them both at pretty much the same time, they wouldn't have been like that, would they? They'd have gone their separate ways. Cactus might have gone home. She might have gone out to deliver a baby or collect someone's washing or whatever she did to make ends meet. And even if they'd both felt ill, how long would they have gone on holding each other while it ran its course? And the bowl's still there, right beside them. Whatever it was, it worked a lot faster than snake venom.'

'I can guess what it was,' my mistress said. 'Tobacco juice.'

I looked at her with interest and a little concern. 'Pardon?'

'Tobacco juice. You press the leaves and leave the juice to evaporate in the sun. What's left will knock you out in moments and stop your heart before the day's out. But it tastes bitter – so you mix it with chocolate.' She returned my stare. 'What's the matter with you?'

'How do you know that?' I asked weakly.

She gave me a thin smile. 'My father told me. He learned it in the lowlands, while he was trading there.' Suddenly she laughed. 'Don't worry, Yaotl! How often do you think I'm likely to offer you chocolate?'

'With these ingredients, once would be enough!'

'I'll remember this next time I want my pipe,' said Lion drily.

'Someone obviously gave it to them, mixed with the chocolate,' I suggested. 'The question is, who?'

'Gave it to them – or one of them.' Lily glanced over her shoulder into the house. 'I bet it was Cactus who was the lucky recipient. He was supposed to be the curer, wasn't he? The one who could get the herbs she needed to ply her trade?'

I took up the idea. 'But if he was the fake I think he was, then someone must have given the stuff to him. Slender Neck thought so.

He was just a middleman, really. So whoever his supplier was must have decided it was time to get rid of him – with poisoned chocolate. But he chose to share the treat with his girlfriend Gentle Heart.'

'Poor woman,' Lily said softly.

' "Poor woman"?' Handy had settled himself against the wall of the house, a little apart from the rest of us, and up until now had squatted there in morose silence, keeping his thoughts to himself. Now that he chose to voice them, it was as an outraged cry. ' "Poor woman", you say! That poor woman killed my wife!'

'Did she, though?' I said thoughtfully.

'You know she did! You were there, you heard what Slender Neck told us. You were the one who said she and Cactus were in it together. And what about those herbs he offered to Slender Neck? They were intended for Star, weren't they? And he tried to kill the midwife when she refused them.'

I corrected him. '*Someone* tried to kill her. We don't know who that was. Now suppose Cactus genuinely had no idea what was in those herbs? When he tried to get Slender Neck to take them, he may just have been trying to drum up business. What if the same person gave poisoned herbs to Gentle Heart, only she was more gullible, or not skilled enough to know them for what they were? In fact... That's it!' I looked around at all of them excitedly, forgetting for an instant that we were talking about the deaths of Handy's wife and the two people in the house beside us. 'Whoever it was gave the poison to Cactus. He obviously persuaded him to offer it to Slender Neck, but she wasn't having any. So she was put out of the way and Cactus was told to palm the stuff off on Gentle Heart instead. And when he wanted to give you those herbs, Handy, I bet he really thought they'd help –

because the sorcerer had suggested it to him!'

Lily said: 'Then he'd have to know Handy and his family pretty well, wouldn't he?'

The commoner gaped at us both while he absorbed what we were saying. 'You're saying both Gentle Heart and Cactus were used by someone else? But who? I don't know any sorcerers!'

'What about your brother in law?' Lily suggested gently.

Handy made a rude noise through his nose. 'Flower Gatherer? He'd never have the guts, or the brains!'

'Whoever it was, you haven't explained why he came back to kill these two now,' Lion pointed out.

'Maybe they weren't useful any more.' I considered the question. 'He was afraid one of them would sooner or later figure out what had gone wrong with Star's pregnancy, and didn't want to risk keeping either of them live any longer than he had to.' I looked at Handy. 'I'm sorry, my friend, but the thing you're going to have to accept is that Cactus and Gentle Heart were as much victims of this thing as your wife was. And there's someone else out there, some associate of the otomi, who murdered all three of them.'

7

We walked from Gentle Heart's house to the parish hall in Atlixco. It was not such a long distance that there was much to be gained by taking the canoe, which in any event was laden with the bodies of the midwife and Cactus. Lion intended to leave them to the authorities in the dead woman's own parish. 'They'll need to record the deaths,' he explained, 'and it's one less problem for us!'

As the sun set and a blue-grey twilight enveloped the mountains, we found ourselves in the centre of Handy's home parish. The plaza outside was all but empty, the traders having packed up their their wares and reed mats and gone. Now, shadowed as it was, with the squat bulk of the parish's pyramid looming above it, the empty space had an air of menace that made me think twice about crossing it to get to the parish hall, even in company. And when I caught sight of a lone figure apparently trying to conceal himself against the outer wall of the building, I was convinced my worst fears had been realised.

'Look out!' I hissed at the others. 'It's an ambush!'

To my amazement, Handy responded with a laugh. 'No it isn't, Yaotl. It's only the Prick! Didn't you tell me old Black Feathers was sending him out here as part of your escort?'

'Him!' Lily cried indignantly. 'If we've got to deal with the otomi, I'd sooner do it alone than with him protecting me!'

Huitztic detached himself from the wall and walked towards us. I noticed he was limping. I wondered whether that meant lord Feathered in Black had ordered some of his followers – perhaps the hefty men who carried his litter – to vent his displeasure on his steward.

My brother looked at him critically. With the limp and the extra weight he carried about his midriff, the Prick did not make a very convincing warrior, despite the sword that swung from his right hand. Lion and the steward were probably of an age – if anything, my brother may have been slightly the elder – but the Guardian of the Waterfront had never let himself go and despised anyone who did. He glanced scornfully at the weapon the other man was holding and said: 'Are you sure you can remember how to use that thing?'

Huitztic drew in his breath with a sharp hiss and I saw the sword in his hand twitch threateningly, but he thought better of whatever he had been about to do. Instead he tossed his head indignantly in the direction of the building behind him. 'They won't let me in!'

'Who won't?' I asked, trying to conceal my amusement.

'The morons in there! I told them I was the chief minister's servant, but they kept going on about someone called Kite, and saying this was his parish, and he'd said... Well, you won't believe it...'

'Try us,' I suggested.

He swallowed audibly. 'He'd let the chief minister in if he came in person and asked nicely, but not some... some...'

'Flunky?' my brother suggested.

'Not imaginative enough,' I said. How about "Some overweight geriatric who thinks he used to be a warrior?"'

The steward stared at me. 'How dare you!' he spluttered. 'Have you forgotten who I am?'

'No, but by the look of you, you aren't exactly in favour at the moment.' I noticed he had acquired a couple of prominent bruises since our last meeting. 'Probably that had some influence on them in there. Maybe if you went home, gave the bruises a chance to heal, lost a bit of weight...'

'Besides,' Lion added, 'they're not wrong. This is Kite's parish, and if he's the man I remember, he won't have anyone else throwing their weight around here as long as he can do anything about it. And telling them you were from old Black Feathers's household wouldn't have helped much.'

Huitztic glowered at us. For a moment he stood where he was, clearly uncertain what to do, but it did not take him long to make up his mind. Slowly, like the flow of blood from a shallow wound, a grin spread itself across his face.

'Very well,' he said. 'Then you can just go in there and tell them from me that they had their chance. And that they may have more to worry about than the chief minister, for all his power!'

With that, he shouldered his sword, turned around and walked off into the gathering darkness.

'Now what was all that about?' Lion wondered aloud.

'Who cares?' I said.

'Not me,' Handy muttered. 'He's always been trouble, even when he was bringing me work. Though if there's any truth in what you told me, Yaotl, about that time you met him, when he got pushed in the canal, then I wouldn't mind a chance to ask him about it. I'd still like to know just how he knew about my wife and Red Macaw!'

'Come on,' my brother urged. 'Let's see if they'll let *us* in.'

For a man who would defy the chief minister's servant, Kite presented a wretched figure.

They had strapped him to something resembling an infant's cradleboard, so that he could move his arms but everything else seemed to be held fast. He wore no cloak and instead of a breechcloth, his hips were swaddled in bloodstained bandages, from the top and bottom of which wooden splints projected. His skin appeared to hang off his bones, as though he had neither eaten nor drunk in an age.

The men – a handful of the men of the parish, headed by my old acquaintance, Quail – had placed him by a brazier in the centre of the parish hall's courtyard, and now hovered about him like moths around a torch, attending to his every need. Hence he appeared comfortable enough, and the voice in which he greeted us, although weak, was cheerful.

'It looks worse than it is,' he assured us. 'And I'm allowed to have sacred wine, which is good. Mind you, I've been warned not to expect to take any more captives!'

Lion told us about our encounter with the steward.

The policeman's response was a laugh which turned into a dry cough. When he recovered he whispered: 'He was looking for you, Yaotl, and he wouldn't have it when my men told him you weren't here. In the end I lost patience and told them to tell him to sod off. It sounds as if he got the message!'

'It does,' I agreed, 'but all the same, I wonder where he went? Back to his master?'

'Who cares?' Handy replied. He squatted on the ground a little apart from the rest of us, as seemed to have become his habit, at the edge of the circle of warmth from the brazier.

'You ought to,' Kite remarked. 'Don't you rely on him for work?'

'On old Black Feathers, yes, sometimes. But from what you tell me and what we saw out there this evening, I don't suppose Huitztic has much say in it any more. Besides, we've two less mouths to feed now, haven't we?'

Nobody could think of an answer to Handy's bleak statement.

The sky's hue deepened from blue to black, while the first stars began to show themselves, and the parish temple, the only nearby building tall enough to be visible above the walls surrounding us, became a vague shadow whose very shape would shortly dissolve into the night.

There was no sound. The whole vast city spread over the island around us seemed to have gone to sleep; either that, or it was holding its breath, waiting for something to happen.

I looked at the prancing shadows thrown against the sides of the courtyard by the brazier's flickering flame, and felt suddenly uneasy. To calm myself, I talked. 'It's funny. Apart from the fire in front of your little temple there, we could be the only creatures alive anywhere.'

The temple fire was like a star: a little twinkling pale orange light.

'We aren't, though,' Handy reminded me. 'There's at least one otomi out there tonight. I ought to be getting home, in case he attacks again.'

'He didn't come last night,' I reminded him.

'You'd be better off staying here,' Lion advised. 'This must be the most defensible building in the parish. If you set off now you might

Tribute of Death

risk running into trouble in the dark.'

Handy said: 'Last night he was busy getting his warrior costume back, and moving Star and Red Macaw.' He shivered, and shuffled a little closer to the fire. 'Why did they do that, do you think? And where did they put them? Will we ever get her back?'

'Lord Feathered in Black said there might still be some power in your wife's remains,' I recalled.

'Is that true?' asked Lily.

'Not that I ever heard of,' I admitted, 'but then, the chief minister may know more than I do. As Lion said earlier on, he probably has sorcerers of his own.'

Handy's face glowed in the firelight. 'I just want to find her,' he said simply. 'When you and Spotted Eagle told me what had happened, I couldn't believe it. And you were so close!' His features were briefly wrinkled with pain.

'I'm sorry.' It was all I could think of.

He sighed. 'I'm all right, though. But it's not easy, you know? I keep thinking I'm getting over what happened, and maybe I am, but I'm beginning to realise that it won't ever be easy.' He took a deep breath. 'You know what the hardest part was? It wasn't this morning, when I learned about the bodies being taken. It was when Slender Neck told us about Gentle Heart. It was a shock. We trusted the woman, and… well.' He sighed again. 'Now she's dead too, and we're no nearer to knowing who was really to blame. It's the children I'm worried about. That's another reason I need to go home, because I'm all they've got. And there's Goose and her brood. Flower Gatherer can't have been much of a husband to her, of course, but still…'

Lily said: 'What about Goose's and Star's parents? Won't they help?'

Handy laughed bitterly. 'I bet they will – they'll help so much, by the time they've finished I doubt if any of my children will ever talk to me again!' He scowled. 'Not that they don't love their grandchildren. They dote on them, in fact, spoil them rotten.' For some reason at that point he looked at me, as though he expected me to come up with a response to his next question: 'Do you suppose that's why they hated me and Flower Gatherer so much? Maybe it wasn't that we weren't good enough husbands for their daughters. I wonder if they just thought our kids deserved better fathers!'

'That's not a question I could answer,' I said shortly. It was not a subject I cared for; I had been no sort of father to my own son.

An awkward silence followed. It was as if everybody was waiting for someone else to speak first, and the fact that we all knew what it was that needed saying did nothing to loosen our tongues.

I looked through the gateway at the void beyond it and saw how the plaza outside had become one featureless, empty expanse of night.

There are times when you can know what you need to do, and have made up your mind to do it, yet find that the impulse to move somehow fails to reach your muscles. I must have willed my mouth to open several times before the words finally came out of it.

'Come on, then,' I said roughly. 'If you're really intent on going home, I'll come with you.'

Lily gasped indignantly. 'Yaotl! What are doing? How dare you! You're mine, I forbid you to go out there!'

I said: 'We can't let Handy go alone. It's not far and it'll be safe enough. It's not as if the captain can take us by surprise.' I wished I could have made it sound more convincing.

Quail appeared next to me. He was carrying three swords, one of which he handed to me without comment. He gave Handy another and kept the third.

'Thanks,' I said, as my hand closed around the weapon. It was not a crude relic like the one Spotted Eagle had given me the day before; its polished shaft gleamed in the firelight and the blades set into its edges were fixed in two unbroken, flawless rows. 'I'll try not to hurt myself with this! Who's the third one for?'

'I'm coming too, but let's get this over with, shall we?' I could not help glancing across at my brother, who still stood beside Kite and the brazier. He was very still, with his head bowed and his fingers wrapped tightly around the handle of his sword. Looking at him more closely, I noticed the white of his teeth, which where clamped rigidly together, and then I realised with a shock why this was: it was to stop them from chattering.

Suddenly he whirled around and strode towards us, walking straight past me towards the gap in the courtyard wall.

Quail stared at him. 'What...?'

'He's afraid of the dark,' I hissed. 'Come on. It's not far. We'll be fine if we all keep together, won't we?'

Another figure appeared beside me then. I stared at Lily, aghast. 'What are you doing here?'

She smiled. 'We really must get this owner and slave relationship sorted out, Yaotl. I'm supposed to ask you questions like that!'

'But you can't come! It's dangerous!'

' "We'll be fine if we all keep together",' she quoted. Then, more firmly, she added: 'I can't let you go without me. I have a lot of money invested in you, remember?

We all stood at the gateway, gazing out into the night and hesitating like swimmers contemplating a plunge into icy water.

'Like the desert out there,' Lion muttered, 'only without any owls.'

'Is it always this quiet here?' I asked.

'Nobody likes going out after dark,' Quail said. 'But I suppose with all these murders, and all of them at night, and the rumours of what might be out there, it's not surprising if people are even warier than usual.'

'I don't blame them,' Lion said morosely. 'Give me a horde of screaming barbarians any day – anything but this!'

'What if he comes here?' Lily asked suddenly.

'Who?' I replied.

'The otomi. What if he comes here instead of going to Handy's house? There are only Kite and a couple of young boys with him to defend the place.' I had to smile at that description; Lily's 'young boys' were fully grown one-captive warriors, not equal to the captain but still armed to the teeth and able and willing to give a good account of themselves. Only Kite's direct order had prevented them from joining Handy's miniature army, and they had shown the greatest reluctance to obey.

'Why would he come to the Parish Hall?'

'It's you he wants, and you're here.'

'But he doesn't know where I am – does he?' The words were barely out of my mouth when a voice bawled out of the gloom ahead of us and told me just how wrong I could be.

'Hey! You in there!'

It was the otomi captain.

8

The shock of hearing the captain's voice turned our brave little band into a flock of terrified fugitives, scattering helplessly, like wild peccaries driven by huntsmen. For a moment fright drove every thought from my head, and in the urge to save myself I forgot Handy, my brother and even Lily. I was only aware of the harsh, mocking calls behind me and the feel of the ground under my bare feet. I was halfway up the steps towards Kite's rooftop garden before I came to my senses.

The otomi was not running after me. He was still shouting. The sound of it came out of the night, from somewhere beyond the gateway, although it was hard to tell precisely where because of the way it echoed off the sides of the pyramid and the walls of the buildings around it.

I stumbled to a halt between one step and the next and turned slowly to survey the scene around me.

Kite and the two men who had stayed with him were still where we had left them a few moments before, the three of them standing or lying in the middle of the courtyard beside the brazier. My flight had carried me right past them. Long, wavering shadows in the firelight told me where three of the others were. Lion and Handy had pulled up short next to the gateway, and were standing on either side of it, while Quail was slowly walking back towards them from the bottom of the steps.

I could see nothing beyond the walls of the courtyard, but I would have bet that the captain was standing in the middle of the plaza outside, his sword by his side, bellowing out his taunt as brazenly as if he were in the midst of a battle-line.

I could not see Lily.

I looked wildly about me. I peered into the shadowed corners of the courtyard, hoping I might have missed her the first time I looked. I ran down the steps, calling her name.

'I'm up here!'

I spun around and looked up. My mistress stood at the edge of the roof, near the top of the steps.

At first I was too astounded to be relieved. 'What are you doing up there?'

'I felt like doing some gardening,' she shouted over the sounds from outside. 'There's a prickly pear here that's ripe for harvesting – what do you think? I ran, the same as everyone else!'

'What's going on?' Kite shouted. 'What are you all doing back here? And who is that out there?'

The answer came back immediately. 'You know who I am and what I've come for! Is Yaotl in there with you? If he is, send him out here now!'

Lily ran down into the courtyard, the slap of her feet accompanying the captain's bellowing like a two-toned drum beating the rhythm of a hymn.

'We have to get Kite up onto the roof,' she cried breathlessly as she came up to me.

I stared at her.

'Yaotl, listen! He can't run or fight. His only chance is if we get him up there and barricade him in somehow while someone else gets help. Do you understand?'

I understood. I turned to the two young soldiers and between us Lily and I managed to convince them of what they had to do, ignoring their chief's protests.

'Forget it!' Kite said angrily. 'I can stay here. I'm not skulking on the roof while that madman makes free with my parish!'

Beside the door, my brother raised his own voice in answer to the captain's. 'And if he isn't here?'

'Then you tell me where he went. Or it'll be the worse for you!'

Lion seemed to think about that for a moment. He turned to me and beckoned with a sharp gesture. I ran towards him while Lily supervised Kite's short journey up the steps.

'I'm waiting,' came the voice from outside. 'Do I have to come in there and look for him?'

I had only half the courtyard to cross to join my brother by the gateway, but it seemed much farther. Every step that took me closer to the roaring man in the square felt as though it might be my last. I seemed to be walking slowly, and when I looked about me I was like a dying man filling his sight with familiar things for the last time: the small square space of the courtyard, the brazier at its centre, the flat-roofed rooms surrounding it on three sides and the gateway to the plaza on the fourth side. The brazier's flickering light made the entrances to the rooms look like the mouths of caverns. The doorways opened out into the central space, including one on either side of the stairway. At the top of the steps, crowning the rooms and so overlooking the courtyard from three sides, was Kite's well-planted patio, whose owner was now, under protest, being settled among his cacti and succulents.

I was tempted to make a dash for it, run indoors and cower behind a large clay pot or a wicker chest, but I did not. I knew the captain would not leave or give up now until he had found me.

'He's in there, isn't he?' the captain yelled. 'I'm going to count to twenty, and you'd better send him out before I've finished!' There was a brief pause before he began, in a voice loud enough to be heard all over the Valley of Mexico: 'ONE!'

Handy, standing beside the far gatepost, muttered an oath. 'Why's he want to drag this out?'

'TWO!'

I looked at Lion, and he looked back at me, with his eyes hard and unblinking and his mouth set in a grim line. Now that his enemy had come out to confront him, he longer showed a trace of fear. 'Yaotl…'

'THREE!'

'All right,' I gasped. Somehow I managed to drag one foot in front of the other. 'I'm going. Sorry about all the trouble, but…'

'FOUR!'

He seized my arm, gripping it so hard that the pain cut through my misery and fear, making me flinch. 'You stay there!' he snapped. 'You're no good to anyone as a corpse!'

'FIVE!'

I gaped at him but he was not looking at me now. He beckoned to Quail and Handy. 'We can't just stand here waiting for him.' The observation met with a growl of approval.

'SIX!'

I looked about me as if waking from a dream. 'But…'

'SEVEN!'

'I wish he'd pack that in!' Lion said, to no-one in particular. He turned back to me. 'You're going nowhere. Forget that you're my brother. I wouldn't give that bastard what he wants, even if he were demanding old Black Feathers' liver fresh from the griddle.'

'EIGHT!'

'We could rush him,' Handy suggested.

'NINE!'

I stared at the commoner. 'You're crazy! We can't take him on! Don't you know what he…'

'TEN!'

'Of course I do,' he replied. 'But we can't just stand and wait.'

'ELEVEN!'

Lion said: 'Handy's right. It's all we can do. Yaotl, get back up on the roof. Tell Kite and Lily what we're about and send those two lads down here.'

I stared stupidly at the top of the building.

'Go on, move! If he attacks first then we'll hold him off down here as long as we can. If he shows himself out there first, we'll charge him. He won't be expecting that. If we can at least wing him –'

'TWELVE!'

'– you may have a chance. Now go!'

I looked at the roof, at my brother's tense, determined face that was already swinging away from me towards the doorway, at Quail and Handy, standing firm although the swords shook in their hands, at the doorways leading into the interior of the building with their false promise of safety, at Lion once more, and I took them all in so fast I made myself dizzy.

'THIRTEEN!'

I made up my mind. I could stand here and argue with my brother or I could do as he said. I ran towards the steps as the next number rang out in time to the pulse beating in my head.

'FOURTEEN!'

I burst onto the rooftop. Lily dashed towards me, a cry forming in her throat, but I waved her away.

'No time,' I gasped. I stammered out the instructions Lion had given me.

Kite's men looked at each other uncertainly.

'FIFTEEN!'

'Go on!' the policeman cried hoarsely. 'You can't do anything for me up here. Get down into the courtyard and fight!'

They ran to obey. I started after them, but Lily called me back sharply.

'Where are you going?'

'I can't let Lion and Handy and Quail do this on their own. I've got to help,' I said.

'You can help me.'

My mistress had her bandaged hands on one of the plant containers that decorated the rooftop patio: pots with mesquite shrubs, maguey plants, prickly pears and other cacti. She was trying to manoeuvre one of the thornier specimens towards the top of the steps. 'We've got to make a barricade. If he comes up here after us then he'll have to fight his way through a hedge.'

'SIXTEEN!'

I did as I was told. I dropped my sword and the two of us hauled as many plants as we could to the edge of the patio, with me standing at the top of the steps, dragging the pots, and Lily pushing them as best she could with the palms of her hands.

'SEVENTEEN!'

The cry stung my ears. 'Didn't know he could count up that far,' I grunted.

'Will it be enough?' Lily wondered.

'It'll have to do,' I said. I took a step backwards, surveying the makeshift barricade. I had intentionally put myself on the wrong side of it, meaning to run down the steps to be with my brother. Now it formed a wall between me and Lily, one which, I realised with a pang, neither of us might live to cross.

'Go on,' she said brusquely.

'EIGHTEEN!'

'And don't forget your sword!' She turned away without another word. I opened my mouth to speak, thought better of it, picked up the weapon and dashed back down into the courtyard.

'Where is he?' one of Kite's men was asking.

'No idea,' Handy muttered. 'We can hear that madman all right, but we can't see him.'

Lion had taken charge, directing Handy, Quail and the others into their positions with a few gestures. Now he and Quail were crouched, on one side of the entrance to the courtyard, with Handy and Kite's young warriors facing them.

With a silent jerk of the head, my brother summoned me to his side. 'Keep quiet,' he hissed. 'For all we know he might be right outside. When I give the order, I want everyone through the gateway at the same time. Then we spread out. Hopefully we can confuse him, make him waste a heartbeat or two choosing his target.'

I looked ruefully at the sword in my hand. 'I've not used one of these in years. Any tips?'

'Just hit him with the bloody thing.'

I lifted my eyes to look again at the plaza outside. As before, I saw nothing.

'NINETEEN!'

The only illumination came from the stars and the little brazier burning at the top of the pyramid.

There was something strange about the light from that brazier. I noticed that it was growing stronger, as though someone had stoked the fire. I wondered briefly what the priest, who ought to be tending it and keeping watch from the pyramid's summit was doing: hiding in the sanctuary at the back of his temple, perhaps. Possibly he had had some premonition of what was going to happen tonight and remembered a prior engagement elsewhere.

A peculiar shape seemed to be dancing in front of the pyramid, and for a moment I wondered what it might be, before I remembered the idol that lived at its summit, and the long, grotesque shadow it would cast in the light of the temple fire. The flames' flickering would make the shadow seem to gyrate, I thought, although it seemed to prance about too vigorously for that.

I felt my mouth suddenly go dry as I realised my mistake.

'It's the sorcerer,' I gasped. 'Look! Dancing on top of the pyramid!'

'With my wife's forearm?' Beside me, Handy started forward.

I caught his arm. 'Where are you going? You can't do anything from here!'

'But don't you see?' He cried. 'He's got…'

'TWENTY!'

Handy fell silent.

I glanced up at the rooftop patio, but could see nothing beyond the barricade of plant pots.

The men around me in the courtyard were like carvings.

There was silence, broken only by the crackling of the temple fire.

The fire was crackling much too loudly.

As the sound grew, becoming impossible to ignore, I found my eyes drawn towards its source.

At first it was hard to make sense of what I saw. The glow at the top of the pyramid was growing, becoming more intense and somehow spreading. From the coals on the brazier, flames and sparks were leaping like frenzied demons, darting up and spreading out, breeding little copies of themselves that in turn flew skywards in swarms, like flies off the surface of the lake in springtime. The glow became a red glare, the idols in front of the temple seeming to stand up before it in strange, distorted postures before the flames swirled around them and engulfed them.

'I don't believe it!' I cried 'He's set fire to the temple!'

9

I stood transfixed, my eyes fixed on the sight of the burning temple. I knew, without asking, that anyone else who saw what I was looking at would be feeling the same as I. Shock, fear and despair tumbled into and out of my mind, leaving behind them only a kind of hollowness.

The thatched roof of the shrine had caught now. The crackling had become a roar, as the flames reared up, lighting up the plaza and the surrounding streets. As I watched, there came a loud crash and a sheet of yellow fire enveloped the top of the pyramid: the roof had collapsed.

This was more than an audacious act of vandalism, more even than sacrilege. The captain and the sorcerer had burned the temple. It was the gesture that ended wars, for to seize and destroy your enemy's temple signalled to both friend and foe that the fighting was over. No Aztec, certainly no man who had ever served in an army, could see it without knowing at once what had happened or to whom the day belonged. That was why they had started the fire. The otomi wanted us to know that he had won, and that there was nothing we could do now but settle with him on whatever terms he allowed.

It was no use hoping someone in authority would notice the fire and come to put it out. Everyone would assume that the parish police would deal with it, or call for help if they could not. But the parish police were helpless, as mesmerised as I was by the sight of their temple in flames. The first sign of movement that distracted my eyes from the leaping flames was the men around me in the courtyard relinquishing their posts to stand together in the middle of the entrance, staring up at the blaze while their shadows danced behind them.

Then came the sound of laughter.

It was unearthly. It was laughter unlike anything I had ever heard before, like a girlish giggle but deep, as if it came from a throat large enough to give it a hollow ring.

I stared at the middle of the plaza.

There was a solitary figure there, plainly visible now in the spreading firelight. He stood quite still, as though rooted, directly in front of the entrance to the parish hall. Only his long shadow moved with the flickering flames. No more words came from him but his unmoving presence was like a challenge. It was as if he were daring us to come out and fight him.

I watched, appalled, as Lion prepared to take up the dare.

I did not hear the order. The first I knew of it was when my brother was through the courtyard and racing out into the open, the plaza ringing with his war-cry. The others were close behind him and then, caught by the same urgency that drove them, by the same pent-up anger and fear, so was I, the scream of rage tearing itself free of my throat as I ran.

Nobody remembered their orders. Instead of spreading out, we all ran straight ahead, converging on the lone figure in the plaza like wasps on a honeycomb. Incredibly, we seemed to have taken our foe by surprise. He made no move, even when Lion was upon him, swinging his sword and then leaping backwards to avoid the counter-blow while first one and then the other of his followers ran in to the attack. For a moment our enemy was the eye of a storm of whirling blades and flying blood. Before I got to him he had fallen, hitting the ground with an audible crash.

'We got him!' Lion's cry of triumph rang in my ears as I ran up my comrades. My footsteps slowed as I stared at the scene, taking it in with a mounting horror that made itself known by the churning in my guts and a small, helpless noise forcing itself out of my throat.

Handy yelled: 'We did it, Yaotl! We...'

I pushed my way through into the middle of the little group around the dead man. I stared at the corpse. It was badly mangled but the face, contorted with agony though it was, was unmistakable. So were the ropes that had been used to secure it and the wooden frame it had been tied to.

I whiled to face Lion. 'That's not the otomi!' I yelled. 'Where is he?'

My brother stared blankly at me. 'What are you talking about?'

'It's Huitztic! It's old Black Feathers' steward! They killed him and left him here as a decoy!' I screamed. 'Now where's the otomi? And where's the sorcerer?'

Even as I posed the question, I knew it was too late.

He had stationed himself against the outer wall of the parish hall, just paces away from where my brother and I had been crouching. Now, while we stared stupidly at the decoy he had set up for us, he sprang his trap.

He did not look like a human. He was a dark shape, casting a shadow that could have been made by an animal, a tree, a tower or a god. But he was moving with more purpose than any animal, coming across the plaza with a measured tread that showed contempt for his enemies in every step he took.

I had never seen him in his full uniform before.

It was not merely a means of distinguishing himself from others or rallying the men under his command. The close-fitting suit of green cotton that covered his arms, legs and trunk like a second skin, the golden bone through his lip and the tall, teardrop-shaped back device, bedecked with green feathers and topped with long quetzal plumes that fluttered and danced in the wind stirred up by the flames: these were a weapon in themselves, as deadly as the sword in his right hand. As he strode toward the middle of the plaza, he knew most of us would be so helpless with fear at the sight of him that he would scarcely need to fight.

He screamed once and charged.

One of Kite's men did not move at all. The other one did, but far too late, and they were still too close together when the madman struck.

The nearest of his victims was on the captain's left. The sword flew from one hand to the other to be swung deftly into his opponent's arm before the man had a chance to raise his own weapon. I heard the bone crack. The injured man shrieked and reeled aside. At the same time a kick took his neighbour, a sandalled foot catching him in the midriff while he was still backing away. He fell sprawling, and the last thing he would have seen as he stared helplessly up into the sky was the blades of the sword as they swept down towards his face. The otomi turned back towards the man with the broken arm and finished him off with a single slash.

The rest of us backed away instinctively. I looked out of the corner of my eye at my brother. I saw the way he held himself, with his knees flexed, his feet braced just so, his head thrust intently forward, and there came straight back to me the games he had loved playing as a boy, pretending to be a warrior in our parents' courtyard. I knew he was preparing to spring.

It was suicide, and I could not let him do it.

I was slightly nearer to the enemy. Without knowing what I was doing, I leapt at him, howling, the sword raised in both hands as I swung it wildly. What had my brother's advice been?

Just hit him with the bloody thing.

The captain smashed the weapon out of my hands with a blow that numbed my wrists and sent ripples of pain up into my shoulders. The force of the blow made me stagger and set him whirling in a half circle. He was facing away from me when he raked my left leg with the heel of his sandalled foot, driving it downwards in a backwards kick that peeled a strip of skin from knee to ankle and sent me crashing to the ground.

I fell at his feet, writhing in agony, my leg twisting itself uncontrollably as though trying to snatch itself from a fire. The only thing that stilled me was a foot planted heavily in my stomach, pinning me to the ground.

I struggled for a moment and lay still. My breath came in shallow gasps. I was faint and dizzy from shock and pain.

The temple blazed. The flames may have abated a little now, much of their fuel consumed, but the smell of wood-smoke and burned resin from the shrine's store of incense hung thick and sweet in the air.

Tribute of Death

When I looked up, I saw the otomi's face clearly, glistening in the orange light. His few teeth gleamed in his monstrous half-grin.

His horrible four-bladed club was poised over my face. Warm fluid dripped from it onto my forehead.

I could imagine him mulling over which bit of me to cut open first. However, he was not looking at me.

'That's right,' he snarled. 'Keep backing away. Further than that. Make it far enough and I might kill this piece of offal with one blow. Well, maybe just a couple!'

'Let him go,' my brother cried, his voice high-pitched with strain. 'Let him go and we'll forget we ever saw you.'

'It's too late for that,' the captain rasped. The weapon in his hand twitched, spattering me with more fresh blood. 'Do you think I'm interested in running away? You're the Guardian of the Waterfront, aren't you? Well, I'm looking forward to fighting you. It's a long time since I took on anyone who was worth the trouble of killing. Ah... Not so fast!'

I flinched as the blades flashed by within a hair's breadth of my nose. Then came a cackling laugh.

'Nearly lost him then!' the captain cried. 'Now stand back if you don't want his end to be any more horrible than it needs to be. I can crush his skull in my own time. If you rush me I'll wind his guts three times around this club before you even get close! Now, I've been looking forward to this, Yaotl, so I do hope your brother doesn't go and spoil it for all of us... Oh, here comes someone else. Well, I don't think you need an introduction. You've met.'

My head snapped round to follow the captain's glance.

I could just about make out, against the light of the burning temple, the shadowy figures of my brother, Handy and Quail. Something moved behind them; a fourth figure, shorter and slighter than any of them, mildly stooped and walking with a shuffling gait, which it interrupted every few steps by stopping and spinning around.

It was holding two things. Its right hand grasped an incense ladle, of the kind used by priests, a bowl full of hot coals and smoking copal resin. In its left was a pale object that I had seen before. The captain was correct: the newcomer and I had met, on the night when they had together attacked Handy's house.

I stared fearfully at the strange figure as it stepped and twirled towards me. Its path took it past Lion, Handy and Quail, but none of them made any move to interfere. They seemed fascinated, like rabbits transfixed by a weasel.

I dared not speak. *Do something, you fools,* I mouthed in silent desperation. *It's not as if she's a real sorcerer!*

And then, surprised by my own words, I thought: *She?*

'Come to watch?' the captain smirked.

The sorcerer made no answer. I could only look on with mounting dread as the outlandish creature danced slowly towards me, and past me. It began circling the otomi, stopping behind the great warrior's back for one more twirl.

'I wish you'd stop that,' the captain said irritably. 'It's beginning to get on my nerves!'

Still silent, the sorcerer danced away obediently. It was only afterwards, playing the scene back in my mind, that I realised that the left hand was now empty.

'That's better. Now, where shall I cut?' He raised the sword.

From very far away I heard shouting voices and running feet, but all my senses could take in then were those obsidian blades, glittering in the firelight.

I shut my eyes, ready for the impact.

The roar of flames filled my ears. Smoke scorched my throat and stung my nostrils.

An age seemed to pass, and nothing happened.

Was this what death was like, I wondered, waiting forever until the way through the Nine Hells opened up before you?

A piercing, unearthly cry broke out of the darkness around me, a scream of inhuman pain and fury, and suddenly to the smell of blazing wood and thatch was added something new, a bitter, oily reek that I struggled to identify.

When I opened my eyes again, it was to watch my enemy dying on his feet. As he stood, smoke swirled above and around him, and yellow flames and sparks were leaping over his head. The sword, still poised, twitched violently in his hand. He screamed once more, just at the moment when I recognised the smell of burning feathers.

He jumped, dropping his sword as he leaped and whirled, and the light of his flaming back-device, the cloth and feathers and reeds blazing like pitch, became a brilliant streak, like the sun's reflection on the lake, as he ran from it.

My brother, Handy and Quail ran up. For a moment they could only stand and stare, too astounded to move.

The otomi pranced about, bellowing and cursing, beating at the flames behind him. Lion jumped out of his way as he blundered blindly towards him.

'The club, Lion!' I yelled. 'Get his club!'

Finally coming to his senses, Lion darted towards the discarded weapon. He was too late. He had to jump out of the way again as the anguished, infuriated otomi bore down on him.

The captain's foot slammed down on his own blades and his cry shot up in pitch as sharp edges of obsidian sliced through sandal leather and flesh and toe-bone alike.

He crashed to the ground, and the burning cloth, feathers and reeds fell over him, burying his head in fire.

On the ground beside him lay the sorcerer's incense ladle. It still smoked faintly, although there were no coals in it, because the sorcerer had tipped all of them over the wicker frame on the captain's back.

10

Lion, Handy and Quail helped me to my feet.

'Be careful! That hurts! What do you mean, can I stand? What does it look like? Don't touch the leg! I'm likely to lose it as it is!'

'Ignore him,' Lion said. 'He's like this with a nosebleed. Just get him back to the parish hall.'

Handy was looking at the incense ladle. 'What's this doing here?' he asked.

'The sorcerer dropped it,' I said. 'I can explain when I can sit down and rest this leg – that's if I haven't fainted first! And I need a drink.'

I never finished the sentence, because Lion interrupted me.

'Look at the parish hall!'

The temple was all but burned out by now. Yet for some reason the light seemed to be growing rather than diminishing, and I became aware of sparks dancing about me, and something pricked the back of my neck: a piece of burning vegetation. The air was alive with bright orange fireflies, dancing and coupling amid thickening clouds of white smoke.

I followed Lion's gaze to stare in horror at the flames that were leaping up over the parish hall. A falling ember had caught one of the plants at the top of the steps. Soon they would be ablaze, and Lily and Kite were up there, trapped by their own barricade.

'We've got to get them out of there!' I cried fatuously. There was no answer. When I tore my eyes from the sight I realised that Lion and the others were already running towards the blazing building. I lurched and limped in their wake, reaching the courtyard in time to see them frantically tearing at the barricade, braving the heat and the thorns and cactus spines in their efforts to get through it.

It was not working, I realised with despair. As I watched, Lion reeled blindly away down the steps, coughing and gasping, driven back by the flames. A few moments later he staggered back up them, but by now it was hotter still, and Handy and Quail had been forced to retreat as well.

There was no sign of Kite or Lily.

I stumbled to the bottom of the steps just as Quail toppled down into the courtyard for the last time. 'It's no good,' he gasped. 'The roof's going to collapse. There'll be nothing left up there after that.'

Lion came down, grabbing me by the arm and tugging me away with him. 'I'm sorry, Yaotl,' he yelled. 'We were too late. There's no sign of life up there anyway. We've got to go before the whole place comes down around us!'

I could only stare stupidly at him while he told me the woman I loved was dead. I did not scream at him or shout 'no' or curse the gods, the way I have heard people are supposed to. I just allowed myself to be led quietly away, while the parish hall of Atlixco burned to the ground.

Tribute of Death

They were waiting for us in the plaza outside: what looked like all the menfolk of the parish, and not a few of the women and children too. It was as dense a crowd as would gather for the local market. They were far too late to be of any use, of course, but still in time to enjoy a good blaze, and marvel at the carnage we had left behind: the bodies of two of their own, the otomi, and lord Feathered in Black's steward.

'Out of the way!' Lion barked, shoving people roughly aside. 'No, I'm not telling you anything, because I know bugger all myself!'

Handy helped me stagger along in my brother's wake. One elderly man – the very same man I had accosted on the morning when Star's body had gone missing – called out: 'Hey, I know you! What's this all about, then?'

I looked at him, the eyes in his lined and leathery face gleaming with curiosity like a child's, and felt suddenly sick. I could have told him what he wanted to know by now – all of it, from the beginning – but I was too tired.

We stopped by the steward's body.

'Poor old Huitztic,' Handy said magnanimously. 'I never liked him, but I don't know that he deserved that.'

'I do,' I said huskily. 'And he did.'

The commoner stared at me. 'What makes you say that?'

I sighed. 'Can it wait till the morning? For now, let's just say that he brought it on himself.'

Lion said: 'It's a pity we didn't get the sorcerer. You reckon we might have done, if it hadn't been for the fire?'

'I saw him!' someone called out.

'Really?' Lion cried eagerly. I glanced at the man who had spoken, noting indifferently that he was no-one I had seen or heard before, just a tonsured commoner in a plain, brief cloak and breechcloth. 'Where did he go?'

The man gestured towards the path that led towards Handy's house and the lake. 'That way. He was running. He must have been near the temple – that's how I know who it was – and he was screaming and trailing sparks like his cloak had caught fire!'

Lion grinned at me. 'You stay here. I'm going after him. Handy, you can come too, if you want to get your hands on the man who killed your wife!'

Pain and fatigue and a peculiar sense that none of what I could see or hear was really happening were beginning to overwhelm me. My head was spinning. My voice fell almost to a whisper, but I just about managed to make myself heard: 'Don't bother!'

Handy and Lion stared at me, slack-jawed. Eventually my brother said: 'You can stay here, then. No-one's asking you to go. But if we don't move now, we'll lose him.'

'No you won't,' I said weakly. 'That wasn't the sorcerer.' I stumbled dizzily forward, stopping only when Lion seized my arm and held me upright. I looked at him and Handy, taking in both of their shocked faces in turn. 'You'll get your sorcerer,' I assured them, 'and the man who ran away – you'll get him too. But they'll keep, both of them. There's plenty of time.'

As Lion lowered me to the ground, there was a disturbance near the edge of the crowd. Heads turned and feet started to move in the direction of some new spectacle, and I heard voices calling for help: a blanket, a couple of men to carry something, a brazier for warmth. Considering that flames were still crackling in parts of the parish hall, this last request struck me as funny. To find myself giggling inanely at

Tribute of Death

such a time was all part of the unreality that surrounded me.

Handy disappeared into the crowd for a moment to find out what the fuss was about. He burst back out of it almost immediately.

'Yaotl, you really need to see this,' he said, grasping my wrist and pulling me to my feet again.

'Let me go!' I protested feebly, but the words died in my throat as he tugged me after him.

There was a small clear space at the edge of the plaza. In the middle of it was a large puddle. In the middle of the puddle, with water still dripping from her hair and clothes, sat Lily. Kite lay next to her, still strapped to his board. Both were clearly very much alive.

Handy thrust me towards them and then stood behind me, holding me up.

My mistress looked me up and down. I must have presented a sorry sight, covered in blood and soot, with my clothes and hair singed. She, on the other hand, looked well, apart from the bandages on her hands and the fact that she was soaking wet and still shivering slightly.

For a long moment neither of us said anything. Then we both uttered the same words at once: 'What happened to you?'

I added: 'I thought you were dead! I thought you'd been burned alive!'

She frowned at me. 'Why would you think that?'

'But... how did you get down?'

'Yaotl, you can be so dense. Have you forgotten about the canal? It runs right past the building – or at least it did, before the building burned down. I had to push Kite off the roof – which wasn't easy with these hands – and hope he didn't drown before I got in to save him. It's a good thing I'm a strong swimmer!' She grinned then. 'I'm surprised at you. You really don't know me very well if you thought we were just going to sit up there waiting to be cooked!'

FIVE WIND

·····

1

From the outside, the house looked almost as it had when Lily, Kite, Snake and I had last visited it. The only small difference was that the wicker screen had already been drawn back.

'As if we were expected,' Lion said.

'We are,' I said.

'Do you want me to call out?' Snake asked.

'No, I think we can go straight in.'

We were a larger party this time: no Kite, but Lion, Spotted Eagle and Handy were with us. The two last looked about them warily as we followed Snake into the house of Red Macaw's mother. I had promised them there would be no sorcery and they in turn had promised not to wreak some bloody revenge on the owner of the house. I suspected that by the time we were done they would have lost whatever appetite they might have for vengeance.

Precious Light was kneeling in her courtyard. She barely looked up at us as we filed in and variously squatted, kneeled or stood by the walls. She was intent on patting down the earth she had used to fill in a small hole in the ground beside her.

There was an earthenware cup by one of her knees. I eyed it warily. It was positioned so that she could snatch it up in an instant, but were its contents a weapon or a means of escape?

'You're later that I expected,' she remarked.

'I was late rising,' I said. 'It was a long night, last night.'

She looked up then and smiled. 'Is your leg troubling you?'

'A little,' I admitted. I had remained on my feet. My leg was too stiff to bend easily, and the bandages swaddling it from the knee down did not help.

'I can give you something for that, you know.'

'I'm sure you can.' I decided the pleasantries ought to end there: I could sense Handy and his sons becoming impatient. 'But would it be anything like what you used to give Cactus?'

If I expected her to break down into some tearful confession, or even launch into a spirited denial, I was to be disappointed. 'No, nothing like that,' she said calmly. 'Only a poultice.'

Handy could not contain himself any longer. 'Why?' he cried suddenly. 'Why did you do it? You tried to use Cactus to get at Star through Slender Neck. When that didn't work you put her out of the way and replaced her with Gentle Heart. You sent someone to the House of Pleasure to tell them my wife didn't need a midwife – or was that you?'

'It was me,' the old woman responded calmly.

'You even tried to use the curer to kill me, but why? What was it all for?'

'You made my son unhappy.'

'That's ridiculous! What did I do to him? What about what he did to us?'

'Oh, I understand all that. I don't mean you did anything; but the fact that you and Star were alive, that was the cause of his

Tribute of Death

unhappiness. Do you see? I just wanted to get rid of that, the thing that was making him miserable. That was all.'

'And you wanted to kill us for that?'

She looked up, frowning slightly, an expression of puzzlement. 'No, I didn't *want* to kill you. I needed to.'

Spotted Eagle said: 'Where's my mother's body?'

'I made the otomi rebury it. It's in the plot just to the south of yours. Really, I'm surprised it's not been found yet.'

'Why did you steal it in the first place?' the young man cried piteously.

Precious Light's answer to this was a sigh. Her hand drifted towards the bowl beside her. Alarmed, I said: 'We don't mean to weary you. Why don't I try to answer the questions? Then if you'd be kind enough to fill in any gaps, we would be... grateful.' I shot a warning look at Handy and Spotted Eagle.

Precious Light laid her hand on the earth beside the bowl. 'I'll tell you what you need to know. In a way, I owe it to you. You've only been doing what you had to as well. But not too many questions. I'm tired. It was a long night for me too.'

'I don't know where this starts,' I continued. 'I suppose with the otomi, looking for a way to get his revenge on me and Handy.'

'He wasn't that interested in Handy,' Precious Light said. 'You were the one he wanted. But it was a mutual arrangement, you see: he got his revenge, I removed the obstacle to my son's happiness, we helped each other.'

'Right. Anyway, somehow he got the idea of consulting a sorcerer, and maybe getting hold of a charm to make himself invincible.'

'It was the other way around. I found him.'

'Through Huitztic, the steward?'

'That's right. Everyone knew he came to the parish to see Handy, and I made a point of getting to know him.'

'The steward,' I said ruefully. 'That's someone else that hated me.'

'Yes,' she said in a matter-of-fact tone, 'but I don't think you were that important. It was the captain that mattered to the steward. He wanted to do something for the otomi – to make a friend of him, I suppose. He was terrified of him, but he seemed to be fascinated by him as well. When he talked about him to me, about how he'd come back to the city and what he wanted to do, I realised I could make use of them both.'

'And pretending to be a sorcerer – to know how to do the dance with dead woman's forearm – whose idea was that?'

'It was the steward's. I didn't care for it, but he said the otomi would accept it, and he did. I scared him as much as he scared Huitztic. And Cactus was so easily impressed.' The corners of her mouth turned down, as if the gullibility and folly of others were a source of regret. 'Cactus would take any potion or herb or mushroom I offered him, if I assured him I had a second soul and could turn myself into an animal at will. And apparently lord Feathered in Black's sorcerers would give his steward anything we needed.'

Handy said to me: 'You said last night that Huitztic brought it all on himself. Is this what you meant?'

'Yes.' I looked at him, Lily and Lion. 'If you remember, I kept wondering what the link was between the otomi and the sorcerer. In fact, the answer was staring us in the face. It had to be Huitztic,

Tribute of Death

because apart from lord Feathered in Black – who admittedly would have been my first choice of suspect, if the captain hadn't made it clear they no longer had anything to do with each other – he was the only person who knew the otomi. I remember how surprised he was to see me, the day after Star's funeral. He knew what the otomi and Precious Light had in mind and didn't expect ever to see me alive again. And then, the otomi found us right after Huitztic vanished last night. I don't think they met by chance. I think the steward went to tell the captain where he could find me. Unfortunately his reward was to be used as bait!'

I turned to Precious Light. 'It was Huitztic who told the captain where I was going when I came back to the city, but he also led me to you in the end. He knew about Star and Red Macaw. There are people born and raised in this parish who don't know the facts about that, and none who will talk about it to outsiders. He had to have got it from you.'

'That's true enough,' the old woman conceded.

I went on: 'That wasn't quite the only thing that pointed to you, of course. There was Red Macaw's behaviour as well. What was he doing following Star's funeral procession? Why did he go out to the *chinampa* plot?'

Spotted Eagle said: 'He wanted to see my mother. He told you that before he died.'

'No, he didn't. "Wanted to see her": those were the words he used, but we never asked who he meant by "her". It wasn't Star he wanted to see at all, was it, Precious Light? It was you. He wanted to stop what you were doing. He used that word too – "Stop". He knew you were part of the funeral procession for a reason – because you were planning to interfere with the body. And he found out where you'd reburied her, and I guess he wanted to try to talk to you there too. Only the captain got to him first.' I looked at Handy. 'He tried to warn you, if you remember, on the afternoon of the funeral. He didn't want to implicate his mother, so he couldn't spell it out, but he did tell you there'd be trouble if he was left out of the procession.'

'But he failed,' Lion said. 'They got the body.' He addressed Precious Light himself. 'Tell me, why did you rebury the body at all? Why not just chuck it in a canal?'

The woman shuddered. 'If you knew the Divine Princesses, you wouldn't ask that! I was risking enough taking her hair and forearm.'

'You did leave a body in a canal, though. It belonged to lord Feathered in Black's spy. Why did you do that?'

'That was the captain's idea. He knew who this man was, and thought if his body were found, the chief minister would immediately have the place swarming with warriors searching for the killer. If the man just disappeared, his master might assume he'd gone to ground somewhere. It was just to slow the pursuit down. Of course, with the second one – the one he killed outside Handy's house – there wasn't time for that.'

I took up the tale again, wondering all the time when the woman's patience would wear out and her hand move toward that cup. 'You were with the funeral procession. The otomi followed it: we know that because he was seen. I'm guessing that you bided your time until we'd all fallen asleep, and then he attacked.'

'What happened to my brother-in-law?' Handy asked.

'I don't know,' she said. 'I presume he ran away. We didn't kill him, if that's what you mean.'

Tribute of Death

Handy and I exchanged glances. He was no doubt wondering whether that meant Goose's husband was still alive after all. I knew the answer to that one, but I was more interested, now, in learning all that the woman had to say.

'What happened then?' I answered my own question. 'The captain followed me. He lost me, luckily, and went back to the plaza. Did he fall in with old Black Feathers' man on the way?'

'He did.'

'And he killed him. And the next day you tried to kill Handy.'

'I gave Cactus some herbs and urged him to pass them on to Star's husband, yes.'

Handy growled angrily.

'I told you,' she replied, 'it was for my son. Remember, you were the man who pretended you'd fathered his child.'

That was very nearly the last we heard, as the commoner, incensed, suddenly leaped up from where he had been squatting. However, and to my surprise, it was his son who restrained him. 'Father, don't. We need to know. And Yaotl's right: it's not for us to end this.'

As his father's rage subsided into angry muttering, I began again. 'Everybody thought you were Cactus's customer...'

'It was the other way around. I gave him his healing herbs – the ones Huitztic had given me. But everyone needed to believe Cactus had found them for himself.'

Carefully, aware that she might cut short the interrogation at any time she chose, I took her through what had happened after we had buried Handy's unborn child. She described how Gentle Heart had become suspicious, and how, when Cactus had mentioned this to her,

Precious Light had given him the poisoned chocolate, knowing he and the midwife would share it. She told me how she and the captain had attacked Handy's house, hoping their newly acquired charms would help them, and been driven away by me and Spotted Eagle, though not before killing lord Feathered in Black's other spy. She recounted the following day's events in the marshes, when her son had come upon the captain and received his death wound.

'The otomi was scared,' I recalled. 'He was afraid of what you would do when you found out he'd killed your son. That's why he made me bury him on top of Star's body.'

'He still needed me then, which was why he tried to conceal what he'd done. That was while this young man was chasing me through the rushes, wasn't it?'

'Pity I didn't catch you,' said Spotted Eagle sullenly.

'You nearly did. I had to pretend to be gathering stone dung with the other old men and women to escape. You ran past me, very close.' Handy's son stared at her, while a look of disgust formed on his face.

'I took my son's body back, after that,' she added. 'We moved them both, so that you wouldn't guess what I'd taken and why. But of course I wanted to burn it decently, and bring the ashes here.' She lowered her head to look at the place where she had been patting down freshly-dug earth. 'Here, where they belong.'

'He never went to join the army, did he?' I said.

'No, of course not. He lied to Kite about that to protect me, but really he was trying to stop us. He'd never understood what was wrong with him. The sick often don't, do they? That's why we have curers. He needed me to tell him that he would never be able to live as long as Star and Handy were around. But when I did something about it, he

Tribute of Death

wouldn't accept it, which I suppose is always the way.'

'Why now, though?' I asked. 'Your son and Star hadn't seen each other in a dozen years. What made you do this thing now, after all that time?'

'The sickness was getting worse, all of a sudden. It was the boy. He was growing into a man, and Red Macaw could talk to him, promise to help train him as a warrior, get news about his mother. I think it made him dwell on what he'd lost.' When she looked up and turned her gaze on Snake, her eyes were wet. 'In the end, I did what any mother would.'

Lily had been watching and listening in silence, with narrowed eyes and a deepening frown. When she spoke, it was to say simply: 'No, you didn't.'

Lion asked: 'Why did you go on helping the captain after you found out what he'd done to Red Macaw?'

'I didn't.'

'Yes, you did. You were there last night.'

'I wasn't there to help him,' she insisted. 'I was there to kill him.'

'But you were dancing with my wife's forearm!' Handy cried indignantly.

'It was a ruse. It got me close to him. He wouldn't trust me otherwise – he certainly wouldn't let me give him anything to drink! But I knew as soon as he got you in his power his guard would drop. And that was my chance.'

And so she had killed the otomi, pouring burning coals over the feathers and wickerwork on his back because he had murdered her son. It suddenly occurred to me that this had been the only thing she had done in anger, her only act of revenge.

I turned to Handy, intending to say as much to him, and in doing so I missed the final movements of the hand towards the cup, the cup towards her mouth. The first I knew about it was when my brother started forward with a cry of dismay.

When I turned back, she was kneeling as before, with no apparent change in her expression.

'Handy,' she said softly, 'I am sorry for the pain you've had to suffer. But Star would have told you what it's like. You were hurting my son, even if you didn't mean to. And a mother will do anything to protect her child.'

Then she died.

2

'I should think it was the most frightening thing I've ever known,' my brother was saying. 'No, really, I have to admit it – I was scared. There was this creature, strutting and gyrating in front of me, with your mother's arm in her hand, and I just knew I wouldn't be able to move a muscle if I tried.'

It was the evening of the day Precious Light had killed herself. We were standing in Atlixco Plaza, by the base of the temple. In front of us, a paving slab had been prized up, revealing a hole large enough to receive a human body. Handy had found Star where her killer had told him to look for her, and he was determined to lay her to rest once and for all as soon as he could.

Snake's brother, Buck – the one who had gone with him to take a message to Lily's house two days before – had been listening, enraptured, to the Guardian of the Waterfront's tales of military prowess. In all fairness, these were mostly as true as they were exciting. However, he frowned in puzzlement when he heard Lion's account of how Precious Light had bewitched him. 'That's pretty much how my father described it,' the youngster said carefully, before turning to me. 'She didn't have that effect on you, though, did she, Yaotl?'

'That's because she was fake,' I replied shortly. I regretted my brusqueness immediately, but the boy kept reminding me of his brother. I had not seen Snake since we had left Precious Light's house that morning. He was not here now, although he ought to be. How was he going to recover from learning that his father was not his father, and that both his parents had died horribly – not to mention his grandmother?

I remembered what I had told the boy on the way back from my parent's house, about obsidian and stone, and wondered which he would grow up to be. Would what had just happened turn him one way or the other?

My brother exclaimed indignantly: 'It's easy for you to say she was fake, with your priest's training, but let me tell you, when she was this far away...' He held his hand up, the thumb and forefinger a hair's breadth apart.

'I'm sure the effect she had on you and the others was real enough,' I assured him. 'But you knew you wouldn't be able to move a muscle, so you didn't try. Sooner or later you would have done, if only to scratch an itch. You just need to ask yourself how many genuine sorcerers there are and what the odds are against Red Macaw just happening to have one for his mother.'

'She was insane, wasn't she? No normal mother would do what she did.'

I found myself wondering about the same thing. My mistress had had a son, now dead, for whom she had once been prepared to sacrifice me. I wondered what more she might have done if she had had to. So far I had not had the courage to ask.

While I pondered this I surveyed the wreckage of the plaza. The temple above us was a charred ruin while the parish hall had been reduced to a heap of rubble. Yet the space between them was filled with reed mats spread with merchandise, many of them surrounded by crowds of men and women, haggling enthusiastically. The parish had suffered grievously, two more of its men having been killed just the night before, yet life went on.

A little procession made its way around the edge of the plaza. Most of the people ignored it. The few that turned to look turned hastily away again. They might sympathise with Handy's grief, but his wife, the woman reborn as a Divine Princess, was still a fearful object. For the same reason, our little group beside the burned out temple was let well alone.

Her husband and her eldest son carried her, now decently wrapped in a shroud. She was almost entire, I knew, for we had found her forearm in Precious Light's house; only the hair had perished with the otomi, burned to ashes.

'Now, this will be interesting,' I remarked.

'You said that before,' my brother said, 'But you wouldn't tell us what you meant. What's the big mystery?'

I peered at the procession and felt a grin beginning to break out over my face as I saw who was walking behind the men carrying the body, confirming my suspicions.

Just then Buck called out: 'I don't believe it! That's my uncle – Flower Gatherer!' Sure enough, Goose and her husband were there, walking side by side but an arm's length apart.

The lad turned an awed face towards me. 'Where's he been? How did you know?'

'She doesn't look happy, for a woman who's just found out she's not a widow,' Lion remarked. Handy's sister-in-law had a strained, pinched expression, as though she were holding her mouth shut for fear of what might come out if she opened it.

Lion looked at me resignedly. 'All right, Yaotl, since you're going to tell us anyway: what's the answer? He was supposed to have run off, wasn't he? What made you think he'd be here?'

'Where else? Really, I'd have thought it was obvious.' I never could help dwelling on my own cleverness and now I was making the most of the fact that my mistress had gone home. I suspected she would have been quick to pour scorn on any showing off by her slave. 'It was just that he had to be somewhere. His wife couldn't imagine him running away to fend for himself. He clearly wasn't the kind to stand and fight, and since there was no sign of his body it was a safe bet he hadn't been killed. So he must have gone to ground. When that man last night described someone fleeing with his cloak on fire, I realised he must have been hiding out in the temple all along – skulking in the dark at the back of the shrine, stealing offerings for his food, I shouldn't wonder. That's why I didn't think it was worth chasing after him: he was bound to come home the moment he knew the captain was dead.'

'That's pathetic!' cried Buck.

'Well, judging by the way she's not looking at him, his wife appears to agree,' I told him. 'But look out, she's coming over here.'

Goose had detached herself from her husband's side and hurried on ahead, overtaking Handy and Spotted Eagle and their burden in her eagerness to speak to us.

'Yaotl, thank you for coming,' she said. 'I don't know what we'd do without you.'